Kandy Shepherd swapped a career as a magazine editor for a life writing romance. She lives on a small farm in the Blue Mountains near Sydney, Australia, with her husband, daughter and lots of pets. She believes in love at first sight and real-life romance — they worked for her! Kandy loves to hear from her readers. Visit her at www.kandyshepherd.com.

Christine Rimmer came to her profession the long way around. She tried everything from acting to teaching to telephone sales. Now she's finally found work that suits her perfectly. Visit her at www.christinerimmer.com.

Discover more at millsandboon.co.uk

BEST MAN AND THE RUNAWAY BRIDE

KANDY SHEPHERD

A MAVERICK TO (RE)MARRY

CHRISTINE RIMMER

MIX
Paper from
responsible sources
FSC C007454

This book is produced from independently certified FSC™
paper to ensure responsible forest management.

For more information visit: www.harpercollins.co.uk/green

Printed and bound in Spain
by CPI, Barcelona

MILLS & BOON

First Published in Great Britain 2018
by Mills & Boon, an imprint of HarperCollinsPublishers,
1 London Bridge Street, London, SE1 9GF

Best Man and the Runaway Bride © 2018 Kandy Shepherd
A Maverick to (Re)Marry © 2018 Harlequin Books S.A.

Special thanks and acknowledgement to Christine Rimmer for her contribution to the Montana Mavericks: The Lonelyhearts Ranch continuity.

ISBN: 978-0-263-26510-1

38-0718

BEST MAN AND THE RUNAWAY BRIDE

KANDY SHEPHERD

In memory of my dear friend Patrick J Houston,
married to his soulmate, my friend Louise,
for more than forty years after proposing
to her on their second date.
Charismatic, big-hearted and very handsome,
he was truly a real-life romance hero.

CHAPTER ONE

WHERE WAS THE BRIDE? She should have been at the church a half-hour ago. Max Conway paced back and forth on the pavement in front of the historic sandstone building. As best man at the wedding, he'd been despatched outside to report on the bride's arrival status. Again, he glanced down at his watch. Traditionally a bride was tardy but this much late was ridiculous. No wonder the groom, standing inside all by himself at the altar, was grim-faced and tapping his foot.

Organ music drifted out through the arched windows of the church. The notes had a trill of desperation as the organist started her wedding repertoire for the third time. Anticipation levels inside would be rising as the congregation waited—and waited.

Max checked the traffic app on his phone to see if there were problems. All roads leading to the church in Sydney's posh eastern suburbs were clear. The bridesmaids had arrived without any problem. *But still no bride.* He was about to turn on his heel and go back inside to give the glowering groom an update—a task he didn't relish—when the bridal car approached. His shoulders sagged with relief. *She was here.*

Through the tinted window of the luxury limousine

he could see a froth of white veil framing a lovely female face. Nikki Lucas. Max recognised her straight
away, though he'd only met her for the first time at the
rehearsal two nights before. Honey-blonde hair. Soft
brown eyes. Tall and slender. A truly beautiful bride.
Well worth the wait for the lucky groom.

At the rehearsal she'd greeted Max with a smile so
dazzling he'd been momentarily stunned. She'd been
warm and welcoming to her fiancé's best man—a total
stranger to her. If she'd realised who he was—who he
had once been—she'd been too well-mannered to mention it. The rehearsal had gone smoothly and he'd got the
impression Ms Lucas was efficient and organised. Not
the kind of woman to be so late for her own wedding.

The wealthy father of the bride sat next to her in the
back seat. Why hadn't he hurried his daughter along?
Max found such lack of punctuality unpardonable. What
was Ms Lucas's game? If this were his bride—not that
he had any intention of marrying any time soon—he
would be furious. The limo slowed to a halt. No doubt
he'd be greeted with a flurry of excuses. He would cut
her short, bustle her inside and get this tardy bride up
the aisle pronto.

He ran to the bride's door and yanked it open. 'You're
here,' he said through gritted teeth, swallowing the
where the hell have you been.

He didn't get so much as a smile in response. In fact
the errant bride looked downright hostile. Her face was
as pale as the layers of tulle that framed it, her mouth
set tight. She swung her long, elegant legs out of the car,
shook off the hand he offered her to help, and stood up
in a flurry of fluffy white skirts.

She gave no apologies, no explanations, no excuses.

Just a tersely spoken command. 'You have to get me out of here.'

Max stared at her. 'Get you up the aisle, you mean,' he said. 'You're late. There's a church full of guests waiting for you. Not to mention your groom.'

'Him.' She shook her head so vehemently her long veil whipped around her face. 'I'm not going to marry that man. I thought I could go through with it but I can't.'

By now her father had clambered out of the car to join them. The limo took off with a squeal of tyres, the driver muttering he was late for his next job.

'Think about this, sweetheart,' said the older man. He handed her the bouquet of white roses that she had left behind her on the car seat. 'You can't just walk out on your wedding.'

'Yes, I can. You can't talk me out of this, Dad. If you won't help me, Max here will.' She spat out his name as if it were a dirty word. 'It's the least he can do as best man to the creep who convinced me to marry him under false pretences.' She glared at Max through narrowed eyes. 'That is, unless you're just as much lying pond scum as he is.'

Max wasn't usually lost for words. But the insult came from nowhere. Where was the smiling charmer from the rehearsal? Behind the perfect make-up the bride was grim-faced and steely eyed. 'I don't consider myself to be pond scum,' Max said through gritted teeth. 'But my duty as best man is to get you into the church for your wedding.'

'There isn't going to be a wedding. Your duty as a decent human being is to help me get away from here. Now.' Her hands shook with agitation and she kept looking anxiously towards the church.

Max's first reaction was to back away from the bride. He wasn't good with crazy. This was something more than pre-wedding nerves. There was no trace of the joyous, vibrant woman he'd met at the rehearsal. But then her lush pink mouth trembled and her eyes clouded with something he couldn't quite place—fear, anxiety, disappointment? It made him swallow a retort. How well did he actually know the groom? He'd played tennis with him back in high school but had only reconnected with him just weeks before the wedding—had been surprised to be asked to be best man. The groom could well be pond scum these days for all he knew. But he'd made a commitment to be best man. That made him Team Groom.

The father took her arm. 'Now, Nikki, there's no need to—'

The bride turned on her father with a swirl of white skirts, glaring back at Max as she did so. 'I'm sorry, Dad,' she said, her voice unsteady. 'I can't do it.'

She indicated the church with a wave of a perfectly manicured hand. Her large diamond engagement ring flashed in the afternoon summer sunlight. 'Please tell everyone to party on without me. Don't let all that food and wine go to waste.' Her mouth curled. 'Maybe someone could have the fun of smashing Alan's lying, scheming face into the wedding cake—all three tiers of it.'

'Maybe not,' Max said, trying not to let a smile twitch at the corners of his mouth at the thought of the somewhat supercilious groom facedown in the frosting.

He made his voice calm and reassuring. 'I know you must be nervous.'

Pre-performance nerves. He knew all about them. There was nothing more nerve-wracking than stepping out onto the centre court at Wimbledon with the world watching him defend his title.

'Nervous?' Her cheeks flushed and her eyes glittered. 'I'm not nervous. I'm mad as hell.' She brandished the cascade of white roses as if it were a weapon. Max ducked. 'The wedding is cancelled.'

'Why?' At the rehearsal she'd seemed to be floating on a cloud of happiness. For one long, secret moment he had envied her groom his gorgeous, vivacious bride-to-be. Despite his success at the highest rank of his chosen sport, and all the female attention that came with it, at age thirty Max was still single.

'You want a reason?' She raised her perfectly shaped brows. 'How about four reasons? His two ex-wives and two children.'

Max frowned. 'You knew Alan was divorced.'

'Divorced *once*. With no children. He lied.' Her voice ended on a heart-rending whimper. 'One of the reasons I fell for him was that he told me he was longing for children. Like…like I was.' Her face seemed to crumple; all the poise Max had admired melted away to leave only wide-eyed bewilderment.

'How did you find out?' he asked.

'His first ex-wife called to warn me off Alan. Didn't want to see me get fooled and hurt by him like she had been. He called her a vindictive witch. Then the second ex-wife wife called to tell me about their three-year-old twin sons and how he'd deserted them. Oh, and warned me he was on the verge of bankruptcy now that he'd gone through all her money.'

Max gasped. The dad hissed. Nikki was a successful businesswoman. Being both beautiful and wealthy made her quite the catch—and vulnerable to a fortune hunter.

'You believed her?' said Max.

She shook her head. 'I trusted my fiancé. But I had her investigated. Definitive proof she was telling the truth came just as I waved off my bridesmaids and was about to get into the limo.' Her breath caught on a hitch, dangerously close to a sob. 'I can't marry a liar and a fraud.'

'Go in there and tell him that,' said Max.

'I couldn't bear the humiliation.' She looked up at him, her eyes pleading now. 'You know all about humiliation.'

Max grimaced. Of course he did. Evidence of his disastrous final game where he'd injured his elbow so badly still circulated on the Internet: the thrown racket, his writhing in pain on the grass court surface of Wimbledon. People had even made memes of it.

'Yes,' he said through gritted teeth, not appreciating the reminder.

'Please help me get away. I can't run down the street to hail a cab dressed like this.'

Tears glistened in her brown eyes, making them luminous. Max had a weakness for female tears. But he was also a man of his word. He was the best man. An honourable position with duties he took seriously. It would take more than tears to recruit him to Team Bride. As she looked up at him, a single teardrop rolled slowly down her cheek. He had to fight an impulse to wipe it gently away with his thumb. *She was another man's bride.* She sniffed and her voice quivered as she spoke. 'You say you're not pond scum, now prove it to me.'

Nikki held her breath as she looked up at Max Conway for his answer. She hadn't expected to find him standing guard outside the church, ready to corral her inside. In fact, she hardly knew the guy. Just was aware he was a celebrity athlete and had a well-publicised love life.

The first she'd known that her groom's best man was the world's golden boy of tennis—featured in countless 'sexiest men alive' media round-ups—was when she'd met him at the rehearsal. Just another of her former fiancé's secrets, she thought with a twist of bitterness.

She could read the struggle on Max's face—with his spiky light brown hair and blue eyes, he was every bit as handsome as his photos. Duty warred an obvious battle with gentlemanly instincts to help a bride in distress. The media did not consider him a gentleman. She didn't care. All she wanted was his help to get away. The clock was ticking. Her father had reluctantly gone to tell everyone that the bride would be a no-show. If she was going to escape, she'd have to do it now.

'Are you quite sure you want to do this?' Max said.

'Yes, yes, yes,' she said, unable to keep the impatience from her voice. At any moment Alan might come raging outside. She shuddered at the thought.

'There'll be no going back. It's Alan who'll be humiliated.'

'*Huh!* Finding out the truth about him from his ex-wives rates high in humiliation. Being foolish enough to have believed his lies even higher.'

She clutched Max by the sleeve of his dark best-man suit. Looked with trepidation across to the Gothic-style arched wooden doors that led to the interior of the church. People were beginning to spill out down the steps. Ahead of the pack was the wedding photographer, brandishing his camera aimed at her. Forget Max. She gathered up her skirts. Got ready to run. Risked a final glance up at him. 'Are you going to help me or not?'

'I don't like liars.'

'Is that a "yes"?'

In reply he took her by the arm. Through the sheer fabric of her sleeve she could feel the warmth and strength of his grip. 'My car is around the corner. We'll have to run.'

She started to run but only got a few steps before she stumbled. The combination of bumpy pavement, long skirts and high, skinny heels wasn't conducive to a speedy escape.

'Ditch the shoes,' he said tersely. She kicked them off. One after the other they flew into the air and landed side down on the pavement. 'And the flowers.' The white flowers landed near the white shoes with a flurry of petals, forming a tableau of lost dreams on the grey of the tarmac. She didn't look back.

They had rounded the corner from the church when she heard the first shout. More outraged bellow than civilised protest. She cringed at the anger in Alan's voice. Max's grip on her arm tightened as he hurried her along. 'We're not going fast enough,' he said.

She wished she could tear away her long skirts. 'I'm moving as fast as I—'

Her protest ended in a gasp as he effortlessly swept her up to cradle her in his arms. 'Hold on tight,' he said as he broke into a run—at twice her speed.

Max Conway was a tall, powerfully built man famed for the relentless power of his serve. Instinctively Nikki looped her arms around his neck and pressed herself close against a solid wall of muscle.

'You...you don't have to carry me,' she managed to choke out.

'I do,' he said. She noticed he wasn't the slightest bit out of breath even while running at full stride weighed down by the burden of a bride. 'That is, if you really want to escape from your groom.'

The edge to his voice made her stiffen in his arms. Did he think this was some kind of attention-seeking ruse? That she would let Alan catch her and lead her triumphantly back to the wedding? She went to retort but realised he didn't know her any better than she knew him. She would never behave like that. But he wasn't to know.

It seemed like only seconds before he stopped by a modest sedan parked by the kerb. Wouldn't a sports celebrity like Max Conway drive something flashier? Unless he wanted to stay under the radar for some reason. In this case, it would serve her well if Alan tried to follow her. Once in the traffic, this car would be anonymous.

Max put her down by the passenger door. The pavement was warm to her stockinged feet. She was in a wedding dress and no shoes. It made her feel vulnerable and aware of her predicament. For the first time she questioned the wisdom of begging a stranger to take her away. But there was something about Max's assured, take-charge attitude that made her feel she could trust him.

He unlocked the car with a fob on his key ring and held open her door. 'Jump in,' he said. 'And be quick.'

That was easier said than done with a voluminous full skirt to tuck in around her. With fumbling fingers, she'd just managed to fasten her seat belt when the car took off with a jolt and a screech of tyres. 'We've got company,' Max said by way of explanation.

Nikki glanced behind her to see what he meant. Heading towards the car was a red-faced Alan, followed closely by her sister, resplendent in her bridesmaid's dress, her sweet face screwed up in anguish. The wedding photographer followed—snapping gleefully away at the runaway bride. Nikki's heart started to race and she choked on her breath. For the first time, she realised the enormity of what she had done. How it would affect so many people other than herself. She hadn't even told her beloved sister.

But she'd make it up to them later. Far better to offend a few people than to chain herself in marriage to the wrong man. 'Step on it,' she urged Max.

It wasn't long before they'd reached her older style waterfront apartment in Double Bay. She'd bought it with her first big profits from her business.

Max pulled into the driveway. 'Have you got keys?'

'No need. The entry is security coded.'

She expected him to bundle her out into the courtyard and speed off. Instead, he got out of the car to come around and open the passenger door for her. She realised Alan had never done that. Not once. Why had she let herself be so swept off her feet by him?

'Ouch!' The gravelled courtyard was not kind to stockinged feet. She started to pick her way across it, wincing as she went.

'Allow me,' Max said. Before she could protest she was swept up into his arms again as he carried her across the courtyard to the front door.

'This is very chivalrous of you,' she said, flushing.

'Nothing is chivalrous about the best man running off with the bride,' he said with a wry twist to his mouth that didn't quite pass as a smile.

'But the bride is very grateful,' she said. 'More grateful than she can say.'

He continued to hold her as she coded in her password. Then kicked the door open and carried her inside. It was as if he were carrying her over the threshold like a *real* bride on her wedding night. The thought was way too disconcerting. She struggled to be put down. He immediately set her back on her feet. She fussed with her dress to cover her confusion.

'What now for you?' he asked.

'I intend to barricade myself in my apartment.'

'And then?'

'I have a plan.' She didn't really. The plan had been to spend the night with her new husband—she shuddered at even the thought of it—in a luxury city hotel then next day set off to a honeymoon in an even more expensive hotel in Dubai. Alan's choice. 'But I'm not going to tell you about it. Then you can truthfully tell people you don't know where I am.'

'You mean Alan?'

She nodded. 'I really and truly don't want him to find me. And I don't want to make things more awkward for you than I already have.'

'I get that,' he said.

'Just one more thing.' She tugged the diamond engagement ring—that she had worn with such optimism for the future—off her finger. 'Can you give this to him, please? I have no further use for it.'

'Like a best man's duty in reverse.'

He took the ring from her, his warm fingers brushing against hers as he did so. She snatched her hand back, not welcoming the tingle of awareness that shot through her. She'd been about to wed another man, for heaven's sake. How could she feel such a flutter of attraction to his best man? Especially a guy who had cheated on his tennis-player girlfriend—a woman as famous as he was—and been involved in a highly publicised paternity dispute.

An awkward silence fell between them. She shifted from one stockinged foot to another, not wanting to meet his gaze. 'Thank you for helping me,' she said finally. 'It was very good of you.'

'Good doesn't come into it. I'm not proud of myself for helping you run away. I went against my principles. I'm not convinced it was the right thing for you to do either. I seriously hope you don't regret it.'

The full impact of what she'd done might not hit her until Max left her alone in her apartment, surrounded by the disarray of her wedding preparations and honeymoon packing. But he didn't need to sound self-righteous about it. It wasn't for Max Conway to sit in judgement against her. Grateful though she was for his help.

Anger flooded through her. 'There's one more thing you don't know about your friend Alan. After his twins, he had a vasectomy so he couldn't have more children. The man who used to toss names for our future kids around with me. Spent hours discussing what colour eyes they might have. Was he ever going to tell me he was shooting blanks? Or let me go through fertility treatment when I didn't fall pregnant?'

'I have no words,' Max said, tight-lipped. No criticism of his friend, of course. Not when the famous tennis player himself had cheated and lied.

'I'll never regret walking out on that despicable excuse for a man. But letting my family and friends down?

Not doing due diligence on the man before I agreed to marry him? I suspect I'll always regret my lapse in judgement. I wouldn't have done a minor business deal without all the facts, yet I was prepared to commit my life to a person I didn't really know. I wanted that life so much…the husband and kids.'

'I can only wish you good luck in whatever you end up doing,' he said. Looking serious suited him and it struck her again how good-looking he was. No wonder the public was so fascinated by him.

'What I don't regret is putting my trust in you to help me,' she said. Max might be pond scum in his personal life and be friend to a cheating, lying fraud. But he had come through for her. That was all that counted.

On impulse she leaned up and kissed him on his smooth, tanned cheek. She was stunned by the sensation that shot through her at the contact, brief as it was. He didn't kiss her back. Why would he? She'd just run out on his friend. 'I won't say I'll return the favour for you some day because it's not the kind of favour you want to call on, is it?'

He half smiled at that and turned to leave. She watched him as he strode back to his car, broad-shouldered and athletic. Unless she glimpsed him on television, slamming a tennis ball at his opponent in some top-level tournament, she would never see Max Conway again.

CHAPTER TWO

Six months later

MAX HADN'T COME to the small Indonesian island of Nusa Lembongan for fun. On previous visits to nearby Bali he had stayed with friends in luxurious private villas the size of mansions, with all their needs and whims catered to by a team of attendants devoted purely to their comfort. Near the beach in fashionable Seminyak. Overlooking the sea on a cliff top in exclusive Uluwatu. High in the treetops of Ubud.

Not this time.

The last six months had been hell. Everything that could have gone wrong had gone wrong in both his professional and personal life. He had come to this small island, off the east coast of the main island of Bali, on his own. Not to party. But to make plans to reinvent himself.

Yesterday he had checked in to the Big Blue Bungalows, a small family-run hotel on the beach at Frangipani Bay on the south-west end of the island. He'd come with just a backpack and his laptop. The accommodation wasn't backpacker basic, nor was it the five-star luxury he was accustomed to. Built as a collection of traditional-style bungalows and small villas with thatched roofs, the hotel was comfortable without being overly luxurious—and not without its own rustic charm.

Lembongan was much quieter and less touristy than Bali, with more scooters and bicycles and few cars on the narrow streets. He hadn't been there twenty-four hours and he'd already cycled halfway around the island on a pushbike he'd borrowed from the hotel. The friend who'd recommended the island had warned Max he might get bored after a few days. Max doubted that. He just wanted to chill, far away from anyone who had expectations of him. He particularly wanted to escape media attention.

The thing he hated most about his life as a *celebrity sportsman*—he loathed that label—was media intrusion into his private life. Ever since he'd been thrust into the public eye the media had published exaggerated and erroneous versions of events in his private life. A lunch date with a colleague blown up into infidelity. Such fake news had led to a rift with his former girlfriend and, even worse, the inciting incident that had led to his disastrous accident.

His return to Sydney had been purposely under the radar. He'd agreed to be best man to Alan in a low-key, private wedding. Now it seemed Alan had wanted his wedding out of the public eye for his own underhand reasons. Surprisingly to Max, the groom had not traded on the best man's celebrity. It wasn't paparazzi that had taken all those photos. It was the wedding photographer who had fully capitalised on his luck in being in the right place at a scandalous time and sold the pictures everywhere.

As a result, Max's role in the 'runaway bride' story

that had so captivated Sydney had catapulted him head-first into a rabid feeding frenzy of press speculation. Right when he'd most needed his privacy. He shuddered at the memory of it. Especially the photos of him carrying another man's bride in his arms—accompanied by salacious headlines—that had featured on magazine covers all around the world.

Boring would do him just fine. Today, he anticipated the joys of anonymity.

He'd cycled from Frangipani Bay to the village of Jungut Batu, where the fast boat service brought people from Sanur on the mainland across the Badung Strait to Nusa Lembongan.

Max had taken the fast boat ride himself the day before. On arrival, he'd enjoyed a particularly tasty *nasi goreng* from one of the local *warungs*, small family run cafés, on the road that ran parallel to the beach. He fancied trying some other speciality from the menu for lunch, washed down with an Indonesian beer. This was the first time he'd travelled so simply, blending in with the backpackers, without agenda. Already he was enjoying the slower pace.

His talent for tennis had shown up when he was barely tall enough to handle a racket. For many years afterwards, school vacations had been devoted to training. There'd been no gap years or budget bus tours around Europe with friends his own age. Later, vacations had often been linked to promoting events managed by his corporate sponsors. And always there had been tennis. Even on a luxury vacation, he'd trained every day of the year. Training on Sundays and even Christmas Day, when his rivals didn't, had helped give him the edge.

As far as he knew, there was no tennis court on Nusa Lembongan.

Already he was starting to wind down. Felt the warmth of the sun, the sparkling of the endless aquamarine sea, even the spicy scents so different from his everyday life loosening the stranglehold concern for his after-sport career had on his thoughts. The people of this part of the world were known for their warmth and friendliness—their genuine smiles were also contributing to the gradual rebirth of his well-being.

Cycling in the tropical humidity of the day had made him hot; prickles of perspiration stung his forehead, made his T-shirt cling to his back. He decided to walk down one of the narrow alleys that led from the street to the beach to cool off, maybe even plunge into the water. His clothes would dry soon enough.

A nearby boat was offloading passengers, including backpackers and tourists from all over the world. Max paused to watch them. There was no dock. Boats were tethered to shore by mooring lines that ran up the beach. Passengers were helped off the back of the boat and had to wade through the shallow waters to dry land. As people disembarked, he heard excited exclamations in German, Dutch, French, Chinese as well as English spoken in a variety of accents. Fascinated, he gazed at the local women who got off the boat then walked away with heavy boxes of supplies balanced on the tops of their heads.

A young woman with a large backpack turned to thank the boat crew with a wide, sunny smile. Idly, he wondered where she was from, where she was going. She looked like a typical backpacker in loose, brightly patterned hippy pants pulled up to her knees in preparation for her paddle through the water, a gauzy white top and a woven straw hat jammed over wind-tangled blonde hair. As she waded through the aqua-coloured water to the sand, she turned to a fellow backpacker and laughed at something he said. Max froze. That laugh, her profile, seemed familiar.

For a moment he thought... But it couldn't be. Then she turned to face the beach and he caught sight of her face full on. *No.* Not *her.* Not here. The last woman he ever wanted to see again. He blamed her in large part for the hell his life in Sydney had become.

'Terima kasih.'

Nikki thanked the crew as she left the boat to wade the few metres onto the beach shore, cool waters lapping around her calves. She'd been to Sanur to pick up supplies from the pharmacy for her friend Maya. Mission accomplished and back on Lembongan, she turned her thoughts to work and the snorkelling trip she was guiding that afternoon, currents permitting. July with its excellent weather was one of the busiest months for tourism here, coinciding with school vacations in both northern and southern hemispheres.

The island didn't get as overrun as some of the more popular areas of the main island of Bali. But in this peak season there were both day trippers and new guests arriving all the time. Tourists from all around the world seeking a more off-the-beaten-track Bali experience came to Lembongan.

As she neared the shore, she became aware of a man's intense gaze on her. The guy standing on the beach was hot. Tall, broad-shouldered, hair bleached from the sun, a sexy scruff of beard growth. Blue shorts and a white

T-shirt showcased an athletic, muscular body. But she wasn't looking for masculine company. Not now. Maybe not ever. The experience with Alan had left her too shattered to imagine ever trusting another man again. She ignored the stranger.

But his gaze didn't drop. In fact it turned into a distinct glare. Was he some discontented dive-boat customer? Some of the tourists were determined to swim with the manta rays or *mola mola* fish, no matter the time of year or conditions on the day they took a tour. They didn't understand how unpredictable the sea currents could be here and would go away to vent their anger on Internet review sites. She'd prefer them to express their disappointment to her. How would she have forgotten a man as attractive as this?

But as she got closer she realised exactly who the man was. *Max Conway.*

Anger and frustration rose in her so bitter she could taste it. After six months surely Alan had given up trying to find her? Now it seemed he'd sicced his watchdog best man onto her.

She marched across the sand to confront him. There was no call for niceties. 'What the hell are you doing here?' she demanded.

His blue eyes were intense with dislike. 'I could ask the same of you.'

She didn't owe him any explanations. 'Did Alan send you to drag me back to Sydney? If so I—'

'No. Why would he? And why would you think I'd jump to his command if he did?'

'He hasn't stopped hunting for me.'

Max shrugged. 'That's nothing to do with me. I

haven't seen the guy since your wedding day.' His tone was so decisive, his gaze so direct, she believed him.

His hand went to his nose in a reflex action he didn't seem to know he was doing. She noticed it was slightly crooked. The slight flaw only made him look more handsome. *So it was true.*

'I believe Alan didn't take it kindly when you returned my engagement ring to him.' She felt bad about what had happened. All her fault for dragging the unwilling best man into her drama. Not that she regretted it for a moment. She still shuddered at the thought of how lucky she'd been to escape marriage to Alan.

'You heard right,' said Max. 'His response was to try to knock me out.'

She cringed. The photos of the best man and the groom brawling had been all over the press. The erroneous implication being they were fighting over her. The photographer she had hired for her wedding had cashed in big time. 'Did he break your nose when he punched you?' She found herself mirroring Max's action by touching her own perfectly intact nose.

'I've had worse injuries.' He smiled a not very pleasant smile. 'Trust me, he was hurting more than I was when I punched him back.'

Secretly, she was glad Alan had been hurt. After all he'd done to her, his ex-wives, and others she'd since found out had been damaged by his underhand behaviour, her former fiancé deserved more than a whack on the nose.

'But you were friends,' she said.

'I wouldn't go so far as to call it friendship,' he said. 'I met him at tennis camp when we were teenagers and we became mates of a kind. He wasn't good enough to make the grade competitively. When he stopped play-ing tennis we pretty much lost touch. Until recently. I was back in Australia after years of living abroad. He'd returned to Sydney after living in Melbourne for a long time. I was surprised when he asked me to be his best man, but he said his friends were in Melbourne.'

'By marriage number three—thwarted marriage number three, I mean—he might have run out of best-man options.' Nikki couldn't help the cynical edge to her voice.

He frowned. 'Perhaps.'

'I didn't mean that as an insult,' she said hastily. 'He was lucky to have you.'

He shrugged. 'I was the sucker who said yes.'

'So you weren't pond scum after all. Not that I ever really thought you were.' It was a small white lie. She'd thought him pond scum by association. But when he'd picked her up and run with her in his arms, Max had redeemed himself in her eyes. There was still his media reputation as a love cheat but that had nothing to do with her.

'No. But he proved to be particularly unpleasant.' Should she offer to pay for plastic surgery on his nose? Perhaps not. He might be insulted. Besides, she hadn't been the one to swing that punch.

She looked up at him. 'I'm sorry if—'

He caught her arm. 'Can we move somewhere more private? I don't want an audience.'

She followed him to a quieter part of the beach, tak-ing care not to trip over the mooring ropes that snaked along the sand. Max stopped under the shade of a spiky-leaved Pandanus tree. She slung off her backpack and placed it by her feet. A backpack was best for carrying shopping to keep her hands free when hopping on and off boats. 'I'm sorry for being confrontational,' she said. 'I associated you with Alan. Even though you were so kind about helping me.'

He nodded in acknowledgment of her apology. *He looked so good with that beard.* 'So why are you here if not to track me down for Alan?'

'Why does anyone come to tropical islands?' he said. 'But I don't want people to know I'm here on vacation. I'd appreciate it if you kept it quiet.'

'How long are you here for?' she asked. Most people only stayed a few days. There wasn't a lot to do if you weren't into surfing or snorkelling.

'Two weeks.'

Nikki didn't know whether to be concerned by his reply or not. Only her family and very closest friends knew where she'd fled to six months ago. She'd prefer to keep it that way.

He indicated her backpack. 'What about you? Are you here just for the day?' He didn't have to say *I hope so.* She could see it on his face, hear it in the tone of his voice.

'I live here.' There was no way she could conceal it.

'What?' She could take his alarm as an insult. But their last meeting hadn't exactly led to sunshine and moonbeams for him. The media had been ruthless in their pursuit of him after the scandal of the wedding. Determined to drum up a romance, at the very least an affair, between the runaway bride and the best man. She'd run all the way up here. He'd been left in Sydney to bear the brunt of the intrusive attention.

'Do you remember I said I had a plan?'

He nodded.

'Well, I didn't. I escaped up here the day after the wedding to stay with my Indonesian friend while I thought about what to do. She was a boarder at the girls' school I went to in Sydney. We've been great friends ever since. She'd come to Sydney for the wedding, one of my bridesmaids, and I went home with her. I knew she'd keep my whereabouts secret. What I didn't know was that she was pregnant and suffering severe morning sickness that went on and on. She and her husband run a hotel here. I stayed to help her. And I'm still here.'

He shrugged. 'The island is small. Just four kilometres long, I believe. But large enough so we can stay out of each other's way,' he said.

'True,' she said. 'I promise to keep your whereabouts secret if you do the same for me.'

'Done,' he said. His shoulders visibly relaxed. She hadn't realised how tense their chance meeting had made him. If it weren't for what she had dragged him into six months ago she might feel hurt by his aversion to her.

'Where are you staying?' she asked. 'So I'll know which resort to steer clear of.'

'The Big Blue Bungalows in Frangipani Bay,' he said.

Nikki's mouth went suddenly dry and her heart sank somewhere below sand level. She couldn't look at him. 'It…er…might be difficult for you to avoid me. That's the hotel run by my friend Maya and her husband, Kadek. Not only do I work there, I live there.'

CHAPTER THREE

EVER SINCE HE'D helped Nikki flee her wedding, Max had been haunted by dreams of the lovely runaway bride. Dreams, not nightmares.

The real-life nightmares had been played out in his waking hours with the photos of the best man and the runaway bride splashed all over the media, rabid with speculation about a relationship between them. *'Cheater Best Man'* was one of the most innocuous. His past dating history had also been dragged out and picked over—again and again. Would they ever leave him alone?

He was, in his own way, famous. The media had become interested in him when he was still a teenager and had snatched the glory of winning the Australian Open from a much older international player. Then he'd dated a rising female tennis star until their conflicting commitments and ambitions had ended it.

Though apparently, it wasn't a juicy enough story that he and Ellen didn't make it because of their careers clashing. In London, a reporter had used an intrusive lens to shoot him and a female friend having a quiet lunch together and blown it up into a 'Love Cheat' scandal. The resulting headlines had made it impossible for him and Ellen to retain any kind of friendship. She'd been convinced he'd cheated on her while they were still together. If he ever played against her in a doubles game it was always a 'grudge match', according to the press. His love life—or lack of it—was of continuing interest.

What he hadn't realised was that Nikki had a public profile too, as daughter of a wealthy property developer and in her own right as a successful entrepreneur. That had ramped the interest in them as an illicit 'couple' up to a higher level. Those few weeks after the wedding when they were hot news had been nightmarish.

His ongoing dreams of Nikki might not be nightmares but they were unsettling.

The dream always started at the same moment. He was back at the wedding rehearsal in the church on the Thursday night before her wedding. As best man, he was standing next to Alan near the altar. Nikki walked down the aisle, slowly and gracefully, just as she had that night. She was wearing the same short, sleeveless blue dress and silver sandals. Her hair was tied back off her face in a ponytail. She carried a bunch of fake flowers so she could practise handing it to her sister, the chief bridesmaid. All just as it had been.

What differed in the dream was that Nikki veered away towards *him* not Alan. Her smile, the loving anticipation in her eyes, was for him. *He* was the groom. As she neared him he held out both hands to her and drew her close with a possessive murmur. She looked up to him and raised her face for his kiss. He dipped his head to claim her mouth—

And that was when he always woke up. Confused. Yearning. Disconsolate. Until he shook himself into consciousness and a return to common sense.

The dream was all kinds of crazy. For one thing, he

had no interest in getting married. Not now when his injury had turned his life upside down. Not until his life was sorted. And not until he could be sure his marriage was for keeps. He'd seen the stresses the life of an elite sportsperson could place on a relationship. He wanted the for ever kind of happy marriage his parents had. That meant stability and certainty. Right now all his energies were single-mindedly focussed on his new post-tennis direction.

Besides, he wasn't interested in Nikki Lucas in that way. He *couldn't* be. She was attractive, yes. Not just in her looks but also her warm, engaging personality. If they'd met in other circumstances perhaps he would want to pursue that attraction. But she'd impulsively stood up her groom and left him standing at the altar. That showed a certain messiness of thought that alarmed him. Max had abandoned all the rules that had governed his life to aid and abet the runaway bride. And paid the price with his name all over the scandal sheets. *They'd both paid the price.* The only way he could deal with the adverse press was the knowledge that he had nothing to hide. He could truthfully plead he was innocent of any romantic intent towards Nikki. No affair. No ongoing relationship. *Just those cursed dreams.*

And yet here she was. Not the Nikki of his memory or his imagination. But just as lovely. Just as appealing. *Just as off-limits.* With the uncertain future that lay ahead of him, he needed to stay scandal free with no appearances in the press for the wrong reasons. His behaviour that day had been quite out of character for him. To get where he had in the ultra-competitive world of international tennis, he'd had to stay focussed. He planned. He strategised. He drove himself with iron self-discipline. He did not let his emotions get the better of him.

Now Nikki looked up at him, not with the loving gaze of his dream but eyes again narrowed with suspicion. 'How did I not know you were staying at Big Blue?' she asked. 'I help out at the check-in desk. I didn't see your name.'

'I'm checked in as Maxwell James. James is my second name. It's a privacy thing.'

Her feet were firmly planted in the sand. She looked as combative as someone could in billowing hippy pants with the light breeze blowing her hair around her face. He noticed she didn't wear any make-up. She didn't need it. 'Why the Big Blue? Why Lembongan island? Isn't it a remarkable coincidence that you should end up here?'

'That's all it is. A coincidence. I'd never heard of the island until recently. And my travel agent booked me into the hotel. It ticked all the boxes for what I wanted.'

Her brows drew together. 'You really didn't know I was staying there?'

'Absolutely not. I would have steered clear if I'd had any idea.'

Hurt flashed across her face at his words. Max mentally slammed his hand against his forehead. 'Please don't take offence. I didn't mean to be rude. But you must realise that after our time in the headlines, I wouldn't want to see you again. To risk all the media speculation starting up afresh. That was hell.'

She took a moment to reply. 'It must have been awful for you. Being up here, I escaped the worst of it. Though my unavailability for comment sent them into a frenzy. I stopped reading after someone claimed to have sighted me with you hiding in a…in a love nest in Fiji.' She flushed high on her cheekbones at the words *love nest*. Max had to force himself not to conjure up images of how it might play out if that were actually true.

He cleared his throat. 'Yeah. I stopped reading them after a while too. Then, thankfully, the stories dwindled away when the next big beat-up scandal took over. I don't want to give them something new to gossip about.'

'Me neither,' she said fervently.

'I'll move to another hotel. Maybe you can recommend one.'

She shook her head. 'No need for that. Big Blue is a great place to stay this end of the beach. My friends only took it over not so long ago. They won't want anyone cancelling a two-week booking. I especially don't want that to be because of me.'

Max didn't know how to talk about avoiding her without sounding offensive. He remembered how he'd felt—as if his heart were melting—at the sight of her tears on the day of her wedding. He didn't want to upset her, or feel any urge to comfort her. He didn't want any kind of relationship with the woman who had thrust him back into those hideous headlines. 'We'll have to steer clear of each other.'

But she didn't sound offended—in fact it seemed she wanted to avoid him as much as he wanted to avoid her. 'We can do that. For one thing I'm part of the staff, unofficially that is, and you're a guest. That means few opportunities to mingle. What room are you in? One of the *lumbung* on the beach?'

'*Lumbung?*'

'Over two levels, the traditional thatched roof, the woven bamboo ceilings, the open bathroom.'

'No. I'm in one of the two larger new villa-style bungalows further back from the beach. Number two. I have my own lap pool. I thought it would be more private than facing the beach.'

'Oh,' she said, her blush deepening. 'That…well, that could be another problem. I'm staying in the adjoining villa.'

Not just on the same island. In adjacent rooms. Nikki lying in bed just a stone wall away from him. What kind of dreams might that inspire? He swallowed a curse. 'Imagine if the media got hold of that? They'd have a field day. I *must* move to another hotel.'

She put up her hand in a halt sign. 'No. Don't do that. I'll move to the staff quarters at the back of the resort. I can have a room there. It's pretty basic but—'

'I can't allow you to do that.'

She scowled. Which made her look cute rather than fierce. 'It's not a matter of you *allowing* me to do anything. It's only for two weeks. I'm not such a "spoiled Sydney princess" that I can't deal with it.'

Her voice wobbled on the words. So she'd read that offensive story too. It had been immensely unflattering about both of them. He'd felt outraged on her behalf. Had thought about contacting her to offer his commiserations. Had decided against it. He could not be linked to her again. Besides, no one had known where she was. *Now he did.*

'And after the two weeks? What then for you?' he asked.

'Back into my own room, I guess,' she said.

'I mean, what are you doing up here?'

'Helping my friend Maya. Making plans. You know I sold my business?'

'I saw that,' he said.

The night of the rehearsal, when he'd first met Nikki, he had looked her up and read about her success story. How her sister had a very sensitive skin and couldn't use any of the commercial products. How Nikki had developed a range of products that worked for her sister. How she hadn't sought conventional distribution but got in early with her online store, stocking first her own products then other brands. Word of mouth and canny marketing had made it a very profitable hit. Just days after the wedding debacle he'd been surprised to see she'd sold out to one of the huge international cosmetic conglomerates under the headline *'Runaway Bride Cashes In'*.

'Congratulations,' he said. 'Did you sell because of what happened with Alan?'

She shook her head. 'The sale was put in motion before the wedding I thought offloading my very demanding business would give me more time to devote to...' Her voice hitched. 'To family life.'

'I'm sorry,' he said, not sure what else he could say.

She shrugged. 'As it turned out the timing was right—after all I needed a sabbatical from work, some time to put myself together again. Everything had fallen apart. I... I wasn't coping very well with the aftermath.'

'Understandably,' he said carefully.

She raised her eyes to his. 'You know, I really thought I loved Alan. And that he loved me. I'm nearly thirty. I wanted to get married and start a family. It was devastating to find out the truth about him. How horribly he'd lied. That he wasn't at all the person I'd thought he was. I didn't run away from the wedding on a whim, you know.' She scuffed the sand with the toe of her sandals, averting her gaze.

'I know you didn't,' he said. She'd been too desperate for it to have been whim. When the media speculation had been at its fiercest, he had asked himself whether, if he had the time again, he would have aligned himself with Team Groom and refused to help her. He hadn't had to think long.

'Almost to the time I got to the church I thought I'd go through with it,' she said. 'That he'd change. That I'd be the one to make him change where other women had failed. Deep down I knew that wouldn't happen. My father came good when he went into the church to tell Alan and the guests. But in the car he wouldn't hear of helping me bolt. My behaviour would have reflected badly on him. Then I saw you and—'

'And the rest is history,' he said drily. 'I don't regret helping you. I'd do it all again.'

She looked up, her eyes widened in surprise. 'Despite the aftermath?'

'Yes,' he said.

There were two defining moments that had made him certain he'd done the right thing that day. The first was when she'd kissed him. A polite kiss of thanks. And yet for these few seconds her soft lips had been pressed against his cheek and he'd breathed in her scent he'd felt something he hadn't felt in a long time. An awareness. A stirring of excitement, more thrilling perhaps because it was forbidden. *Out of bounds.* He couldn't share that moment and the feelings it had aroused in him with her. But the second moment he could.

'When Alan went for me, there was a moment when his eyes went dead,' he said. 'All the charm and bonhomie gone, unable to mask a ruthless violence that I suspect was habitual. I was very glad I'd helped you escape marriage to the man.'

Nikki gasped and her hand went to her heart. 'You recognised that? His first ex-wife hinted at abuse on that first phone call. Then confirmed it afterwards when I sent her flowers in gratitude for the warning.'

He pushed away the unimaginable dreadful thought of Nikki suffering at the hands of her ex. Thank heaven he had been there for her. 'You had a lucky escape.'

'Yes,' she said. 'Thanks to the people who helped me.'

Max couldn't help but wonder what kind of woman would be so generous as to send flowers to the woman who had warned her off her ex-husband? She was something, Nikki Lucas.

'Why didn't I recognise him for what he was?' she said. 'How could I have been so blind?'

'If it's any consolation I was taken in by him too. Why else would I agree to be best man to a guy I hardly knew? He was persuasive. Played on a long-ago friendship. The fact I was back in Sydney after a lengthy absence and looking to establish a new circle of people.'

'Did you know I agreed to marry him after only a few months? He knew exactly how to play me,' she said with a bitter twist to her mouth. 'Made me believe that everything I wanted from life, he wanted too.'

What did Nikki want? Max realised how very little he actually knew about her. And how tempting it would be to find out more.

Nikki had not intended to confide in Max about The Abominable Alan, the nickname Maya had given her former fiancé. But it was a relief to discover that his best man had been fooled by him as well. Alan had probably had an ulterior motive in his dealings with Max, as he had with her. Max was a very wealthy man. A multi-millionaire. That fact had come up again and again in the media stories about him. She wondered if Alan had approached him to invest in some dodgy enterprise.

She didn't dare ask. Max had given her the impression of being contained—a private person, in spite of his public persona as a love cheat. There were tennis players who threw tantrums, were known for bad behaviour. Not Max. He was renowned for being courteous and well-mannered on the court, the smiling assassin with his killer serve. That first night at the rehearsal, once she'd got over the shock that her groom's best man was a tennis superstar, she'd found him surprisingly reserved. She'd done her best to make him feel comfortable in a room full of people who were strangers to him. Not that it had been a hardship. Not only was Max heart-stoppingly handsome in that strong, athletic way, he'd also made her laugh with his wry comments about wedding procedure. She'd liked him. A lot.

It was ironic, she thought now, that her groom had turned out to be a stranger to her while the unknown best man had done her a favour. But even one moment of her brainpower directed towards Alan was a moment too many. Seeing Max here had brought back feelings that she'd believed six months away from her old life had insulated her against. The discovery of Alan's perfidy, the shattering of her happy-ever-after illusion had left her broken. Her time on the island had helped the healing process. She didn't want the plaster ripped off old wounds. Or any controversy about her and Max stirred up again. They each had much to gain by staying out of each other's way.

'You know we really shouldn't be standing here chitchatting,' she said. 'I doubt anyone on this beach would recognise me. But you could be a different matter. I know your hair is longer and you're growing a beard—which by the way looks really good and suits you—but you're famous in a way I'm not. It would only take one fan to spot you and—'

'Disaster,' he said, taking a step back from her.

'May I suggest you wear a hat as a kind of disguise?' she said. 'You'll need to wear one anyway for the heat. The weather gets really steamy here.'

'It gets so hot on the uncovered courts at the Australian Open that players have hallucinated and collapsed during a game,' he said.

'But not you?' she said with a challenging tilt of her head.

'Not me,' he said. A smile tugged at the corners of his mouth.

'You laugh at the heat?'

In response she had the full impact of the slow, lazy grin he was famed for. Her heart beat a little tattoo of awareness. *He* was hot.

'I wouldn't say that. But I grew up in the central west of New South Wales where the summers are blazing. When I wasn't playing tennis I was helping my dad on the family farm.'

She'd like to ask him about that too. *'Boy from the bush made good'* was a popular description of him. She would have to content herself with looking him up on the Internet rather than engaging in the kind of first-date conversation she could never have with him.

'It's a different kind of heat here. It took me a while to get acclimatised.' Though the temperature seemed to rise just standing near him.

'I'll take your advice and buy a hat,' he said.

She bit her tongue to stop herself from offering to help him choose a style that suited him. *Not a good idea.*

Instead she gave impersonal advice. 'There are a few shops selling hats up on the main street. Well, it's the only street, really.'

'I saw a place that seemed to sell everything including hats near the *warung* where I plan to have lunch.'

'You're having lunch here? I was going to have lunch in the village as well. I like to have a change from eating in Frangipani Bay.'

They fell suddenly, awkwardly silent. Nikki looked up into his blue, blue eyes. She was aware of the gentle swishing of the water on the sand. People from the boats calling to each other in Indonesian. Laughter that would soon turn to squeals from the tourists decked out in orange life jackets climbing aboard the banana float that would be towed out to sea at speed by a small boat.

The words hung unspoken between them. *Why not have lunch together?*

When she finally spoke she knew her words were tumbling over each other too fast. 'Obviously that plan is out the window. I'll go straight back to Big Blue and grab a bite there. But I have a favourite café here. Excellent food. You must try it. I'll tell you the name.'

He frowned. 'Why should you miss your lunch? You go to your café. If my *warung* is too close, I'll find another one. I'm sure it's not the only one serving *nasi goreng.*'

Again the nervous giggle. *What was wrong with her?*

'It most certainly wouldn't be the only one. *Nasi goreng* and *mie goreng* are probably the most commonly served meals on the island.'

'What's the difference?' he asked.

'*Nasi goreng* is a spicy fried rice served with vegetables and maybe prawns or chicken and usually an egg. But then you know that as you've already tried it. *Mie goreng* is fried noodles made in a similar way. I actually prefer it.'

'Do you speak Indonesian?'

'A little. Quite a lot, actually. Maya taught me when we were at school. I'm much better at it than I was when I first arrived.' *Well, that was stating the obvious.* 'There are differences in Balinese and Lembongan, of course. You won't need to worry. Everyone dealing with visitors speaks English. They learn it in school.'

If Max thought she was gabbling he didn't show it. Again that slow, lazy smile. 'That's useful to know. I wish—'

'You wish what?'

Time seemed to stop as he looked down into her face. 'You could be my guide to all things Lembongan,' he said slowly.

A dangerous thrill of anticipation shot through her. She would like that very much. 'But that can't be,' she said, stamping down firmly on that feeling.

'I know,' he said, regret underscoring his words.

'We both know we can't spend time together. Not if we don't want to risk ending up sharing headlines again. I don't think I could deal with a new onslaught of that kind of attention.'

'If we had met under different circumstances, if we

were different people, perhaps—' She felt her heartbeat trip up a gear. *What was he saying?*

'Perhaps?'

'It would be a different story,' he said abruptly. Nikki wasn't sure that was what he had intended to end his *perhaps* with but there was little point in pursuing it. It was enough to know that the spark of interest wasn't completely one-sided. Not that she could do anything about it.

'So how should we handle this, Maxwell James? Pretend we don't know each other?'

'That could work,' he said.

'We'll make it work,' she said. 'We'll have to take Maya and Kadek into our confidence. She was there on the church steps. She saw it all.'

His eyes narrowed. 'Can you trust her?'

'Absolutely without question,' she said. She took a deep breath, took a step back from him. 'We need to start as we mean to continue. You go your way and I go mine. Strangers who happened to chat with each other on the beach about the difference between fried rice and fried noodles.'

'Yes,' he said. Was that regret shadowing his eyes? Or just the reflection of her own feelings?

'How did you get here to the village?' she asked.

'I rode one of the hotel's mountain bikes.'

'That was brave of you. The roads in some places are more potholes than surface and there doesn't seem to be much in the way of road rules.'

'I noticed,' he said in the understated way she was beginning to appreciate. 'You?'

'The hotel truck will come to pick me up when I'm ready.'

'The troop carrier?'

She smiled. 'That's one way of describing the taxis here.'

Transport on the island comprised mainly open-backed trucks where the passengers sat facing each other on parallel benches in the back. No seat belts. No safety rules like back home. It had taken some getting used to. But the drivers were considerate and courteous. And now Nikki never gave the fact she could be risking her life every time she climbed on board a second thought. That was how you lived here and there was a certain freedom to it that she liked. There were different risks and perils back in Sydney.

She reached down to pick up her backpack from where it rested on the sand. Max leaned down at the same time. 'Let me carry that for you.' Their hands brushed just for a moment as he reached for the strap but long enough for that same electric feeling that had tingled through her when he'd carried her over the threshold. She snatched her backpack back to her.

'That's very chivalrous of you. Again. But to see you carrying my bag might kind of give the game away, mightn't it?'

'I get that,' he said. 'But it goes against the grain to let you lift that heavy pack.'

'Must be your rural upbringing,' she said. It was part of the Max Conway mythology that he'd started playing tennis on a rundown community court in a tiny town in the central west of New South Wales.

'There's that. But I grew up seeing my father treat my mother well. He would have done that wherever we lived.'

'How refreshing,' she said, unable to suppress the

note of bitterness from her voice. She seemed to have spent a good deal of her twenty-nine years around men for whom treating women well was not a priority. Like her father—now divorced from wife number three. Like her cheating high-school boyfriend with whom she'd wasted way too many years in a roller coaster of a relationship. And then there was Abominable Alan.

'It's not always appreciated,' he said. Nikki remembered that as part of the 'best man betrayal' frenzy, one of the big women's magazines had run an interview with Max's hometown girlfriend who had nursed a grudge against him. Just another in a line of 'love cheat' stories about him.

'Trust me, I would appreciate it,' she said with rather too much fervour. 'But I've been looking after myself for a long time and am quite okay about carrying my own backpack.'

She picked up the bag and heaved it onto her back. It would have been crass to shrug off his help with getting the straps in place across her back. Even if she did have to grit her teeth against the pleasurable warmth of his touch through the fine cotton fabric of her top.

'Feel okay?' he asked as he adjusted the strap.

'Fine,' she said as nonchalantly as she could manage with the sensation of his fingers so close to her skin. *It wasn't the balance of the backpack that felt fine but his touch.* 'It's not very heavy, anyway.'

She straightened her shoulders. 'Now you need to go your way and I need to go mine. You head off up the alley through those two shops. It will take you onto the street. The café I like is to the right, so you turn to the left. About six shops down there's a great little *warung* serving Balinese food.'

'Hey, that's the place I was heading for with the great *nasi goreng*. Seems you know what pleases me.'

'Just a lucky guess,' she said, flustered by his tone, not wanting to meet his gaze.

'If I see you on the street, I ignore you, right?' he said. 'No hard feelings?'

'No hard feelings,' she said. 'I'll do the same.'

She watched him as he strode away. His back view was as impressive as his front—broad shoulders tapering to a tight butt, lean muscular legs. He was a spectacular athlete on court, leaping and twisting high in the air to connect with the ball in an incredible reach. Not that she'd ever taken much notice before their encounter at her wedding. But in her down time here on the island, she'd discovered there were many online videos of Max Conway's greatest sporting achievements to enjoy.

As he headed towards the street, she realised she wasn't the only one admiring his good looks and athletic grace. A group of attractive girls watched him too, through narrowed, speculative eyes. For a heartstopping moment Nikki thought they recognised him. But no. They just thought he was hot.

So, heaven help her, did she.

CHAPTER FOUR

LATER THAT AFTERNOON, Max sat out by the lap pool under the shade of a frangipani tree in the small, private court-yard outside his room. He was trying to concentrate on a proposal from his agent for a new role—something very different that had potential to be either an exciting new direction or a monumental sell-out. But the words on the screen blurred before his eyes.

There was no reason he should feel so distracted. This place was a private paradise. His one-bedroom suite was spacious and comfortable, traditional with its thatched peaked roof and woven bamboo ceiling, modern in its stylishly appointed open-air shower and air-conditioning.

The courtyard was surrounded by high stone walls and planted with a profusion of lush, tropical plants. The pool was long enough to swim laps, the water cool and sparkling. It was quiet, with just the occasional cooing of doves and echoes of distant laughter coming from somewhere else in the resort to break the silence. The place had everything he'd wanted for his vacation. Se-clusion. Privacy. Time alone with his thoughts.

Trouble was his thoughts were no longer his own. *Nikki Lucas.* Since their encounter earlier in the day she had been flitting in and out of his mind, getting in the way of everything else, tripping up his concentration.

As if the recurring dream weren't bad enough, now he was haunted by the image of her on the beach, laughing up at him, the turquoise sea behind her, green glints in her warm brown eyes, her gauzy shirt clinging to her curves. She had agreed so readily to stay out of his way. As wary, it seemed, as he was about adverse publicity. It was refreshing that she wasn't grasping after him.

He was used to women who, when it came to him, had an agenda. He was wealthy. Wealthier even, thanks to canny investments, than many people suspected. Reasonably good-looking. And, until the elbow incident, at the top of his game. That brought with it a lot of female attention. Not all of it the right type. At first he'd been dazzled by the attention—what red-blooded young man wouldn't be? But he'd soon learned he wasn't a bed-hopping kind of guy. He wanted more, a real relationship, a partnership, but his dedication to his career made that something for the future. Along the way, he'd been burned by women with no interest in him as himself, as just Max, but instead only as a celebrity sports star and what they could get from him.

Even his high-school girlfriend, Lisa, had proved herself to be not immune to the lure of his bank account. From the get-go he'd made it clear he could not commit to her. That his career, with its arduous training schedules and constant travel, came first and would for a long time. He'd broken up with her when he'd moved away for good.

But he'd held happy memories of her and in a moment of nostalgia had hooked up with her on a whirlwind visit to his parents. Only later to be hit by news she'd had a baby and a demand for child support. If it had been true, he would have totally stepped up to his responsibilities. But a DNA test had proved he was not the father. How the episode had leaked to the press he had no idea. But the speculation had not been pleasant. Though how they'd made *him* out to be the 'love cheat' in that case had been beyond him.

Perhaps Lisa's resentment of him had been behind her recent hostile interview where she'd claimed he was selfish, without scruples, and exactly the kind of man who would run away with his friend's bride just because he could. He shuddered at the memory of it—her words, untrue though they were, had hurt. No wonder he was wary, didn't easily place his trust in women. No wonder he hated the intrusion of the media.

But Nikki seemed different. After all, she'd already got what she'd wanted from him—help to escape from her wedding. He had done so and moved on. She needn't have any further role in his life. Avoiding her should be easy.

He forced his attention back to the screen. All of his adult years had been devoted to tennis—and a good deal of his young years as well. His tennis career had meant a tight schedule where every minute of every twenty-four hours was arranged and accounted for. Others had laughed to discover that he practised even on Christmas Day—but he'd felt the joke was on the people who didn't train at his level of intensity. It gave him the edge.

But deciding on a new direction that would satisfy his need to excel was not proving to be straightforward. It wasn't that he needed the money. He need never work again if he didn't want to. But he wanted a purpose, something to drive him forward, a focus. Sitting still had never been his thing. By the time he'd spent two weeks here he was determined to have made a final decision.

Just minutes later, he was surprised by the chiming of the wind chimes hanging by the gate that acted as a doorbell. He hadn't ordered room service. And it was too early for the bed to be turned down.

He opened the ornately carved wooden doors at the entrance to the courtyard. Nikki stood at the threshold. She was carrying a circular wooden tray of snack-sized foods wrapped in banana leaves and an array of sliced fruit, which she held out in front of her like an offering. Max was too surprised to do anything but stare.

She was dressed in the hotel staff uniform of a batik patterned sarong in shades of blue and a hip-length white lacy blouse, finished with a wide blue sash around her trim waist. Her hair was pulled tightly back from her face in a small bun into which was tucked a spray of delicate white flowers. The effect was both charming and quietly alluring. While modest, the outfit discreetly outlined her shape making no secret of the swell of her breasts, the curve of her hips. *She was beautiful.*

But what was she doing there? 'Nikki! I thought we'd agreed not to—'

She gave a quick, furtive glance over her shoulder. From where he stood it didn't seem that anyone was observing them. 'May I come in?' She sidled through the gate and pushed it shut behind her with her hip. 'Indonesian afternoon tea,' she explained. 'Delivering it made a good excuse for me to visit your room.'

Bemused, he took the tray from her, inhaled the delicious spicy aromas that wafted upwards. The food was enticing, it had been a while since lunch, but his thoughts were firmly on Nikki. He placed the tray on the nearby outdoor table.

'I'm sorry but it turns out I can't move into the staff quarters,' she said. 'Maya has assigned the room to a new housekeeper. The rest of the resort is completely booked out. That means—'

'You're still next door.' Why was there elation mingled with his dismay?

'I'm afraid so. My first thought was I could move out for the duration of your stay, perhaps to the mainland. But Maya begged me not to. It's their busiest time. The baby is very young. She needs me.'

'Then there's no choice but for me to move out to the mainland. That would solve any proximity problem.' *He would never see her again.*

Her eyes widened in alarm. 'Please don't do that. Sooner or later the news will get out that you booked in here. Hopefully long after there could be any connection to me. But for a celebrity like you to cancel his stay would be bad publicity for Big Blue. Kadek's family is in the hotel business. This place was run down and badly managed when they bought it. Kadek is a second son. It's his chance to prove himself by making a success of it. His and Maya's.'

Max gave himself time to think. 'Is it such a big deal to be in next-door villas? After all, there are no connecting doors.'

Her eyes brightened. 'Keep to our own side of those high stone walls and there shouldn't be a problem.'

He knew she was as worried about them being seen together as he was. Yet she was prepared to risk it for her friend. Her loyalty to Maya was appealing. Besides, what she said made sense. He looked around him. The high walls, the frangipani trees, the screen of large-leaved foliage acted like barricades against the outside world. Then he looked back to her. 'It's so secluded and private, right now no one would know we were here alone together.'

As if every throbbing cell in her body weren't aware of that. Of her proximity to one of the hottest ever sports stars in the world. Nikki knew the media interest in the scandalous runaway bride and the best man wasn't because of her but because of public fascination with *him*.

She could quite see why. Max was wearing only a pair of black swim shorts. He must recently have been in the pool. His hair was slicked dark and drops of water glistened on his broad shoulders, the super defined muscles of his chest and arms, his flat belly. Nikki had to force her gaze away. It was a real effort to maintain a conversation with him. She'd had to hand him the afternoon tea tray as she'd feared she might drop it because of hands that were suddenly shaky. Now she concentrated on three creamy frangipani blossoms that were floating on the surface of the pool. *Eyes off the best man.*

'You're right.' She forced her voice to sound normal. 'If we're careful, there's no need for either of us to move out of our accommodation.'

'That's done, then. You stay on your side of the wall and I'll stay on mine. But while you're here...' His eyes strayed to the tray of snacks on the table. 'That's like no afternoon tea I've ever seen. I suspect those intriguing parcels would go very well with a cold beer. Join me?'

Nikki glanced down at her watch. She was scheduled to help out on the desk but not just yet. 'Do you think it's wise for me to stay?'

He shrugged those magnificent broad, very naked shoulders. 'Probably not. But you're here, it's private and you're dressed as staff. I think we'd be safe.'

She pushed aside the promptings of her better judgement. 'I'll pass on the beer as I'm due soon at the reception desk. But a cold mineral water would be welcome.'

He headed inside the sliding glass door to the bar fridge. Nikki felt light-headed at the sight of him. She flushed and had to hold onto the back of a chair to steady herself. Could a man have a better rear view? At the beach, she'd thought he'd looked good in his shorts and T-shirt. But with those impressive muscles flexing under suntanned skin and damp swim shorts moulding the best butt she'd ever seen, her appreciation level shot off the scale.

Sadly, when he returned with the bottle of water and a glass, he'd put on a T-shirt. Covering up that chest was a crime. Inwardly, she sighed. Perhaps it was for the best. She couldn't allow herself to fancy Max Conway. She couldn't trust herself to fancy any man. Not after the monumental error of judgement she'd made with Alan. Come to think of it, she'd never been a good judge of men. Seeing in them what she wanted to see, not the reality that they were after no-strings fun or access to her money. Perhaps both. Leaving her with her heart broken and wondering where she'd gone wrong. Feeling like a fool.

'You look flushed,' he said. *If only he knew!*

'Er, yes. It is very hot today.'

'Sit down in the shade and have a cool drink,' he said.

Nikki took the cane chair he offered, one of four set around an outdoor table under the shade of a sweetly scented frangipani tree. She had the exact same furniture in her villa. But no outrageously handsome man solicitously pouring her a drink. 'Thank you,' she said. 'Just what I needed.'

He was just what she needed.

She pushed the errant thought from her mind. For six months she had been without a man's company. Wasn't sure she ever wanted to link her life with a man again. *Needs*, though. That was a different matter. The presence of Max Conway, all six feet two of him, sitting just knee-nudging distance apart was reminding her that her body had needs even if her heart had been put on hold.

She edged her chair a less distracting distance away from him, making the excuse of moving it further into the shade.

Max pushed the wooden tray closer to her. 'What am I looking at here? Samosa? Spring rolls?'

'Spring rolls are called *lumpia* here and those fried pastries are like Indian samosas. There's also *ayam sisit*, which is a shredded chicken dish, and a selection of spicy savoury fritters. For something sweet there's *dadar gulung*, a yummy coconut pancake, fried banana, then fresh pineapple and papaya.'

'You choose first,' he said. 'Be quick. I could probably demolish the whole tray in two minutes.'

She laughed. 'I guess a sportsman would eat a lot.'

Again she was treated to that big, lazy smile. 'I've had to watch every bite I eat for so long. Followed strict dietary guidelines for optimum performance. Had a nutritionist rapping me on the knuckles if I strayed. Now I'm eating what I want. I have a big appetite and love good food.'

Another of those disconcerting shivers of awareness travelled down her spine. Nikki refused to speculate about his other appetites. She really shouldn't be here alone with him. Thank heaven he'd put on that T-shirt, though it really didn't do much to disguise the strength and power of his awesome body.

She wasn't very hungry so she nibbled on a spicy vegetable samosa then a piece of papaya with a squeeze of lime juice. As Max reached out for his third snack, she noticed a small scar on his elbow, white against his tan. 'How is your elbow now? Is it fully healed?'

He stopped with a *lumpia* halfway to his mouth, put it back down on its banana-leaf wrapping. All trace of humour fled from his face and the air seemed to chill around him. 'Why do you ask?' he said, eyes narrowed.

Had she said the wrong thing? Didn't the whole world know he had injured his elbow in a spectacular manner? 'I was thinking—not that I think much about you, of course I don't—that this is summer in the Northern Hemisphere and the tennis season and you—'

'Should be competing?' His expression was bleak and Nikki wished she'd never raised the subject.

'Well, yes,' she said. 'I'm sorry I brought it up.'

'Don't be sorry. It's a valid question. One that more people than you have been asking. I can't avoid answering it any longer.' He sighed, a great heaving of manly shoulders that made her want to reach out and comfort him. But even a reassuring hand on his arm wouldn't be appropriate. Not when they couldn't even be friends because of the scandal that linked them—the fear of it erupting again when she was healing from her emotional wounds. 'Fact is, the elbow is healed. But not well enough to take the stress of competitive tennis.'

'Oh,' she said, not sure what else to say. She couldn't say she was sorry again. 'I'm sad to hear that.'

'The injury was serious. Tendons torn. Bone fractured. From the get-go, the doctors weren't optimistic that I'd ever get the strength back in it. But I refused to give into that diagnosis. I spent a year in intense rehab at a facility in California. I had orthodox treatments by the top practitioners in their field. Unorthodox treatments that seemed to have more hope than science behind them. I was willing to try anything.'

The anguish in his voice gave her no hope for optimism on his behalf. 'But nothing worked?'

'For everyday use, thankfully my arm is good. But not for elite tennis. If I can't play at the top of my form I don't want to play at all. No exhibition matches. No charity matches. There's been no announcement yet, but I'm retiring. That's another reason I'm staying out of the spotlight.'

There was a depth of sadness to his words that struck at Nikki's heart. 'I can't begin to imagine how difficult this is for you.' There was a fine line between sympathy and pity and she didn't want to cross it.

He shrugged but his voice was strained when he spoke. 'I'm not the first athlete it's happened to and I won't be the last. The constant risk of injury is something we live with. Every elite sportsperson has to move on at some time or another.'

'But you weren't ready.'

'At twenty-eight I was nearing the peak of my game.' Regret tinged with bitterness underscored his voice.

'With a serve speed of over one hundred and fifty-five miles an hour?'

'That's right,' he said.

She paused. 'I'm trying to see a silver lining here, but is it a good thing that you got out at your peak?'

'*If* that was indeed my peak. I felt I had further to go. Now I'll never know what I could have achieved.'

The depth of sadness and regret in his voice tore at her heart. She had to try and cheer him up. Without giving into the temptation to give him a hug. 'How many people come nowhere near what you achieved? In any field, not just tennis. You can be really proud of your amazing career.'

His mouth had turned down and she saw the effort he made to force it into the semblance of a smile. 'That's what my dad says. He's always been my number one cheerleader. My mum too. I've spent a lot of time with them over the last months, coming to terms with it.'

But no significant other to discuss his future with? *Not that it would matter to her.*

'So,' she said, not sure how far to go with her questions. 'What will you do?'

He shrugged those impressive shoulders. 'I've never done anything but played tennis. I started a university degree but it was impossible to continue with my sporting commitments. I never really thought beyond tennis. I'm in the same boat as many sports people who didn't plan beyond the next game.'

Only not all of them were multimillionaires. 'Someone as talented and well known as you must have options coming at you from all sides,' she said.

'There are offers on the table. That's one reason I came here. To consider them. And it's another reason I can't get caught up in any further scandal. The role I favour most is with a company with very conservative owners.'

At the pointed reminder, she wiggled uncomfortably

in her chair. 'And here's potential scandal, sitting right next to you eating your papaya.'

She was relieved to see some of the tension lift from his face and the return of that engaging smile. 'If you put it that way,' he said.

'Seriously though,' she said. 'I feel for you. It wasn't easy for me to sell my business. I started it from nothing. So much slog went into it. It was my baby.' Though at the time she'd been happy to trade it for a fat cheque and the prospect of a real baby in her arms. 'I thought I might feel rudderless without it.'

'Do you?'

'Surprisingly, no. Since I've been up here I'm dreaming up new ideas.' Now with no prospect of a family anywhere in the near future—if ever—she needed a new business baby to keep her occupied.

She'd put her cosmetics business before everything, social life, dating. According to her sister, Kaylie, she had done that as much to prove herself to her father as to help Kaylie with her skin allergies.

But Nikki had never really wanted to hear that. Her relationship with her father was fraught at the best of times. Deep down she didn't know if she could ever forgive him for the death of her mother. She had died just a few days after Nikki's twenty-first birthday of a fast-acting form of breast cancer. Nikki and her sister were convinced their mum had died of a broken heart. She'd never got over the discovery of her husband's infidelity with a much younger woman on his sales team, the subsequent divorce and her father's hasty remarriage. But Nikki had no intention of discussing that aspect of her life with Max.

'Did Alan know you were planning to sell your business?' Max's face tightened and she realised there really was no love lost there. The groom had shown his true colours to the best man. Along with his fist.

'Yes. He pressed me to sell. In hindsight, I think that's the only reason he proposed—the prospect of sharing in the bounty.'

Max frowned. 'Surely you don't believe that was the only reason?'

'Looking at what he turned out to be, I can only conclude he was marrying me for my money. His anger when I ran away from him was more about loss of a potential windfall rather than of his bride.'

She knew she had failed to keep the hurt from her voice. In spite of what a jerk her former fiancé had been, in spite of her full knowledge of her lucky escape, that fact still chipped away at her self-esteem. How could she ever again trust her judgement of a man's character?

Max leaned over towards her. He frowned. 'You can't be serious. You're smart, beautiful, kind—what man wouldn't thank his lucky stars you'd want him in your life?'

His gaze drilled into hers for a moment too long. 'Uh, theoretically speaking, of course,' he said, leaning back into his chair.

'Of course,' she echoed, dropping her eyes, unable to stop her spirits from lifting. *He thought she was beautiful.* 'Thank you for those kind words.' It was amazing how soothing they were.

'True words,' he said. 'Every one of them.'

She glanced down at her watch. 'I'd love to hear more. But duty calls from the reception desk.'

But she made no move to get up from her chair, reluctant to go. This kind of chat with Max wasn't likely to happen again and she was enjoying his company. Not because he was a famous tennis star sharing his doubts and hopes for the future but because she felt relaxed in his company. *She liked him.*

But she shouldn't. *Like, love, lust.* All were off the agenda for her. She no longer trusted herself to know the difference. She wasn't ready to think about men. Not for a long time. If ever.

Max indicated the tray. 'Have some more fruit before you go. Or take that last samosa.'

'You have it,' she said. 'I really do have to go.' Not just because duty called but also because it was disconcerting to be so close to him sharing food and conversation. *Enjoying it too much.*

Max reached for the samosa. As he picked it up, the fried pastry cracked to reveal the filling. Nikki jumped up from her chair. 'Max. Be careful. Don't—'

Too late. He bit into the pastry with gusto, then stilled, spluttered, swore, and threw the remaining half on the table. What was left of a big, mean green chilli pepper protruded from the pastry. Max's face flushed red as he pushed away from the table and stumbled up, clutching his mouth. 'Chilli. Burning. Agony.' He repeated the same swear word six times in a row.

He went to grab her bottle of mineral water. Nikki stopped him with her hand on his wrist. 'No. Water will make it worse. Milk. I'll get some.' She ran into his room to retrieve from the refrigerator the milk provided for coffee and tea. She didn't waste time pouring it in a glass but thrust the ceramic jug at him. 'Swill the milk around your mouth. It will help neutralise the burn.'

'Thanks,' he choked out as he gulped down the milk.

She handed him a piece of pineapple. 'Try this, too. The acid in the fruit helps with the heat.'

He followed instructions. She didn't try to engage him in conversation. Eventually a smile struggled through his obvious discomfort. 'I didn't know you were a nurse, Miss Scandal in Waiting.'

She was so concerned that she hadn't warned him about how hot some of the local food could be that she barely smiled her acknowledgment of his teasing comment. 'I got caught out by the heat in the chillies when I first arrived here. I know how much it burns.' She grimaced at the memory of her first encounter with those particular chillies. 'The one you just ate had seeds and the pith and they give lots of extra heat.'

Max went to wipe his mouth. 'Don't touch!' Again she stayed his hand with hers, her fingers resting on his wrist. She noticed his pulse accelerated, no doubt from effect of the chilli on his system. 'Let the milk and the acid of the pineapple do their work. The pain will ease.'

He rolled his eyes. 'I come up here for some peace and quiet and get burned. Max Conway, unbeaten champion, felled by a chilli.'

'I saw it too late to warn you. I should have thought—'

'After all those years of never eating anything that might upset my stomach before a tournament and I bite into *that*. I didn't know they grew chillies that hot.'

'I feel so bad about it. I wish I'd taken you up on the offer to eat it instead of—'

Before she could finish her words, Max started to laugh. His blue eyes were lit with humour, his laugh was deep and rumbling and utterly infectious. After a startled pause, Nikki started to laugh too, so hard she bent over from her waist. Her laugh ended in splutters but when she looked up at him again he widened his eyes and it set them both off again.

Somehow during the laughter her hand on his arm had become her hand in his hand and she was standing close to him. Now his fingers moved to hold her hand firm. 'If you feel so bad about it, why not share the burn?' he said.

Then his lips were on hers. Briefly. Fleetingly. Her lips tingled and her heart raced at the contact. 'Do you feel it?' he murmured against her mouth. Shaken, she pulled away. Not from the slight buzz of the chilli on her lips. But from the other sensations coursing through her. Awareness. Excitement. The dizzying impact of his closeness.

'I feel it,' she said shakily, all laughter dissipated by the heat of that sizzling kiss. Heat that had not been generated by anything as straightforward as the chemical compound *capsaicinoid* that lurked in the chilli.

He wasn't laughing either. 'So did I,' he said, his voice unsteady. She wasn't talking about the chilli. Was he?

This was too much. The empathy she'd felt when he'd told her about his injury. The pleasure in his company. The flare of awareness at that fleeting touch of his mouth, not intended as a kiss, she felt sure, but as a sort of meaningless game. She found him too attractive to be playing with this kind of emotional fire. She had to stay away from him. Not just because of the need to avoid any kind of publicity and the risk of further scandal. But for the sake of preserving her own hard-won composure.

She pulled her hand away from his. 'I have to go,' she said and fled. The last thing she wanted while she healed from the deep emotional wounds caused by her encounter with a liar and a fraud was any kind of involvement with a well-publicised love cheat.

CHAPTER FIVE

MAX HADN'T BEEN anywhere near Nikki for a day. To be precise, it had been two long nights and an entire day. A few times he'd seen her in the distance. Once walking head to head in deep discussion with a beautiful young Indonesian woman he assumed was Maya. Another when she was alone and rushing along the wooden pathways that connected the various areas of the resort.

But her eyes hadn't made contact with his. Either she hadn't seen him or she'd pretended not to see him. He couldn't feel offended because it was what they had agreed. She might very well be angry with him. He had not kept to his side of the bargain with that impulsive kiss. *Feel my chilli burn.* He cringed at the thought of it. Of all the stupid moves in the book he had to pick that one. With a woman who had made it very clear she had no interest in him. Who was, anyway, out of bounds. *He had to keep it that way.*

The resort was proving more than big enough for two people intent on avoiding each other. Not so the proximity of their rooms. Despite those high stone walls, he was aware of her presence in the villa next door. The odd snatch of music. The gentle splash-splash of someone swimming in her lap pool. Did she swim in a bikini? Or nothing at all? The courtyard was secluded enough for the latter. Then there was the shower—open to the sky, and paved with smooth pebbles. In the still of the early morning, he'd heard the splash of water coming from what he thought must be her bathroom and driven himself crazy with imagining her in there as she showered, soaping her lithe body, holding her face up to the water as if for a kiss.

That he heard evidence of Nikki being in residence so close by had nothing to do with the fact he'd pushed the outdoor tables and chairs nearer to the common wall. That was just to take advantage of the shade as he worked through the despatches from his manager. Or the moonlight as he drank a solitary beer by his pool.

Then there was that darn dream.

He'd had it again last night. The same but different. This time his lips actually brushed hers before he woke, seething with the same mixed emotions the dream always aroused. It didn't take much thought to link the progression of the dream to that real-time kiss they'd shared. That impulsive ill-thought-out move had generated heat that had nothing to do with the chilli and everything to do with Nikki's sweet laughter, the scent of flowers in her hair, her slender warm body close to his. The realisation that not only did he find her very attractive—a given since the moment he'd met her on the eve of her wedding to another man—but also he found her so easy to talk to.

He wasn't a guy who easily shared confidences and yet he'd found himself opening up to her. In truth, he hadn't enjoyed a woman's company as much for a very long time. But he was also a man who did not let his life run on impulse. This time on the island was scheduled for serious career planning. Not distraction by a woman. Especially one who, if he was seen with her, could drive his name back into those hideous headlines. The kiss had been a bad idea. *It couldn't happen again.*

Because of all those very serious reasons, he found it difficult to admit to himself that it was driving him crazy not being able to see her. Even though it made utter sense not to. Just because he enjoyed her company didn't make the fact that further scandal, if he were to be linked to her, could be any less disastrous. The directorship he'd been offered was with a very conservative company. People could speculate all they liked about his role in the 'runaway bride' scandal but the truth was he had had no relationship with the bride. To appear ethical, he had to keep it that way.

As he stood beneath his own outdoor shower, he reflected that so far his time on Lembongan was working out as he'd intended. He was getting all the privacy he needed. All the quiet time to reflect. But he was on edge, restless. *Since when had private become lonely?*

After a lifetime of extreme activity he was already going a little stir crazy. He was used to his life being timetabled to the max. In years past, he'd had so little chance to relax he didn't really know how to do it. The word had never been part of his lexicon. He wasn't dealing well with 'civilian' life after the regimented life his tennis career had demanded. No wonder he was spending too much time thinking about Nikki. It might be an idea to return to a timetable allocating time for exercise, eating, time at the computer, sleeping.

As a start, he'd booked a snorkelling trip for this morning. He'd told the guy at the desk yesterday afternoon he wasn't interested in being one of a boatload of tourists. The guy had suggested he engage a small traditional fishing boat, known as a *jukung*, manned by a fisherman who knew the local tides and currents. He'd also need to hire a guide.

Max had refused a guide until it had been gently pointed out that the currents were notoriously unpredictable around the island and could be very dangerous. That local knowledge was required to find the reefs with the best coral and tropical fish. And that, for safety reasons, the hotel could never recommend that a guest snorkel alone. Reluctantly Max had agreed.

He had always enjoyed the water. He'd grown up swimming in creeks and billabongs in the country town where he grew up. The annual family vacation had involved the long trek to the coast, usually Sydney but sometimes Queensland and the Great Barrier Reef. Until the family vacation had no longer included him because he'd been playing tennis. He now realised how narrow the focus of his life had become—the process starting when he was scarcely out of his teens.

At school, he'd been encouraged to compete in the pool but tennis had already taken a hold of him and his competitive efforts had been directed there. Later, swimming had been relegated to part of his training regime. Backstroke and freestyle helped build muscular endurance and strengthened the upper body and shoulders, which powered his serve.

In recent years there hadn't been much chance to swim for pleasure. Let alone snorkel at leisure in warm, tropical waters.

He'd bought himself some fins, a mask and snorkel in a small dive shop not far from the hotel. No need for a wetsuit in these warm waters. He ate the breakfast he'd had delivered to the room and headed down to the bay for an early start. He felt truly excited for the first time since he'd been on the island. Except for when he'd given beautiful Nikki that red-hot-chilli kiss. But that was a very different kind of excitement.

As he walked down to the bay through the hotel's lush, tropical gardens, Max marvelled at the colour of the sea glistening in every shade of aquamarine interspersed with darker blues. At nine a.m. the sun was already hot, burning down from a blue sky. He was glad he'd worn the hat Nikki had suggested he buy.

His spirits lifted even further when he saw the small traditional outrigger fishing boat, powered by an outboard motor, moored near the beach. It was painted bright yellow and red. He thought it looked like a water spider floating on the calm turquoise surface of the bay. As he made his way down the sand, the boatman waved him over with a cheerful greeting.

The guide seemed to be already in the boat, with his back to Max, wearing a black top and leaning over to rummage under the seat in the front of the boat. The boat was small, no more than five metres long by his estimation, and Max wondered if there would be enough room for him and two other men.

But as Max neared the boat the guide turned. Not a man but Nikki, wearing a black swim shirt over a red swimsuit, pulling out a life jacket from where it had been stored under the wide slat that formed a seat. She looked ready to call a greeting but her eyes widened in alarm and she dropped the life jacket when she saw him.

'What are you doing here?' she said at the same time he spoke.

'What are you doing on my boat?' he said.

'Your boat? It's not your boat. It's booked for…' She straightened up to face him, her eyes narrowed. 'You must be James.'

'*Mister* James,' he said.

'The desk told me I was guiding for a man named James.' The drawing together of her eyebrows said *I didn't expect it to be you.*

Max was aware they had an audience of the boatman and the people already basking in the sun on the beach. They had an agreement to act in public as though they didn't know each other. 'And you are?' he said.

She cleared her throat. Obviously not a natural-born liar or used to pretence. 'Nikki,' she choked out. 'Your snorkelling guide.'

He decided to give her an 'out'. 'Pleased to meet you, Nikki,' he said. 'But I don't need a guide. I'm a strong swimmer and I've snorkelled before.'

She shook her head. 'You have to have a guide. These beautiful waters can be deceptively dangerous to people who don't know them. Wild, spinning undercurrents can come from nowhere. You cannot go out alone.' She indicated the boatman. 'Wayan grew up around here. He knows how to read the waters, be aware of changes in weather. If he thought it wasn't safe, we wouldn't be going out today. But he stays on the boat. You need someone with you in the water.'

'And that would be you.' He tried to keep the sudden surge of pleasure at the thought out of his voice.

'Yes. But I can try and find someone else for you if you'd rather not go with me as your guide.' Now she was giving him an out.

'That won't be necessary…Nikki,' he said. 'If I'm going to have a guide I'm happy for it to be you.'

Happier than he should be considering their agreement to stay out of each other's way, considering the awkwardness he felt that the last time they'd met he'd kissed her and she'd turned and run from him.

He couldn't tell whether she was glad or annoyed that he hadn't chosen to have another guide. She nodded. 'I'm a certified dive instructor and though I'm not a local I have extensive experience of diving and snorkelling here. Between me and Wayan, you'll be in good hands.'

Max thought about that. 'I surrender myself to your hands,' he said. She flushed high on her cheekbones and glared at him. 'And Wayan's hands, of course,' he added.

'With pleasure, Mr James,' she said coolly.

Max put his waterproof bag containing his snorkelling gear and a bottle of water onto the boat, then stepped over the outrigger to climb on board. With his added weight, the boat rocked from side to side. Nikki put her hand on his arm to steady him. He didn't really need it—good balance was a skill that served a tennis player well—but he left it there because he liked it.

She took the opportunity to lean in towards him to whisper, 'How did this happen?' Today she smelled of salt and fresh air and the lemongrass shampoo provided in their bathrooms.

'I have no idea,' he replied in a hushed undertone. 'I inquired about snorkelling at the desk at Big Blue and the guy suggested hiring Wayan's boat. He also stressed the unpredictable currents and insisted he book me a guide. He didn't say who it would be and I didn't ask.'

'He wasn't to know we knew each other, or how. Only Maya and Kadek know we're acquainted.'

He didn't want to get off that boat. 'Perhaps it's not such a big deal. No one is likely to see us out at sea. And a mask and snorkel would be a good disguise.'

'We still need to be careful,' she cautioned. 'There are quite a lot of people on the beach. There will be other boats out there too, though you make a good point about the mask.'

'It's agreed we'll be careful,' he said, tugging his hat down further over his face.

Nikki pulled away from him, as far as she could in the very confined space of the narrow boat. 'So, let's enjoy our time snorkelling,' she said out loud, speaking as impersonally as if she were, indeed, a total stranger to him. 'I'll need to get you a larger life jacket.' She reached back under the seat and handed him an orange life jacket. Then strapped herself into a smaller one. She spoke a few words to Wayan in Indonesian and within minutes the boat headed out of Frangipani Bay.

Max sat next to her on the wooden bench that spanned the boat. It was just wide enough so they could sit without touching, even with their torsos bulked up by the life jackets. She didn't talk, just looked straight ahead, calm, unconcerned. But she betrayed herself by the way she nervously twisted the strap of her life jacket.

Max looked straight ahead too. 'I…uh…must apologise about the incident with the chilli.' He couldn't bring himself to say the word 'kiss' to her.

'I'm sorry I didn't prevent it.' Did she mean the kiss? 'I mean, sorry I didn't warn you to be careful of the food until you got used to it.'

'I didn't mean that. I'm sorry that I—'

'Played that trick on me about the burn?' She still

looked straight ahead, her voice pitched higher than usual, as if it took an effort for her to control it. 'Don't worry about that. It was funny. Something my sister and I might have played on each other when we were young. You have a younger brother, don't you? Perhaps you and your brother did something similar. Though maybe not. Boys wouldn't ki— Do that.'

'No. They wouldn't. My brother and I were more for rough and tumble games. The farm was our play-ground.' No surprise when his brother had grown up wanting nothing more than to take over the family farm. As his father had taken over from his father, Max's grandfather.

So the kiss would be ignored? She obviously hadn't felt what he'd felt when he'd held her close. To her it had been a silly game of no consequence. 'No need for any further apologies, then,' he said. 'On either side.'

'Okay,' she said. Finally she turned to him. He drank in the sight of her face, make-up free, cheeks flushed pink, utterly lovely. How had he thought her eyes were plain brown? Those green flecks seemed to make them appear a different colour each time he saw her. Or maybe that was because he was looking more closely. 'I did enjoy the laughter though,' she said with, he thought, a touch of wistfulness.

'As did I,' he said.

She smiled.

'So we're good, then?' he asked, relieved. He'd felt uncomfortable with her initial chilliness.

'All good. Now hold on, the water gets choppy once we get out past the reef that surrounds the island and onto the open sea.'

The ride did become bumpy with water spurting over

them as the boat increased speed. 'This is fun,' he said, exhilarated by the splash of the spray, the thump as the boat rode the crest of the wave then slapped back onto the water. He gave up holding onto his hat and squashed it under the bench. Nikki had tied her hair back off her face but a few stray wisps waved wildly around her head in the wind.

'Better than a fairground ride,' she said, laughing.

Her laughter. It was warm and melodic and engaging. More than anything, he thought, that was what had prompted the chilli kiss. There was something very sensual about shared laughter with a beautiful woman. With *this* beautiful woman.

'Where is this wild ride taking us?' he asked.

'That depends,' she said.

'On what?'

'How competent you are in the water. You may be a champion top-ranking tennis player but I have only your word as to how safe a swimmer you are.'

'I think you can take my word on that.' Max couldn't help but feel affronted. He wasn't used to having his athletic prowess questioned.

'As your guide, I have to make my own judgement on that.' This time when she turned to look at him there was a spark of mischief lighting those extraordinary eyes.

'So you like having me in your power?' he said. Over the sound of the outboard motor and the swishing of the water, he doubted Wayan could hear what they were saying so felt free to skip the pretence they were strangers.

'Whatever made you think that?' she said with what looked suspiciously like a smirk hovering around her mouth.

'Just a thought,' he said, unable to stop an answering smile. Or to prevent thoughts of what it might be like to be in her power in a more intimate way.

'Seriously, I'd be remiss in my duty if I let you just dive in without knowing if you can stay afloat. You'd be surprised how many people tell me they can swim when they really can't. But I haven't lost a snorkeller yet.'

'That's reassuring,' he said with as good grace as he could muster. She was only doing her job—though how she'd ended up in a job like this was beyond his comprehension. From all reports she had been a supercharged CEO of her own company, with a business degree to boot.

'We're heading for the mangroves at the other end of the island,' she said. 'You know the island is only four kilometres long, right?'

'I cycled down to the mangrove forest yesterday,' he said.

He'd taken a boat ride through the quiet, dark waterways under the overhanging mangrove trees and passed the exposed roots that reached into the clear water. It had had an eerie peacefulness. Sitting by himself as the boatman had punted them along, again he had been struck by his aloneness.

The driven life of a professional tennis player had been followed by the rigid regime of rehabilitation. He'd been so determined to prove the doctors wrong and restore his career it had left room for nothing else—not even a flirtation with a cute physical therapist who had made her interest obvious. Looking back, he saw all the activity had masked the essential emptiness of his life.

Yet his solution was more control—timetables, schedules, goals set out and achieved. Control over himself, control over his time, control of the people he'd gathered around him to ensure he was the best he could be. One goal attained, another to reach for, no room in his life for someone to share it with him.

'Don't leave it too long to get hitched, son,' his father had said on his last visit. 'We don't want to be doddery old grandparents.' But marriage and a family of his own were still on hold as he determined a new future. He had loved Ellen, his tennis player girlfriend, but it hadn't been enough to keep them together when it had come to conflicts in their tournament and training schedules. When they'd broken up he'd played the worst tennis of his career—a fact noted by the sports media.

'We're heading for Mangrove Point,' said Nikki. 'The spot on the reef where we're taking you has a gentle current and is a great introduction to snorkelling off Nusa Lembongan.'

'And then?'

'If I think you can handle it, we'll take you to Crystal Bay around on the larger island of Nusa Penida.'

'So, baby steps first,' he said.

'If you put it that way.'

Max went to protest that he didn't need babying but he swallowed the words. Actually he didn't really care where they went. He was back in Nikki's very enjoyable company and out here on a small boat on a big sea they were about as private as they could be.

'How did you end up acting as a guide?' he asked.

'I lived in Manly on the northern beaches until I was a teenager and never far from a beach after that. I loved the sea—swimming, surfing, snorkelling. When I was old enough I learned to scuba dive. The first thing I did when I got here was dive the reef and I totally fell in love with the place.'

'Swimming on the reef is one thing. Taking people out as a guide is another.'

She shrugged. 'It's temporary, isn't it? Like a vacation job really.'

'That makes sense,' he said.

'I was too distraught the first few days I got here to do much but go out snorkelling or curl up in my room. Either activity meant I didn't have to talk to people. That eventually passed and I began to take note of what was happening here.'

'You mean with your friends' venture?'

She nodded. 'I could see Maya and Kadek had done an amazing job renovating and rejuvenating the hotel. They built the wonderful villas we're staying in to extend the range of accommodation. But there were a few areas where they could generate more revenue. Guests wanted to snorkel or dive or take a trip around the island. They'd just refer them to the existing businesses. My friends were too flat out with getting the buildings up to scratch to cut deals with operators and book them through the hotel, or even keep good boatmen and guides on retainer. I thought maybe they could build up to having their own dive shop attached to the hotel one day, buy their own boats.'

'Ever the business person,' he said. *'Sydney's energetic entrepreneur, Nikki Lucas'* was a common label applied to her in the media.

'My father says it's in the blood.' She smiled. 'I'm not so sure about that but if I see a way to make money—honestly, that is—I want to chase it. Luckily, Kadek didn't think I was interfering and welcomed my advice—not that he didn't have plenty of good advice from his own hotelier family, of course.'

'Has it all worked out?'

'So far, really well. They organised things in their own way, keeping staff and family on board. I'm happy to fill in as a guide when required.' She gestured around her to the glorious water sparkling and dancing in the morning sun, the large volcano over on Bali, Mount Agung mysteriously shrouded in cloud in the distance on the mainland. 'How could you possibly call this work?'

She looked up at him, her face shining with enthusiasm and a kind of joy that warmed Max. He wished he could have more quiet time with her. He'd like to bounce some of the ideas he'd had for his future off her. He'd like to— *No*.

Sitting so close to her, her curves accentuated by the tight stretch fabric of her swim shirt, her slender, bare legs so tantalisingly close to his, he couldn't let his thoughts stray to kissing her—properly this time— holding her, making love to her. Not when they were so scandalously linked they couldn't afford to be caught together. Not when he had nothing to offer her in the way of a relationship. Nikki was so obviously not a no-strings-fling kind of woman. And that was all he had to offer at this time of his life, retired from tennis and determined to focus on the transition from the man he used to be to the man he wanted to be now.

Not that she'd shown any such interest in return.

'Not work at all,' he said. 'Unless you find I can't swim and you have to save me from drowning and give me the kiss of life and—'

She raised her eyebrows, but a smile danced around her lips. 'Really? I can see where this is going and I—'

At that moment, Wayan shouted something from behind them. The wind caught the boatman's words and Max couldn't make out what he'd said.

But then Nikki pointed past the starboard side of the boat. 'Dolphins!'

All attention was then on the small pod of frolicking dolphins just a few metres away from the boat. And he never did get to hear where Nikki's thoughts on giving him the kiss of life—any kiss—were going.

CHAPTER SIX

NIKKI KNEW IT was probably a waste of breath to suggest that Max keep on his life jacket for his first foray into the water at Mangrove Point. But she felt obligated to do so.

'No. Flat out *no*,' he said. Then scowled in masculine outrage. 'I'm an Aussie, Nikki. We swim. You know that. I was swimming in the creek at the farm when I was three.' About the same time he'd first picked up a tennis racket, she remembered reading.

'I know,' she said. 'But some people freak out when it comes to swimming in deep water in the open sea.' And more people than she would have imagined—even Australians—either couldn't swim well enough to handle themselves in the sea or couldn't swim at all.

'That isn't going to be me,' he said emphatically as he took off the life jacket and tucked it under the bench. He pulled his white T-shirt up over his head, leaving that magnificent chest bare, just touching distance away from her. She caught her breath, mesmerised by the play of his muscles beneath his smooth, tanned skin even as he made the simplest movement. Like reaching into his kit bag to pull out his snorkelling equipment. *The guy was built.*

'Look, I can even put on my mask without any help, snorkel too.' He proceeded to put on his mask with great exaggeration and a running commentary that made her laugh.

'I concede you're a master at putting on your mask,' she said. A smile tugged at the corner of her mouth as she pulled her own mask over her head and secured it in place over her eyes and nose.

'While you, however, need help with yours,' he said, with a distinct note of triumph. 'You have some of your hair caught up in it. That will stop your mask from getting a good seal and salt water will leak into your eyes.'

'I was going to fix that,' she said in protest.

Too late.

He reached out to tuck the errant lock away from her forehead where it had tangled near the straps. 'Ouch,' she said.

But it didn't hurt. In fact she had to close her eyes at the pleasure of his touch, his fingers firm and gentle as he proceeded to straighten and adjust the strap.

How could something as mundane as helping a fellow swimmer with her mask turn into a caress? Did she imagine that his fingers lingered a touch longer than necessary, brushed across her cheek tantalisingly near her mouth? Did it thrill her because she'd been so long without a man's touch? Or was it because it was *his* touch?

Sadly, she thought it had everything to do with Max and how attractive she found him. What red-blooded woman wouldn't swoon at this gorgeous man's slightest touch? She was no more immune than the fans who'd voted him to first place in those 'sexiest man alive' polls. Only she was fortunate enough to be in close proximity to him.

For a moment—for a long, fervent moment—she wished they'd met some other way so they'd be free to pursue at the least a friendship. But even that, if detected by the media, could draw the kind of attention neither of them could bear to endure again.

'Th...thank you,' she stuttered.

'My pleasure,' he said.

How crazy, here they were both wearing masks that covered half their faces and smiling at each other. It would be comical if she weren't finding being so close to him so disconcerting. She needed to plunge into that water to cool off. Pronto.

But first she took Max through some common hand signals used in diving, to communicate both with each other in the water and with Wayan watching from the boat. When she suggested they keep each other near as they swam, Max didn't argue with her. She went to put on her snorkel. And hesitated.

There was something inherently unattractive about the effect of a snorkel on a person's mouth, she thought, as she held it in her hand. Inserting the mouthpiece so you could breathe easily pushed your lips into an extreme pout that she found a tad grotesque. She was reluctant to put hers on in front of Max. A silly vanity, she knew. Ridiculous, really, as it had never bothered her before.

Max had no such inhibitions. His snorkel was on in seconds. He grinned as well as he could around the mouthpiece and didn't look odd at all. Fact was, he was so good-looking it didn't matter. And he was so confident he wouldn't care anyway. She couldn't help a grin in return as she slipped in her own mouthpiece. He gave her the 'okay' signal.

From the side of the boat, she slid into the water and watched Max do the same. She needn't have wasted any worry about his swimming ability. It was immediately apparent he was as competent and confident in the water as she was. As he struck out away from the boat, facedown in the water, she followed him.

As soon as her head was under the water she was lost to any other thought save the wonder of exploring the underwater world that revealed itself to her. Vibrantly coloured fish darted through the coral, the sun filtered through the clear blue water in shafts right down to the floor of the sea, illuminating a waving sea plant, exposing tiny cobalt-blue fish camouflaged against brilliant blue coral. The feel of the water sliding over her skin.

She turned to see Max gliding through the water beside her, arms by his sides to reduce drag, just the kick of his long fins to propel himself forward. Yes, he'd snorkelled before, there could be no doubt about that. She swam alongside him and could see his pleasure in the water, his head turning to follow the path of a shoal of blue-and-yellow-striped angel fish, as he swam in an easy, well-paced rhythm.

Nikki suspected Max was a natural athlete. No doubt good at any sport he tried. Among the best in the world at the one he had chosen to excel at. Who knew what he might still achieve?

As she watched him, he dived down and swam deeper propelled by strokes of his muscular arms, the strength of his powerful torso. He stayed under, holding his breath longer than she could have imagined anyone could—but then as an athlete in peak condition he must have an amazing lung capacity.

On land, he seemed strong and athletic with an insouciant physical presence. His confidence underwater added a further element of gracefulness to his athleticism. His perfectly proportioned body was as streamlined as if he were himself a magnificent sea creature, riding the current rather than fighting it. To her, watching from above, it seemed he belonged there as much as the coloured coral and the sea plants waving gently in the water, the schools of brilliantly coloured reef fish darting in and out of the underwater landscape. He turned and twisted with, she thought, the sheer joy of his physicality.

As she watched him, Nikki felt torn by a yearning to be part of whatever it was he was experiencing. To be with him. She couldn't put a name on what she felt. It ached but it wasn't anything sexual. Or was it? As she watched him glide through the turquoise depths of the sea, the realisation hit her with full force. She flushed, even with the coolness of the water on her face. Yes, she admired him. But not in a dispassionate way. *She wanted him.*

During the time she'd avoided him, her growing desire had pushed insistently against her defences. Defences she'd rapidly put up when he'd held her in his arms as he'd helped her flee from her wedding—and she'd liked it. Liked it too much. That was what all that tingling had been about. Sheer sensual awareness of the best man. She'd taken it for nerves, relief, even embarrassment at the situation she'd got herself into.

The more she'd fought it, the more that desire had pushed to be acknowledged as she'd tried to ignore his presence at the resort. Tried to forget the feelings that had surged through her at his brief, unforgettable kiss. Even pretended she hadn't seen him when he'd crossed her path. When in fact she'd thought of little else but him. Had even found herself on her side of the common wall between their villas alert for sounds of his presence. She'd spent rather too long wondering if he swam in his lap pool in the black swim shorts he currently wore or nothing at all.

Now that dammed-up desire burst through, shattering her defences and leaving her vulnerable to him, to her awakened needs. She would have to make every effort to mask it. Nothing had changed. They still couldn't be seen to be in any way linked to that old scandal if they didn't want to be splashed all over the media again in such an unpleasant way. How foolish she'd been to even contemplate a friendship between them. Being platonic friends with Max wouldn't cut it for her. Not when she hungered for the physical.

He'd been under the water for so long she realised she was holding her own breath as she watched him. How long had it been, he swimming, she lost in admiration and newly acknowledged desire? She dived down to join him.

As she reached him, he pointed down to a brilliant blue starfish for her to admire then turned. They powered up to the surface together, emerged from the water at the same moment. Blew the water from their snorkels in plumes. He looked around to find her. Even through his mask she could see his exhilaration, the eagerness to share his underwater experience with her. She'd felt the same when she'd first snorkelled here. Her heart skipped a beat at the sight of him; she knew how difficult it would be to pretend indifference to this man. How much fun it had been for her to swim with him, like-minded, matched in their skills. How much more she wanted.

Now, she swam up beside him, removed her mouth-piece so she could talk to him, treading water. He did the same. His hair was slicked flat to his head, dark with water, his eyes bluer than the bluest patch of the sea. She was treated to his most dazzling smile yet.

'Wow,' he said. 'Just wow!'

Wow! Yep. That was exactly her reaction when she saw Max's half-naked body emerging from the water like some gorgeous mythical merman from his enchanted underwater kingdom. *Just wow.*

She had to swallow hard to make her voice sound normal. 'I'm so glad you enjoyed it,' she said, genuinely pleased at his reaction. One of the things she liked about helping out as a guide was introducing people to these beautiful waters and the marine spectacle that lay beneath the serene aquamarine surface.

'Thank you for bringing me here,' he said. 'It was brilliant. Better than any expectation.'

She forced her voice to sound how a swimming guide should sound, impartial yet encouraging. She the guide, he the client. 'Crystal Bay is even better,' she said. 'Deeper water, more coral, more fish, more colour.'

'So I'm being allowed to move up to the next grade?' he said, with just a touch of sarcasm.

'If you put it that way,' she said. 'Obviously, you're a really good swimmer and experienced at snorkelling. But you understand why I had to see for myself. Safety is paramount.'

'I understand,' he said. 'At the time I felt insulted by your refusal to believe me but—'

'Insulted? I didn't mean—'

'I know.' The smile dimmed. 'I guess I might have to get used to people questioning my skills at anything but tennis.'

She frowned. 'I'm sure that's not going to happen.'

'It will. It has. Taking a new turn in life is never straightforward.'

'No, it's not,' she said, thinking of the way her own life had gone since she'd made that fatal decision in the car on the way to her wedding. How she couldn't stay hiding on this island for ever. How maybe one day she might trust a guy enough to consider a relationship. But not now. And certainly not with a man she'd have to share with thousands of adoring fans who hung posters of him in their bedrooms. A man trumpeted in the media as a love cheat. Much as she might want him. 'But I'm sure with your skills and contacts, you will be successful in whatever you choose to do. I… I'll watch your new career with interest.' *From a distance.*

'I'll keep you posted,' he said politely. But she suspected he didn't mean it. How likely would it be that their very different paths in life would cross again after his two weeks on the island were up?

She looked across to the boat. 'Wayan has put the ladder down so we can easily get back on board. Crystal Bay is quite a way away. We have to go around Nusa Ceningan, which is even smaller than Lembongan, then around to the east coast of Nusa Penida, which is the largest of these three islands. *Nusa* means island, by the way.'

'How did I not know about this fabulous place?' he asked as he effortlessly pulled himself up out of the water and onto the boat.

She averted her eyes from the sight of his gorgeous, near-naked back view. *Eyes off the best man,* she had to remind herself yet again.

Max didn't feel much like talking in the boat on the way back from Crystal Bay. The water there had been everything Nikki had promised. More. As he'd swum in that underwater paradise he had realised for the first time since the accident he had felt happy, relaxed, and living in the present rather than angsting about the past or worrying about the future.

He'd enjoyed a non-competitive sport, swimming with Nikki for fun, not seeing her as a rival he had to beat at all costs. To crush his opponent had been his mindset for so long he'd found it difficult to switch out of it enough to enjoy a sport for sport's sake. That had been his only motivation during the gruelling year of full-time rehab. To focus both physically and mentally on getting back in shape so he could win again. The pressure had been so intense the knowledge that he wouldn't compete again had led to an immense letdown. Followed by an immediate drive to find a new direction in life that didn't hang on numbers on a scoreboard.

But today he'd forgotten all that. Thanks to Nikki.

Nikki was relaxed, easy-going, non-judgemental. He had soon realised she wasn't a particular fan of tennis, or of him as a tennis player—and he was okay with that. More than okay. She knew of him, but he suspected he hadn't really been much on her radar until he'd turned up as best man for her groom at her wedding. He felt he didn't have to prove anything to her, to be someone he was no longer.

Today they'd slipped into an easy companionship, swimming together, marvelling at the same beauty of the underwater world that revealed itself to them. In sync. Obviously, she was a kindred spirit in the water. And out of it? He had an overwhelming urge to find out.

Now she turned to him. 'Have you done any scuba-diving?'

He shook his head. 'Not interested. I don't want to be fussed with all that equipment. I'll stick with snorkelling where I'm in control.'

'I can see that point of view,' she said. 'However, there are deeper waters around these islands I'm sure you'd love that can best be appreciated by diving. The island is a good place to learn.'

'That rather depends on who my teacher would be,' he said. His eyes caught hers in an unspoken question.

She met his gaze full on, unblinking. 'I can recommend a good dive school.' There wasn't a trace of flirtation in his snorkelling guide's voice. She apparently had no interest in him as anything other than an inconvenient client foisted upon her by a misunderstanding. A happy misunderstanding from his point of view. Obviously not from hers.

'I'll keep that in mind,' he said, determined not to reveal any trace of disappointment. 'In the meantime I want to snorkel as much as I can while I'm here. Can I hire Wayan and his boat to be on standby for every day of my stay? I'd pay the full day fee, of course, whether I use him or not.'

Her eyebrows rose. 'No one has ever asked that before. But I guess it could be arranged. We'll have to ask Wayan.'

'What about my guide?'

She stilled. For a long moment she looked back at him. He was so intent on her face as he waited for her reply he was barely aware of the constant spray, the rhythmic slap of the water on the hull as the boat navigated the rougher waters of the open sea on the way back to Frangipani Bay.

'I'm not for hire, nor can you keep me on retainer. I might go out on the water with you if it suits my schedule. If not I can arrange for a different guide.' There was a distinct chill to her voice that had nothing to do with wind cooling them in their wet swimwear.

'I don't for one moment think you're for hire. I don't know what your arrangement is with your friends who run the hotel. But today has been…special for me. I doubt it would have been that special with another guide.'

'Thank you. I really enjoyed it too. You were great to swim with.'

She hadn't given him any indication that she felt anything at all for him beyond that. Except, perhaps, annoyance that he was on the island at all. Even further annoyance that he had crashed *Mr James's* boat trip. But she was too professional to show it.

He leaned a little closer. Not that he thought Wayan could hear him but it was important his words weren't snatched away by the breeze. 'Nikki. I enjoy your company. I like you.'

She flushed and dropped her gaze, seeming to fixate on her discarded swim fins on the floor of the boat. 'I…er… I like you too.' The flutter of her lashes, the slight stutter made her words sound like a major admission. Max was surprised at the relief he felt. But he could almost see the cogs in her brain wondering where this was leading.

He considered his words. 'This vacation is shaping up to be the best I've had in a long time.'

She looked up. 'That's really good to hear. Maya and Kadek will think so too.'

He shook his head impatiently. 'I don't mean that. Well, yes, I do. The resort is great. The island is wonderful. But what I'm trying to say is that today is all thanks to you. And I want to spend more time with you.'

Her eyebrows raised in alarm. 'But we agreed—'

'Yes, we did. But out here, on this boat, in this water, the media and all the scandal seems so far away. It's like we're operating on a different clock with different rules for the way time passes.'

Jam karet,' she said. '"Rubber time", they call it here.'

'There's a name for it? *Jam karet.'* He rolled the unfamiliar words around on his tongue. Thought about what it meant to someone who had always been ruled by timetables, obsessed with punctuality. Could there be a different way for him? 'That's not a concept that would fit my old life. But here… I get it. Yeah, I like it.'

'Me too. Although I was so strung out when I first got here it took me a while to get my head around a different attitude. Now, I hope I'll take some of that relaxed feel back with me when I return to frantic Sydney.'

'What about we relax our attitude here? Out on the water, actually *in* the water, no one has recognised me—or you. I haven't seen a flicker of recognition from anyone, tourist or local.'

She assessed him through narrowed eyes. 'I think it's the beard. Even in the days you've been here it's grown. You look different. Maybe not to one of your rabid fans, but to a casual observer.' She shrugged. 'As for me, blonde Australian women are a dime a dozen in Bali.'

As she sat next to him, her damp hair a wild tangle, the imprint of her mask still around her eyes and nose, her cheeks reddened by windburn, he had never seen a more attractive woman. 'Women like you are not a dime a dozen *anywhere*, let me reassure you of that.'

That won him a self-deprecating smile. 'Thank you, it's very sweet of you to say so. But *you* being seen here, or *me* being seen isn't a problem. It's if we're seen *together* that there could be trouble.'

'The longer I'm here, the less I'm believing it,' he said thoughtfully. 'This island is hardly party central. Not a place where paparazzi are popping out of the undergrowth.'

'Perhaps not,' she said slowly.

'Maybe it's a good place to spend time with a person you like.'

'I guess it could be,' she said, not sounding very convinced.

He angled himself closer to her, injected a note of urgency into his voice. 'I'd like to spend some time with you, Nikki. More snorkelling, tomorrow perhaps. Maybe lunch today.' He glanced down at his waterproof watch. 'I'm grateful for those nuts and snacks you brought on board with you. But right now I'm starving.'

She sighed and he could see her conflicting thoughts play across her face. 'During those weeks after the wedding I felt ill every time I opened my laptop. The things that were said about me, about you. I wish there wasn't so much at stake if we were to be discovered enjoying each other's company by the media. No matter how innocent it might actually be.'

Innocent. Was that the right description for his feel-ings towards Nikki? They certainly weren't platonic. In fact, they were growing less innocent each minute he spent in her company. He wanted more time with her, more opportunities to get to know her.

Max wasn't used to giving into impulse or emotion. The times he had let his feelings rule had led him into trouble. The worst had been his reaction to the unprofes-sional opponent who had been taunting him both on and off court in an effort to break his concentration. He'd es-calated from the professional to the personal. The final insult had been a snide comment about the doubt over the paternity of his former girlfriend's child. During that all-important game his sudden surge of anger in reaction to the guy's smirk had made him forget tactics, forget self-control and smash the guy with everything he had—re-sulting in the injury that had ended his career.

But there was something implacable about this im-pulse to be with Nikki. Something that urged him not to hold back for fear of possible consequence. That his time here with her was limited and the opportunity to act on that impulse might never come again.

Back there in the water with her he'd felt something he didn't think he'd ever felt before. Not just apprecia-tion of her beautiful body, gliding through the water with effortless grace. Of her spirit, her beautiful smile. There'd been a harmony between them, as if he and she together were meant to be. Now he felt compelled to grab the chance to see if she felt in any way the same.

He found himself urging her to a course of action when only days before he'd been pressing for the op-posite. 'If we're discreet. If we're careful. If we both wear hats and sunglasses—like everyone does here anyway—I'm happy to risk a lunch together. Maybe down at the mangrove end of the island. It seems quieter there.'

'I know a wonderful family-run restaurant there,' she said. 'Small, rustic but the food is incomparable.'

'Sounds perfect,' he said. 'Count me in.'

But the tone of her voice led him to believe there could be a 'however' coming and he wasn't wrong.

'However it's a risk,' she said. 'And not one I'm ready to take.'

Something made him wonder if she was referring to something altogether different from the risk of exposure by the media. There was something in her eyes he couldn't read. Wariness? Fear? Surely not fear of *him*?

His spirits plummeted. He hadn't realised how much he was counting on her saying yes. But as he started to plan his next strategy for winning her over, he realised she hadn't stopped speaking.

'But I'll think about it,' she said slowly, weighing out the words. 'I need some time.'

Despite the urge to want to ask her every five minutes if she'd thought about it yet, he and Nikki spent the rest of the boat trip back to Frangipani Bay in silence. He gave her the space she'd asked for. He knew it was a big ask. A turnaround. There was still risk they might be discovered, that his worst nightmare of press intrusion might rear up again. But there was a greater risk of future regret. He had ten days left on this island in near proximity to Nikki. After that it was highly likely he would never see her again.

By the time the boat headed into Frangipani Bay she still hadn't said a word—yea or nay. But he held his tongue. Until they had to slip back into the pretence that they hadn't known each other before this day.

As Wayan anchored the boat in the shallow waters. Max took off his life jacket and handed it to Nikki.

'I need to stay on board the boat,' she said. 'Tidy the life jacket, talk with Wayan.'

'Have you thought about what I said?' He realised he was holding his breath for her answer.

She paused, then slowly nodded. 'Your time on the island is short. I… I think I might regret it if I don't take the opportunity to…to get to know you a little better.'

He let out his breath in a whoop of relief, stopped short of punching the air. 'Yes! Lunch. Now. Nikki, I—'

She put up her hand to stop him. 'Not lunch. But I have a thought for dinner tonight. Don't make any other plans.'

'Right,' he said. Having got her this far, he wasn't going to argue.

'You might get a call from Maya. If so, just do as she suggests.'

He made a mock salute. 'Yes, ma'am.'

She laughed. 'Now, Mr James, I suggest you thank your boatman and your guide for a great day's snorkelling and get off the boat.'

His instinct was to hug her. But common sense told him that would not be the right move. She had met him more than halfway. The next move had to come from her. He thanked both Wayan and Nikki, jammed on his hat, put on his sunglasses, picked up his kit bag of snorkelling equipment and got off the boat. He waded through the water and onto the beach without looking back.

CHAPTER SEVEN

LATER THAT AFTERNOON, Max did indeed get a call from Nikki's friend Maya. She apologised for not having made contact earlier and invited him to come to her house at the back of the resort complex for six p.m. to meet her and her husband Kadek.

Max was intrigued. Was this an invitation to have dinner with them and Nikki? If so, he had mixed feelings. Yes, it was one way of seeing her again safe from the public gaze. But he would so much rather see her one to one. No chaperones. Just him and her. Alone and getting to know her better. Anticipation shivered up his spine. When had he last felt this way about spending time with a woman? Not just a woman. *This* woman.

The friend who had warned him that he might get bored in Nusa Lembongan could not have been further from the mark. Max hadn't experienced a moment's boredom since he had seen Nikki step off that boat and back into his life.

He arrived at Maya's house promptly at six. Although finding himself seduced by the concept of *jam karet*, he wasn't yet won over. Punctuality was deeply ingrained in him. The house sat in its own garden behind the last row of bungalows. He entered through traditionally carved wooden gates into a stone courtyard complete with lush greenery, a water feature and eye-catching Indonesian artefacts.

A petite, lovely dark-haired woman in an elegant, traditionally inspired top and wrap skirt in a batik print greeted him with a welcoming smile. 'Hi, I'm Maya. So pleased you could come.' She introduced him to her husband, Kadek, tall, handsome in a high-collared white shirt over a boldly patterned sarong type garment. In this kind of heat, Max thought, a sarong would be a good idea. He'd always dressed conservatively, never knowing when a photo of him might be snapped by paparazzi. He must ask Kadek about the best type for a Westerner to wear.

'I've been looking forward to meeting you both,' Max said sincerely. Maya had obviously been a true friend to Nikki; that predisposed him to like her.

'We've kind of met before,' Maya said. 'I was one of Nikki's bridesmaids but I couldn't make it to the rehearsal so you might not recognise me.' She spoke perfect English with a distinct Australian accent.

Max narrowed his eyes as he thought. 'I think I remember seeing you getting out of the car with the other bridesmaids at the church. But I was watching out for the bride.' Already the bride had been running late and he'd been edgy.

'You did a great job on rescuing Nikki from that dreadful man. Her friends thank you for that.'

'Uh, yes,' he said, uncertain as to where this was going. *Where was Nikki?*

Maya laughed. 'You're probably wondering what you're doing here. Come on through.'

She and Kadek led Max through to an open living

area with a polished stone floor scattered with bright rugs and traditional Balinese wooden carved furniture. But it was the carved wooden settee, piled with colourful cushions, that drew Max's attention.

Nikki sat in the centre, cradling a tiny, dark-haired baby. She looked up to greet him and her eyes were still warm with a doting kind of love that had obviously been directed at the baby. 'You're here,' she said. She got up, baby still in her arms. 'Meet Putu, Maya and Kadek's firstborn son.'

Max was reeling at the sight of Nikki looking so at home with a baby in her arms. But as she took careful steps towards him he began to think he was hallucinating. She was wearing the same blue dress as at the rehearsal, as in his recurring dream. Her hair was pulled back the same, only now it was fixed with a spray of white flowers. She was wearing the same silver sandals. And her eyes had that dreamy look of love that was so disconcerting in his dreams. Though the love was for the baby, not for Dream Max. 'Nikki,' he managed to get out of a suddenly choked throat. Why did he feel as if he'd been aced?

'Isn't he cute?' she asked, in a doting tone of voice that did not completely disguise an undertone of yearning.

Max cleared his throat. 'Uh, yes. Very cute.'

He hoped she wouldn't ask him to hold the baby. He wasn't used to babies. Didn't know how to handle them. What to do with them. It had to be admitted—babies scared him. In more ways than one. Their unpredictable digestive systems scared him; their propensity to scream blue murder if placed in his arms scared him; but what scared him most of all was the effect an unplanned pregnancy could have on a guy's life. His brief legal battle with his former girlfriend had shown him that. Her baby had not been his, but before that had been proven by DNA he'd thought a lot about how he could do the right thing and maintain a relationship with the child.

But little Putu was cute, very cute, with fine black hair and merry dark eyes. 'He's a great little guy. You must be very proud,' he said to Kadek.

'We are,' said Kadek, the warmth in his eyes speaking to the truth of his words.

In fact, each of the other three people in the room were united in looking adoringly at the baby, eyes glazed with fondness. Secure in Nikki's arms, little Putu chortled with glee at the attention, waving his tiny hands about. Until suddenly he stilled and his face went very red and strained. A symptom, Max suspected, of something alarming happening in that baby digestive system. At one end or the other.

To Max's intense relief, Maya expertly swept the baby from Nikki. 'I'll see to him and be back as soon as I can,' she said.

Kadek made small talk and offered drinks from a tray on the carved wooden coffee table. 'Nikki tells me you enjoyed your snorkelling trip today,' he said.

'Very much so. I can't wait to get out there again,' Max said. But he was finding it difficult to concentrate on what the other man was saying. It was as if everything and everyone were out of focus, the spotlight shining only on Dream Nikki.

'I've seen you in that dress before,' he said, not attempting to hide his admiration. In fact, he remembered almost to the very minute when he'd first seen her wearing it.

The tall woman in the blue dress had caught his eye when he'd got to the church for the rehearsal. She'd been laughing at something an older lady was saying. He'd been struck not so much by how she looked—though he'd thought her very attractive—but what could only be described as her aura of warmth and vivacity. Not that he believed in actual coloured auras that psychic people claimed to see surrounding a person. In fact he didn't believe in anything supernatural of any kind. But there had been something about that girl in the blue dress that had drawn him so his gaze had kept returning to her again and again. He well remembered the intense stab of disappointment he'd felt when he'd discovered she was the bride, about to marry his recently rediscovered 'friend'.

'When did you—?' She answered the question herself. 'The rehearsal. I was wearing it that night, wasn't I? It was so hot.'

She was so hot. And he'd seen her many times in the dress since then in his dreams. He certainly had no intention of telling Nikki that. She'd think he was crazy and run screaming. He wouldn't blame her. Maybe he *was* a tad crazy when it came to her.

How sane was it to suggest they see each other alone when he knew what the outcome could be if they were discovered together by the media? His civil break-up with Ellen had degenerated into enmity thanks to the media casting him so unfairly in the role of love cheat. A reputation further cemented by the 'runaway bride' episode. If the press caught them together again his totally unwarranted reputation as a sleaze would endure. Yet seeing her here, he wanted to be with her more than ever.

'It's a lovely dress,' he said lamely. 'You look, uh, lovely.' What was the matter with him? He was usually not short of a reply, of banter and repartee to keep a social conversation going.

'Thank you,' she said. 'I'm glad you were able to come tonight.'

'How could I not?' he said. Nothing could have stopped him from accepting Maya's invitation.

'If you're willing to take a risk of being seen out together, I can help out Maya and Kadek at the same time. That's what you're here to talk about.'

Just then Maya swept back into the room. 'Putu is in bed and now we can return to adult conversation.' She turned to Nikki. 'You were explaining the plan to Max?'

'I'd just started,' Nikki said. 'Max, you know Maya and Kadek are working hard on making Big Blue an even better resort than it is already. They've made a lot of improvements.'

'But more to come,' said Maya.

'We want to make our restaurant a destination in its own right, not just somewhere for guests to have meals,' said Kadek.

The Big Blue restaurant was in a rotunda-type building right on the beach. Max hadn't eaten there yet—he'd had room service when he'd actually been at the hotel for meal time. Including, of course, the memorable afternoon tea. The food had been consistently good.

Nikki continued. 'Maya asked me to visit some of the island restaurants to check out their new menus.'

'To see if there was anything we could be doing better,' said Maya.

'Maya and I were going to go out together tonight to one of the good restaurants not far from here,' Nikki said.

'Even though there are risks in that,' Maya said. 'I might be recognised as a rival hotelier.'

Nikki directed her words to Max. 'You, however, would not.'

'What better front than a couple enjoying a nice dinner for two?' said Maya.

'While surreptitiously photographing the menu,' said Nikki.

'And taking photos of the plated meals supposedly for social media but really to show to our chefs,' said Maya.

'You mean me? Me and Nikki?' asked Max, bemused.

He looked to Kadek. Kadek threw up his hands. 'This is something the girls cooked up.'

'We would be like the secret shoppers they send into stores to check the service,' said Nikki. 'Only we'd also get a really good dinner.'

Her eyes pleaded with him to say yes. Max thought he would do anything she asked of him. 'Sign me up. I'm in.'

'Wonderful,' said Nikki. She and Maya gave each other a high five. Max couldn't help wondering what was more appealing to her, the dinner or his company. He'd take his chance on making sure the pleasure of his company won out.

Maya tucked her hand into the crook of Kadek's elbow and looked up at him lovingly. 'Good. I get to have a quiet night in with my husband.' Kadek put his other hand over his wife's and looked down at her with equal affection. Max felt a stab of something uncomfortably like envy.

What would it be like to have the kind of loving security that Maya and Kadek so obviously shared? As his parents did, even after all their years together? The closest he'd come to the kind of partnership he held as the ideal was with Ellen. But it had never developed past initial high hopes. He wondered if they'd both known deep down that the relationship had no future—that it would always come second to their careers. The breakup had hurt at the time, hurt more when she'd quickly moved on to date and ultimately marry the physiotherapist who travelled with her on tour.

Kadek stepped forward. 'If you're ready to go now, I will drive you both in the truck to the restaurant.'

Max frowned. 'Won't it look suspicious to have us arrive in the truck with a Big Blue logo on the side?'

Nikki shook her head. 'Not at all. It's common to drop off guests to other destinations. The restaurant would send its own truck to get us if we booked it. But we thought that would be drawing too much attention to us.'

Us. He and Nikki having dinner together. No matter the pretext, he was going to enjoy it. 'Okay. Let's do it,' he said.

The Big Blue truck was like the others on the island, open at the back and sides with just a canopy over the top that offered little protection from rain. Luckily the sky was clear. Nikki accepted Max's offer of help to climb in from the rear. Not because she needed it but because, in spite of her resolve to ignore her attraction to him, she couldn't resist the opportunity to enjoy the sensation of his hand on her arm. Even that light, casual touch sent shimmers of awareness through her. It was doubly intoxicating as she now recognised those shimmers for what they were—the stirrings of desire.

Once in the truck, she settled herself on one of the narrow, padded benches that formed the seating. She slanted her legs neatly to the side, aware that her dress easily rode up to expose rather too much bare leg.

'Be warned, there's not much padding on these seats,' she said to Max as he swung himself aboard. She was tempted to offer him a hand up but decided that might be just too obvious. With his athletic build it was very apparent he didn't need help.

'I'm tough,' he said, as he sat next to her at a polite distance.

Tough in body and, she suspected, tough in spirit. He must be to have got where he was in his sport. To be one of the top-ranked tennis players in the world. It was a mind-boggling achievement and she could only imagine the perseverance it had taken him to get there. For the umpteenth time she wished she could get to know him better. Tonight might give her that opportunity.

Kadek was a careful driver, but the roads were narrow with unexpected ruts, and tourists riding motor scooters two or three abreast. They were not long out of the hotel when the truck swerved and Nikki was swung hard against Max. 'Sorry,' she said in that ridiculous way she did when apologising for something for which she wasn't responsible.

He looked down into her face with the slow, lazy grin that made her melt. 'I'm not sorry at all,' he said, his voice low and husky.

They'd been thrown together so closely their thighs

were touching. It would be crass to move away. To tug down her skirt from where it had, predictably, ridden up. As if she found his nearness distasteful—which was far, far from the truth. Nikki let her shoulders relax and leaned against him. She realised how long it had been since she'd been as close to a man. But she gave no thought to other men. Just this one. *Max.* She breathed in the scent of him: lemongrass, a hint of cologne, healthy, fit male. Heady. Intoxicating. Dangerously close to arousing.

He made no attempt to move away either. In fact he wedged his legs closer, which kept her from sliding in her seat but also brought them kissing-distance close. 'Where are we headed?' he asked. Did he mean something deeper by that than a question about the truck's direction? *Don't overthink things,* she told herself.

She took a deep breath to steady her racing pulse. Tried to speak normally. Even so, her words came out rather too quickly. 'The restaurant is right on the beach near the most western point of the island. We're passing through the village now. Those beautiful buildings are the temples where families worship. Over there is the elementary school.'

'So you're as good a local area tourist guide as you are a snorkelling guide,' he said, teasing.

'I do my best to excel,' she replied in the same tone.

She spoke with mock modesty but it was true. Nikki did try to excel at whatever she did. Which was why it was a constant nagging undercurrent to her life that, while she'd succeeded in business, done well with investments, had long-time close friends, she didn't seem to have what it took to succeed in a relationship with a man. Here she was staring thirty smack in the face with nothing but failure—spectacular, public failure in the case of Alan—behind her. No wonder she was terrified of trying again, of ever letting herself trust.

'Is the restaurant far?' Max asked.

'Just a few more hair-raising twists and turns. We should be just in time to catch the sunset.' She was about to say the sunset was very romantic but decided against it. This wasn't a date. They were on an information-gathering mission.

Kadek stopped the truck a short distance from the restaurant. Nikki called a 'thank you' to him then went to get off the back of the truck. Max jumped down first. 'I'm here if you need help,' he said.

'Of course I don't need help,' she said as she prepared to jump. 'I've done this lots of times and—oh!' She stumbled a little on the uneven ground and landed heavily against him.

'Whoa,' he said as he caught her and steadied her with his hands on her upper arms.

'Th...thank you,' she stuttered.

'You okay?' He looked down into her face.

'Fine,' she said. And feeling finer every second he kept his hands on her arms. His tennis-player calluses felt pleasingly rough against her sensitised bare skin, his fingers strong and firm.

When she didn't move away he pulled her closer, so close she could sense the hammering of his heart, breathe in the exciting maleness of his scent, thrill at the warm strength of his body. She slid her arms around his waist and looked up at him, feeling nervous, excited, uncertain, on the brink of something unexpected. His eyes seemed a deeper shade of blue in the waning light and the intensity of his expression made her breath come short. For a very long moment their gazes locked in what seemed a series of unspoken questions with only one answer. *Yes.*

She was only vaguely aware of Kadek driving away. The world had shrunk to her and Max. Her lips parted in anticipation and she murmured her pleasure when he kissed her. His mouth was firm and warm against hers, his beard surprisingly soft against her skin. She tilted her head so she could more easily kiss him back.

'Is this because we're pretending to be a couple,' she murmured against his mouth.

'No, it's because I want to kiss you,' he said.

'I want to kiss you too.' She licked along the seam of his mouth with the tip of her tongue. 'No chilli this time. You're naturally hot.'

'You think so?'

'Oh, yes.' She wound her arms around his neck and pulled him to her, deepening the kiss. What had started as tender very quickly escalated into something intense, demanding, passionate, so all-consuming all she could think about was Max and the heat they were generating. Desire burned through her. She pressed her body to his as lips and tongues became more demanding.

This. Him. Max. *She wanted him.*

She didn't know how much longer they would have stood there in the middle of the narrow lane kissing, oblivious to their surroundings, if another truck hadn't driven up to deposit visitors to the restaurant. At the sound of its blaring horn, she came plummeting back to reality. Reluctantly she pulled away, immediately had to hold onto Max's arm to steady herself on legs that had turned to jelly. She blinked with bewilderment.

'What happened?' She choked out the words.

Max looked equally shaken. He took in a deep, shuddering breath. 'The inevitable,' he said.

Nikki didn't have to ask what he meant. No matter how she'd tried to deny it, they'd been heading towards this.

'The…the question is where do we go from here?' She knew her voice sounded strained and uncertain.

Max reached out and gently smoothed the strands of her hair that had come loose back off her face. She stood very still, briefly closed her eyes at the pleasure of his touch on her skin. 'Wherever it leads us,' he said.

Could she do that? Could she risk it? The thought was terrifying.

The people from the bus rushed towards them. She and Max stood aside to let them past. 'They're hurrying so they don't miss the sunset,' she explained. 'We should do the same. We need to go.' She went to turn away.

He put a finger under her chin, tilted her face upwards so she was forced to look at him. 'Regretting it already?'

'No. Yes. I… I don't know.'

He released her but then took her hand in his. 'I'm not usually an impulsive person. But I feel compelled to follow where this is taking us—wherever it might be.'

'I'm not sure. I—' She could be impulsive, had used her quick decision-making to her benefit in the past. But feeling like this, about him, was scaring her. *She wanted him too much.*

'We don't have to think any further than tonight,' he said as he looked down into her eyes. 'Just tonight, Nikki. One night.'

CHAPTER EIGHT

THE RESTAURANT SAT by itself on the edge of a small, sandy beach lashed by fierce surf. People at the front tables could wiggle their toes in the sand. To the left were limestone cliffs where wild waves rolled in at all angles and crashed onto the cliff walls. The sunset was glorious, an enormous glowing red orb casting a fiery pathway onto the sea as it slowly sank into the horizon.

Nikki knew the sunsets on this coastline were reputed to be among the most splendid in the world. But she scarcely noticed nature's splendid display. She only had eyes for Max. His face seemed infinitely more interesting. Equally nature's masterpiece. Quite the best-looking man she had ever met. *And hers for tonight.* A thrill of pleasure and anticipation shimmied through her.

She was seated next to him at a table discreetly set towards the back of the restaurant. While the ones at the very front overlooking the beach caught the best view, the people seated there were also on display. Nikki's choice of table was as private as it could be in the well-patronised, fashionable restaurant. It was just as well no one was looking at them for several reasons, not least of which was that she was entranced by Max and he seemed equally entranced by her.

So much for having to pretend to be interested in each other as she and Maya had planned. The waitress had to ask them twice if they were ready to order—neither she nor Max had even noticed she was there. Such bumbling spies they'd turned out to be. More interested in each other than in analysing the menu and service in the interests of Big Blue. She would have to do better on the spying front. But not just yet. Being with him had suddenly become the overwhelming interest in her world. She kept reliving that unexpected kiss. *Wanting more.*

Max was holding her hand under the table. In fact he'd scarcely let go of it since they'd kissed outside the restaurant. 'How are we going to eat when our meals arrive?' she murmured.

'One-handed?' he suggested. 'You with your right and me with my left.'

She laughed. 'I guess it's possible.'

He leaned closer to her. 'I don't want to let go of you. I have to keep touching you to reassure myself you're still here with me.' There was an undertone of surprise to his words that she totally related to. This thing between them had flared up so quickly. *And could burn out as quickly,* she reminded herself. It wasn't something she could place any trust in.

She entwined her fingers with his even closer. 'I feel the same,' she said, her voice a little wobbly with wonder.

'I have to pinch myself that you actually said that.' He lowered his voice. 'You know, I didn't think you were interested in me at all.'

'I couldn't allow myself to be. Not when we'd been

so singed by the scandal I dragged you into. Not when I'd been the bride and you the best man.'

'But now we're two people without ties and—'

'Are you? Without ties, I mean,' she said. 'I wondered. After all, I'm talking to the guy voted sexiest man alive.' How could he be single?

He groaned. 'Don't remind me of that stupid title. I'll never live it down. You should hear what my father and brother have to say about it. There's nothing like the ribbing of two blokes from the bush to keep a guy from getting a swelled head. Though I think my mother was secretly tickled. But in answer to your question, there's no one. Hasn't been for a long time.'

Nikki realised she'd been holding her breath for his answer. She let it out on a silent sigh of relief. 'I see,' was all she managed to say.

'After the accident I was totally focussed on getting fit enough to play again. Obsessed. There was no room for the distraction of dating. What about you?'

'No one. I... I think I'd have to know a guy for ten years before I'd trust him enough to date.' Her comment was meant to be light-hearted but she couldn't help a note of bitterness from slipping through.

His brows raised. 'Really? Ten years?'

She nodded. 'The thing with Alan was that bad. To find out someone I'd believed in had lied to me about something so fundamental caused serious damage.'

Max's other hand went to his nose, once again, the slightly crooked bend showing in the evening light, as evidence of his encounter with Alan's fist. 'Bad for you too,' she said. 'If it's any consolation I think the new-shape nose suits you. It adds a touch of edginess. Make you look even...even more handsome.' She was going to say *sexier* but thought better of it. Not when she was clueless about where this was going. *But she had tonight.*

'I'll take that as a compliment,' he said.

'Please do,' she said. She would like to kiss that nose if she got the chance. Oh, yes, she'd like to kiss him, taste him, explore him. Now that she'd had her first taste of intimacy with Max she wanted more.

The waitress brought drinks, an aptly named sunset cocktail for her, a local beer for him. Still Max didn't let go of her hand and she didn't free it. Instead he demonstrated how well he could pour a beer using his left hand. Picking up her glass with her right was hardly an achievement as she was strictly right-handed. But it was fun. *He* was fun.

'Did you ever see me play tennis on television?' he asked after the waitress left.

'Yes,' she said, wondering where he was going with this. 'I enjoy watching the tennis. And it would have been difficult to avoid seeing you, reading about you. The entire country was behind you when you kept winning those big tournaments. And of course you were so hot you turned a lot of besotted young women onto tennis.'

'The more fans, the better. Good for the game.' It would be false modesty if he tried to deny his celebrity status. She was glad he didn't. 'So when did you first see me?' he asked.

'I think it might have been when you first won Wimbledon.'

'Men's singles. I was twenty-two.'

'I was twenty-one. Finishing uni and starting my own business.' Still with Ray, the high-school boyfriend, thinking they were headed for marriage when he'd been cheating on her for six months with the woman he eventually left her for. Ray, her first big fail when it came to men.

Max let go her hand, made a show of counting on his fingers. 'By my calculation, you've known me eight years.'

'What?' His statement was so audacious, she had to laugh. 'You have got to be kidding me.'

'I could be.' He shrugged. 'Or I could be seriously suggesting you take that first time you watched me on television as our introduction. Eight years ago. Two more years to go before you could trust me.'

'There's something seriously flawed in your logic.' She tried to sound serious but couldn't help laughter infusing her voice.

'Makes sense to me,' he said.

'Except for the fact *you* didn't actually see *me* unless you could somehow beam vision from the centre court at Wimbledon to my house in Sydney.'

He grinned. 'Maybe. Maybe not.'

'I think we'll go with "maybe not",' she said, laughing again. 'As far as I recall, the first time you ever laid eyes on me was at the wedding rehearsal. By my count, that makes nine and a half years to go before—'

He sobered. 'Before you could trust me. Or any other man.'

'That's right,' she said, thinking she'd dug herself into a ditch. 'Though there could possibly be time reduced for good behaviour.'

He leaned closer to her, concern warming his eyes. 'Why, Nikki? Why such distrust? It's not just Alan, is it?'

'No, it's not,' she said, unable to stop a hitch in her voice. 'I had a long-time boyfriend and that didn't end well. A few other disasters when I started to date again. But I don't know that I want to talk about all that. It's a bit heavy for a first date.' She frowned. 'That is, if this is what you'd call a date?'

'It can be whatever you want it to be,' he said. 'I don't much care for labels.'

'We said one night only.' Already the hours were counting down. *One night wouldn't be enough.*

'May I remind you I still have ten more nights on the island after tonight. We could make it ten nights. I can't speak for after that—I don't know where I'll be. It wouldn't be fair to say otherwise.'

'I could be exaggerating about the ten years. But I'm not ready for a relationship. Not sure when I ever will be ready.'

'I'm not in a position to offer one. I don't even know where I might be living. Anyway, "relationship" is just another label.'

'I'm glad you said that. Tag me in a relationship and it's doomed.'

Nikki hated that she sounded down on herself. She was strong, intelligent, had everything going for her. She knew that. But she chose the wrong men. Trouble was she didn't know they were wrong for her until she was already in too deep to easily extricate herself. Perhaps it was because she didn't want to admit she'd made an error of judgement. Or perhaps she was too willing to try and see the best in people and forgive them when she shouldn't. She got that trait from her mother, who had never said a bad word about her duplicitous father, right up to the day she'd died. Given Max's reputation—perhaps he was a mistake too.

'The media, they made a big deal about you and Ellen Trantor. That you...that you cheated on her.'

Max's face set grim. 'I was never unfaithful to Ellen. Ever.'

'That photo...' Nikki hated to dig when it so obviously made him uncomfortable. But she had to know.

'That photo of me having lunch with a female friend was taken after I'd broken up with Ellen.'

'But I thought—?'

'That we were still together? The press certainly took great delight in pointing that out. Fact was we'd split weeks before. But Ellen was facing one of the most important tournaments of her career. She knew the media would make a song and dance about a break-up and asked me to keep it quiet as she didn't want to be distracted from her game.'

'Then they broke the story about your date with the other girl.'

'Which made it look like I was cheating on my girlfriend. Ellen was furious on two counts. The adverse publicity put her off her game and she lost. Then she refused to believe that I hadn't been dating the girl during our relationship. For the record, the girl I was lunching with was an account executive from the sportswear company that sponsored me. There was nothing romantic between us, and there certainly wouldn't have been after that whole thing blew up. As the so-called "other woman" she was hunted by the press everywhere she went, even had paparazzi popping out of the flower beds at her parents' house. She hated me.'

'Wow. I'm sorry. I had no idea.'

His mouth twisted into a bitter line. 'You can see why I despise press intrusion into my private life. That incident cost me several matches, too. I've never played so badly. It also lost me the friendship and respect of Ellen, a woman I had deeply cared for and a peer. Playing against her in a doubles match became a nightmare—every time a "grudge match" according to our media "friends".'

'And that other girl? The former girlfriend from your home town who gave that horrible interview in that magazine?' She shuddered at the memory of those vindictive words.

He grimaced. 'How did I get cast as the villain in that case? I was single, she told me she was single when we met up again on one of my flying visits home to see my parents.'

'You mean you had ex-sex?'

'No strings. By mutual consent. But she couldn't have been single at the time because I was definitely not the father of her child.'

'Yet you got branded as the love cheat?' she asked, puzzled. 'How did that happen?'

'Turns out the father was a guy I'd known at school. Not difficult in a small school in a small country town. The media made out I was cheating on a friend.'

'Then you were made out as doing the same thing with me—the best man betraying his friend the groom. Which was utter nonsense, of course.'

'*All* of it utter nonsense. But the gutter press breeds on creating scandal. That kind of beat-up story gives their readers and viewers a temporary "ooh-ah" kind of thrill. Makes them think they "know" a celebrity. But it changes the lives of those involved and not for the better. Mud sticks. There are people who believe there's no smoke without fire. Each time it's happened to me, people I respected thought less of me.' His eyes were clouded with disbelief that he should have been judged so unfairly for something he hadn't done.

'I think more of you for sharing that with me.' He took her hand again. She tightened her clasp on his hand when what she really wanted to do was hug him and comfort him. 'And I appreciate you want to take a chance on me, in spite of the consequences if we're discovered.'

If the press who hounded him could blow up something as innocent as a lunch date, what might they make of the best man and the runaway bride 'hiding out' on an island six months down the track?

'Why don't we take it day by day?' Max said. 'One night at a time.'

Her heart kicked up a beat. 'Are we talking a fling? A no-strings fling? If so, I've never had a fling. I don't know how—'

'Just another label,' he said.

'So a no-label fling?'

'If that's what you want to call it. But I'd rather forget about labels altogether.'

'No labels…no expectations,' she said slowly.

'Just enjoy each other's company without worrying where it's headed,' he said.

It was a refreshing thought. She'd always worried about where a relationship was headed before it had really started. Here, away from her life back home, could be the right place to take a risk on something different. With a man so very different from anyone she had ever met before.

'Yes,' she said. 'Get to know each other in the time we have.'

'The clock has already started ticking on that time,' he said. 'There's so much I want to know about you. So many questions I want to ask you.' She was surprised at how urgent he made that sound.

'Fire away,' she said. 'I'm ready to answer your questions. Like you answered mine. But there's one thing I want to get out of the way first. I… I haven't been completely honest with you about something important.'

Dread clutched Max deep in the gut. Just when he was allowing himself to relax into the real-life scenario of being with his dream girl in the blue dress. That kiss had taken his dream a whole lot of steps further from where it usually ended. Nikki. In his arms. Passionate. Exciting. *Real.*

A hundred hideous reasons for Nikki being dishonest with him churned through his brain. He had always placed great store on honesty and trust, even before he'd been played by the press. He let go of her hand, placed his on the table. Immediately felt bereft of her touch. 'What do you mean?' He braced himself for her reply.

'I said I was dreaming up ideas for a new venture. Truth is, that venture is well and truly in the development stage.'

'A business venture? And you didn't tell me that because—?'

Her eyes flickered nervously. 'It's that trust thing again.'

'So why confide in me now?'

'Because I don't think you look at me with dollar

signs flashing in your eyes.' She looked down at the table. 'Like Alan so obviously did.'

He was so relieved he nearly gagged. 'Dollar signs are not what I see when I look at you, Nikki, I can assure you.' What he saw was a woman exceptional, not just in looks, but in nature. How could any man let her go? No wonder Alan had whacked him in the nose. Nikki underestimated herself if she thought a man would only be interested in her money. Even Alan must have been hurting at her loss from his life.

'I also think you probably have enough of your own money not to be interested in mine,' she said.

'You're right there. I've been caught too often by people more interested in what I have rather than who I am.'

Nikki nodded. 'Just Max. Not Max the celebrity. Not Max the millionaire. The Max I've got to know and to…to like.'

'Exactly,' he said. 'And I like you for the you I've got to know over the last days. Not just beautiful Nikki—that's a given—but smart, clever, kind Nikki. I can assure you your personal wealth has no interest for me.'

I have more than enough for both of us. Max swatted the thought from his mind. He wasn't thinking of a future with Nikki. He couldn't. He was a single-minded kind of guy. Needed to get his life sorted before he could consider a relationship. He had to be careful he didn't raise expectations of anything he couldn't fulfil. Especially when he was beginning to realise the damage that had been done to her by unscrupulous men in her past. He didn't want to be another man who hurt her.

'So as far as wealth is concerned, we're on an even playing field,' she said.

'And perhaps I've gained a few minutes' credit in the trust department?' he said.

'Maybe even a few hours,' she said with a smile that made her eyes dance.

He wanted to kiss her, but fought the urge. Holding hands under the table was one thing in terms of possible exposure. Kissing in a crowded restaurant was another, even if most people's focus was on the last minutes of the setting sun.

'Tell me about your new venture.'

'Private swimming clubs for women back home in Australia,' she said. 'Since I've been here I've been shocked at the number of people who can't swim but want to enjoy the water or to keep their kids safe. Australian women from various backgrounds who didn't learn to swim for one reason or another but are embarrassed to admit it. I think they'd value a safe, private environment where they could be taught. Not just to swim but to snorkel and dive, even surf. Remember you said to me, "I'm an Aussie, we swim?"'

Max nodded.

'That's not always the case. The Australian statistics on non-swimmers are quite alarming for a country where death by drowning is a real issue.'

He smiled at her enthusiasm. 'Sounds like a worthy idea. But would it be profitable?'

'I'm looking into that.' Her eyes narrowed in an expression of concentration that was almost sensual in its intensity. 'The clubs would be luxurious without being intimidating. Stroke correction as well as beginners' classes for a wider customer base. A health and beauty spa. Branded swimwear. A swim travel company to take postgraduate clients to destinations like Frangipani Bay and Greece and Croatia for fabulous swimming tours.'

'You thought of all that since you've been here?'

'I would never have thought of it otherwise.'

He realised both her ideas for businesses sprang from a desire to help people, a generosity of spirit he admired in her. First her sister with her skin problems and now women who yearned to be able to swim. He could learn from her. His thoughts for his future had focussed on his needs, not the needs of others. Perhaps he needed to re-think that. Could he, after so long focussing on his need to win? Could he ever share his life with someone else?

'How far advanced are you with your plans?' he asked.

'As far as I can be from up here. I'm working through my father's property development company to search out potential sites, talk to architects.'

'You're on such good terms with your father?'

'I haven't always been. We clash. Perhaps we're too alike. But he and my mother started the company together—she was an interior designer, he a real-estate agent. They started by flipping houses and went on to apartment blocks and commercial developments. The partnership fell apart when he left her for his assistant. But the point is, my mother left me and my sister her shares. So of course I work through the company.'

'You're at a crossroads in your life,' he said.

'So are you,' she said. 'I'm interested in what path you might take after tennis.'

Work. She was talking about work. Did he have to walk that path alone?

He would usually keep such matters very close to his chest. But suddenly he wanted Nikki's opinion, her business smarts and maybe— No. He was *not* seeking her approval. That would imply something he didn't want to acknowledge.

'Okay. The options. I'm tempted by a directorship of a big sporting goods company.'

She nodded. 'Could be a plan. Keeps you in the world of sport and is prestigious. As long as the directorship would be an active role, not just there for them to have you on their masthead for prestige. I suspect you would get easily frustrated by a passive role.'

'You're right about that,' he said. She was both shrewd and perceptive. 'There's also an opportunity with an elite tennis coaching ranch in the US.'

'Might you find it too difficult to be training others when what you really still want to do is to be out there competing yourself?'

'You've nailed it,' he said, shaken at how she seemed to read his mind. It was disconcerting.

'There is another option.'

She smiled. 'Now I hear some excitement in your voice.'

'Excitement and a touch of trepidation,' he admitted.

'Spill.' She leaned a little closer to him.

'Sports commentator for one of the big cable networks. Covering the major tournaments. All around the world.'

'Wow. You've got the knowledge, the screen presence, the personality. I could really see you doing that.'

'But it would involve the kind of peripatetic lifestyle I've been living since I was a teenager. Perhaps I want to put down roots.'

'Where?'

He shrugged. 'Ideally Australia. It's home and my

parents aren't getting any younger. But I've lived in the UK and the US too.'

'It's all very exciting for you, isn't it?' she said.

Not half as exciting as being here with you.

He looked up to see a waitress heading their way bearing a tray. 'I see our starters heading our way,' he said, welcoming the opportunity to change the subject. 'I'm ready to eat.'

'Me too,' she said. 'But we can't touch a thing until I've taken shots with my phone for Maya. We mustn't forget the reason we're here. I don't want to let my friends down.'

Max pretended to grumble. Made to snatch up the little 'fusion' tacos with an Asian filling before she finished her photo. Complained he would faint of hunger if she didn't let him start on the tuna slices with a spicy soy dipping sauce and a wasabi mayo. Told her it was torture to keep him from the fritters.

But he liked her loyalty and commitment to her friends. Loyalty wasn't something he'd experienced from a female companion. But then perhaps he'd been too focussed on his game to be able to give it in return.

'Okay, we can start now,' she said. 'Sorry to have made you suffer.'

'You don't look sorry at all,' he said. 'I think you enjoyed torturing me.'

'I'm admitting to nothing,' she said with a delightful curve of a smile.

He held back on his hunger. *Ladies first* had been a strict rule at his house when he'd been growing up. He always followed it. At the table. When it came to opening doors. In bed when his lover's pleasure was as important as his own. He watched Nikki as she savoured her tuna, making little oohs and aahs of appreciation and tried not to think of how she would react if he were to make love to her. He had to suppress a groan at the thought.

'Aren't you having any?' she asked, innocent of the not so innocent thoughts that were occupying him.

'Of course,' he said. 'I was waiting for you to go first.'

'Why thank you, I appreciate that,' she said, oblivious to any play on words.

'Try the corn fritters—they're scrumptious.' She caught his eye. 'Watch out for the sambal that accompanies them, though. It's really spicy. I know you don't like it too hot.'

He might surprise her, if he ever got the chance. 'Yes, scrumptious,' he said as he sampled the food. How he wanted to sample *her*.

'What do you think about the restaurant and the menu?' she asked. 'What shall we report back to Maya?'

'I'm no foodie,' he said. 'But it's a bigger menu than at Big Blue, going by their room-service menu.'

'You haven't actually eaten in the Big Blue restaurant?'

'Privacy and anonymity, remember,' he said.

'Of course,' she said. 'Though I don't think anyone has recognised you here tonight.'

'They were too busy taking selfies in front of the sunset to notice anyone else, I think,' he said.

'I know,' she said, rolling her eyes. 'The last time I was here one girl had three changes of clothes for her photographs.'

'Now they're all heads down eating. Which is just

what I want to do too. I hope the main courses won't take too long.'

'Be patient,' she said. 'The service is very good here. Another thing to report back on.' He was good at being patient when it came to the food, impatient when it came to having her in his arms again.

The sun had finally slid into the sea and the place was lit by strings of glowing lanterns. The white foam of the surf glistened where it caught the light. Even over the chatter of guests and the clatter of dishes he could hear the water pummelling the cliffs. 'It's very atmospheric,' he said. He'd nearly said *romantic* but caught himself in time.

'It is, isn't it? I might suggest to Maya they invest in some of those lanterns. I really like the effect.'

'It's an impressive menu too,' he said. 'A good mix of Indonesian and Asian food with Western dishes too. People from all around the world come to this island. The variety is excellent. Vegetarian and vegan choices too.'

'It's impressive all right. I notice here they specialise in barbecue foods. I wonder if Big Blue should specialise to make their menu stand out.'

'Desserts,' he said immediately. 'Really fabulous desserts. That would draw the punters in, I reckon.'

Her eyes widened. 'I didn't think of you as a dessert fiend.'

'I had to suppress a lot of cravings when I was training. There's a lot you don't know about me.'

Her eyes glazed over, narrowed a little. 'And I have ten nights to discover it,' she said, her voice low and husky.

Max was too astounded to reply. He wondered if he had underestimated lovely Nikki when it came to the not so innocent thoughts.

CHAPTER NINE

WOULD MAX EXPECT her to go to bed with him tonight? It was all Nikki could think about as she stood shoulder-to-shoulder with him in front of the carved wooden gate to her villa. Surely the thought must be playing on his mind as much as it was on hers? Not to mention the urgent signals her body was sending her. *My needs, remember?*

She wanted him. She *really* wanted him. But she still didn't know him very well and to be intimate with someone who was still virtually a stranger had never been part of her romantic game plan.

She'd always been a commitment type of girl. Admittedly she'd been a schoolgirl at the time but she'd dated Ray for six months before they'd made love— her first time.

Perhaps it was to do with her upbringing by her religious mother. One of the reasons her mother's last years had been so miserable was because her religion didn't recognise divorce. While in the eyes of the state her mum had been divorced, in the eyes of her church she wasn't. There'd been no thought of a second marriage for her, despite her father having wed his mistress to make her wife number two. Her mum had drummed into both the girls that sex should be part of a committed relationship. Nikki had discovered the truth in that herself. Now she wasn't so sure.

Maybe now was the time to stir up her life a little and do things differently. Take what she wanted without worrying about where it might lead. By agreeing to the no-label fling she'd taken the first step. *With Max.*

Kadek had picked her and Max up at the restaurant in the truck. He'd just said goodnight and was headed back to Maya and the baby at his house at the back of the resort. Nikki listened to her friend's footsteps on the wooden walkway until they faded into the distance then disappeared altogether.

The silence between her and Max seemed to stretch out for too long—although it was probably only seconds. She became intensely aware of the sounds of the evening on the warm, tropical night. Birds rustled in the trees above them. Some kind of insect gave an intermittent chirrup. The sea swished gently onto the sand of Frangipani Bay. There was the distant crow of a rooster—they seemed to crow without timetable at all hours of the night. And her own breathing, too rapid, making her feel faint. Perhaps from the rich fragrance of frangipani that hung in the air. Or was it because she was alone with Max for the first time since that hungry, passionate kiss had changed everything between them?

It was ridiculous to feel so nervous. She was a grown-up woman of nearly thirty. Not a starstruck adolescent. She turned towards him. His face was illuminated by the lantern above the gate. He looked very serious and impossibly handsome. She was awestruck at the thought she had him in her life, even if the time had limits on it.

'I…er…would like to ask you in for a nightcap.

But—' She stuttered away into nothing. How did she say this?

Without speaking, Max gathered her into his arms and held her close. It felt so good to be back close to him, his warmth and strength. Her dress swooped low at the back and he stroked her bare skin until she relaxed against him. 'But you're worried I might try to seduce you,' he said, his voice deep and rich and laced with humour, his breath ruffling her hair, his hands warm on her body.

She pulled back within the circle of his arms so she could look up at him. A hint of his endearing grin lingered and his eyes were warm. Her heart seemed to flip over inside her chest. 'How did you know?'

'A lucky guess,' he said. 'Or it could be that I'm learning to read you.'

'Oh,' she said, disconcerted that he could understand what she was feeling without her having to say a word. 'It's not that I'm *worried*. Just… I want to. I want *you*. But it seems too soon. I… I told you I haven't had a fling before. I don't know the rules.'

'No rules, no labels, remember?'

Wordlessly she nodded, bowed her head so she looked down at her feet, feeling awkward and more than a little foolish. If they only had the one night she would probably rush him inside to the bedroom. But it was a big turnaround for her to contemplate sex as part of a fling with no future. She would feel so much happier if she knew him a little better before she took that step. Even though it might be a kind of torture to wait. Even though he might lose interest if she put him off.

He tilted her chin with his fingers so she was forced to look up at him. His eyes searched her face. She could

see an undisguised desire in them but also a warmth
of understanding that surprised her. *Sexiest man alive.*
This man could pick and choose from a waiting list of
women who wouldn't hesitate to take their clothes off
for him.

'Of course I want to take you to bed,' he said. 'You're
gorgeous and sexy and I can't think of anything more
wonderful than making love to you, Nikki Lucas.'

She thrilled to hear his words and an answering desire shimmied through her. 'Me too. I mean, I want to
make love with you too. But—'

'When you're ready,' he said.

'It's not that I'm a prude or anything but I—'

He laid a finger on her mouth to silence her. 'You
don't have to explain or make excuses.'

'It's just that I've always—'

He followed his finger with his mouth in a brief kiss
that left her breathless. 'I tell you what,' he said. 'How
about I leave it for *you* to seduce *me*?'

'What do you mean?'

'When you're ready, I'm sure you'll be able to find
a way to let me know you want to have your way with
me.' He gave an imitation of a wicked leer that made
him look more handsome than devilish.

'Oh, I think I could manage that,' she said, laughing. She could already think of several ways. *When
the time was right.* She felt instantly more relaxed and
happier once he'd taken off the pressure. Pressure, she
realised, that was self-imposed. He hadn't tried to push
her into anything.

He kissed her again. She wound her arms around his
neck and kissed him back—a long, slow, exploratory
kiss. It was a kiss that acknowledged mutual desire, that

agreed they both wanted more than kisses and—importantly—that insisted there be mutual respect.

'Are you going to invite me in?' he asked, still holding her close, his breathing not quite steady.

Nikki hesitated for only the merest fraction of a second but it was obviously enough for him to pick up on. 'I'll sit on one sofa and you can sit on the other, look don't touch,' he said.

'That's a plan,' she said, not liking it in the slightest but seeing sense in it.

He put on a woeful expression. 'It's not late and if I go next door I'll only sit out in the courtyard and think of you on the other side of the wall.'

So he did that too? 'Would you really?' she said, wondering if she should admit to doing exactly the same thing, deciding she should maintain at least a semblance of mystery. She most certainly wouldn't admit she fantasised about him soaping his magnificent body in his outdoor shower.

'Of course. Then I might dive into the pool and wonder if you might be doing the same thing.' If he did that, and she heard him splashing, she'd drive herself crazy imagining it and wondering if he swam naked. Her breath caught. *She wanted to see him naked.*

'You…you could come into my courtyard and swim. Or…or we could sit on the sofas opposite each other as you suggest.'

'Or do both?'

'What about—?'

'I can swim in my shorts,' he said.

He must think she was a real prude if he'd picked up on her thoughts about what he might wear to swim in her lap pool tonight. She wasn't ready for naked just yet. But she wasn't a prude—and she looked forward to showing him that. But not tonight.

She reached into her purse for her key. 'I'd only sit on this side of the wall and think about you if I let you go,' she said. She inserted the big, old-fashioned metal key in the door. 'So please do come in.' He followed her over the threshold.

'Ah, the bliss of the air-conditioning,' she said, holding her arms up to the chilled air. Even at night it was hot and steamy.

Max looked around him with obvious interest. 'It's just like my villa but the mirror image. Nice to see you've added some personal touches. I like the Balinese puppets on the wall and the prints you've got propped up against the desk.' He picked up one of the framed photographic prints. 'Is this the abandoned seaweed farm near here? The colours of the water are incredible.' She nodded. Tourism was beginning to overtake the traditional industry of seaweed farming. 'And this black and white view of Mount Agung is so atmospheric.'

'They're by a local photographer,' she said. 'I bought some other knick-knacks too, so I could personalise the place.'

'The more I look around, the more I see,' he said.

'I've lived here for six months. The villas had only just been finished when I arrived. It's my home. For the time being at least.' When she'd first come to the island she'd thought she'd never want to go back to Sydney.

She noticed he put the frame back in the precise spot he'd taken it from. 'How long do you think you'll stay up here?' he asked.

'Not much longer. I'll need to be in Sydney to decide on sites for my swim clubs.'

'Are you frightened of going home?' he said quietly.

She felt herself flush. 'Frightened? Of course not. All the fuss with the media will be over. Hopefully the runaway bride is yesterday's news.' But she'd go back to Sydney single. The thought of having to face the dating scene again was not an appealing one. Especially when she'd be comparing every man she met to Max.

'Are you worried about Alan?' he said.

She shrugged. 'Not really. When I first saw you here I thought he'd sent you and I felt fearful. He continued to make threats against me for months after the wedding. Scary stuff.'

Max's hands curled into fists. He cursed in extremely uncomplimentary terms about Alan.

'Don't worry,' she hastened to assure him. 'My father paid him a visit and there have been no more threats. In fact, my sister informed me just yesterday that Alan has recently been seen around town with a wealthy widow.'

'It didn't take long for him to bounce back,' he said, his distaste for his former friend evident.

'Perhaps the ex-wives will warn her off like they did me.'

Max moved towards her, his stance protective. 'Make sure you don't do the warning. I suggest you stay right out of it.'

She shuddered. 'I intend to. I want absolutely nothing to do with that man.'

'But you're worried Sydney might be too small to contain both you and him.'

Again he seemed to read her mind. 'Maybe,' she admitted. 'But I have to suffer the consequences of my own actions, don't I? I was the one who was foolish enough to be taken in by him.'

'But you were also the one who found the courage to leave Alan.'

'I keep telling myself that,' she said, but couldn't help a catch in her voice. 'And I know I have to go home soon.' She headed towards the small kitchen area. 'But here I am, offering you a nightcap and all I'm doing is talking. Beer?'

Nikki carried two local beers and a packet of spicy pretzels into the sitting area, and put them on the coffee table. She sat down on one of the sofas and Max, true to his word, sat on the other facing her. It seemed a vast distance over the low, carved wooden table.

'You look lonely over there,' he said.

'I am,' she said. 'It was you who suggested separate sofas.' She patted the cushion next to her.

He needed no further urging and came over to sit next to her. When he put his arm around her, she snuggled close with a happy sigh. 'That's better,' he said, as he pulled her closer.

'So much better than being on opposite sides of the coffee table and certainly opposite sides of the wall,' she said.

The door to the bedroom was open. The staff had been in to arrange the mosquito net canopy over the traditional carved wooden bed. It was a big, lonely bed and she wondered if she was making a mistake by not taking Max by the hand and leading him in there. 'So, do you want to watch a movie? The Wi-Fi is good here so there's a choice.'

Nikki only offered to be polite. She would so much rather talk to him.

'Why would I want to watch a movie when I can

sit here on the sofa with my arm around a beautiful woman?'

She looked up at him and was struck by the admiration in his eyes. Admiration and something more she couldn't put a word to but which might have been longing, yearning even. But she had to be careful not to read into it what she wanted to see rather than what was there. She'd been so easily fooled by Alan. For all her jokes about ten years to trust, she didn't know Max well enough to trust him.

For all his denial of any wrongdoing in those publicised cases, she couldn't be sure he was trustworthy in other ways. If she did have an affair with him—no label, no strings, whatever she might choose to call it— if the press found out and her bad choice was once again emblazoned all over the media for the world to know, she didn't think she could endure it. But she could not admit that to him, to anyone.

But right here, right now, she wanted him and she wasn't thinking past that. 'When you put it that way…' she said, letting her voice trail away.

'There's something I didn't get to ask you over dinner,' he said.

'Fire away,' she said.

'You once told me that Alan knew how to play you,' he said.

'Yes. He was a master manipulator.' And how gullible she'd been to be taken in by him. Would she ever be able to trust her judgement in men again?

'You said something like he made you believe everything you most wanted in life, he wanted as well.' Max's gaze connected with hers. 'So after everything, what is it that you most want from life now, Nikki? I'm really curious to know.'

* * *

Max was surprised at how the shutters seemed to come down over Nikki's face, blanking her expression. She edged away from him on the sofa so she was no longer touching distance.

'If I tell you, will you promise not to run screaming from the room?' she said. If she was attempting humour, it fell flat.

'I can't ever see myself running screaming from you under any circumstances,' he said.

'You might change your mind when you hear what I have to say.' Her eyebrows lifted. 'Seriously.'

'I very much doubt it. Don't keep me in suspense.'

'Okay. The truth is, I still want what I wanted then. And what I most wanted was to be married and starting a family before I was thirty,' she said.

He knew he shouldn't be surprised. She'd alluded to that a few times. But not stated so bluntly.

'No chance of it happening now as I turn thirty in September,' she continued. 'But when I met Alan it was feasible.'

'Okay,' he said cautiously, not sure where she was going with this. 'And he said he wanted that too?'

'I told him after our first few dates.' A black mood descended over Max at the thought of Nikki dating another man. He had to shake it off. He had no right to be jealous.

'That was my dating policy,' she said. 'There was no point wasting time with a man who didn't want what I wanted.'

'Like other guys you'd dated?'

'Yes. You might be surprised at the number of commitment-phobic men there are in Sydney. Maybe everywhere in the world, according to my girlfriends. An epidemic of men just wanting to have fun.'

Max hated the cynical twist to her mouth. And yet, could he not count himself among the commitment-phobes? Not for ever. One day he wanted all that. *Just not now.*

'But Alan didn't run screaming?'

'Far from it. He seemed delighted to meet a woman who wanted a family as much as he did. Reminded me of my advancing age. Suggested we get married as soon as we could, while I was still fertile. Of course, he didn't mention he'd had a vasectomy.' She twisted her face into a mock comic expression but didn't manage to disguise the hurt in her voice. *Was she completely over her former fiancé?*

'We all know what a pack of lies that was,' she continued. 'I would have had a family quickly all right—stepmother to his twins. Those poor little kids having a father like him. How I despise him.' *Guess that gave him his answer.*

'You didn't ever meet a man who shared your views?'

'I didn't actually date enough to find out,' she said. 'Between the time I broke up with the long-time boyfriend and the time I met Alan, I was working insane hours establishing my business.'

'What happened with the long-time boyfriend?' he asked. He hated the thought of lovely Nikki with some other loser who'd wounded her. But he had to know.

'We met in my last year of high school. Lasted all through uni. I actually thought he was "the one". We were unofficially engaged for years.' She paused. 'Are you sure you want to hear all this? It was years ago now.'

'Yes,' he said. He needed to know what made her

tick. He'd always made it his business to thoroughly re-
search an opponent to give him any advantage. Not that
Nikki was an opponent. Fact was, she fascinated him.

'Okay,' she said. 'Cracks started to show around
when I started the business. He didn't like the idea I
was more successful than he was, I think. I lost count
of the number of times we broke up and then got back
together and plastered it all over.'

'What happened in the end?' he said through gritted teeth.

'I was looking at engagement rings while he was
cheating on me.' She said it so matter-of-factly, yet it
must have hurt like hell at the time. 'I discovered she
wasn't the first. He confessed his first infidelity was
when I was mourning my mother. Didn't give him
enough attention at the time, I suppose.' She shrugged
but he could still see tension in her shoulders. 'Worse,
he got the last woman pregnant and married her, not
me.'

'Your first lucky escape, by the sound of it,' he said.

'I can see that now,' she said.

'And I can see where your ten-year trust again thing
comes from,' he said.

'You get a few more hours' credit for recognising it,'
she said, in a dismally failed attempt at humour.

'Thank you,' he said, gathering her into his arms
again, breathing in her closeness, the scent of the flowers in her hair. 'Please note that I haven't run screaming from the room.'

'No need to worry with a no-label fling is there?
We've both been honest about what we expect from the
time we plan to spend together. Both realise it can't be
more than that.' She kissed him, her mouth sweet and

tender on his. 'Besides, I might have to rethink what I want from life. By the time ten years rolls around and I trust someone enough to consider marriage, I'll be heading for forty.'

'Women have babies in their forties.'

'I guess,' she said sounding doubtful. 'I think my only babies are going to be my businesses.'

He went to protest but she spoke over him. 'Look, can we not talk about this stuff any more? Now you know all about my dismal dating past and I don't particularly want to rehash it. Right now I'd rather look to the future than the past.'

'Meaning?' he asked.

'Meaning you've got Wayan and his boat on a retainer for the rest of your stay. I happen to have the day off tomorrow but I'm happy to be your guide if you'd like that.'

'I'd like that very much,' he said.

She smiled. 'Good. I thought maybe some more snorkelling and perhaps we could take a kayak out, just the two of us, currents permitting. That can be a lot of fun.'

Just him and her in a minimum of clothes alone together out on the sea? 'I can't wait,' he said.

CHAPTER TEN

THERE WAS SOMETHING very sexy about secrecy, Nikki thought as next evening she sounded the door chime to Max's villa. 'Room service,' she called in her most official voice, trying not to give the game away by laughing at the surreptitiousness of it all. Anyone passing by would see a staff member. Nothing suspicious.

The night before, she and Max had discussed how they still needed to be circumspect about being seen together. It was important to both of them to avoid any kind of adverse publicity. Behind the high walls of their villas seemed to be the best option for privacy. Hats and sunglasses when they were out in public. The pretence of her as staff and he as 'Mr James' at other times.

She was wearing the hotel's traditional style uniform and bearing a large covered tray containing dinner from the restaurant. One of the girls in the kitchen had remarked that it was a lot of *mee goreng* for one person. In response she'd laughed and said Mr James must be very hungry. After all the exercise she'd done throughout the day she was hungry and was glad he had ordered for big appetites.

Underneath her modest clothes she was wearing her favourite pink bikini. The previous night she and Max had never got around to swimming in the lap pool. In fact they had drowsed off together on the sofa. She'd awoken, startled, in his arms at the same time he had. Just as he'd done on the day of the wedding, he'd picked her up, then carried her into her room and laid her on her bed under the mosquito net. He'd kissed her and left. She'd drifted back off to sleep feeling, safe, happy and something not at all expected from a no-label fling—cherished.

Not that she read anything into that. Max was a gentleman—he'd shown that from the beginning in spite of his reputation. He liked her. He desired her. He was honest about his intentions. As far as she could ascertain, he was not pond scum. That was all there was to it.

She'd woken up alone, happy she'd made the decision not to invite him into her bed before she'd got to know him better. A perfect day had followed, snorkelling in a different spot at Crystal Bay, lunch at a quiet table in an out-of-the-way *warung* at the mangroves end of the island, followed by taking out a double kayak in the waters around Frangipani Bay and around to the next beach. She couldn't remember when she'd had more fun. She'd done all those things before. But being with Max had made them magical.

The door opened. Max stood before her, framed by the doorway, clad only in a sarong slung low on his hips and that winning smile. Nikki was struck speechless, all the breath knocked out of her body.

The sarong was in a Balinese *ikat* print in multiple shades of blue and contrasted with his smooth golden tan. Blue eyes, blue sarong and a whole lot of muscular male perfection in between. With a hungry gaze she took in the sight—broad shoulders tapering to narrow

hips, his hard defined belly, the rippling muscles in his
torso, the strong arms that had powered his killer tennis game, and seen them surging through the water in
the kayak earlier that day.

Yes, she'd been with him all day when he'd been
only wearing swim shorts. But that was for swimming.
This was altogether different. This was…more naked
somehow. *Was he wearing anything under that sarong?*

'What do you think of the sarong?' he said. 'I bought
it from the hotel store. Kadek advised me on how to
tie it.'

She swallowed hard. 'You look hot.'

He frowned. 'Do I? The idea is that a sarong is cooler
than shorts or trousers in this climate.'

'I didn't mean that kind of hot.' She could feel her
eyes glazing over. If she wasn't holding the tray she
thought she might simply swoon and fall at his feet.

'I'm glad you think so,' he said. 'It's a guy thing in
this country but not where we come from. I was concerned I might look ridiculous.'

'Not ridiculous,' she said. 'Very…very manly.' She
had to clear her throat again. 'If they put a photo of
you looking like that on a poster for your fans it would
sell out.'

'Thank you. But I'd rather keep my new look just
between us,' he said.

'Me too,' she said. A sudden possessive urge swept
over her. *She wanted him all to herself.*

If she just undid that one knot at the front, would she
see the sarong fall away from him? Perhaps it was as
well that her hands were firmly clenched on the tray.

'Let me take that from you,' he said, taking the

meal from her. He inhaled. 'Smells good.' He carried it through to the circular dining table in the living area.

Then he turned to her again, put out his arms. 'I'm glad you're here,' he said. 'And not just because you come bearing food.'

She laughed and went willingly into his embrace. All she wanted was to be close to him, to be near to him, to be kissed by him. She couldn't let her thoughts stray further than that.

She put up her face for his kiss and a few blissful moments followed. How could she ever imagine sharing such a thing with anyone else? Excitement built as the kiss intensified. *Take what you can, while you can,* she urged herself. Spending all day together had accelerated the 'getting to know him' process. Too well. It had been a wrench when she, as guide, had said goodbye to 'Mr James' on the beach. In just the few hours since, she'd missed him with an intense sense of loss. Maybe it was time. Maybe tonight.

'Today was one of the best days of my life,' Max said, his voice deep and husky.

Nikki's heart gave a little lurch at his words. Being with him, enjoying the same experiences, laughing with him. His presence nearby had added such a wild joy to the day she'd found herself wishing it would never end. Had he felt the same about her?

'It was for me too,' she murmured. What if he didn't mean being with her at all? What if he'd been referring to the water and the weather? She stepped back from him. 'Yes, it was a perfect day,' she added hastily. 'Those beautiful fish, the coral, the lunch and—'

He reached for her, swivelled her so he could look deep into her face. He traced his finger down her cheek.

'All that. But it was the company that made the day. Being with you, Nikki. That's what was so special for me. You.'

An unreasoning hope soared to life in her heart at the expression in his eyes. 'Thank you. For me too. I mean you. Your company. I… I can't remember when I last enjoyed a day as much.' *Enjoyed a man as much.*

But she couldn't let herself think that this was any more than two people thrown together by circumstance with limited time on a beautiful holiday island. She forced her voice to sound steady. 'You're a mean hand with a kayak. All that upper body strength. You did all the work. I scarcely had to paddle.'

'We were in perfect rhythm together.'

'Yes, we were,' she said, feeling a little breathless. Within minutes on the kayak they'd found their rhythm with the double-bladed paddles, in sync with each other, propelling through the sparkling aqua water in perfect harmony. Even when they'd hit one of the notorious unpredictable currents they'd worked effortlessly together to get the kayak out of trouble. Of course her thoughts had wandered to how their rhythm might match under other circumstances. After all, she was a red-blooded female with needs clamouring to be acknowledged.

'I missed you,' he said, tracing her lips with his thumb.

'It's only been a couple of hours.' She couldn't show how affected she was by his touch, by his words. *She didn't trust this feeling.*

'Those couple of hours away from you seemed very long.' *Was this genuine or a practised seduction?*

'I missed you too.' The words blurted out despite her

best efforts to hold back. 'I... I've been counting down the minutes until I saw you again.'

'The wait seemed interminable. But I couldn't very well storm in next door and drag you in here.'

Why not? she thought. It might make it easier for her if he kissed and caressed her senseless until she thought of nothing but making love with him. But she wouldn't want to feel overwhelmed by caveman tactics. 'I... I guess not,' she said.

He looked unbearably appealing in that sarong. Sexiest man alive and then some. Because of her reluctance he was waiting for her to make the first move. *Her call.*

Was now the time? She didn't know how to deal with this. Nothing had prepared her for the way she felt about Max. Why couldn't she allow herself to look at sex simply as an appetite to slake rather than something special to share between two people who cared about each other? What had she got herself into by agreeing to the no-label fling?

She couldn't let him read those thoughts on her face. Instead she took the few steps over to the table and took the cover off the tray. 'What have we got here? *Mee goreng*—my favourite, thank you.'

He walked over so he was behind her, looking over her shoulder. Too close for her to be able to keep a clear head. All that bare skin and muscle with nothing but the light cotton of her top between them. 'I remembered you said you liked it,' he said.

'And *tom be siap*, steamed chicken wrapped in banana leaves with a lemongrass salsa. That's yummy too. So is the tuna *bakar*—it's a grilled tuna fillet with a spicy Balinese sauce. You chose well.'

'They all sounded good,' he said. 'I was hungry.

All the swimming and kayaking today. I thought the kayaking might have made my damaged arm ache but it didn't.'

'That's good news. I'm glad.'

He put his hands on her shoulders and turned her halfway towards him so there was no escaping his gaze. 'For the first time in a long time I feel relaxed. Able to think clearly about the decisions I have to make. It's like I've turned some kind of corner. Thanks to you, Nikki.'

She picked up a fork and started to pull apart the banana leaf wrapping from the chicken. Anything but look at him. 'Any good guide would have done the same,' she said, purposefully misunderstanding him. She'd felt it too out there with him. The magic. The happiness she'd felt at being with him. At playing at being a couple. Struck in unguarded moments by an inexplicable longing for it to be real.

'That's not true and you know it,' he said. 'It was more than that.'

Again her heart gave that painful lurch. It would be only too easy to develop feelings for Max. But she couldn't allow that. He'd made it very clear he wasn't looking for a relationship. She had only just recovered from the emotional fallout from her failed engagement. She couldn't let herself fall for a man who only wanted a fling.

She screwed up her eyes in a kind of despair. *Don't let yourself fall in love with him, Nikki.* She could lie to herself all she liked but she knew she was in serious danger of losing her heart to this man.

She looked up at him. 'We're away from home, in an exotic environment. Both escaping trauma of a kind. It would be easy to think there's more to some vacation

fun than there really is.' She was trying to talk herself
into believing that as much as she was him.

'You can say that,' he said, his voice controlled. 'That
doesn't stop me from believing it was an exceptional
day and that the reason it was exceptional was the company of a wonderful woman.'

Max tried to sound on top of the situation but inside he
was in turmoil. Things with Nikki were not going as
planned. He had intended a no-strings vacation affair.
Something warm and sexy and fun that would help them
both heal from the calamities that had driven them in
their own separate ways to this island.

It should be something easy to walk away from at the
end of his time here. He had his farewell speech prepared—something along the lines of it would be awkward to stay in touch. They both had lives to get back
on track. No point in trying to prolong something that
had a limited life. No need to exchange phone numbers.

Trouble was, it wasn't turning out like that. *He was
falling in love with her.* Head over heels and so rapidly
he could hardly keep his feet on the ground. Or that
was how it seemed.

It wasn't what he wanted. Not now. Not even in the
foreseeable future. Not when he was forging a new post-
tennis life. When he got married, he wanted all his
ducks to be in a row so he could have the kind of relationship his parents had. One that lasted. Where he
would be there for his wife and children. Not absent. It
hadn't just been conflicting training schedules that had
ended his relationship with Ellen. It had been what she
had called—what she had screamed at him when she'd
ended it—his absence both physical and emotional.

Truth was, the career he'd striven for most of his life had defined him. He was used to being a champion. A winner. He needed to be back on top with whatever new path he chose before he could ask a woman to share his life.

Nikki could be the right girl at the wrong time. *Perhaps he should back off.*

Although it was hardly likely that she reciprocated any deeper feelings. In fact she'd just given him a nice little lecture about how he shouldn't mistake a vacation fling for anything more significant. He should take heed of her advice. Hope like hell she hadn't read anything deeper into his compliments about how much he'd enjoyed her company.

And stop speculating whether that was a pink bra or a pink bikini giving him tantalising glimpses of the top of her breasts through her lacy white cotton uniform top.

'This dinner will be getting cold if we don't eat it soon,' he said. 'Do you want to eat inside or out in my courtyard? There are citronella candles to keep mosquitoes at bay.'

'The courtyard, please,' she said. 'Do you mind if I change into my swimsuit first?'

No, I'd rather you stayed completely covered up so I'm not tempted by your lovely body. 'Sure,' he said. 'Whatever is most comfortable for you.'

Would she do a striptease in front of him? If so, might he offer to help her undress? First that lacy blouse slid over her shoulders and breasts, then the long skirt, sliding it down over her legs and—

'If you'll excuse me for a moment, I'll pop into the bathroom to change,' she said, heading in that direction.

He suppressed a groan of frustration, turned it into an awkward cough.

'You okay?' she said, turning back.

'Chilli fumes wafting up from the food, making me cough.' He faked another cough. 'Nothing to worry about. You just go.'

'Are you sure? I've seen how chilli can affect you.'

'I'm *okay* with the chilli,' he said, tight-lipped. Would he ever live down that earlier incident? 'You go. I'll unpack the food.'

Just minutes later she came out wearing just a pink bikini top and an orange-and-white-striped hotel towel wrapped around her waist. It stopped short of covering her legs. 'I hope you don't mind if I borrowed a towel,' she said.

Lucky towel. 'Of course not,' he said through a suddenly choked throat that had nothing to do with chilli fumes. Did she realise how artlessly sexy she looked?

'I feel much cooler now,' she said, stretching up her arms so her breasts threatened to fall out of her bikini top. 'That long-sleeved blouse is actually quite warm when it's this hot.'

She was hot. He hadn't seen her before with so little clothing—she wore a sun protective swim shirt out on Wayan's boat. In the kayak she'd worn leggings and a life jacket. Now, the triangles of the bikini top drew attention to the swell of her breasts as much as covered them, emphasised the shadow of her cleavage. Her body was lithe and strong—her slender waist, the flare of her hips, her firm, finely muscled arms in perfection proportion. The more he saw of Nikki, the more he wanted her.

But that was all it was. A healthy sexual attraction.

A friendship of sorts. Not anything more. *Of course he wasn't falling in love with her.*

She sat down in the chair opposite him at the outdoor bamboo table and served herself her favourite noodles. 'You didn't order dessert?' she asked.

'Nothing really appealed,' he said. 'I've ordered the caramelised bananas a few times already.'

'I told Maya what you suggested about spectacular desserts. She agreed. In fact she's organised a meeting with her chefs to discuss a new dessert menu. She said to say thank you for the suggestion.'

'She's so welcome,' he said. 'Can you tell her I'm volunteering to taste any new dishes?'

Nikki laughed. 'I'll pass that on.' She sobered. 'Although it's likely that will be happening after you go home.'

'Shame,' he said. Truth be told, he hadn't been thinking that far ahead. Without being consciously aware of it, he had abandoned timetables completely and given in to 'rubber time'.

'Don't worry, I'll send you photos to drool over and…' Her voice trailed away. There had been no mention of any future contact between them after the eight remaining nights. She flushed and looked embarrassed. 'Or…er…not.'

'I'd like that,' he said. But he knew his voice came out sounding half-hearted.

The sudden silence between them stretched out too long to be comfortable, even taking into account that they were eating a meal. She was the first to break it. 'I have news,' she said. 'A very good friend of mine might be coming to the island tomorrow.'

Her news came from left field. 'A friend?' *Male or female?*

'Yes. Sammie and I go way back to high school. She's friends with Maya too.'

Suddenly his wariness about being seen with Nikki returned in full flood. 'Why might she come to the island?'

'First and foremost to catch up with me and Maya. But she wants to write a profile on me. She—'

Max got up from the table, pushed his chair back so hard it fell over, clattering on the paving. 'She's a journalist? You're inviting a journalist here? After all we went through with the media?'

Nikki got up too, not one to let herself be put at a disadvantage. 'She's not *that* type of journalist. Sammie writes for one of the weekend newspaper magazines. She's in Bali for a short holiday. But Sammie being Sammie never switches off. Her boyfriend is a photographer, he's here with her and—'

'A journalist *and* a photographer? What are you thinking?'

Nikki frowned. 'Sammie is one of my oldest, dearest friends. Another of my bridesmaids. I trust her implicitly.'

'What if she sees me here? What if she puts two and two together? Is that what you intend to—?'

'No! Sammie is writing a feature about me as an Australian female entrepreneur. About how one of the biggest cosmetic conglomerates in the world purchased my company that was born as a little, underfunded startup in Sydney. About what my next venture will be. Her boyfriend also works for the magazine. It's absolutely nothing to do with *you*.' Her eyes flared, the green flecks sparking.

'But if she sees me—'

'You could stay in your room. Or leave early and spend the afternoon elsewhere. Go way out to sea with Wayan—'

'Why should I have to hide?'

She put up her hand in a halt sign. 'I haven't finished yet. I was going to say you *could* do all that but you don't need to do anything. Because the alternative is that I go in the morning to Sanur to the hotel where she's staying, for the interview and photo shoot. Then Maya will go over in the afternoon and we'll both stay in Sanur for a girls' night out with Sammie. I really want to see my friend. I haven't seen her for more than six months. But I don't want to put you out either. So that might be the best decision all round.'

In the face of her annoyance Max felt petty and mean. And gutted he wouldn't see her for all the time she was in Sanur. But the fear of media exposure of his affair with Nikki was still very real. Not that you could call it an affair yet. And the way she was glaring at him made him doubt an affair would ever eventuate.

Perhaps this would be a good opportunity to cool things down between him and Nikki before they ever really heated up. Before anyone—he was thinking of her—got hurt.

'You go to Sanur and do what you have to do. I hope the interview goes well for you.' He sincerely meant it.

'Thank you,' she said. 'It will be good PR for my new business. And for me. A positive feature should help re-establish my image as a serious businesswoman after the "runaway bride" scandal. Sammie has promised to completely avoid that term in her profile.'

'Good,' he said. 'Let's sit down and finish our meal.'

Nikki remained standing. 'Sorry. No can do.' She stood there in a revealing pink bikini top with a hotel towel tucked around her waist, her feet bare, yet he could see her morphing into Nikki the businesswoman. Could almost see her thoughts veering away from him and towards her goals for the next day. 'I have to go,' she said, with what seemed to him to be only the merest trace of regret.

How could he have forgotten? Nikki Lucas was a high-powered businesswoman who had admitted to him she'd put dating on hold in favour of her work. She had been as driven to make her company a success as he'd been in his career as a sportsman. The odds of a young woman succeeding so spectacularly in the international market as she had were probably the same as of him winning the US Open.

'It's still early,' he said.

She shook her head. 'Not for all I have to do this evening. I have to call Sammie and tell her I've decided on the Sanur option. Let Maya know—Kadek will look after Putu for the night she's away but she might have to rearrange some staff shifts.'

'I get that, but it won't take long. Surely you don't need to go just yet.' Was he begging? Max swore under his breath. He never had, and never would, beg for a woman's company.

'Sadly I do,' she said. 'Because the shoot won't be happening here, I have to pack and take over stuff I might need in Sanur. I'll need to get an early boat, organise a hairdresser, then grab the opportunity to shop in boutiques in Sanur for a more businesslike outfit for the shoot than I brought with me when I came here. If we'd shot here, Sammie would have brought clothes with her for me but this way is better because I can choose my own outfit. I always like to have control of the image I present.'

'I was the same in my tennis career,' he said. Though in fact it had been his manager who had insisted on control over his image. Max had just wanted to play tennis. *To win.*

'Really? I suppose you would,' she said without any real interest.

The stiff set of her shoulders told him she was not happy with his reaction to her news about her friend's visit. But it wasn't just that. Her thoughts were racing away in a direction that led away from him. And Max wasn't sure he liked it.

CHAPTER ELEVEN

NIKKI HAD STRETCHED out her time in Sanur with her friends, delaying her return to Lembongan for as long as she could. Maya had left on the earliest boat in the morning. But it was late afternoon by the time the speedboat transporting Nikki back to the island was nearing the beach at Jungut Batu.

Nikki was oblivious to the beauty around her, the aquamarine waters, the tree-lined shore coming into view, the excited chatter of first-time visitors to the island. Despite the fun of seeing her friends, the challenge of the interview and photo shoot, she was too preoccupied.

She'd endured some emotional pain in her life, but few things had hurt like the shaft of pain that had stabbed her at Max's response to her thoughtless comment about sending him photos of desserts from the kitchens of Big Blue once he was back in Sydney. Of course she knew the score for a no-strings fling—don't expect anything more. Just walk away and pretend it doesn't hurt. But the obvious discomfort that had flickered across his face that she should dare to presume any ongoing contact with Max Conway, the celebrity sportsman, had made her cringe. Then his instant suspicion of her because she was seeing a friend who was a journalist—someone she'd known since they were fourteen years old—had driven the blade in deeper.

No more Max. She wasn't cut out for no-label flings, one-night stands, or whatever she chose to call them. He was a celebrity used, no doubt, to picking up and putting down women when it suited him. She, for all her business success, was just a girl who'd been wounded by the men she'd misjudged while looking for love and the not unreasonable expectation of marriage and a family. She wasn't good at pretending to be something else.

She liked Max. She liked him a lot. Thought he was the hottest man on the planet. But that closed-over look had told her she was in way above her head when it came to pretending she could easily cope with the aftermath of how she would feel when what Max was offering came to an end. She simply couldn't deal with it.

How could she endure these remaining nights with him on the island? She didn't want to let Maya down but she might have to decamp over to Sanur for the duration.

Not that Maya had expected her to stay as long as she had. They'd talked about that with Sammie on their girls' night out at a restaurant in Sanur. How Nikki had stretched her time on Lembongan for as long as she could—or should. That an exciting new venture awaited her, one that would continue her links with Maya and Frangipani Bay. But her life was in Sydney, not here. Sammie had asked her about her love life, concerned that she might not be getting over the Alan debacle. But Nikki had reassured her friend she was okay. Not ready to date okay, but okay just the same.

Neither Maya nor she had breathed a word to Sammie

about Max being at Big Blue. Privately, Maya had voiced her concern that Nikki might be heading for heartbreak. Which was perceptive of her as Nikki had not even confided in her how she felt about him. She had denied that she and Max were anything other than friends. But Maya's expression told her she knew better but wasn't going to interfere with further advice.

Perhaps, when it all boiled down to it, she should be thinking of flying back home rather than skulking in Sanur until Max checked out of Big Blue. Maybe she'd needed a kick in the butt like this to get back to face her real life.

Nevertheless, as she hitched up her dress above her knees to wade through the shallow water to the shore, it was with a heavy heart. Despite it all, she missed him. Every minute she'd been away from him, she had ached for him. There was something about her connection to Max that went beyond the physical, that called not only to her heart but to her soul.

Which was why she thought she might be hallucinating when she saw him standing on the beach, in the same place he'd stood when she'd last been here. She blinked. It was Max all right. Tall, imposing. The same but different. Even more handsome, if that were possible. His beard was a proper short beard now, not the stubble of when she'd first seen him there. His shorts were grey not blue. And he was wearing the hat and sunglasses they'd agreed to wear in public.

Had he seen her? Could she turn around and take the speedboat back to the mainland? Panic tightened her throat. She wasn't ready for this. Had thought she'd have time to prepare herself before she spoke to him. *What was he doing here?*

He waved to her. There would be no escape. She would have to face him. But she wasn't going to be cowed by his presence.

'Mr James, what a coincidence,' she said lightly.

'It's no coincidence,' he said. 'Maya organised for the truck to come pick you up. I hitched a ride so I could meet you at the boat. I didn't want to hang around at the hotel waiting for you.'

She wasn't going to act all passive aggressive and angsty because he'd hurt her feelings. But she wasn't going to let the conversation get personal either. As far as she was concerned, their no-label fling had fizzled out. 'Thank you, but that wasn't necessary,' she said, forcing a polite smile. 'I trust our driver to get me back to Big Blue.' She knew she sounded stilted. But it was the best she could do. She screwed her eyes shut tight and wished he'd be gone when she opened them.

Nikki looked different, Max thought. Gone were the hippy pants, the tangle of windblown hair. Now her hair was sleek and sophisticated, falling below her shoulders; her eyes made up with some dark shadow; her mouth slicked a deep pink. Her natural-coloured linen dress looked elegant and businesslike, even with the flip-flops she'd worn for the boat. This wasn't his Nikki of the island or the Nikki of his dreams. Not that she'd ever been his, either in reality or dream.

He felt as if there were a sheet of glass between them. And it wasn't because she was wearing sunglasses and a hat and he couldn't properly see her expression.

He offered to carry her backpack for her but she demurred. 'It's nicely balanced,' she said.

'How did the interview go?' he asked as they walked

to the waiting place for the truck. The streets were much too narrow for the driver to park anywhere and they had to wait for him to come back for them.

'Very well,' she said. 'Sammie asked some interesting questions, which really made me think.' She put up her hand as if to forestall a question from him. 'Rest assured, your name wasn't mentioned at all. The wedding incident was a no-go zone so you didn't even come up in reference to your role as best man. It was strictly business.'

'Good,' he said, relieved to hear it. He still worried at the wisdom of her meeting with a journalist. Journalists went for blood at the slightest sniff of a story, the more scandalous the better. And if it wasn't a scandal, they turned it into one—as he'd learned to his peril. If the press hadn't got hold of the paternity dispute story, it wouldn't have given his opponent the fuel to goad him into the ill-timed shot that had ended his career. He was glad he hadn't had to meet Sammie. It would have been difficult to be polite to her.

While he waited with Nikki for the truck they made small talk about the hotel she had stayed at with her friends in Sanur. She was polite, pleasant, not a trace of snark in her voice or demeanour. But he realised she had not once met his gaze.

He'd blown it with her.

They sat on opposite benches on the back of the truck all the way back to the hotel. Max tried not to think of the last time they'd sat there together, Nikki with her blue dress slipping up her thighs, he trying not to stare too blatantly. Or to remember the previous night when his 'Nikki in her blue dress' dream had turned into a nightmare.

It had started as usual with her gliding up the aisle towards him, then lifting her face for his kiss. Only instead of kissing her, he'd watched as she'd turned away from him back to her groom. A groom who suddenly wasn't Alan but some anonymous dude gazing at her in adoration. The symbolism was painfully obvious—he couldn't give her what she wanted so she'd found someone else. In the dream the pain of his loss had seared through him. He'd awoken in a sweat and never returned to sleep, tossing and turning, thoughts and regrets churning through his brain.

He was beginning to realise that relationships were a fluid thing. Opportunities for something exciting and unexpected could slip away while he was trying to make everything perfect. There wasn't a perfect time for a relationship. You had to *make* the time. He might have good balance when it came to being nimble on his feet. What he didn't have was balance in his life. He *could* have both a career and a relationship. What appeared so patently obvious to others had been a revelation to him. Look how Maya and Kadek worked so harmoniously together—a business, a happy marriage, a child.

When it came to Nikki, it seemed he'd kept his eye off the ball and lost the game, forfeiting the prize that had been right under his nose.

Nikki looked unseeingly out of the truck as it bumped its way back to the hotel. Seeing Max, wanting him, was too difficult. It was impossible for her to stay in any kind of proximity to him. She would have to get right away from here, from Bali, from anywhere in Indonesia. Time to move on. Tonight she would get online and book a flight home. Many of the flights to Sydney left from the Ngurah Rai international airport in Denpasar very late in the evening so she would almost certainly be able to leave tomorrow. Maya would understand.

When they reached the hotel, Nikki accepted Max's offer of assistance with her backpack but not his hand to help her down from the truck. Not after what had happened last time. She flushed at the memory of that passionate, public kiss, furious at herself for the wave of longing for him that swept through her. Now Max kept at a polite distance but she was as aware of him as if they were skin-to-skin close. His scent, his warmth, the essence of his Max-ness. It was too painful. She had to go, and go quickly.

Packing up to leave Lembongan wouldn't take long. She hadn't brought much with her when she had fled Sydney and hadn't acquired much during her stay. Just the knick-knacks she'd bought to personalise her villa, a couple of gorgeous sarongs, this dress she'd bought for the interview.

Oh, and her heart. She'd been at risk of leaving that behind with the best man. It had been a close call.

She thanked the driver. He wasn't known to her, so she was very careful to stay staff-guest distance from Max and to address him as Mr James. But when the truck drove away from the driveway nearest to their villas she was left alone with Max. Most likely for the last time.

He refused to give her back her backpack, saying he would carry it to her villa for her. She walked the short distance to her door aware every second that he was only a few steps behind her. They reached her villa. He put her backpack down.

'Thank you,' she said. 'That was kind of you.' She

went to fish in the outside pocket of it for her room key but her hands were shaking too much to make a connection. She closed her eyes in despair. This was dreadful. They'd been so at ease with each other. To be reduced to this level of awkwardness was unbearable.

'Let me,' he said, deftly retrieving her big old-fashioned key with the wooden tag and handing it to her. A gentleman to the last.

She took it, being ultra-careful their hands didn't brush in the process. 'Thank you,' she said again, in an excess of politeness to cover how she was crying in her heart that it had come to this. She feigned a yawn. 'I'm so tired, can't wait to get inside.' She'd been about to add *and out of this dress* but stopped herself in time.

'You left your uniform in my villa the other night,' he said. 'The top, the sash and the sarong.'

Nikki snatched her hand to her mouth. 'How careless of me. The housekeepers would have seen it and drawn their own conclusions.' She groaned. 'So much for being discreet.'

'They couldn't have seen it. I packed it away in my suitcase in my closet to keep it hidden until you came back.'

'Good idea,' she said. She would just leave the clothing there. Maya could retrieve it after she'd left.

'I could bring it out to you,' he said.

'That won't be necessary,' she said.

'Or you could come into my villa and get it,' he said.

'I… I don't think so.' She couldn't bear to be alone with him in the privacy of those high walls.

She looked up and finally caught his gaze, intensely blue in the fading light of the day. 'Please come in, Nikki,' he said. 'Please.'

CHAPTER TWELVE

NIKKI TOOK A deep breath to steady herself. Now would be as good a time as any to tell him she intended to fly back to Sydney tomorrow evening. After all, he hadn't actually done anything wrong. She had simply decided not to accept the terms he was offering. Her choice. They should part on civilised terms.

Mutely, she nodded.

She followed him through the courtyard and into his villa. He closed the door and stood with it behind him, facing her. 'I missed you, Nikki. Every minute you were away I missed you. This place was so empty without you. I know you were angry with me. I was—'

Her carefully rehearsed explanation of why she was going fled from her mind. 'I missed you too,' she said, something she had had no intention of admitting. 'Every second I wished you were with me. I couldn't sleep for thinking about you. Yearning for you. But I can't do a no-strings fling, Max. And I actually don't see at this stage what's stopping us from treating this like a normal boy-meets-girl scenario. Okay, so we want to avoid media intrusion, keep things private. We're on the same page there.'

'Yes,' he said vehemently with a curse that told her exactly what he thought of the media.

'But we're both single. Free to see whoever we want. We've both been burned before in other relationships. I… I'm scared of getting hurt again. I admit I have trust issues. But I also really enjoy being with you. More than any other man I've ever met. A few days here has established that. If we like each other why—?'

'Can't we just date and see where it leads to?'

'I was going to say why hedge ourselves with restrictions like one night but you said it better. I deserve better than to be seen as a no-strings fling to be picked up then discarded. And so do you.'

He looked at her quizzically. 'That's not the kind of thing a girl usually says to a guy. That he deserves more than a passing encounter.'

'I mean it. But if you still don't think you can fit a meaningful relationship into your new life after tennis, then say goodbye for good now.'

Their gazes held for a long moment. The hunger she saw in his eyes was surely reflected in hers. She swayed towards him. All thoughts fled her mind except how much she wanted him. *Max*.

'I don't want to say goodbye,' he said.

He kissed her and she kissed him back without hesitation. They skipped the tender, questing kind of warm-up kiss and went straight to demanding and urgent. He bunched her hair in his hand and tugged to tilt her face upward to deepen the kiss. The tug on her hair should have hurt but it didn't. It thrilled her. *He* thrilled her.

Pent-up desire ignited and flamed through her. He pulled away from the kiss, to say something, she thought. But there had been enough words. She pressed her mouth back against his to silence him, slipped her tongue between his lips, demanded more. She slid her arms under his shirt, around his waist to hold warm, bare skin. He slid his hands down her shoulders past the curves of her breasts to hold her bottom. Her nipples tightened and tingled and she pressed her body close to his. Close, closer, not close enough. *She wanted more.*

She murmured deep in her throat. Pleasure, want, hunger. He groaned and held her closer. She stepped back, trying to drag him in the direction of the bedroom but she met an immovable wall of muscle. Then he propelled her forward. Then they were stumbling towards his bedroom, laughing when they bumped into the wall and knocked a wooden carving askew, laughing when they got tangled up in the mosquito net, laughing when they met a recalcitrant zipper or tore off a button in their haste to strip each other of their clothes.

'This would be so much easier if we were wearing sarongs,' she murmured in mock complaint.

'Or a towel and a pink bikini,' he said.

Then their laughter slowed to murmurs and sighs and moans as they explored each other's wants and needs.

Nikki woke up and thought for a moment she was in her own bed in her own villa. The bed was identical. Same mosquito-net canopy. Same ceiling fan with cane blades flicking languorously around. What was different was the warm male body next to her, hand resting possessively on her thigh. Max. *Her lover.*

And what an awesome lover he was. Passionate, energetic, inventive. Not to mention thoughtful and considerate. They had seemed to instinctively know what pleased each other. After their first time together, they had fallen asleep in each other's arms. It was dark when they'd woken, ravenous, and ordered pizza from room service. *Nasi goreng* didn't seem quite the thing to eat in bed.

He'd then fulfilled all her built-up fantasies of him—and she his—in his open-air bathroom as they'd showered together. When they eventually fell asleep again it was the deep sleep of the totally exhausted.

Now shafts of sunlight were filtering through the blinds, picking up the gold in Max's beard, the fine hair on his chest and legs. Heaven knew what time it was.

She stretched out her satisfied, pleasurably aching body. Max lay asleep on his back beside her, his limbs sprawled across the bed in the same confident possession of space that had become so familiar. His hand stayed on her thigh and she tentatively covered it with hers.

She didn't think she had ever felt happier. She wanted this. Wanted *him*. There was no use in denying it any further. *She was falling in love with him.*

The first thing Max saw when he woke was Nikki smiling into his face. She lay next to him, her head turned to his. With her hair dishevelled and spread across the pillow, dark smudges of make-up under her eyes, her lips swollen from his kisses, she had never looked more beautiful. She was naked and unselfconscious, her lovely body gilded with sunlight.

He noted with a stab of guilt slight marks from his fingers on the smooth skin of her thighs. But he remembered when he'd given them to her and she hadn't been complaining. A fierce possessiveness surged through him. She was perfect in every way. *She was his.*

'Hey, you,' he said, dropping a kiss on her mouth.

'Hey to you too,' she said, nipping on his lower lip.

'This is nice,' he said, knowing the words were grossly inadequate to express how he felt.

'Yes,' she said, and he knew he didn't need the words. 'Do I wish we'd done this the first night we knew we wanted to do it?'

'Do you?'

'No. It wouldn't have been the same.'

'I think I could have been okay with it that first night,' he said. In fact he knew so. He had wanted her from the get-go. 'But I want more.'

'Now?' she said, wiggling closer to him.

He stroked the fine strands of her hair back from where they were falling across her face. 'Yes,' he said, immediately ready for her. 'But what I meant was I want this to continue. Us, I mean.' He laughed. 'I'm not very good at this. If I was sixteen I'd say I want you to be my girlfriend.'

'That's not a bad way of putting it even for a thirty-year-old,' she said. 'I know exactly what you mean. I'd like to be your girlfriend.' She stroked his face with delicate fingers from his cheekbone to the corner of his mouth. 'Very much so.'

'I want to enjoy all the time we can have together here and then afterwards. What are your plans? I could try to get up here as often as possible, but it would be easier if we were in the same city. Sydney, I mean. For the foreseeable future anyway.' If he took the sports announcer job he could be based anywhere. But rather than thinking he had to make those decisions on his own, he realised with a surprising sense of relief he might make them with Nikki. Make a decision based on what she wanted as well as his own needs.

'I was talking about that with my friends last night,' she said. 'Me moving back to Sydney, I mean. Going back to my old life.' Her voice trailed away and he realised she was still nervous about going home.

'Not quite the same old life with a new boyfriend,' he said.

Her eyes brightened. The way the green seemed to appear among the brown at different times continued to fascinate him. 'What an exceedingly appealing thought,' she said, her lips curving into a luminescent smile. 'That makes me much happier about going home—sooner rather than later.'

'Good,' he said. Later he might broach the subject of her coming back on the same flight as him. That and the other vexed topic of how they would handle being seen together in the public eye. Perhaps he could talk to his publicist about making a media announcement, keeping the public perception of his relationship with Nikki under his control.

But right now she was snuggling close to him and pressing a trail of little kisses across his chest and up towards his mouth. Thoughts of an entirely different nature took over and he rolled Nikki over so he could kiss her back. She wound her arms around his neck and whispered exactly what she'd like to do to him. Who was he to resist?

CHAPTER THIRTEEN

WHEN NIKKI NEXT woke, the sun was seriously bright in Max's bedroom and her mobile phone was vibrating all over the bedside table. Blearily she reached out to get it, blinked herself awake when she noticed the number of messages, both voicemail and text, that had come in.

Alarmed, she sat up in bed, now wide awake. Was something wrong back home?

She opened the urgent text from her sister.

Nikki, you need to look at this. Then call me.

With fingers that were suddenly unsteady, Nikki clicked on the link to the website of a popular tabloid newspaper. The words screamed up at her: *'Runaway bride and traitor best man enjoy raunchy romp in tropical love nest!'*

For a shocked second she thought it was a rehash of the 'secret Fiji love nest' beat-up that had run six months ago. Then she focussed on the photos that ran below the headline. And had to swallow against the nausea that rose in her throat.

The photos had been taken here on this island. Recently. The main shot was a zoomed-in image of her and

Max kissing in the laneway outside the sunset restaurant, her blue dress rucked up and exposing an indecent amount of bare thigh as well as bare back. The kiss was hungry and passionate—as indeed it had been. But the way the image had been cropped made it look seedy.

The next one was another of her with Max, their heads very close together, smiling intimately at each other at the restaurant table. They looked like lovers. In fact it was captioned *'The Look of Love?'* Under any other circumstance Nikki would think it beautiful and want a copy.

The final shot was of her and Max, shoulders touching, wading out of the water together at Frangipani Bay, she in her high-cut red swimsuit and the tight black swim shirt that, when wet, revealed every curve and indent of her body. Max was wearing just his black swim shorts, the rest of his magnificent body bare and glistening with drops of water. She was laughing up at him as if she was besotted. That one was captioned *'Hot Stuff!'*

And of course, under those photos, there was an old one of Max running away from the church, carrying her in his arms.

Other captions referred to Max's tennis career: *'Tennis star not too injured to enjoy sexy tryst with friend's fiancée!'* was the only one she could bear to read.

She closed her eyes but it was all there in front of her when she opened them again and she was plunged back into the nightmare she'd thought she'd left behind. *Dear heaven, how had this happened?*

She scrolled down her messages. They were from other friends alerting her to the article. Reporters asking for comments. Her father demanding to know what the hell was going on.

She gagged as she forced herself to read through the rest of the story, under the byline of *'Our reporter on Lembongan Island'*. She and Max had let themselves believe they'd had privacy in this out-of-the-way place. How naive they'd been.

Beside her, Max stirred. Looking over to his side of the bed, she could see his phone was flashing with messages too.

He opened his eyes. Smiled at her as if it was the happiest thing ever for him to find her there in his bed. But her expression must have told him something was wrong. He sat up. 'You okay?' he asked, wary.

Nikki shook her head, fighting tears. She wanted to scream and cry and shout. But she managed a choked, 'Not okay.' Without another word, she handed him over her phone open at the offending article.

'Why have the bridesmaid when the best man snagged the bride?' was another headline.

Oh, it was awful. What was beautiful between them was now being made to look sleazy. But at least this time they could face the media united as a couple.

Max's face darkened as he read. He cursed. Threw her phone on the bed. Then scowled. 'Your friend Sammie.' He spat out the words. 'Some friend she is. How did you let this happen, Nikki? I thought you said you could trust her.'

'You think this is Sammie? This isn't her. She's not that type of journalist. It's some tourist with a smartphone. Everyone is a paparazzi these days. He—the photo credit is a he, probably a fake name—most likely recognised you then realised who I must be. Then he's stalked us. Taken the opportunity to make some cash to fund his vacation by selling the photos to the trashy tabloid. They've then got some desk hack to cobble together an article.'

She picked up her phone from where Max had thrown it and scrolled through some more. 'Thank heaven he didn't get behind our courtyard walls.'

Max glared at her. 'Only because I stopped your friend from coming over here.'

'That's ridiculous,' she said.

Nikki pulled the sheet up over her breasts. Felt uncomfortable in front of him now when she'd been so uninhibited all night.

'Is it? You shouldn't have talked to a journalist, Nikki.'

She gritted her teeth. 'This has got nothing to do with me talking to Sammie.'

'She could have shared her information with a mate on the tabloid. These photos were taken with a long-distance lens. A professional camera.'

'Smartphones can have adjustable lenses. I'm telling you this is an opportunistic amateur trying to make a tidy sum from invading our privacy.'

Max swung his legs over and sat on the edge of the bed, his bare back to her. He muttered an inventive string of curses. 'You'd better get back to your own villa now this has hit the fan.'

'What? You're kicking me out?'

He turned to her. 'We don't want your "opportunistic tourist" seeing us like this.' He cursed again. 'Don't you see how bad this is? Last time, the media could lie all it liked but I knew the truth. I had behaved with honour. Now it looks like I ran away with you for a quick—'

'Don't say it. That disrespects me. And you. How do you think I feel about this? It's always worse for the woman. My father will be spitting. My sister is upset too.'

'My parents won't like it either. They wouldn't see this as honourable behaviour. Even though my father didn't particularly like Alan when we played tennis together all those years ago.'

'Actually it was an honourable thing you did by helping me escape what would almost certainly have been a disastrous marriage. This interest in us is only because you're a celebrity. You're news. I'm not. *Any* female "frolicking" with Max Conway would be news.'

'The way you look in the red swimsuit makes you news,' he said through obviously gritted teeth. 'And good publicity for your swim school.'

'Are you serious? You can't mean that?'

'Of course not,' he muttered. But she was shocked he could even think it.

'Max, can I be the voice of reason here? This is awful. I'm not saying it's anything less than despicable that these people have tried to drag our names through the mud. But we actually haven't done anything wrong. Nothing underhand or sordid. The wedding was six months ago. Alan has moved on to more profitable pastures. So we met when you helped me run away? Big deal. Isn't that what the movies call "a cute meet"?' The stubborn set of his face told her she wasn't getting through to him. 'Viewed through a different lens, I might have thought the way we met and then reconnected by accident on this beautiful island was…was romantic.'

He picked up his phone and groaned. 'There's nothing vaguely romantic about *"Tennis star not too injured to enjoy sexy tryst with friend's fiancée!"'*

With what seemed to Nikki like morbid interest, Max continued to scroll through the story. 'The comments from readers are even worse.' He cradled his head in his hands.

'Well, don't read them,' she said. 'I didn't.'

He didn't seem to notice when she tiptoed around the bed, still wrapped in the sheet, to retrieve her dress, then her panties and bra from where Max had tossed them on the floor last night.

She ran into the bathroom with her clothes clutched to her front. Quickly she slipped into her underwear, then pulled her crumpled linen dress on over her head. She wet a tissue and wiped away the worst of her mascara panda eyes. Then dragged Max's comb through her hair. Her worst fear—one she didn't dare share with Max—was that there would be photographers waiting outside Max's villa hoping to catch her leaving in a morning-after-the-night-before 'walk of shame'. As Sydney was two hours ahead of Lembongan in time difference, and the news mightn't have hit here yet, she might be lucky.

Max barred her way at the doorway from the bedroom. Standing there stark naked, he looked so magnificent she had to force herself not to stare. Not to take him by the hand and lead him back to the bed. But she was beginning to doubt whether she actually wanted to be his girlfriend. A good relationship needed more than good sex. Like trust. Particularly trust.

'Where are you going?'

'You told me to get next door and so I am.'

If he let her slink out there by herself without him by her side to support her, it was over.

'I'm not sure that's a good idea,' he said. 'There might be more of those leeches out there.'

She glared at him. 'Max, what's wrong with this picture? We should be dealing with this together. Instead you're blaming me.'

'I didn't say that.'

'You're refusing to believe I didn't slip an exclusive to my journalist friend.'

'You must admit the timing of her visit is suspicious.'

'We went to that sunset restaurant on Thursday evening. She and her boyfriend didn't fly into Bali until Friday afternoon. She, or her boyfriend, couldn't possibly have taken those photos. Besides, she writes serious stuff for quality media, not tabloid rubbish. It might have been someone in that group of people who brushed past us in the laneway. It could have been anyone with a smartphone.'

He brandished his phone. 'There's a lot of good publicity for Big Blue in this article. According to it, the resort is a perfect place for a "raunchy romp".'

'As it turned out, it actually was perfect for that purpose.' She caught his eye. If he laughed she'd give him more credit on his trust account. He didn't laugh. 'But surely you're not pinning any of this on Maya or Kadek?'

He paused for a second too long. 'Of course not.'

She screwed up her face in what she hoped he would recognise as a look of loathing. 'Not in a million years would they do this to me.' Not content with calling her, in not so many words, a liar, now he was casting slurs on the honesty of the most scrupulously honest people she knew. He was right back there with the wounding words, one stab for her and two more on behalf of her friends.

'Not them, but perhaps someone on the staff.'

'I didn't realise you were so stubborn,' she said. 'We're victims here, me as much as you.'

'Tenacious is how my game was described,' he said. 'I won't give up until I find out who did this to us.'

Did this to *you*, she thought. He didn't seem to give a damn about the effect on her. She was surprised to realise how self-centred Max was. How gutted she was to realise it. When she thought back to it, this…this *affair*—because she now realised that was all it was— had been all about him. His need for privacy, his need to re-establish himself. He hadn't uttered one word of comfort to her. All she wanted was for him to take her in his arms and tell her they were in this together and he was by her side. *Wasn't going to happen.*

'I told you trust is important to me. You don't believe I'm telling the truth. Can you imagine how painful it is for me to be considered a liar? You don't trust me. And I can't trust you to support me. You deal with this in your own way. I'll deal with it in mine.'

She marched to the door outside to the courtyard. Hoped he might follow her. Realised that would be impossible as he didn't have a stitch on. If there was indeed a photographer lurking, Max Conway naked after 'lusty night with busty blonde' would be the money shot of that photographer's career.

She couldn't look back. If she managed to get on a plane tonight that might be the last time she saw Max and she didn't want him to see the tears that she could no longer stop from cascading down her cheeks. Once again she had totally misjudged the true character of a man she had fallen for. She was disappointed in herself as much as him. She'd really thought he was everything she wanted.

CHAPTER FOURTEEN

MAX IMMEDIATELY REALISED he had made one of the worst mistakes of his life. Nikki had hit him with the news of the latest media outrage as he'd woken up from a new and improved version of the 'Nikki in the blue dress' dream. Nikki had been in the church wearing the blue dress but not for a wedding rehearsal. She'd been holding a baby in her arms and they were there for a christening. At first it was black-haired baby Putu with Nikki but then, in the way of dreams, the baby morphed into a blond-haired baby that looked just like Max's baby photos. His baby.

His and Nikki's baby.

In his dream, she'd held their baby out to him and he'd been overjoyed, which was odd as he wasn't at all comfortable with holding babies. That was probably why he woke up. But he'd been only half awake. Awake enough to register the joy of finding Nikki naked in his bed, asleep enough to be about to murmur, *Did we have a boy or a girl?* Then her real-life expression had alerted him to the fact that something was very wrong.

He'd overreacted big-time to what he'd seen on her phone. Thinking on his feet had stood him in good stead on the tennis court. But it had let him down badly here.

Worse, he'd been unable to let go of the idea that Nikki had somehow contributed to the disaster through her journalist friend, Sammie. He'd just looked Sammie up to find what Nikki had said was true. She was a serious, award-winning journalist. Not only would she be unlikely to stoop to tabloid trash, he doubted she'd betray her friend. Nikki inspired loyalty from a group of long-term friends. He, having just asked her to be his girlfriend, had been guilty of stunning disloyalty in not believing her and supporting her. He'd virtually called her a liar.

Fact was, he'd been so determined to pin down the nearest scapegoat, because he knew who was really at fault. Him. As soon as he'd seen that photo of him kissing Nikki in that laneway he'd known the whole disaster had been because of him. In spite of his past history with the tabloids he had been so enchanted with her he'd let down his guard. He had given in to the impulse to kiss her in that laneway even though there had been people about. And as such, he'd failed to protect her. It was that photo that had led to the others. To some creep stalking his lovely Nikki.

The other fact was he simply was not used to thinking as a couple. What had Ellen accused him of being? *'Max first, Max last, and Max in between.'* That might have been true then, when his entire focus had been on his game. But it shouldn't be now. He'd gone into his default protect-his-reputation-at-all-costs mode as soon as he'd seen those scurrilous headlines—so like the headlines that had plagued him before. It was like when he'd got completely immersed in 'the zone' before a game. No one could reach him once he'd reached that state.

But he wasn't playing competitive tennis any more. He'd zoned out and been impervious to the common-sense explanations that Nikki had repeatedly tried to get him to accept. Worse, he had hurt her. Hurt the woman he had realised was vital to his future happiness. Possibly scuppered his chances to make any kind of life with her.

He had to find her. Apologise. Explain. Make amends.

He quickly showered and headed next door. She wasn't there. Or was refusing to acknowledge him. He sounded the chimes. Shouted into the intercom. Even gave an impatient kick to the heavy carved wooden door. Which wasn't a good idea when he was wearing flip-flops.

Kadek approached from the boardwalk just in time to see him kick the door. 'Sorry, Kadek, I'll pay for any damage,' Max said immediately.

Kadek looked amused. 'You're more likely to damage your foot than that door,' he said. Max could hardly look the guy in the eye. Kadek had invited him to dinner at his house the night Nikki had stayed in Sanur. And in return he had included him in his list of suspects. He had a lot of amends to make.

'If you're looking for Nikki, I saw her heading down to the beach. She said she was taking a kayak out.' Thankfully Kadek didn't mention any media reports. He'd see them soon enough, if he hadn't already. Something good might come of it if it helped put Big Blue more on the map for potential guests.

Wayan was on the beach when Max got there. He confirmed Nikki had taken out a kayak. Even though he had warned her that the currents might be unpredictable today. He pointed out to Max where she'd gone.

Shading his eyes against the sun, Max could see

Nikki in her red swim shirt and yellow life jacket paddling to the headland at the south end of the beach. *What the hell was she doing?* Around that headland were wild surf beaches, including the beach at the sunset restaurant. He recalled with a shudder how those waves had pounded against the limestone cliffs. Even in a special surf kayak it would be highly dangerous.

Nikki. She seemed very small in a very big sea out there by herself. As he watched, she disappeared out of sight around the headland.

Max ran to Wayan. 'Let me have your boat,' he said.

Within minutes he was heading out after Nikki in Wayan's *jukung.* As he neared the headland the currents came at him from all directions, buffeting the boat. Nobody should be in a kayak in these waters. Fear gripped his gut.

He gunned the motor. The boat surged through the water. He had to get to her. Had to make sure she was safe. Had to tell her…had to tell her so many things. How sorry he was. How much he regretted the way he'd behaved, not just this morning, but since he'd been on the island. How he'd let his loathing of the media make him hide her, as if she were some guilty secret, instead of shouting to the world how lucky he was to have this beautiful, perfect woman in his life. How blind he'd been to place her behind his career plans instead of putting her first. First in *everything.* Most of all he had to tell her how much— Max stopped his crazy flow of thoughts as the truth hit him harder that the most powerful wave. *How much he loved her.*

Love. He'd tried to deny to himself that he had fallen in love with her. But he'd been kidding himself from the word go. He'd fallen a little in love with her as far back as her wedding rehearsal. That was another reason he'd overreacted to the media interest in them. Deep down, when he'd helped her run away from her wedding, hadn't part of his heart wished he were running away with her for himself?

That was what all the dreams had been telling him—his subconscious shouting out to him what his conscious mind refused to acknowledge. *He loved Nikki Lucas.*

He rounded the first headland, scanning the water for her. Nothing. Not even other small craft. Sensible people did not go out in this kind of current. Why had Nikki?

The current got stronger, the water choppier; he had to fight with the steering wheel to keep the boat on course as he rounded the next set of jagged cliffs.

He saw the oar first. A lone paddle floating on the surface, pulled inextricably by the water towards where it would be smashed against the rocks. So close it wasn't safe for him to retrieve it. In the next split second he saw Nikki. Lying draped across the hull of her capsized kayak. She was very, very still. Injured? Unconscious? Worse? *No!*

He hit the gas so hard the boat reared up out of the water. 'Nikki!' he shouted, the word reverberating around the empty sea.

As he neared her, she lifted her head. 'Max. Thank heaven,' she gasped. Her face was pale, which made the blood trickling down her mouth seem shockingly red in contrast.

He manoeuvred the boat as close as he could get to her. Fear strangled his voice. 'I'm coming for you,' he choked out.

'The kayak capsized. I tried to grab the hull to pull

it back over to me, like I've done a hundred times before.' A choppy wave broke over the kayak, pushed it forward and splashed into her face, sending her sliding back into the sea. 'Aargh!' she spluttered. 'But that keeps happening.'

His first instinct was to dive overboard and get her. But that would leave them both bobbing in the ocean while Wayan's boat drifted away. 'Grab the outrigger,' he said as he manoeuvred the boat closer.

Nikki was an excellent swimmer. She was wearing a life jacket but she was bleeding. His gut roiled as he watched her wait for a lull in the choppy sea and then push herself forward until she was gripping the outrigger. He reached out to haul her in but she was just out of reach. He cursed. Then remembered the ladder. He quickly put it in place. 'Swim to the ladder,' he urged her.

Then he had her in his grasp as he pulled her on board. She was in his arms, wet, shaking, *alive*. He guided her onto the bench, where he sat next to her. 'You're bleeding,' he said, wiping the blood away from her chin.

'Am I?' she said, putting her hand up to her face. 'Oh. That. Bumped my nose. It's nothing. I'm fine.'

'Nothing!' Anger surged through his relief. 'I thought you'd drowned. What the hell were you thinking, coming out here by yourself? How many times did you warn me against it? Don't you ever do something so foolish again.'

Nikki stiffened and shuffled herself along the bench as far away from him as she could without toppling back into the water. As he manoeuvred the boat away from the rocks and back towards the shore, he realised with a chill that went right through to his heart that she wasn't just putting a physical distance between them.

'I'm glad you came along,' she said finally after what felt like hours of silence. They were nearly at the beach when she continued, 'Appreciate the help. But I don't owe you an explanation. Not as your ex-girlfriend of less than twenty-four hours' standing.'

'You're my ex-girlfriend before you've even had time to be my girlfriend?'

'Why would I want to be the girlfriend of a guy who calls me a liar, who refuses to listen to me, who can't act as a boyfriend-girlfriend team, who kicks me out of his room after we'd spent the night making love?'

As he hauled the boat onto the deserted beach, he moored it, finally turning to help her out of the boat. Her eyes were red-rimmed, her face splotchy. Not just with salt water. She'd been crying, crying for some time. Her words were tough but he could see the deep level of pain in her eyes. *He'd hurt her badly.* That was why she'd gone out there by herself. To get as far away from him as possible. *He'd lost her.*

But Max Conway didn't easily accept defeat. He waited until she stood beside him on the sand before finding the words he needed to say.

'Nikki, I'm sorry. You're right. I'm a rotten boyfriend who doesn't deserve you. I've been an idiot. Not just this morning but since the day I watched you step off that boat at Jungut Batu and wade back into my life. For too many stupid reasons I've handled this so badly.'

'Handled what, Max?' she said, her chin still held at a mutinous angle but her expression softened into wary anticipation.

'The fact I'm head over heels in love with you. That nothing else matters but that I'm with you. Not career, not reputation, nothing. That I fell in love with you that first night at the rehearsal of your wedding to another man. I had to deny it then. But I don't have to deny it now. I love you, Nikki.'

Nikki wondered if she'd been knocked unconscious by the edge of the kayak and was hallucinating. Perhaps she was still drifting along in that glorious sea, dreaming of what she wanted most in the world. That Max loved her.

Then she felt the touch of his hand on her arm. Saw the trepidation in his eyes as he waited for her response. *Max loved her.*

'Is there a chance you might love me too?' he said. 'Or is it only about the hot sex for you?'

Her joyous laughter pealed out across the empty beach. 'I love you too, Max.' He kissed her, warm and passionate and tender and *loving* all at the same time. 'And I love the hot sex too,' she murmured against his mouth. They kissed for a long time, each repeating those magical words 'I love you' with increasing wonderment and joy.

'When—?'

'Did I first fall in love with you?' she said. 'I realised I was attracted to you when you carried me away in your arms at the wedding. But here, on this island, on this sea, exploring the underwater paradise together, I realised it was so much more than that. When you kissed me at sunset I knew I was in love.'

'We wasted so much time,' he said.

'Only a few days, though it seems longer,' she said. 'Can we truly fall in love so quickly?'

He smiled. 'Thirty-two years ago my father spotted my mother across the hall at a country dance. He was smitten. Fortunately so was she. They married three months later and are still the happiest couple I know.'

Her breath caught. 'Do you take after your dad?'

'Definitely. I don't need more time. Will you marry me, Nikki?'

Her heart seemed to swell with her love for him. 'Yes, Max, yes.'

'I want to give you everything you want, Nikki. Marriage, children when you're ready. Most of all a husband you can trust to love you and care for you for the rest of our lives.'

'All I want is you,' she murmured through a suddenly constricted throat. 'Everything else will be a bonus.'

He kissed her again for a long time. She couldn't think of a more perfect proposal on the beautiful empty beach, with the vastness of the ocean stretched out before them, in this magical place where they'd each found their for ever love. That they were both wearing life jackets was something to tell the grandchildren.

He broke away from the kiss. 'Instead of hiding us from the media, I should have taken out an advert in that dreadful tabloid and screamed it out in tall black headlines: *"Best Man Loves Runaway Bride."* Only now I'd add, *"And Makes Her His Wife".*'

She laughed. 'Sounds like a plan,' she said, as she drew him to her for another kiss.

CHAPTER FIFTEEN

Three months later, Nusa Lembongan

THIS WEDDING WASN'T strictly their wedding. Nikki and Max had discovered it was legally more straightforward to actually get married in Australia and have the wedding blessed in Indonesia. But this was the place they'd fallen in love and the place they wanted to make a public declaration of their commitment to each other. With a big party to celebrate.

In Sydney, Nikki and Max had got married in the tiny chapel at her old school with just a handful of guests comprising family and their very closest friends, including Max's mother and father, who Nikki already adored. She'd had just her sister Kaylie as bridesmaid and Max's brother had been best man. Her father had given her away and she'd been surprised to see him shed a tear as he'd told her how much he wished her mother could have been here for her special day.

Now here she and Max were on the beach at Frangipani Bay under an arch covered with frangipani and gold-painted ceremonial flowers. She wore a long, white dress trimmed with handmade lace, her feet bare in the sand. Max wore white trousers and shirt, his feet bare too. Kaylie was bridesmaid again, along with Maya and Sammie.

The entire resort had been booked out for the guests they had flown up to the island. They included staff members from the residential tennis training college Max had started to give talented kids from underprivileged backgrounds the same opportunities to excel that he'd had. He'd told Nikki he was enjoying his involvement with it more than he could have imagined. But he got a different kind of satisfaction from his directorship of the sporting goods company. He had a team working on the swimwear for Nikki's first swim club, which was nearly ready to open its doors—already there'd been a lot of interest and advance bookings.

The wedding was being covered by the same classy magazine that had published the feature on Nikki and Max's romance to set their story straight, from the 'cute meet' as runaway bride and the best man, to the happy coincidence of their meeting again six months later on the island.

As they joyously repeated their vows, Max kept Nikki's hand firmly held in his. 'There's no way you're running away from this wedding,' he said.

'Why would I,' she said, looking up to his beloved face, 'when I'm already married to the best man?'

* * * * *

A MAVERICK
TO (RE)MARRY

CHRISTINE RIMMER

For everyone who's loved and lost
and dared to try again.

Chapter One

"I can't believe you're here at last," said Eva Rose Armstrong with a tender little smile. "When you pulled up in your fancy car yesterday, I almost wondered if I was seeing things."

"I'm here and I'm staying," Amy Wainwright replied. "You won't get rid of me until the wedding, no matter how hard you try," she spoke firmly and did her best to ignore the growing sense of dread that had her stomach feeling queasy and her nerves on a thin edge.

"Thirteen years," Eva scolded fondly, "do you realize that? Thirteen years it's taken us to get you to come back to town." *Us* included Eva and her older sisters, Delphine and Calla. Growing up, the Armstrong sisters had been like family to Amy. In the years since Amy had moved to Colorado, the Armstrong girls had come to visit her often, but Amy had always found some rea-

son she couldn't make the trip to Rust Creek Falls—
and in actual fact, it had been nine years, not thirteen,
since Amy had last set foot in Montana. But Eva didn't
know about that other visit and she never would.

"It took you getting married to do the trick." Amy
strove for a light tone. "But I'm here now. And I'm
going nowhere until I see you walk down the aisle to
the man that you love."

Eva laughed. "You don't have to look so grim and
determined about it."

Relax, Amy reminded herself for the umpteenth
time. *It's going to be fine.* "Grim?" She reached out
and took Eva's hand. "Are you kidding? I'm thrilled
to be your maid of honor." It was coming face-to-face
again with the best man that had her belly in knots and
her heart stuck in her throat.

They stood near the sunny front window in the living room of the farmhouse where Eva lived with her
fiancé, Luke Stockton. The best man would be joining
them any minute now. And Amy would get through this
meeting with her pride and her dignity intact.

She was going to smile in a cordial sort of way, just
smile and say hello and ask him how he'd been. She
would treat him as exactly what he was—a guy she
knew way back when. An old high school boyfriend,
nothing more.

What had really happened between them all those
years ago was their secret, his and hers. And Amy could
see no reason on earth why it shouldn't stay that way.

"Now, we just need to find a way to keep you here
forever," Eva said with a definite smirk.

"Highly unlikely." Amy lived in Boulder. She owned
her own home and she worked for a major accounting

firm as a digital forensic accountant. Most people's eyes glazed over when she talked about her work, but Amy had always been a math whiz and a computer nerd. She totally loved stopping hackers and fraudsters dead in their tracks.

"You never know," Eva teased, "you could finally meet the man of your dreams right here in Rust Creek Falls. This town is magic when it comes to love and romance, you just ask anyone."

Once, long ago, Amy would have agreed with her friend. Now, though? Not happening. No way, uh-uh. "If you say so…"

Eva tugged on her hand. "Come on." She led Amy to the sofa and chairs grouped around the coffee table. Eva and Luke had moved to Sunshine Farm last winter. Slowly, they'd been fixing up the old farmhouse, stripping dated wallpaper, installing new countertops and appliances in the kitchen. The furniture was mostly family hand-me-downs and stuff picked up at estate and yard sales, but Eva had a great sense of style and the effect was homey. Welcoming. "Sit down," Eva said, "and have a cookie."

Amy took one of the two wing chairs across from the couch—and a lemon-praline macaron. Eva was a baker by profession, her cookies as irresistible as her sunny smile.

The doorbell chimed.

It's him…

Adrenaline spurted. Amy's throat locked up tight on a bite of macaron.

Calm down. You're okay. Breathe. She gulped a sip of iced tea and somehow managed to swallow the bite of cookie without surrendering to a choking fit.

Across the room and through the open arch, in the small foyer, Eva pulled open the door. "Viv!" It was the wedding planner, Vivienne Shuster. Not *him*, after all. Amy's heartbeat slowed a little as Eva ushered the other woman into the living room.

Vivienne, a tall, striking blonde in a simple tan skirt and a white shirt, took a seat on the couch. She set down her stack of pastel binders and her tablet, shook hands with Amy and said yes to a glass of iced tea and a butter-pecan sandy.

For a few minutes, the women chatted about nothing in particular. Viv was relatively new to town, just getting started with her wedding-planner business. "Eva, the house looks great."

"We keep working on it," said Eva. Luke had grown up at Sunshine Farm, but the place had fallen into disrepair when his parents died and the Stockton family was torn apart.

Viv had obviously heard the whole heartbreaking story, including the current state of affairs. "It's wonderful," she said, "that Luke and his brothers and sisters are reunited now—or almost." Her bright smile dimmed a little. "Any word on Liza?" Liza Stockton was the only one of Luke's siblings who had yet to be located.

"No. But we're still looking. We'll never give up."

"Well, you're certainly bringing the family ranch back to life again." Viv picked up one of her binders and flipped to a tab labeled *Barn Weddings*. Like Luke's brother Danny last Christmas, Luke and Eva's wedding venue would be the big yellow barn right there on Sunshine Farm. "So, we're still going with holding the ceremony outside, and then the reception dinner in the barn, right?" At Eva's nod, Viv continued, "Good, then. I have a few new ideas to run by you."

Amy heard boots out on the front steps. Her mouth went dust-dry and her ears started ringing.

But it was only Luke coming in from the horse pasture. She took slow, deep breaths to settle her absurdly overactive nerves as Luke left his muddy boots by the door and slipped on a pair of soft mocs. "Am I late?"

"Nope." Eva got up to offer a quick kiss and pull him into the living room. "You're right on time." *They look so happy together*, Amy thought. She was glad for her friend. A born romantic, Eva had survived more than her share of disappointments in love. But she never gave up. And now she'd finally found the perfect man for her.

The doorbell rang again. Amy's stomach lurched and her heart beat so hard, she knew it would pound its way right out of her chest.

"That'll be Derek," Luke said. "I'll get it." He returned to the door as Amy practiced slow breathing and prayed she wouldn't sink to the floor in a dead faint like the heroine of some old-time novel, felled by her own secret past. "Come on in," said Luke.

And then, there he was.

Derek Dalton. In Wranglers and a soft chambray shirt. He took off his hat and his hair was just as she remembered it, thick and unruly, sable brown. *He* was just as she remembered—only bigger, broader. A grown man now, not a nineteen-year-old boy.

He hung his hat by the door. Luke signaled him forward and he entered the living room, filling it with his presence, with their past that seemed to suck all the air right out of her lungs. He greeted Eva and Viv. And then he turned to Amy, those leaf-green eyes homing right in on her. "Hey, Amy. Long time, huh?"

She stared up at him, unable to speak. But then he held out his big, blunt-fingered, work-roughened hand. She forced herself to take it and the shock of touching him again after all these years sent a bolt of lightning straight up her arm—and jolted the necessary words out of her.

"Hey, Derek." She pulled her fingers free of his grip and somehow managed the barest semblance of a smile. "Great to see you again."

"You, too." With that, he turned away at last and lowered his big frame into the other wing chair.

The meeting began.

Viv opened a binder, pulled the rings wide and took out a small stack of papers. "Derek." She handed several sheets to him. "And for you, Amy." She passed Amy the rest. "You each now have the phone numbers and email addresses of everyone in the wedding party. Also, you'll find a series of suggestions for the joint bachelor-bachelorette party, which is slated for the Saturday before the wedding. You two will be working as a team to pull it together. Invitations have already been sent and we're counting on a big crowd. I threw in a few brainstorming sheets. It always helps to have those— just as a way to get the ideas flowing, you understand."

"Wonderful," Amy said, because Viv was looking at her and it seemed important that she say something.

"As for the bachelor party venue," said Viv, "Maverick Manor is a dream setting, luxe and rustic at once. A real coup that we got it." She gave Derek a nod. "Big thanks to Derek."

"Don't thank me," Derek said. His voice was a little different somehow, deeper than Amy remembered. The sound of it reached down inside her, stirring up memories, reminding her of tender moments she really needed to forget. He added, "Nate Crawford's the one."

Eva asked, "You remember Nate, Amy?"

"Yeah. Of course." Nate had been four or five years ahead of her in school, but everybody knew him. He was the oldest of six children. His parents, Laura and Todd, owned the general store.

"Nate's become kind of a town benefactor in the last few years," said Eva. "He's a major shareholder in Maverick Manor."

Derek said, "I just mentioned the party to him and he offered the Manor as a good place for it."

"Ah," said Amy, staring straight ahead, unable to make herself look at him though he was sitting right there at the other end of the coffee table from her. "Terrific."

Eva explained, "Instead of separating the girls and the guys, I wanted one big party for all of us—with nothing X-rated, if you know what I mean."

Viv clarified, "No strippers. And the games can be a *little* sexy—"

"—but nothing over the top." Eva patted Luke's hand. "Just good fun, right, Luke?"

"Works for me." The groom nodded.

"It'll be a nice, relaxed get-together for everyone," added Eva, "not only for the wedding party, but also for all of our friends in town. We want it to be loose and easy and the Manor is a beautiful, comfortable place for it."

Viv nodded at Derek and then at Amy. "Food and music are already taken care of, again thanks to Derek."

Wait a minute. Had Derek paid for all this? Or just arranged everything? The boy she'd known in high school hadn't had a lot of money. So then, he'd done well for himself?

Not that it mattered how much money he had. What mattered was that she would make sure the financial burden didn't all fall on him—and wait a minute. Why was she worrying about Derek and his finances anyway?

Really, she didn't even know the guy anymore....

Viv was still talking. "If you need specific songs played or whatever, I'll be happy to pass your requests along to the band. You two will be putting your heads together and coming up with some fun things to do for the event, along with party favors and prizes.

"Mostly, it's a balance. You don't want to pack in too many activities, but you need a few games and such, to get people mingling. I've listed some very basic ideas on your party brainstorm sheets, just to jump-start the process for you. I'll be ready with more suggestions if you need them and to help in any way I can."

Amy tried really hard to focus, to keep her mind in the now, to think about great things to do at a coed bachelor party and what prizes and favors might be cute.

But her brain defied her will. Images assailed her, of those five days all those years ago, the tacky motel by the highway, the sound of the big rigs going by in the night, the reassuring warmth of Derek's strong arms around her. How much she had loved him.

How scared she'd been, her life spinning out of control, nothing going the way she'd planned it.

"Fun activities," she heard herself repeat. "Will do."

From the other chair, Derek spoke up, too. "Uh, yeah. We'll get right on that."

The meeting continued. To Amy, it seemed endless. The memories pressed in on her, making it hard to breathe. But really, no one seemed to notice that she wasn't saying much. Did they?

Eva and Luke seemed relaxed, happy as only two people in love can be. Viv was laser-focused on the wedding plans. Eva, a baker to the core, was all about the food and the cake, while Viv talked flowers and ways to make the barn setting really pop.

They discussed music for the wedding day, too. Luke and Eva had put in hours practicing their first dance. The band—the same group they were using at the bachelor party—had been given a long playlist of the couple's favorites to fill up the evening. Luke joked that of course local eccentric Homer Gilmore would be welcome at the wedding. But they had to make absolutely certain that Homer's infamous moonshine didn't find its way into the punch.

As for Derek...

Well, Amy didn't know how Derek was faring. From the moment he took the chair across from hers, she hadn't been able to make herself so much as glance in his direction.

When it was finally over and Viv was closing up her binders and stacking them to go, Amy longed to race for the stairs and the big guest room up there that would be hers for the next few weeks. She'd brought her work with her. She could power up her computer and concentrate on keeping the giant accounting firm of Hurdly and Main, International protected from cyber-criminals and digital fraud.

But no. She and Derek needed to talk.

She needed to tell him...what? There was nothing

to tell him. It was over and it had been over for years and years.

Still. They really ought to come to some sort of understanding as to how they were going to work together. Not to mention, she needed to know who in town knew about them. And how much they knew. And, from now on, what would be getting said to whom.

Suddenly, everyone was standing and moving toward the door—everyone but Amy. She shook herself and leapt to her feet.

And then once she was up, she just stood there at her chair, dithering over how to approach him, what to say to get his attention before he went out the door and she missed her chance to tell him…

What?

Dear Lord, she had no idea.

She blinked and finally made herself glance in his direction.

He was looking straight at her. "So, Amy, got a few minutes?" Those green eyes gave nothing away. "We should touch base."

Her heart pounding so hard she was lucky it didn't crack a rib, she nodded. "A walk, maybe?" she heard herself offer lamely.

"That'll work."

It took her several agonizing seconds to realize that he was waiting for her to join him. "Oh!" she exclaimed like a total doofus and ordered her feet to carry her toward him.

They all went out to the porch together and waved goodbye to Viv.

Luke shook Derek's hand. "Friday, happy hour. The Ace."

"I'll be there," said Derek.

The Ace in the Hole was the only bar within the Rust Creek Falls town limits. Amy remembered it all too well from her short, unhappy visit to town nine years before.

And then, last year, the Ace had garnered national attention when a reality show, *The Great Roundup*, had filmed final auditions there. Travis Dalton, Derek's cousin, had been on that show and so had Travis's now-wife, Brenna O'Reilly Dalton.

Amy had watched the show faithfully every week. The scenes filmed in town had made her feel all warm and fuzzy, made her long for Rust Creek Falls, made her remember the good times growing up. Best of all, *The Great Roundup* had allowed her to get sappy and sentimental from the safety of her Boulder, Colorado living room. Never had she ever planned to set foot in town again.

But now, here she was, about to get up close and conversational with the very reason she'd stayed away for so long in the first place.

Luke and Eva went back into the house, leaving Amy alone with the gorgeous broad-shouldered stranger who'd once ruled her teenaged heart. She just stood there, like a lump. She had no idea what to say to him.

He had his straw Resistol in his hand. He slid the hat onto his head and tugged on the brim to settle it.

Everything inside her was aching. This couldn't be happening.

But it was.

"Let's go." He started walking. She followed him

down the steps and out into the late-afternoon sun-shine.

He turned for the big yellow barn where Eva and Luke would get married in less than four weeks. Amy came up beside him and they walked together, but not touching, neither saying a word. Somewhere far off, a lone bird cried, the sound faint. Plaintive.

"Here's as good as anywhere, I guess," he said, stop-ping at a split rail fence fifty yards or so from the loom-ing shape of the barn.

For more reasons than she cared to contemplate, she didn't want to look directly at him, so she turned toward the pasture on the other side of the fence. The papers Viv had given her crackled in her hands as she rested her forearms on the top rail and gazed off at nothing in particular.

Silence. Out in the pasture, a bay mare snorted and shook her dark mane.

Derek said, "You look good," and she tried to read his tone. Careful? Thoughtful? Maybe a little angry?

What did it matter, though, what was on his mind? She didn't know him anymore. They were strangers to each other now and she needed to remember that. "Thanks. You, too—and, well, I don't even know where to start." She did look at him then. He was watching her from under the shadow of his hat. Waiting. She swallowed. Hard. "I have been wondering, though…"

"What?"

"Well, it would be good to have some idea of who *knows*," she said, and then wanted to kick herself. Could she *be* any more unclear? He probably had no clue what she'd just tried to ask him.

But as it turned out, he understood perfectly. "About us, you mean?"

"Yeah. About, um, what happened thirteen years ago."

"Nobody in this town," he said. "Nobody but me." A slow smile curved his beautiful mouth. "Well, and you, now that you're here. *While* you're here."

She caught her lower lip between her teeth. "I would like it to stay that way."

"Just between you and me, you mean?"

"Yes, Derek." His name in her mouth tasted way too familiar. "Just between us. Can we keep it that way?"

"You got it. I've never told a soul and I won't start now." And then he frowned. "But what about the Armstrongs? You didn't ever tell Eva or her sisters?"

"No." Her silly throat had clutched and the word came out in a whisper. She knew her cheeks had to be lobster-red. "Ahem." She coughed into her hand. And then she made herself explain. "I never told the Armstrongs the whole story. All they know is that you and I dated in high school. How about Luke? Your family?"

"I meant what I said, Amy. I haven't told anyone. It just seemed better to put the whole thing behind me. It's the past and it needs to stay that way."

"I agree." And she did. Absolutely, she did. She wished that none of it had ever happened.

But it did happen. And it changed her in the deepest way.

Did it change him, too, she wondered?

Not that she would ever ask. She had no right to ask and she needed to remember that.

He smiled again—halfway this time, one corner of his mouth kicking up. "Luke waited until after I said

I would be his best man to tell me that you would be the maid of honor."

A strange, tight spurt of laughter escaped her. She quickly composed herself. "I see Eva all over that."

"What do you mean?"

"She got me to agree to be her maid of honor before she mentioned that you would be best man."

"So, you think she knows more than you've told her?"

"Well, you know Eva, right? She's a complete and unapologetic romantic. I think she suspects there was more than just a high school crush going on between us back in the day." Another tight little laugh escaped her—and then she wanted to cry. Really, she couldn't stand for him not to know what she truly felt, how much she regretted the way things had ended up. "Derek, I..."

"Yeah?" His eyes held hers, a deep look, one that reached down into the center of her and stirred up emotions she wished she didn't feel.

"I, well, I just need you to know that I'm sorry. For everything."

Wow. She almost couldn't believe that she'd gone and done it, apologized straight out. And as soon as the words escaped her lips, she kind of wanted to take them back.

Because really, wasn't *he* the one who'd told *her* to go?

But what else could a person say at a time like this?

"I'm sorry, too," he said.

"But it's fine," she blurted out.

He nodded. "Yeah. You're right. It's water under the bridge. Years ago. Not a big deal."

"Absolutely. Over and done. We've both put it be-hind us. Derek, we can do this. We can be there for Luke and Eva. We can help make their wedding ev-erything they deserve it to be."

He took off his hat, hit the brim against his denim-clad thigh, then put it back on. "Yeah. That's our job and we can do it."

She straightened her shoulders. "We *will* do it."

"Yes, we will," he agreed.

And then they just stood there at the fence, staring at each other.

The silence stretched thin.

He broke it. "Well, all right, then. I'll be in touch." And without another word, he turned and left her standing there.

Chapter Two

Feeling stunned by the whole encounter, Amy stared after Derek as he walked away from her.

Once he reached the turnaround in front of the house again, he climbed into a mud-spattered red F-150 pickup. The engine roared out, the big wheels stirring up a cloud of dust as he drove away.

What had just happened? She wasn't sure. Had they actually forgiven each other?

Well, at least they'd said the words. And that was good, she decided. They didn't need to talk it to death. What was there to say, anyway?

It was all in the past.

Too bad they'd come up with nothing in terms of a plan for the bachelor party. He'd said he would "be in touch." What exactly did that mean?

Annoyance prickled through her. Okay, she got that

she wasn't his favorite person. But they did have to work together. He could have stuck around long enough to set a time and a place.

She glanced down at the papers in her hand. His numbers were right there at the top of the first page—mobile and home. Would the home number be the main house at his family's ranch, the Circle D? She'd had that number memorized all those years ago. It was burned into her brain and she remembered it still. But this home number was different. Did he live somewhere else now?

He'd moved to the bunkhouse in April of their senior year, to give himself a little independence from his close-knit family. Back then, the bunkhouse number was the same as at the main house, but maybe they'd put in a separate line since then.

Not that she cared. It didn't matter to her where, exactly, he lived now. She just needed to know when and where they would meet.

She shook her head at the stack of papers. If he didn't get back to her in the next day or two, she would have to call him.

No big deal.

And really, he *had* said he would be in touch, right? What was she worrying about?

Forget calling him. *He* would call *her*.

And of course, that would be soon...

Amy barely got back in the door of the farmhouse before Eva was all over her. "What did he say? Is it okay between you? Was it hard, to see him again?"

"Eva." She managed a laugh. "Cut it out. It was fine. It was years ago."

"But you *loved* him."

Oh, yes, she had. But she wasn't going there. "It was high school. And it's all in the past. There are no problems between us and you don't have to worry."

"I'm not worrying." Her big blue eyes got bigger. "I just want to know, is the spark still there?"

Amy wasn't answering that one. No way. She kept it light, making a show of tapping her chin as though deep in thought. "Hmm. Is it just me or are you playing matchmaker?"

Eva blushed the sweetest shade of pink. "I would never…"

"Yeah, right."

They both burst out laughing at the same time and Eva said, "Okay, okay. I'll butt out, I promise."

Amy gave her friend the side-eye. "I'll believe it when I see it."

Derek didn't call that evening. And he didn't call on Tuesday.

By Wednesday, the Fourth of July, she knew she should go ahead and reach out.

Maybe a text. She wouldn't even have to talk to him until their actual meeting.

She put his cell number in her phone, hit the message icon and started typing, whipping out five different messages and deleting them as fast as she wrote them. After the fifth attempt, she decided she would just wait another day to deal with the whole reaching out thing.

That night, she went into town with Eva, Luke and his brother Bailey, for a barbecue at their sister Bella's house and to watch the fireworks in the town park later.

That whole evening, she felt on edge just thinking that she might run into Derek.

But she never so much as caught sight of him.

The days were going by. They needed to meet up. But he hadn't called.

And she couldn't quite bring herself to make the first move.

By Thursday evening, as he ate his solitary dinner in the house he'd built for himself on Circle D land, Derek Dalton was feeling more than a little bit jerkish.

He'd told Amy he would get back to her. He needed to call her and set up another meeting.

But even after all these years, it still hurt something deep inside him just to be near her. She looked the same—with long brown hair showing gleams of red in the sun, creamy skin, eyes that seemed to change color depending on her mood, brown to olive green and back again, sometimes with a hint of gold.

Yeah. She looked the same. But even better, so smooth and classy. Luke had mentioned that she'd gone on to graduate school after four years at the University of Colorado. He'd said she had some high-tech accounting job and she owned her own house in Boulder.

None of that information surprised Derek. Amy had been the smartest girl at Rust Creek Falls High, put ahead a year when she was twelve, so they'd ended up in the same grade. She'd been valedictorian of their small graduating class. Her dad was a rich guy from Boulder who'd given up the rat race for a while to become a rancher in the Rust Creek Falls Valley—and then moved back to Colorado when Amy left to go to college there.

Derek never would've had a chance with Jack and Helen Wainwright's precious only daughter if he hadn't needed a math tutor to get him through Algebra II in his senior year.

He shook his head. Him and Amy? That was an old, sad song and they wouldn't be playing it ever again. He needed to get his mind off the past. There was zero to be gained by a trip down memory lane.

Shoving back his chair, he picked up his plate and carried it to the counter. Outside the window over the sink, the sunset turned the bellies of the clouds to bright orange and deep purple.

Maybe he'd head on into town, see if he could scare up a poker game at the Ace.

Then again, he'd had a long day today, moving cattle, putting out mineral barrels. Tomorrow, he needed to be up early. He felt antsy and ornery. If he went to the Ace, it would be too easy to drink too much and do or say something he would end up regretting.

He turned in early and had a restless night.

But it could have been worse. At least he didn't have a hangover at eight on Friday morning when he parked his pickup in front of the old warehouse at Sawmill and North Broomtail Road.

Four years ago, he'd joined Collin Traub in his one-man saddlery business. At first, they'd worked in the basement of Collin's house up on Falls Mountain. But then CT Saddles had moved to the warehouse. The larger space allowed them to buy more equipment and take on more projects. They were still a small shop, but the Traub name was a trusted one and their business kept growing.

Derek thought about Amy constantly that day. Really, it was way past time he gave her a call. But the hours ticked by and he never did.

His failure to get back to her was moving beyond jerkish, heading into jackass territory. But he still failed to pick up the phone.

At five, Collin went on up the mountain to his wife, Willa, and their little boy, Robbie. Ned Faraday, who was sixteen and helping out at the saddlery for the summer, headed home for dinner.

Derek washed up in the saddlery restroom and thought again about how he needed to call Amy. He even took out his phone and looked at it for a good minute or two before shaking his head and sticking it back in his pocket.

At five thirty, he walked down the street to the Ace to meet Luke and his brothers for a drink. It was the five of them—Luke, Jamie, Daniel, Bailey and Derek. They took over a big table not far from the bar and ordered some pitchers.

Jamie and Daniel Stockton were both happily married. Jamie had triplets, Henry, Jared and Kate. They were two and a half years old now. Jamie got everyone laughing with stories of the mischief the three little ones got up to. Danny spoke fondly of his wife and their daughter, Janie.

And Luke? He mostly just sat there, slowly sipping his beer with a contented smile on his face. Everyone in town knew that Luke Stockton was long-gone in love with Eva Rose Armstrong and couldn't wait to make her his wife.

Bailey was the lone unattached Stockton brother. He'd been married and divorced. Like Luke and Daniel, he'd returned to town in the past year after more than a decade away. Now he lived at Sunshine Farm.

He and Luke worked the ranch together, building a new herd, bringing the family homestead back from years of neglect.

That evening, Bailey didn't say much at first. But after a beer or two, he started making his feelings about matrimony painfully clear.

"It's a losin' game is what it is." He raised his glass to Derek, who'd taken the chair across from him. "And you, my man, are the only one at this table with the sense the good Lord gave a goat. You got the ladies all over you, but no woman ever tied *you* down and slapped on a brand."

Ignoring the sudden sweet image of Amy that popped into his head unbidden, Derek forced a wry laugh. "Put a sock in it, Bailey. Your brothers look pretty damn happy to me."

Bailey groaned. "They all start out happy, now don't they?"

"You're getting obnoxious," warned Luke. "Quit while you're ahead."

But Bailey wasn't about to take his brother's good advice. "What I'm 'getting' is honest. It's too late for Danny and Jamie here. They'll just have to learn the hard way that marriage is a game for fools." He leaned close to Luke and stage-whispered in his ear, "Get away. Get away while you still can."

"Knock it off." Luke elbowed him hard in the ribs.

"Ow!" Bailey rubbed his side. "Big brother, you got an elbow on you."

"And you have a big mouth. One you need to practice shutting."

Bailey put on a hangdog expression. "It's hopeless, I tell you. You're doomed, brother. Doomed." He tipped his head back and asked the ceiling, "Oh, why won't anyone listen to a man who knows?"

"Get real, Bailey," said Luke. "You love Eva."

"'Course I love Eva. She's a fine woman. So is Annie, for that matter." That was Daniel's wife. "Fallon, too." Fallon O'Reilly had married Jamie the year before. "It's not the women I object to, it's the institution itself. Marriage. It's what ruins people's lives." Bailey wrapped his hands around his own throat and pretended to choke himself. "Slow strangulation, you hear what I'm sayin'?"

Derek decided to step in before Bailey got too far on the wrong side of his own brothers. "Come on, Bailey. Nine-ball. Two out of three." He nodded toward the pool table.

"Go." Daniel made a shooing motion. "Give the rest of us a break."

Bailey scowled. "I'm trying to *help* you."

"We don't need your help," said Jamie.

Bailey hung his head. "Why does no one appreciate the wisdom I'm offering?"

Derek got up. "Nine-ball. What do you say?"

"Why not?" Bailey rose, grumbling, "I'm not makin' any progress here, and that's for sure."

At the pool tables, Bailey continued to trash-talk marriage as Derek proceeded to win the game. Twice.

"Not only smart enough to stay single," declared Bailey when they started back to join the other guys, "but a pool shark, too. What other talents you got?"

As he considered what to try next to get Bailey to stop annoying his brothers, Bailey muttered, "Uh-oh. Here they come."

They were Eva, Bailey's sister Bella—and Amy.

Amy. Looking like a bright ray of sunshine in a pretty yellow dress.

The three women marched straight to the table where the Stockton men were sitting.

Bailey, still beside him, said something else. Derek had no idea what. All rational thought had fled his mind, along with his ability to understand words. He felt sucker punched. And also guilty.

Yeah, he should have called her. But how could he? Even after all these years, she made him forget the English language, made him blind to everything but her.

Somehow, he did what he had to do—put one foot in front of the other, kept walking alongside Bailey until they reached the table again.

"There you are," said Bella, glaring straight at Bailey.

Bailey widened his eyes. "What'd I do now?"

"Don't play innocent," said Bella. "Nobody believes that act from you. You've been driving everybody in the place crazy, going on about all the reasons men should never get married. We just came over to offer you a ride back to Sunshine Farm."

"Somebody called you to come and haul me out of the Ace?" Bailey huffed in trumped-up outrage. "I don't believe this town. A guy can't express an honest opinion without some busybody callin' his sister to come drag him home."

Luke, who'd gotten up to give Eva a quick kiss, advised, "Maybe you've had one too many, huh, Bailey?"

"I'm not drunk," Bailey insisted.

Eva suggested wryly, "Just opinionated?"

He frowned at her. "And where do you and Amy come in? That's what I'd like to know."

"We were over at Bella's when she got the call."

"The call from who?" he demanded.

Bella shook her head. "You don't need to know."

As the others discussed whether Bailey should go home or not, Derek stood by the table and tried not to look at Amy. When he finally couldn't stop himself from shooting her a glance, he caught her at the moment that her gaze skittered away from him.

Just like on Monday, the two of them sitting there in Eva's living room, both of them trying their damnedest not to look at each other.

They'd had love once, powerful love that he'd believed could conquer anything.

Now they just tried not to look at each other when they met up by accident. And when they *had* to speak to each other, they blathered on about how their secret past was long ago and they were both just fine.

Bailey said, "I'll switch to ginger ale. Will that satisfy you women?"

"And stop running down marriage," said Jamie.

"Yeah," Daniel agreed. "We've heard enough about that."

"Fine, fine. It's hopeless to even try, anyway," Bailey groused. "I got the message, loud and clear. You all can keep your happily-ever-afters, see if I care."

"All right, then," said Luke. He turned to Eva. "Stay for a little?" He sat again and pulled her down into the chair next to him. "Come on, Bella. Amy. Stay."

Bailey helped Derek grab some more chairs and then the two of them went and got another round—including a pitcher of ginger ale for Bailey and anyone else who didn't want beer. When they got back to the table, the chair on one side of Amy was empty.

Derek took that chair because he couldn't bear not to.

Someone put a love song on the ancient jukebox. A girl from out of town grabbed Bailey and pulled him up for a dance.

Luke led Eva out onto the floor. They swayed to the music, whispering to each other. Eva tipped her blond head back and laughed. They looked so damn happy.

Life? Sometimes it just wasn't fair.

Derek couldn't stop himself. He turned to Amy. "Dance with me?"

Her eyes looked almost golden right then, golden, green and softest brown. She swallowed. And then she nodded.

He took her hand—so smooth and cool. It fit just right in his, same as it used to all those years ago. He pulled her up and led her out among the dancers, gathering her close, maybe closer than he should have.

So what? She smelled like heaven—like wildflowers and sunshine. And her body felt just right brushing close to his. Maybe he'd dance with her all night long, never once let her out of his arms.

He pressed his rough cheek to her silky hair. "I'm sorry I didn't call."

"Why didn't you?"

"I don't know. I kept meaning to."

She pulled away enough to turn those big eyes up to him. "Apology accepted. I was going to call *you*."

He stared at her lips too long, caught himself and shifted his glance back up to meet her eyes. "But you didn't call me."

"I didn't know what I would say. I also had a feeling you might not answer the phone or call me back. I felt... out of my depth, I guess. So, I just kept putting it off."

"Yeah, well. All that, what you just said? Me, too."

"We need to stop this. We're two grown adults."

He almost chuckled. "Coulda fooled me."

"Derek, we've got a bachelor party to plan."

He sucked in her scent of flowers and sunshine. "Yeah. We need to get going on that." Holding her like this felt so natural, so completely right. It made the years kind of melt away.

And he really needed to keep a grip on himself. This would go nowhere. It was only a dance.

"So then," she whispered, "we need to make a date to meet and then we need to stick to it."

"A date?" He said it in a playful way and felt stupidly proud of himself that he'd managed to tease her. "You want a date with me?"

She slanted him a sharp glance. "Yeah, a date. But not a *date*."

"So…a *non*-date, then?"

"Exactly. And I mean it, Derek. We need to make it soon. We've got two weeks till the bachelor party. Viv dropped by the farmhouse yesterday and asked how we were doing with our plans. I promised her we'd have it all figured out in the next few days."

Amy was right. No more mooning around like a heartsick fool. It was all over years ago and he needed to stop stewing about it and hold up his end as Luke's best man.

"Tomorrow," he said. "I'll pick you up at six. Ever been to Maverick Manor?"

"No."

"Great. We'll go there and you can get a look at the place. It might give us some ideas."

"All right. That works."

"We'll get a couple of fancy burgers and come up

with a bunch of activities to satisfy Viv Shuster's list-making soul."

"Perfect. I'm in."

The song ended.

Another cowboy tapped him on the shoulder. *Get lost*, he almost let himself say. But not quite. He gave Amy a hint of a smile. "Thanks for the dance."

She nodded. "See you tomorrow, then." And she turned into the other cowboy's waiting arms.

The next day, Amy spent way too much time trying to decide what to wear to Maverick Manor that night. She finally settled on a turquoise halter dress with a handkerchief hem and a pair of matching high-heeled sandals. Why not dress up a little? From what everyone said, Maverick Manor was an upscale sort of place.

True, this was not a real date, but it couldn't hurt to look her best.

Maybe, just possibly, she went a little overboard, pumicing and shaving and getting everything all smooth and sleek. And then she used up a whole hour on her hair and makeup. But taking the time to look good was so worth it, a real confidence-booster. And with Derek, well, she needed all the confidence she could muster.

At five thirty, she was trying to decide between a shoulder bag and a clutch, wondering if she ought to bring a light wrap, when her phone rang.

It was Derek. "Amy? Hey. I'm really sorry, but we've got some fences down and I'm not gonna be able to make it tonight, after all. We'll have to reschedule."

Reschedule.

Her heart sank. It felt like a lead weight in her chest.

How had this happened? Somehow, she'd gone and let herself look forward to the evening, let herself forget that this was only a meeting, a *non*-date.

Tears blurred her vision—which was totally ridiculous. She dropped to the edge of her bed and fiddled with the filmy hem of the dress she wouldn't be wearing tonight after all. "Oh. Ahem. Well, I totally understand. You just give me a call tomorrow, why don't you? We'll set up something else."

"Amy, are you all—"

"Listen." She swallowed down the lump in her throat. "I've got to go. Talk to you later."

"But are you—"

"'Bye, now." She disconnected the call and dropped the phone on the bed. And then, teeth gritted, eyes shut, she willed the tears away. So silly, to get all emo just because an old boyfriend needed a rain check on their non-date. It was in no way, shape or form a big deal.

Except, well, he'd been so much more than just a boyfriend...

But she wasn't going to even think about all that. That was all in the past and it needed to stay there. She'd moved on long ago, gone out with other guys. Once, she'd almost gotten engaged. But when it came right down to it, well, it hadn't been true love and she just couldn't say yes. Not like with—

No. Stop. Not going there.

Besides, her dating history was not the issue. What mattered was that the days were flying by and they really did have to make some plans for the big party. They had a great venue and everyone had already been invited. Music and food were taken care of, or so she'd been told.

Games and activities. That was all she and Derek had to handle. And Eva and Luke were counting on them to do it up right.

Really, she would not allow a single tear to fall. Annoyance was what she felt right now. Annoyance and exasperation that Derek Dalton kept putting off the job they'd both agreed to do.

Down the hall in the bathroom, she washed her face free of every bit of the makeup she'd so carefully applied. She raked her hair up into a ponytail and changed into old jeans, a white T-shirt edged in lace that had seen better days and a worn pair of Converse high-tops.

Then, in her room again, she sat at her computer and spent half an hour brainstorming ideas for the party. When that got old, she logged in at work.

Around eight, she started getting antsy. Grabbing her phone, she went downstairs. Eva and Luke had gone to Jamie and Fallon's for dinner, so she had the house to herself for the evening. She should fix a sandwich or something.

But she didn't really feel hungry.

She wandered out to the front porch and perched on the step. Her phone was synced to her computer. She brought up the list for the party to jot down a few more ideas just as a red pickup rolled into the yard.

Derek. Her pulse started racing and her heart seemed to expand in her chest.

He stopped not far from the foot of the steps and got out. "Hey, pretty girl." He swept off his hat. His hair was damp, his cheeks freshly shaved. He wore dark-wash jeans and a crisp snap-front shirt.

She was really glad to see him and that irritated

her no end. Sticking her phone in her back pocket, she challenged, "I thought you had fences to deal with."

"I did. We had three sections of fence down, cows and calves loose all over the place. But we rounded them up and drove them back where they belonged, fixing fences as we went. When we got to the last fence, Eli said he could handle the rest." Eli was his brother. "I left him to it, cleaned up fast and came right over here in hopes I might still have a chance at that nondate you promised me."

She scowled down at her old T-shirt and busted out jeans. "Do I look like I'm ready for a visit to the local resort?"

His gorgeous mouth twitched at one corner. She knew damn well he was trying not to smile. "Aw, Amy."

"What?" she demanded, feeling sour as a pile of lemons.

"You're all grown-up now, but in some ways, you're still the same girl I remember."

Now her chest felt tight, like a bunch of sweet memories had gotten trapped in there, leaving no room for breath. She narrowed her eyes and pinched her mouth at him. "What is *that* supposed to mean?"

"You never would go anywhere without your hair just so and your makeup just right."

She sat up straighter. He wasn't getting to her. No way. "I like to make a good impression. Something wrong with that?"

"Not a thing." He put his hat to his heart. "I'm sorry, okay? That I didn't call you all week, that tonight got messed up. But when you work cattle, fences go down and you just have to deal with it."

"I know that."

"So then, what's really bugging you is that I didn't call earlier in the week like I said I would?"

She wrapped her arms around her knees, braced her chin on them and considered blowing off his question. But where would that get them? A little honesty never hurt and she might as well at least try to clear the air between them. After all, he'd asked. "Yeah. You said you'd get in touch and you didn't. And then tonight, at the last possible minute, you called it off. It's like you're messing with me or something."

"I'm not."

"And I'm not sure I believe you. I mean, whatever happened in the past, that was then. We need to get over it."

"I know that, Amy." He regarded her solemnly.

"We have a job to do, Derek." Did she sound whiny? Well, why shouldn't she? She certainly *felt* whiny. "People we care about are counting on us."

"You're right." He took a step closer and spoke in a rough whisper. "You want the truth from me?"

Did she? Really? She wasn't sure. But she had too much pride to back down now. "Yes, I do. Tell me the truth, Derek Dalton."

"I didn't call all week because I kept thinking of the past, you know? Of you and me and everything that went down. I didn't trust myself to call you. After everything we were to each other once, I felt like I was going to end up blowing it, saying something way out of line to you. I don't want to do that. And so, I put off calling you."

That hurt. On a lot of levels. But the truth was like

that sometimes. "It's not that easy for me, either," she confessed in a small voice.

He stood there in the fading light of day, just looking at her with those green eyes she still sometimes saw in her dreams. "Amy?"

"Yeah?"

"You mind if I come up there on the porch with you?"

By way of an answer, she scooted over and patted the empty space beside her. He came up the steps, hooked his hat on the finial at the end of the porch rail and plunked down next to her. She got a whiff of his scent—soap and clean skin. All manly and fresh and much too well-remembered.

"I...go back and forth," she said.

He frowned. "About?"

She refused to let her gaze waver. "What to say to you. I mean, we did kind of leave it hanging, didn't we?"

His eyes had shadows in them now. "You sent me the papers and I signed them. Nothing left hanging about that."

"Derek, you *told* me to go."

"You *wanted* to go."

She shut her eyes and turned away. "We shouldn't even be talking about this. I mean, what's the point, really?"

There was a silence, one full of all the things she wasn't sure how to say—didn't really believe she even *should* say.

Finally, he spoke. "How 'bout this?" His voice was gentle now. Coaxing. "Let's start with the picnic."

"There's a picnic?" She faced him again. "What picnic?"

"Well, when I called, you didn't seem happy about my breaking our non-date."

"I wasn't happy. Not in the least."

"So, I figured I needed a backup plan. I decided if you wouldn't come out to the Manor with me now, I would put on my pitiful face and say, 'Then how 'bout a picnic, Amy?' Because it just so happens I have one all ready to go in the truck." He looked at her hopefully.

"Is that it?"

"Is what it?"

She waved a hand in a circle around his face. "Is that your pitiful face?"

He chuckled. "It depends. Is it working?"

She was not going to smile at him. He didn't deserve it. Not yet, anyway. "Hmm. Depends on what's in the picnic."

"You'll be relieved to know I stopped by the main house for the food. I have my mom's fried chicken and biscuits all fancy in a basket. I even brought a big blanket to sit on."

"All of a sudden, I'm starving."

"And there's apple pie, too."

She kind of wanted to hold out against him, leave him hanging at least a bit longer. But then her stomach betrayed her with a hungry little growl. His grin said he heard it. At that point, what could she do but give in? "All right. A picnic, then—but I think we'll need to eat inside." She stared out at the darkening sky. "It's almost nighttime. I'm not sure I want to stumble around in the dark looking for somewhere to spread a picnic blanket."

He leaned closer. "Go in and get a sweater. It's getting chilly out."

"But—"

"Shh." His warm breath tickled her ear. "It just so happens I also brought a lantern."

Two hours later, they sat under the stars with the lantern turned down low providing a soft circle of light to push back the shadows.

By then, they'd agreed on the games for the party: a modified version of *The Newlywed Game*, which they'd dubbed "The Nearly Newlywed Game." Also, they planned a scavenger hunt and some random betting and gambling games in a Western-themed, mini-casino setup. They'd made lists of all the things they would need to buy and assemble for each activity, and he'd been fine with her ideas for the decorations.

Tomorrow, she would shop online, making sure to get expedited shipping. Monday, she would drive to Kalispell and try to buy what she hadn't found online. Monday evening, they would meet again and decide how to find or make whatever items they still needed.

Amy grabbed the sweater she'd brought from the house and stuck her arms in the sleeves for warmth against the nighttime chill. "We should probably talk about the cost of all this."

"It's not a problem. I'll pay you back for anything you have to buy."

"Derek, come on. It's a lot more than the decorations and games. I totally intend to pay for that stuff myself. But there's still food and drinks. And what about the venue and the music?"

"It's covered," he said.

"Covered?" She couldn't help scoffing. "All of it?"

He shrugged. "I told you that Nate Crawford offered the Manor. And he offered it at a deep discount, believe me. Just about everyone in town will be there and that's good PR for the Manor. There'll be plenty of finger food. As for alcohol, Hudson is footing the bill for the champagne and soft drinks." Hudson Jones, a very wealthy man, was Bella Stockton's husband. "I promise I'm good for whatever the final bill amounts to." And then he laughed. "Don't look so worried. I'm not the same broke-ass cowboy you used to know."

"I'm not worried. Really."

"Oh, yeah, you are. But you don't need to be. I'm doing all right. You remember Collin Traub?"

"Of course." Collin had been in their graduating class. "Eva told me that Collin married Willa Christensen." Willa was younger. She'd graduated a few years after them. "Eva also mentioned that Collin's the mayor now. But what has Collin Traub got to do with how we plan to split up the cost of the bachelor party?"

"Collin's uncle Casper had a saddle-making business, which Collin inherited when Casper passed on. I hooked up with Collin a while back. Besides working the family ranch, I make saddles and a variety of fine leather goods. I've kind of built a name for myself— and earned some good money, too."

Leatherwork. He'd always had a talent for that. He used to make pretty beaded leather jewelry for her. And for her eighteenth birthday, he'd made her a leather vest and a fringed skirt. She'd loved them and worn them proudly. Still had them, too, tucked in the back of her closet.

Because she never could quite bear to get rid of them.

"We have a shop on Sawmill Street, at North Broomtail Road," he said.

"CT Saddles, right?"

"That's it."

"I drove by it the other day. And I'm glad that you're doing so well—but, Derek, I want to pitch in, too. I *am* the maid of honor, after all, and I should pay half."

He looked at her for a long time. She felt the sudden presence of the past—*their* past—rising up in the darkness between them.

What had he said?

I'm not the same broke-ass cowboy you used to know.

It wasn't that he came from a poor family. The Daltons had been ranching in the Rust Creek Falls Valley for generations and his dad was a leader in the community, a lawyer with an office in town. Still, back in high school, Derek hadn't had much, not in terms of cash in hand. When they ran away to Kalispell, he'd bought her a simulated diamond ring for forty dollars at Walmart.

She'd thrown it at him the day he told her to get her stuff and go with her dad. Where was that ring now? What had he done with it?

Not that she'd ever ask.

"Okay then," the grown-up Derek said. "We'll go fifty-fifty on the final bill."

"Perfect. Thank you. Now, let me see…" She woke her phone, punched up the party file again and brought up the dual lists of what had to be bought and what would need to be made or otherwise assembled.

"How we doin'?" he asked.

She gave him a nod. "Really well, actually."

"You feel like we're getting somewhere with this party, then?"

"I do. And I think we're pretty much set for now."

Their non-date was almost over.

And somehow, they'd managed to steer clear of the past—mostly, anyway.

All good, she told herself. It was the past, after all, over and done, and they didn't need to go there.

But then he stretched out on his back, laced his hands beneath his head and stared up at the wide indigo sky. "Lots of stars out tonight, Miss Wainwright."

Miss Wainwright.

Their private joke. He'd called her that in their first tutoring session and it had stuck.

"Yes, Miss Wainwright," he would tease her.

"Whatever you say, Miss Wainwright."

"Miss Wainwright, you're the boss."

He looked pretty comfortable, lying there. Not like he planned to get up and leave anytime soon.

Maybe the evening wasn't over, after all.

Chapter Three

Feeling light as air suddenly, and dangerously playful, Amy took his hat off the blanket and put it on. It was too big, and slipped down over her eyes.

Laughing, she tipped her head back. "Yeah. Lots of stars. A beautiful night."

"You forgive me, for not calling?"

"Yeah." She said it softly. "Thank you for the picnic. I...feel better about everything."

He was watching her so steadily. "You're as pretty as you ever were, Miss Wainwright—hell, you're prettier."

She felt the blush as it swept up her neck and over her cheeks. But what with the darkness, she doubted he could see it. She opened her mouth to say something teasing and light. But the memories were pressing in again and somehow, a raw truth slipped out. "I've had a crush on you since I was thirteen."

It was an old confession, one she'd made to him long ago, at a party on New Year's Eve, the night he told her for the first time that she was everything he'd ever wanted.

Her heart had ached with sheer happiness that night. How impossibly young she'd been, young and absolutely certain that nothing could ever tear them apart.

He reached up, took his hat off her head and set it on his chest. "You never would look at me. Not when you were thirteen or fourteen or fifteen…"

"I had no clue you might be looking at me. Not until that first tutoring session."

He grunted. "You were seventeen. And you still wouldn't look at me, even then."

"So, shoot me. I was shy. But it didn't take that long once we were stuck in a room together. By the end of that first session, I *was* looking at you, and right in the eye, too. I started getting the feeling then that just maybe you liked me—but then, I told myself, you liked all the girls."

"Uh-uh." His eyes shone almost black in the moonlight, holding hers. "I only wanted *you*."

"You asked me out." She couldn't help grinning. "I turned you down."

"But I persisted," he said.

"Oh, yes, you did." By Christmas of that year, she totally got that the hottest guy in school was crazy about her. Then at New Year's, he'd said he wasn't looking at any other girl. And he proved it, too. He was all about her, about Amy. And it felt so good to be wanted by a guy at last—not to mention by the sexiest, most charming guy in the whole school.

"My dad taught me that," he said.

"Taught you what?"

"To persist. 'Son,' he used to say, 'above all, if you want something, *persist*.' He always said *persist* with emphasis, you know?"

Amy remembered Charles Dalton as a kind, intelligent man.

"I always liked your dad." She brushed his shoulder, realized that touching him was maybe a bridge too far, and quickly withdrew her hand. "Um, your mom, too."

He stared up at the sky for a string of too-quiet seconds before asking, "How are *your* parents?"

"They're well. My dad retired two years ago. They moved to San Diego. They seem to like it there. My mom's in a bunch of clubs—book clubs, bridge clubs. He plays a lot of golf."

"Well, good," Derek said. He was watching her again, his eyes so deep, she wanted to fall in and never come out.

There had been no love lost between Derek and her mom and dad. They'd checked and found out that he was not a great student and would likely never even go to college. Derek only wanted to live on his family's ranch and work all day running cattle. He wasn't what her parents had in mind for her, their precious only daughter.

Her dad and mom had made it very clear that they wanted her to stop seeing "that Dalton boy." Amy defied them. She stood right up to them and said she would see him anyway, that he was the best thing that had ever happened to her.

They must have realized she meant what she'd said, because they'd backed off.

And after that, she and Derek spent every spare moment together. That New Year's Eve, when he'd said he loved her, she'd believed him and declared her love right back. He promised there would never be anyone but her. Amy wanted him so much and he wanted her and, well, it was young love.

She couldn't wait to have it all—all the kisses, the caresses, the soft, secret sighs. Making love was bound to happen.

And it did. In the early spring.

It was scary, that first time. Scary and a little awkward. But, oh so beautiful.

Already set to go to the University of Colorado on a full scholarship in the fall, Amy turned eighteen in May. In early June, she and Derek both graduated from Rust Creek Falls High.

"Remember graduation?" she asked, lost in the past now.

He made a low noise in the affirmative. "I remember your speech as valedictorian. 'We don't have to be perfect. We just have to do the best that we can every day, as we go forward into a future full of promise and the challenge of—'"

"Please." She cut him off with a groan. "No more. There is no way I was ever that young."

"Yeah, you were." He reached up, brushed a rough-tender finger along her cheek, leaving a sweet trail of lingering sensation in his wake. "So was I. We were *that* young. And you were all set, with a big future ahead of you. I never wanted to hold you back."

"I know that."

"We were *too* young."

She bit her lip, knowing he was right. She'd wanted to go to CU, wanted a good job that challenged her, and she'd doubted she would find that job in their tiny Montana town. At the same time, she hadn't known how she would live without the boy she loved.

He said, "Think about it this way. It all ended up according to plan."

"Right. Just with that big, painful detour stuck in the middle of it."

Because by the end of June, her period was late. She'd waited a week and it didn't come. She went to Derek. He drove her to Kalispell to buy a test and they rented a cheap room where she took that test.

She shivered a little and wrapped her sweater closer around her. "I was so scared when the test came out positive. And you took a knee right there in that motel room."

"I wanted to marry you, Amy. I really did."

She stared down at him, saw the moon reflected in his eyes. "I know. And I loved you. So much."

"It was the Fourth of July. There were fireworks going off all night long, remember?"

Oh, yes, she did. "I remember."

The next day, the fifth of July, they went to the courthouse and said *I do*, just the two of them, two scared kids with a baby on the way.

And for their honeymoon, they returned to the cheap room with its lumpy bed. At night, she could hear the trucks whizzing by on the highway.

"You were sorry, though, weren't you?" he asked. "Sorry from the first."

"It was only that I—"

"Don't lie," he said gently. "Let's just tell each other the truth now, okay, and be done with it?"

"Yeah. All right." She admitted, "I, well, I had serious second thoughts."

"I knew it." At least he didn't sound angry.

But why should he? It was so long ago. And this wasn't any big confession. This was making peace. With the past.

With each other.

This was putting it behind them, once and for all.

She said, "I just had trouble coping, you know? With my whole life turned around and a baby on the way." She really had loved him. But it had all just seemed so overwhelming.

The next day and the day after that, he drove back to the Circle D to work. She stayed in Kalispell. She had a cell phone, though reception in the area was hit and miss back then. Her parents kept calling her. She let the calls go to voice mail for three days and then she finally answered and told them she had married Derek. Her dad demanded to know where she was. She hung up on him.

"And then, the night of the fourth day," she said in a raggedy whisper, "my period came."

Had she lost the baby? Or had she never been pregnant in the first place? Who knew?

"That hurt," he said. "I mean, the baby had turned everything upside down. But suddenly, there was no baby and somehow, that was even worse."

She agreed with a slow nod.

The next day—the fifth and final day—to cheer her up, he'd taken her to visit the Armstrongs while he went to work at the ranch.

Nobody knew that she'd married him—except the two of them and her parents. She'd made him promise not to tell his family until she was ready. When his mom and dad asked questions about where he got off to every night, he just said he was fine and for them not to worry. His parents had let it go at that. After all, he was nineteen, old enough to stay out all night if he wanted to. And besides, their ill-fated elopement didn't last long. Before Rita and Charles Dalton got around to insisting that Derek tell them what was going on, it was over.

That day, the fifth day, when he dropped her off at the Armstrongs', she had longed to confide in her friends—maybe not Eva, who was only thirteen at the time. But Delphine and Calla, definitely. They were like sisters to her.

She just couldn't do it, though, couldn't tell them what she was going through. They knew she was really upset about something and they hugged her and fussed over her. They told her that, whatever it was, it would be all right, that they would always be there for her, no matter what.

She asked Derek, "Did I tell you that Delphine quizzed me about you that day? She wanted to know if something had gone wrong between the two of us." Everyone knew she'd been dating Derek, and the Armstrongs had seen him drop her off that morning.

"No, you never told me that. You hardly said a word on the drive back to the motel in Kalispell."

"I was all turned around inside, so sad about losing the baby, wondering how it was all going to work out."

"I remember." His voice was flat. Bleak. And then he asked, "What did you say to her that day—to Delphine?"

"I just shook my head and promised that I was fine and so were you."

"But she guessed you were lying."

"Yeah. I'll bet they all three did."

"Even Eva? She was so young."

"But she's always been sensitive to what other people are going through."

"That day," he said, staring up at the dark sky, "was the end of it…"

The end of us, she thought. "After that day, I never saw you again until last Monday, right here at the farm."

"Thirteen years," he said, his voice so heavy. With regret? With sadness or maybe bitterness? She couldn't have said and she didn't quite have the nerve to ask him what exactly he was feeling right now.

Instead, she got on with it. "I have no idea how my dad knew to find us at that motel. I never told him where I was. I assumed he'd somehow followed us from the Armstrongs' house. I asked Eva's mom later, before I left for Boulder, if she had called my dad and told him I was there that day. She swore she hadn't." Derek said nothing. He stared at the sky. Somewhere nearby, a lone owl hooted. A shiver ran through her. She peered down at him more closely. "What?"

He shifted his gaze to meet hers. "I didn't say anything."

"I thought maybe you were about to."

"Uh-uh."

She drew in a slow breath. "Well, however he did it, my father figured it out."

Derek stared up into her night-shadowed eyes. Her skin was so smooth, silvered in moonlight.

He knew how her father had found them. But he wasn't going to tell her. What good would that do? Jack Wainwright wasn't a bad man. He'd just wanted the best for his only child and he'd followed them from the Armstrongs', followed them to Kalispell and that cheap motel.

At the sight of her dad emerging from his fancy pickup, looking grim and exhausted, Amy had started to cry.

Derek had hated himself then, for jumping the gun and begging her to marry him, for putting her in this position, for messing everything up.

He didn't know what to do next. Amy had gotten pregnant—or maybe not. She'd lost the baby—or maybe not. Because how can you lose something that never was?

He'd known she was miserable that day, known she regretted running away with him. She'd had such big plans for herself and there she was, a not-pregnant married woman who wasn't going to go to college, after all.

As he'd watched the tears tracking down her cheeks that July afternoon, Derek felt his heart shatter into a million pieces. He and Jack Wainwright agreed on one thing, at least: that run-down motel wasn't good enough for Amy.

And what did Derek think he was going to do next? Move his bride into the bunkhouse with him at the Circle D? Or into the main house where his parents lived? Damn, but the truth he faced then was the hardest one of all.

He'd yet to get a real start in life and would need to depend on his family to help support her. And she? Amy deserved the best. With the baby gone, well, why shouldn't she have the future she'd always planned on? His pride had felt frayed raw at all he couldn't give her.

Now, in the low light of the lantern, she softly accused, "When my dad asked me to come home with him, you said I should go."

He wasn't about to try to make her see how he'd really felt. Better to just confirm what she already knew. "That's right. It's what I said."

"I wondered then if you would be relieved to get rid of me..." She'd had her dad wait outside and she led Derek into their little room. "I did tell you that I loved you."

He could reassure her on that point, at least. "I know you did. I'll never forget that you did."

"I said I did want my education, but couldn't we find a way to be husband and wife, *and* for me to go to CU?"

"Listen. All I felt then was that I was holding you back. I looked in those big eyes of yours and I saw that you needed to be free to live your bright future without being tied down to a guy who couldn't even support you."

"But I *wanted* to be with you."

"Don't." He sat up. "You wanted the future you deserved. There's nothing wrong with that."

She shook her head at him. "Oh, Derek—"

"It wasn't going to work."

"But if we—"

"No. Uh-uh. We needed to let go."

She accused, "That day, you said it was all a big mistake."

"And it was, wasn't it? I mean, there was no baby, or the baby was lost. Whichever it was, we'd just run off and gotten married without thinking things over."

"You said you didn't really want to be married, anyway."

"Yeah, Amy. I did. That's what I said." It was a lie, but it was way too late to tell her that now.

She sat up straighter and tossed her ponytail, defiant, more than a little bit angry. "So, I agreed with you. I said we'd made a mistake and you were right, we just needed to put it behind us. That was when you said I should get my stuff and go with my dad. I threw my ring at you." Her slim shoulders drooped. "I just want you to know I've always regretted doing that. I did love that ring. And you. Oh, Derek, I loved you so much. I'm so sorry that I—"

"Stop." He couldn't stand how he'd hurt her, how they'd hurt each other. "It's okay." He knew he shouldn't, but he reached out anyway. He curled a hand around the back of her neck and drew her close.

"Derek." She sagged against him, wrapped her soft arms around him. He breathed in the scent of her, so sweet, so right.

"I'm sorry, too," he whispered. "About all of it." He stroked the silky hair pulled tight at her temple. There were things he shouldn't say. But he had to let at least a little of the truth shine through. "You were everything to me."

"Oh, Derek. And *you* were, to me."

He took her face between his hands. "We can't go back and do it over. And even if we could, who's to say how it might have turned out? We both had a lot of growing up to do."

Her gaze searched his. "We should have tried. We might have made it."

He gave her ponytail a teasing little tug. "We're never going to know what might have happened."

She pressed her lips together, sniffled just a little—

and smiled. "Yeah. You're right. I know you are. And I'm glad. That we talked about it. I mean, there is no blame here. Things turned out for the best, don't you think?"

What could he say to that, except, "Absolutely."

"And we're over it."

He never would be, not really. But what good would it do either of them to admit that now? "Yeah, we are."

The moment stretched out. She gazed up at him, all soft and trusting. How could he stop himself?

He didn't *want* to stop himself.

He lowered his mouth just enough to brush hers.

Heaven. Kissing Amy was heaven.

Not in years and years had he dared to imagine that someday he would kiss her again.

With a sweet, hungry cry, she surged up onto her knees and slid her arms more firmly around him. She tasted so good, opening to him. Inviting him inside.

He dipped his tongue into all that sweetness and she moaned against his mouth.

More. The word thrummed through his blood. He wanted more of her. He felt sweet desire and a longing so deep—for all that they'd had. All that was lost.

All that he should have sense enough to realize would never be again.

They'd been kids, innocent. Trusting.

Now they were all grown-up. She had her life in Boulder and she would go back to it as soon as Eva married Luke.

The past was just that: done. Over. Gone.

And it needed to stay gone.

With way more regret than he should have allowed himself, he lifted his mouth from hers.

Her eyes slowly opened. She gazed up at him, unspeaking, her expression kind of dreamy. He could have sat there just looking at her forever.

But really, he'd been cradling her beautiful face for much too long. He let his hands drop away.

She sank back on her folded knees, coming to rest on her heels. "Well. That was…unexpected."

"Just a kiss," he said, and way too gruffly.

Slowly, she nodded. "Yeah. Just a kiss."

He saw questions in her eyes. "What? Go ahead and ask."

"You sure?"

"How can I answer until you ask me the question?"

"It's just that I always wondered. Do you still have my ring?"

He shrugged, a lying shrug. But it was better that way. "What can I tell you? I don't remember what I did with it."

"Oh, God." With a soft groan, she covered her face with her palms. And then she slanted him an embarrassed glance. "I am hopeless. Sorry."

"Nothing to be sorry about." For another long stretch of seconds, they just looked at each other. He broke the silence. "It's after eleven. We should probably call it a night."

"Yeah."

They gathered up the remains of their picnic, piled it all in the basket and folded up the blanket. She stuck her big phone in a pocket of her jeans and carried the lantern, lighting their way as they returned to the house and his waiting truck. When they got there, he put the blanket and basket in on the passenger side. She handed him the lantern. He switched it off and set it in the truck, too.

Finally, he shut the door and turned to her.

Luke and Eva had apparently come home and they'd left the porch light on. Amy and Derek stood close together, just beyond the golden circle of light.

"It's meant a lot to me," she said, her eyes so steady, holding his, "the things we said tonight."

"To me, too."

"I feel better about everything. Better about us."

"So do I."

She sank her pretty teeth into her lower lip, glanced away and then back. "I just want you to know that I'm not trying to get anything started."

"I get it, Amy. I completely understand."

"It could never go anywhere."

He wanted only to reach for her again, to claim those soft lips one more time. "You're right," he said, and kept his hands to himself. "But about Monday…"

"Yeah?" Did she sound a little breathless?

Pleasure flowed through him. She might talk about how what they'd had was long over, how they'd get no second chances. But the look in her eyes said otherwise. He tried not to smile. "I'll be at the saddlery all day."

She drew a sharp little breath that sounded a lot like anticipation. "I could meet you there when I get back from shopping in Kalispell. Say at five? You could give me a tour, show me some of your work."

"Five is good. And after the tour, we'll go on out to Maverick Manor for that burger I promised you. You can see the venue, the main meeting room we'll be using and the smaller adjoining room where I thought we would set up the casino."

"Another non-date, right?" she teased, the left corner of her too-damn-kissable mouth hitching up just a fraction, a cute dimple tucking itself into her soft cheek.

"Yep. 'Cause you and me, we aren't getting anything started."

"Oh, no, we are not."

"We're firmly in the friend zone."

"Friends," she repeated. "I'm all for that."

He went around to the driver's side and climbed in. She followed, standing back a little as he turned the engine over. He leaned out the window to tip his hat at her. "'Night, Miss Wainwright."

Her smile bloomed full out. "You are so bad, Derek Dalton."

He gave her a wave and got the hell out of there before he threw all his good intentions out the window, jumped from the truck and showed her just how bad he could be.

Sunday morning, Eva made waffles. When Amy came downstairs, Luke and Bailey were already at the table, chowing down on the delicious food—which, Amy eagerly observed, included fresh fruit and whipped cream and pure maple syrup.

Bailey lived in one of Sunshine Farm's seven cabins, which Rob Stockton, the family patriarch, had built years ago in hopes that his children might stay to raise their own kids on the family homestead. Though Bailey liked his privacy, he often came to the main house to eat. Nobody with a pulse could resist Eva's cooking. Not even a gruff, independent man like Bailey Stockton.

Eva, at the waffle iron, glanced over her shoulder when Amy entered the kitchen. "Pour yourself some coffee," she commanded with a radiant smile, secure in her role as queen of the kitchen. "And have a seat. Your breakfast is almost ready."

Amy savored the excellent coffee and sighed in delight when Eva slid a golden, perfect waffle in front of her. "Eva, you are a goddess of the culinary arts and I love you with all of my heart." Laughing, Eva pulled out the chair next to her and sat down. Amy frowned at her. "Where's yours?"

"I already ate. What's up for you today?"

"Mostly, I'll be upstairs working—and ordering a bunch of stuff online for the bachelor party."

Eva braced her elbow on the table, propped her chin on her hand and remarked with overplayed innocence, "We saw Derek's truck out in front when we got home last night."

Amy ate an amazing bite of waffle, fresh peaches and whipped cream, after which she gave her friend a look of great patience. "We took a meeting in a nice, grassy spot not that far from the barn. It was a very productive meeting, so productive that I actually think we've got this party under control."

Lazily, Eva drew a heart on the table with her index finger. "It was a very long meeting." She stretched out the word *long* until it had about ten syllables in it. "I didn't hear that truck of his leave until after eleven."

"Big party. Lots of planning to do."

Eva glanced across at the men.

Luke met his fiancée's eyes and stood as though on cue. "Come on, Bailey, let's get after it."

Bailey gulped down a last sip of coffee and rose, too. They carried their plates to the sink and went out the back door.

Eva got up, poured herself some coffee and topped off Amy's cup. Then she sat back down again. "I know you really loved him. And he really loved you. And I have to say, the chemistry between you two? Still off the charts."

"Eva, don't exaggerate."

"I'm not. I saw the way you looked at each other Friday night at the Ace in the Hole. And when you were dancing with him?" She made a big show of fanning herself. "It's like you were the only two people in the place."

Amy licked a dab of whipped cream from her upper lip, sipped more coffee—and reminded herself that Eva didn't need to know all the secrets that were better left safely in the past. "You're imagining things."

"Oh, please. I don't think so."

"Derek and I are friends, that's all. Casual friends."

Eva leaned close and spoke softly. "All I'm saying is, maybe give it a chance, you know? Anything might happen. But you have to be open. You have to be ready to let love in."

"I don't think so."

Eva shook a finger at her. "Wrong attitude."

"No. We agreed we weren't going to get anything started."

"We?"

"Eva, please. You know who. Derek and I."

"When, last night?"

"That's right."

"Oh, Amy." Eva fluttered her eyelashes. "You and I both know an agreement like that is just made to be broken."

Chapter Four

After spending much of Sunday ordering party supplies, Amy headed for Kalispell on Monday morning. By four thirty, she'd been to six different stores that sold party supplies, equipment and games—four in Kalispell and two in nearby Columbia Falls. The back of her Audi Q5 was piled high with shopping bags.

She headed for Rust Creek Falls to meet Derek, feeling really good about all she'd accomplished since their meeting by lantern-light Saturday night.

True, the closer she got to seeing him again, the more anxious she felt—an anticipatory sort of anxiousness, complete with flutters in her tummy and a suddenly racing heart. By the time she parked in a space in front of the tin-roofed building with the long wooden porch and the CT Saddles sign across the front, she was a bundle of nerves, but in a giddy kind of way.

And then she saw Derek, in jeans, brown boots and a black T-shirt, looking like every red-blooded girl's fantasy cowboy, waiting on the porch beneath the sign. He came down the steps and pulled her door open for her.

"Nice car." He offered his hand.

She took it and a hot little thrill shivered up her arm. *Friends*, she reminded herself resolutely. *We are friends.* "Thank you." She stepped out.

He shut the door and peeked in the back window. "Looks like you raided every party store in the state of Montana."

"Stick with me." She smoothed her skinny jeans, a nervous gesture and totally unnecessary. Skinny jeans were much too snug to wrinkle. "I know how to shop."

He laughed, the sound deep and free. Easy.

She thought about what Eva had said, that she should be open, give love a chance—okay, maybe not love. That was in the past.

But she did definitely feel the zing of attraction every time she saw him. Being open to whatever might happen, well, that couldn't be wrong, could it?

He leaned close and the flutters in her tummy intensified. "You smell like wildflowers. And you've got a secret kind of smile on your face. What's going on in that big brain of yours, anyway?"

She nudged him with a playful elbow. "I'm all about the party plans. You should see the decorations I got for the casino. Everything in red, white and black. Giant dice stacked at the door. Straw cowboy hats to go with the whole Western theme."

"That secret smile is about party plans?"

"Well, yeah, and seeing what goes on at CT Saddles—oh, and that burger you promised me. I need that soon. All the shopping has given me an appetite."

Her hair was loose. He guided a stray curl back over her shoulder, his finger lightly brushing the side of her neck, stirring up lovely, shivery sensations.

Just friends, she told herself yet again, and tried to believe it.

His finger skated down her arm, causing her nerve endings to spark and flare as it went. He caught her hand.

It felt so right, his touch.

Warm and rough and protective and tender.

And really, she needed *not* to get carried away.

"Come on inside," he said, and pulled her toward the steps.

He showed her his worktables—a butcher block–topped one for laying out patterns and cutting leather, with a huge array of tools on a long, moveable rack overhead. And another for tooling, with a solid slate top mounted on two-by-fours, so the surface had no give in it when he hit the leather to punch in his designs. His hole punches, mauls, chisels and stamps were waiting in a series of racks all around, easy to reach as he worked.

He introduced her to a dark-haired boy in his teens. "This is Ned Faraday. He's working with us for the summer."

Ned set aside the broom he'd been sweeping up scraps with and shook her hand. "Nice to meet you," he said shyly.

"You planning on being a saddle-maker?" she asked him.

"Yes, I am. I like the work…and it keeps me out of trouble." He kind of mumbled that last.

He seemed like a great kid. She couldn't resist asking, "You get in trouble a lot, Ned?"

"Used to," he replied, and got to work with the broom again.

Derek clapped him on the shoulder. "It's after five. You can go ahead and take off now."

"Monday, same as usual?" Ned asked eagerly. Apparently, he loved his job.

"Yeah. See you at nine." As he spoke to Ned, Derek put a hand to the small of Amy's back, a sweetly proprietary gesture that made her feel catered to, cared for. Really, she needed to watch herself or she'd be head-over-heels for the guy all over again. He leaned close. His warm breath kissed her ear. "Let me show you a couple of my projects." He guided her across the room to the rows of saddletrees.

She was vaguely aware of the door closing as Ned left, but mostly she was blown away by the saddle in front of her. "Wow." She reached out and touched the supple, intricately tooled fender. "This is from *Alarica*, right?" She named the wildly popular video game in which robots had taken over the world and gone to war with each other.

"You guessed it."

"Wow," she said again for lack of a word good enough.

"A long way from a leather vest and a fringed skirt, huh?" He slanted her one his almost-smiles.

"I loved that vest and skirt," she informed him and tried to decide whether to admit she still had them, that she never could bear to let them go. But no. To confess that seemed unbearably intimate, somehow. And they were not getting intimate. They were keeping it friendly, easy and light. "This is perfection, Derek." She stroked the barrel of a futuristic weapon, ran her finger down the perfectly pin-hinged hip of the robot temptress, Dellarue, who seduced her challengers before killing them.

"Collin does the classic Western stuff," he explained. "I'm getting known for the weird projects and I like it that way. I did a whole series of saddles for an El Baharian sheikh, scenes from famous battles in the history of El Bahar. This one, though, was commissioned by Lincoln Copes, the creator of *Alarica*. He's got a ranch in Idaho not far from Sundance where he breeds Arabians."

He also showed her saddlebags tooled with exotic twining flowers—orchids, anthuriums, jasmine, hibiscus—and another saddle decorated with stars and moons.

"They're all so gorgeous."

He took her arm and turned her around to face him. "You sound impressed."

"I am. All this is, well, I think I may be running out of adjectives. I knew you had talent for working with leather. I just didn't realize how far you would take it."

"All the way." He touched her hair again, wrapping a curl of it around his finger. The moment felt just next-door to the intimacy they weren't supposed to be sharing and she enjoyed it way too much.

Taking his sweet time over it, he unwrapped that curl and let his hand drop away, after which they shared a long, lovely moment where all they did was stare at each other and grin.

"Tell me about Ned," she suggested after what felt like forever. "What did he mean that working here keeps him out of trouble?"

"His mom died a few years ago."

"That's hard."

"Yeah. He was an only kid, close to his mom. And

he didn't get along that well with his dad. He started acting out."

"After she died, you mean?"

"Right."

"How old is he?"

"Sixteen now. Last year, when he was fifteen, he kind of lost it. Broke into his dad's liquor cabinet and got drunk, wandered over to Crawford's General Store—at night, when the store was closed—and threw rocks in the windows."

"Oh, no."

"Oh, yeah." He backed up a little and sat on an empty saddle stand. Shaking his head, he went on, "Then he came here, broke another window and climbed in it. Didn't do much damage, really, other than the busted window. But he did trigger the alarm. After it rang for a minute or two, he realized he would probably get caught if he tried to hide out in the saddlery, so he jumped back out the window and took off down North Broomtail Road—right past the sheriff's office. Gage Christensen, who's the sheriff now, caught him and locked him up in the jail to put the fear of the law in him."

"Poor kid."

"Yeah. Once he sobered up a little, Ned was scared to death he was going straight to the state pen. Kind of woke up Ned's dad, too. He agreed to get family counseling with Ned. We—me and Collin and the Crawfords—offered Ned the chance to work part-time at the general store and here at the saddlery to pay for the damage he'd done. Long story short, Ned and his dad are getting along better after counseling and Ned found out he likes making things from leather. The kid's got talent for it, too. Once he worked off his debt, he asked if maybe we would keep him on. He works a few hours on the weekends during the school year and twenty hours a week now that it's summer vacation."

"A happy ending, then."

"You could say that." He watched her so closely, his hot gaze tracking from her mouth to her eyes and back again. It sent a happy little thrill rushing through her, the way he looked at her, even if happy little thrills weren't the kind of thing she should be letting him inspire in her.

She gave herself a mental shake. "I love it when bad stuff turns good—and it's so great, what you and Collin and the Crawfords did, giving Ned a way to turn things around for himself."

He shrugged off her praise. "Hey, it's Rust Creek Falls. Everything always ends happily here."

"So they say." Tenderness welled in her. Yeah, he had that sexy edge of the hot guy all the girls sighed over. But he was also a *good* guy, always had been. "And you never could take a compliment." When he made a scoffing sound, she insisted, "I mean it, Derek. You did reach out and help Ned when he needed it. Don't brush me off when I say I admire what you did."

He stood and stepped closer. "All right, then." He smelled so good, of leather and man. Another sweet, endless glance passed between them. "Thank you."

"That's better."

He took her hand. His touch felt so right, stirring old memories, making her wish he might never let go. "Now how 'bout that fancy burger?"

"Sounds great." And much less dangerous than being here alone with him where who knew what kind of mischief she might be tempted to get up to. "I'll follow you."

He rubbed his thumb across the back of her hand. Such a simple caress, yet it stirred her. Too much. "You might as well just ride with me."

Was she tempted? Oh, yes. But somehow, she managed to shake her head. "Then you'd just have to bring me all the way back here to get my car."

"I wouldn't mind. Not one bit." He dipped his dark head a fraction closer, that unruly hair of his flopping on his forehead, just begging her to reach up and smooth it back.

"Derek?" Her voice sounded downright husky.

"Hmm?"

"I'm taking my own car."

Now he was the one shaking his head. "Have it your way."

"I believe I will." She couldn't stifle a slow grin.

"You're acting kind of naughty, Miss Wainwright."

She let her grin get even wider. "Maybe. A little." It was only flirting, after all. And it felt wonderful.

Still holding her hand, he turned for the door.

At Maverick Manor, they parked side by side in the lot by the main entrance.

"Wait a minute," she said, when he stepped up and opened her car door for her. "Isn't this…?"

"Bledsoe's Folly?" He took her hand and she let him. "The one and only." The imposing log home had been built way back in the '80s by an eccentric multimillionaire who later lost it all when the market crashed. "Bledsoe's original log mansion is the center of Maverick Manor."

"It looks great. And even bigger."

"They added on, of course, but kept the log cabin–style throughout."

Inside, he gave her a quick tour—from the giant central lobby with its impressive mural honoring the founding families of Rust Creek Falls to the meeting rooms they would be using for the party. They went outside and strolled the grounds, lush and green in high summer, and then checked out the dining room. Finally, they took seats in the bar and enjoyed giant, juicy burgers with hot, crispy fries. She got out her phone and they went over the few things she'd yet to find for the party.

"Text the list to me," he said. "I'll see how many I can get and then, if we have to, we'll figure out something else to do for the rest."

"You're sure? Because I don't mind—"

He put his hand over hers, tucking his thumb all cozy in the cove of her palm. Little flares of pleasure spiked along her nerve endings. "I've got this. Give me tomorrow to work on it. I'll come by Sunshine Farm tomorrow after dinner. Say, seven?"

"Seven works." She picked up the check. He tried to snatch it from her. "Uh-uh. You brought me a picnic. I'm good for the burgers."

He walked her out to her car. It was almost nine by then, dusk painting the sky in layers of vivid color.

He asked her about her job. "Luke said you track down the bad guys online."

"More or less." She launched into an explanation of the growing prevalence of digital fraud and how her work entailed staying one step ahead of embezzlers, hackers and other internet criminals. "I work mostly at home."

"Doesn't that get lonely?"

"Not really. I make my own hours. Sometimes they're very long hours when the situation is urgent and I need to produce a report in a short time frame. On the other hand, nobody complains if I'm not at my desk nine to five. It's a great job that holds my interest. Never boring, you know?"

"Kind of like fixing fences," he joked.

But she didn't laugh. "Well, you need to keep those cattle where you put them and I need to keep the money in the hands of the people it actually belongs to, so yeah. Kind of like fixing fences."

She could have stood there in that parking lot with him, talking about nothing in particular, all night long.

But when she reluctantly turned to open her door, he reached around and did it for her. She got in. He waved as she drove away.

He knocked on the farmhouse door at seven sharp the next night. She ushered him and he said hi to Eva and Luke.

Eva asked, "Did you eat?" When he said he had, she offered, "How about a fat slice of loganberry pie, then?"

"Eva." He gave her his killer grin. "If you baked it, I'm in."

Derek and Luke sat at the table, eating pie and drinking coffee, discussing alfalfa crop yields and beef prices as Amy helped Eva load the dishwasher with the dinner dishes and wipe down the counters.

It was nice, Amy thought. Homey. The four of them

in the kitchen, the good smells of coffee and the banana bread Eva had baking in the oven, the deep, easy sounds of the men's voices as they talked about everyday things.

Like a fantasy, really. A faint, sweet echo of the life she'd once imagined for herself. This was how it would have been if she and Derek had stayed together and she'd become a ranch wife—while somehow also managing to get her degree and a great job that challenged her.

"What?" asked Eva softly.

Amy realized she was just standing at the counter, staring off into space with a dish towel in one hand and the cut crystal relish plate in the other. "Um, nothing. Not a thing."

Eva's bright blue eyes actually seemed to twinkle. "Yeah, right."

Amy insisted, "Really. Nothing. I was thinking about nothing."

Eva laughed, but said no more.

A few minutes later, out on the porch again, Derek and Amy went over the dwindling list of party supplies they still needed and agreed on substitutes for what they hadn't found. She insisted that he let her look for those.

Then they climbed in his pickup and drove to the yellow barn, where they added the things he'd rounded up that day to the growing pile of goodies Luke had let them store in the tack room.

By the time they finished that small chore it was half past eight—and she just didn't want him to go.

She perched on a hay bale and willed him to sit down next to her. "We should talk about setup, don't you think? I know it's eleven days until the party, but it can't hurt to get everything planned out in advance."

"Fair enough." He hooked his hat on a tack hanger and dropped to her side, right where she wanted him.

Yes, she was being thoroughly bad, to keep urging him closer when she should let him go. But somehow, she couldn't help herself. She never could resist being bad when it came to him. Some things, apparently, never changed.

She'd been the shiest girl at Rust Creek Falls High—until she and Derek had gotten together. After that New Year's Eve when they'd declared their young love to each other, she'd become totally shameless in her need to be near him as often as possible.

"I talked to the manager over at the Manor," he said. "We can get in there to start setting up at 6:00 a.m."

"And the party starts at seven that night..." She tipped her head to the side as though considering what he'd just told her. In reality, her senses were on overload. He was so close, his warm, hard thigh touching hers. "It should be totally doable," she said, biting her lower lip, pretending to be deep in thought.

"Yeah," he replied, drawing out the word, his head turned her way, his gaze on her mouth. "Doable."

It was delicious, this shivery excitement spreading all through her. "Delphine and Calla and their families are driving in the day before, on Friday." Her own voice surprised her, sounding so calm and unaffected. "They'll pitch in, along with their husbands and kids." Eva's sisters, along with Luke's sisters, Bella and Dana, Jamie's wife, Fallon, and Danny's wife, Annie, were all to be bridesmaids. "Dana will be coming Friday, as well." Last born of the seven Stockton siblings, Dana lived in Oregon. She would be staying with Bella and Hudson until after the wedding.

"And you know we'll get Bailey, Danny and Jamie to help," he added. Luke's brothers were the other groomsmen. "Plus, whoever else we can get to volunteer."

"It'll work. Thirteen hours or so should be plenty of time to set it all up."

"Okay, then." He rose.

No! cried the romantic fool within her. *Not yet. Don't go yet.*

But he was already standing above her. "Unless you need me for anything in the meantime," he said, "we're all set until 6:00 a.m. a week from Saturday. If I don't hear from you before then, I'll call you and touch base next Tuesday, just to be sure we're up to speed."

She had the insane urge to grab his hand and yank him back down onto the hay bale with her. Really, this was so weak and wrong of her. They'd agreed that the past was the past and they'd grown beyond it. They were friends by necessity until Eva and Luke walked down the aisle.

"When did you and Luke get to be friends?" The question just burst out of her, sounding slightly squeaky with a weird, desperate edge. And she was desperate. Because she wanted to keep him there and all her good sense had flown out the tack room door.

He didn't answer right away, just gazed down at her with a musing expression. Really, it wasn't fair in the least. He had those beautiful green eyes and that hair she wanted to run her fingers through. And what about that mouth of his? She simply could not stop longing to kiss him again. And then there were those broad, muscled shoulders, those calloused, talented hands.

The man was pure temptation, up close and in person.

"It was just a natural thing," Derek said, and she had no idea what he was talking about. She'd forgotten the question she had just asked him.

Not that it mattered, as long as she could continue to stare up at him, continue to feel this beautiful longing that she would never do anything about.

Uh-uh. No way. Not a chance. Forget about it.

"Neighbors helping neighbors," he said. "When he and Eva moved into the farmhouse, I dropped by to help them get settled in." Right. Luke. She'd asked him about Luke. "There were a lot of fences down on this place. I helped with that. And over at the Circle D, when some of our calves wandered off in a freak spring blizzard, Luke brought Bailey and helped me and my brother Eli and a couple of our cousins track them through the storm." He stared down at her, right into her eyes now.

She wished he would go on like that, just standing there looking at her, for a lifetime. Or two.

"Luke and me," he went on thoughtfully, "we just get along. He had a rough time, back when his parents died, but he came through it strong, you know? He's a man you can count on." Derek chuckled, a warm, rueful sound. "And besides, if I'm his best man, he doesn't have to choose between his brothers."

She laughed, too. "Well, yeah. There's that. Same thing with Eva. She chose me. So, her sisters and sisters-in-law can all be bridesmaids equally. Plus, she's been trying to get me back to town for thirteen years now. She kind of pulled out all the stops when she started in on me to be her maid of honor. Calla and Delphine put the pressure on, too. They were relentless, those three."

"Worked, didn't it?" His voice was low and rough,

like they were sharing a secret, just the two of them. "Eva's a woman who knows what she wants and never quits until she gets it."

"I think she's matchmaking us," Amy said, the words just kind of popping out without permission from her brain.

One corner of that impossibly sexy mouth of his quirked up. "You think so, huh?"

Her cheeks felt so hot, burning red. "I...don't know why I said that."

"Yeah, you do." It was there in his eyes now, clear as day. He knew what she was up to, that she was trying to keep him there though it was past time for him to go.

And still, she longed simply to ask him to sit back down beside her, to talk to her, soft and low, about any old subject that wandered into his mind. She didn't care what they said.

She just wanted him near.

Good gravy, what was *wrong* with her? Enough of this reckless foolishness.

She rose.

He didn't back up, though.

They ended up mere inches apart. If she took a deep breath, her breasts would just about brush his hard chest.

And oh, the warmth of him, the strength and height of him.

The scent of him, of pine and leather.

Everything about him seemed to reach for her, to wrap around her, to reel her in.

And then he did reach for her. He hooked an arm around her waist. She let out a sharp gasp of mingled alarm and delight as he hauled her up tight against him, her breasts to his chest, her thighs pressed to his thighs—and oh, she could feel him, feel the evidence of his desire for her pressed to her belly.

Talk about intimate. "I…"

He bent a fraction closer. "You…?" It was a taunt. His eyes gleamed, so green and deep.

She pressed her lips into a thin, hard line. "You're mocking me." It came out barely a whisper. She was too breathless to give the words much sound.

"Yes, I am. And you're teasing me."

"No…"

"Miss Wainwright." He made a chiding sound. "Don't make me call you a liar. Besides, you know what?"

"What?"

"If you want to tease me, you go right on ahead. I don't mind at all." Derek pulled her closer.

Really, that shouldn't have been physically possible. She was already plastered against the front of him.

But he managed it anyway. He pulled her closer and she felt him even more acutely. Her whole body yearned. Yearned for the innocent passion they'd once shared. And not only that. She yearned for the man he was now, too.

Somehow, her hands had come to rest against his chest. Beneath his soft cotton shirt, she could feel the sculpted muscles, the fierce beating of his heart.

Dear God, she had loved him.

And there was no denying how very much she still wanted him.

There was just something about him that called to her so deeply. Some impossible power he had that made her burn for him even after all these long years.

He said a bad word, low, guttural. His head dipped closer…

And then, at last, his beautiful mouth touched hers.

Chapter Five

They were kissing.

Again.

After promising each other that wasn't going to happen.

Well, it *was* happening. And it was spectacular.

With a soft cry, she slid her hands up over those rock-like shoulders. She opened her mouth and he dipped his tongue in. Her grasping fingers threaded up into that sexy, messy hair of his.

"Amy. Amy," he said her name twice, breathing it into her mouth as he kissed her, lifting his head a fraction, just long enough to slant his kiss the other way.

She didn't say anything. She *couldn't* say anything. She was drowning in him, going down for the third time and loving it. She could kiss him forever, on into the next millennium, kiss him and kiss him and never, ever stop.

But then *he* stopped.

Abruptly.

He took her by the shoulders, ripped his mouth from hers and set her away. "No." His green eyes were like a stormy sea now.

She blinked. "No?"

"We need to stop doing this."

Her mind felt so thick and slow. Her body ached to have his arms wrapped around her again. "Doing…?"

He raked his hand back over his hair, smoothing it. Not that smoothing it did any good. His hair just flopped back over his forehead all over again. "Do I really have to spell it out for you? We've got to stop pretending we're not going to put our hands on each other—and then doing it anyway. It's messing with my head, you know? *Both* heads, as a matter of fact."

She almost laughed, but slapped her hand over her mouth just in time to stop herself—after which she felt thoroughly foolish. Letting her hand drop to her side, she nodded. "Okay. I get it. I'm… Look, I'm sorry. Okay?"

He took another step back from her. "I'm not blaming you, not any more than I'm blaming myself. We're both at fault. It's…what we do to each other."

She sucked in another shaky breath. "Yeah. It's crazy, huh? I mean, for me it's still the same. The, um, feeling I have for you. It's strong." She could not believe what she was admitting, but at the same time, it felt good, right, to lay it out there the way it really was for her. "Even after everything we went through, after all these years, I still feel it so powerfully for you. I was so scared, that first day, when you came here to the farmhouse. I thought I would shatter into a million pieces just at the sight of you. And I almost did."

He looked so young suddenly, his eyes almost hopeful. "Yeah?"

"Yeah."

"You tell me now, Amy Wainwright. Are you with anyone, back there in Boulder?"

"No, I'm not. I promise you. There's no one. What about you?"

A low, rough chuckle escaped him. "Like you even have to ask. It's Rust Creek Falls. If I had a girl, you'd have heard all about it from at least ten different sources by now."

She did laugh then. "Eva, first of all."

"You got that right." His eyes grew serious again and his mouth was a flat line. "You lookin' for a little summer fun with an old flame, is that it?"

She wanted to cry suddenly. "Don't say that. You're so much more than just an old flame to me." *You're the father of the child I never had. My husband. For a while.*

He rubbed the back of his neck again. "I don't know."

Could he be any less clear? "You don't know what?"

"What you want from me, where you're going with this."

She put her hands out to the sides, palms up. "Where are *you* going? And why is it that I'm supposed to have all the answers?"

He didn't say, *You started it.* But he was thinking it. She could see it in his eyes, in the hard set to his square jaw. "I want you, too," he said at last. "It's strong. Really strong."

Her pulse pounded harder. She felt it beating in her neck as a pleasured flush flooded upward over her cheeks. "Well, then…" Seriously? She could not believe what she was about to suggest. "Why don't we just go with it?" She thought about Eva's advice Sunday morning. "Just kind of see where it takes us?"

He wasn't buying. "What if where it takes us is only back to heartbreak all over again?"

So much for putting herself out there. "Here we go again. I know that look on your face, Derek Dalton. You've suddenly got a fence to fix or a poor, lost calf you need to track down and rescue."

"That's right." He scooped his hat off the tack hanger and set it on his head. "I should get going."

Okay, now he was just plain pissing her off. "All of a sudden, I find I am tempted to start making chicken noises."

"You just need to think it over, okay? Think it over, and I will, too. But right now, I really have to go."

Derek did think it over. All the next day and the day after that.

Amy was pretty much all he thought about. Those big, honest eyes. The taste of her mouth and her soft, curvy body pressed up tight to his. The lemony smell of her hair. And the brave things she'd said.

"I still feel it so powerfully for you."

"You're so much more than just an old flame to me."

"Why don't we just go with it? Just kind of see where it takes us?"

He injured himself twice at the shop, punched a hole in his thumb tooling a set of saddlebags and took a slice out of his index finger cutting leather for another project. Blood all over. What a mess.

All because he couldn't keep his mind on the job. It was just like in high school, his brain focused on

Amy all the time, the rest of the world receding into the background.

He knew, over the years, that some people judged him for being one of those guys who played it fast and easy, never sticking with one girl very long.

But no other girl was Amy. So, what was the point of starting anything too heavy? He kept things casual, moving on whenever a girl acted like she might get serious. He'd never been out to hurt anyone. He just wanted a good time on a Friday night.

A good time and maybe not to feel so alone for a while.

Lots of girls felt the same way he had. They weren't looking to settle down.

Now, though?

Well, he was over thirty. A different girl every weekend just kind of made him feel tired. Bailey Stockton might claim to admire him for never settling down, but Bailey was no kid, either. At some point almost every man—and woman, too, he would bet—wanted more than a stranger to take home at closing time.

Amy.

She still cranked his chain in a really big way. But she'd be leaving at the end of the month, going back to her own life. And his life was here.

It just seemed stupid to get anything going with her, stupid and a clear invitation to heartbreak.

By Friday, she hadn't called. What did that mean? She'd found the last few things they needed for the party? Or she'd changed her mind about wanting to "go with it," to "see where it takes us."

Whatever it meant, she hadn't gotten in touch.

And he needed to stop thinking about her.

That made him laugh—and not in a happy way. Stop thinking about her? To stop breathing would be easier.

"You all right?" Collin asked him Friday evening as they were closing up.

He gave his friend and business partner a wry grin and held up his bandaged hand—two small bandages, actually. One on his thumb and the other on his cut index finger. "What? All the blood scared you?"

"You do seem kind of distracted," Collin said mildly. He clapped Derek on the shoulder. "Why don't you come on up the mountain with me? Willa's making pot roast."

"'Night!" Ned called as went out the door. "See you guys Monday."

Derek waved at Ned and said to Collin, "I hate to pass up the best pot roast in Montana, but I told Luke I'd meet him and the boys for happy hour at the Ace. How about joining us?"

"Thanks, but I gotta get home."

They walked out together, Derek trying not to be jealous of an old friend who used to be considered a world-class heartbreaker, all settled down now with a wife and son he couldn't wait to get home to.

In the master bathroom upstairs at Sunshine Farm, Eva touched up her blusher and fluffed her blond hair.

Amy, leaning in the open doorway behind her, asked, "Are you sure about this? The guys might not be too happy about us crashing their happy hour two weeks running."

Eva giggled like a schoolgirl and leaned in closer to the mirror to put on her lipstick. "Of course they'll be happy." She smoothed on a glossy petal-pink shade.

"They'd better be. Because I'm thinking we need to make this a Friday tradition." Eva had invited half the women in town to join them in crashing the guys' happy hour. She capped the lipstick. "Now, get over here." She wiggled her fingers back over her shoulder at Amy, who stepped up beside her. Eva hooked an arm around her waist. They grinned together at their reflections.

Amy said, "You look amazing."

Eva beamed. "And you look just beautiful."

Tonight, Amy wore a short red dress with a flirty hem that left her shoulders bare, and her favorite red-tooled cowboy boots. She'd spent way more time on her hair and makeup than a certain obstinate cowboy deserved. But she did have her pride and she liked to look her best. "You ready?" She kept her smile, though every time she thought of Derek, she wanted to pitch a world-class hissy fit.

Eva glanced at the small clock on the bathroom counter. "Yikes! We'd better get moving. Our girls will wonder what happened to us."

The Ace's dirt parking lot was packed. Amy let Eva out under the flickering neon sign at the entrance and drove around for ten minutes until finally an old guy in a battered pickup pulled out and left a free space. She parked and primped a little, and then got out and headed for the front door.

With every step she took, her hopeless heart knocked harder against her rib cage. Her blood seemed to hum through her veins and her stomach was a big ball of nerves.

All because he hadn't called and she hadn't called

and they'd left it all open-ended last Tuesday night—or rather, *he* had. Telling her to "think it over."

Saying he would think it over, too.

Think it over?

After she'd gone and put her heart right out there, as good as begging him to be with her for the rest of the month, that was all she got? She'd tried so hard to be honest and forthright with him.

And in return, he'd said to think about it—oh, and by the way, he had to go.

Inside the Ace, the music was loud, the dance floor packed. Eva and five other women, friends and family, had joined the group of men at the three large pushed-together tables near the long mahogany bar.

Derek was there, all right, looking like every cowgirl's fantasy in a worn plaid shirt and a straw Resistol. The table blocked her view of his long, strong legs clad in denim and his brown cowboy boots, but she knew he would be wearing them, whether he'd spent his day at the saddlery or working cattle on the Circle D.

A waitress she'd never seen before stood at his shoulder with a tray full of empties. She was really pretty, with a lush, curvy figure and long platinum hair.

She bent close to Derek and whispered something in his ear. He said something in reply. Really, he wasn't flirting with her. He didn't lean close to her and his smile was only casually friendly.

Amy hated them both anyway. Just on principle. Because he'd told her to "think it over." And because why did he have to be the guy every pretty woman wanted to get to know a whole lot better?

The waitress threw back her platinum head and

let out a musical laugh as she turned and strutted to the bar.

Derek spotted Amy then, where she stood watching on the far side of the dance floor. His eyes seemed to burn into hers. He reached out, hooked the seat of an empty chair at the next table over and eased it in between his chair and Bailey's beside him. Then he patted the seat.

As if she was going to trot right over there and sit next to him just because he patted a chair.

Eva caught sight of her. "Amy! There you are!" She waved madly.

Amy ordered her legs to start moving. She marched straight to Eva, who sat between Luke and Viv Shuster on a long bench seat.

"Got room for me?" Amy asked.

"You bet." Viv scooted closer to her fiancé, Cole Dalton, on her other side. As Eva had explained it to Amy, Cole had come to town last year with his brothers and his dad for a fresh start after the family had lost everything in a tragic fire. The dark-haired cowboy was clearly head-over-heels for the wedding planner. He hooked an arm across Viv's shoulders and drew her closer still.

Amy was glad for them. She was glad for all the happy couples in Rust Creek Falls. Too bad love hadn't worked out so well for her, she thought grumpily as she took the vacant space Viv had left for her. Across the table, she could just *feel* Derek scowling at her.

Not that she was going to look at him again. He could just sit there with that empty chair and wait for that waitress to come whisper a few more sweet nothings in his ear for all Amy cared.

There were pitchers of beer already on the table. Eva grabbed a clean glass and poured one for Amy.

"Raise your glasses, everyone," Eva instructed. When the glasses went up, she offered, "To love and happy hour."

The toast echoed around the table. Everybody drank and Eva and Luke shared a kiss, after which Luke took her hand and led her out to the dance floor. Everybody else at the table seemed to think that was a great idea. Most of them, including Cole and Viv, got up to dance. Bailey stayed behind. Bella and Hudson Jones, too.

Across the table, Derek asked, "Dance with me, Amy?"

She pretended she didn't hear him. And when a tall, skinny cowboy asked her dance, she got up and two-stepped with him for all she was worth. Not once did she allow herself to glance at the table or look around to see what Derek "The Lady-Killer" Dalton might be doing.

When the tall cowboy took her back to her seat, she gave him a big smile as he thanked her for the dance. She turned to sit down and her eyes lit on Derek—and that waitress. She was bending close to him as she set a shot glass full of amber liquid in front of him.

Amy shouldn't have looked.

But she did look. And that waitress had some serious cleavage, which she was sticking right in Derek's face.

That did it. There was no point in this.

None at all.

Amy spoke to Bailey. "I think I'm going to take off. Tell Eva I'm fine. I know she can hitch a ride home with Luke."

Bailey opened his mouth to say something, but

then seemed to think better of it, whatever it was. He swallowed and nodded. "Sure thing, Amy. Drive safe."

"Thanks, Bailey." She turned and got moving, her cowboy boots tapping the wood floor swift and sharp, as she skirted the dance area on the way to the exit.

She shoved through to the wide porch in front. Outside, it was still daylight, though the sun had slipped close to the mountains. She ran down the stairs and around to the still-full parking lot.

Almost at her car, she heard swift footsteps behind her.

"Come on, Amy." *Derek*. He had followed her. "Damn it, wait up!"

She kept going, down the dirt aisle between the two rows of cars, feeling hurt and frustrated and angry.

And way too relieved that he'd come after her.

She reached her Audi and marched to the driver's door.

"Amy!"

"Fine," she muttered under her breath to no one in particular. Folding her arms hard under her breasts, she leaned back against the side of the car as he turned from the aisle and strode toward her. "What?" she demanded.

He stopped, whipped off his hat and rubbed the back of his neck. "Look. I got nothing going on with Myra. She flirts. She gets bigger tips that way."

"Oh, her name is Myra, is it?"

"It's no secret. It's on her name tag."

She almost started in on him about the proximity of Myra's cleavage to his face. But that would be tacky. "We both know that Myra's not the issue, okay?"

"Amy, it doesn't look to me like anything is 'okay' between us right at this moment…" His voice trailed off. She could hear laughter and voices a couple of aisles over—and nearer to where they stood, too—customers on their way in and out of the Ace. "We're a block and a half from the saddlery. Would you meet me there? We can talk in private."

"I don't know if that's a good idea."

"Please." He said it softly, sincerely. Like it was really important to him. Like he wouldn't be able to bear it if they didn't work this out.

"Fine," she said tightly. "I'll meet you at the saddlery." He just stood there, looking at her. "What?" she demanded.

"When a woman says 'fine' like that, a man has doubts that anything is fine in any way."

"Your point being?"

"You're not going to take off again, are you?"

"I said I would be there."

"All right. I'll see you in ten minutes, then."

By the time Derek arrived at the shop, Amy was already there. He parked in the space next to her as she got out of her car and ran up the steps.

At the door, she stepped back and wrapped her arms around herself, like he might contaminate her if she happened to actually touch him.

He could think of a few snide remarks he might make about now. But that would get them nowhere. He kept his mouth shut as he stuck his key in the lock and stepped past the threshold to turn off the alarm and switch on the lights.

"Come on in. There's a table and chairs in back. We can make coffee, if you want some." He led the way through the shop to the makeshift lounge area. Once through the open door, he suggested, "Have a seat."

She pulled out a vinyl-covered chair at the scratched-up laminate table and sat down.

He was already sticking a pod in the coffee maker. "You want some coffee?"

"Sure," she said, her mouth pinched, as if even the thought of drinking his coffee was annoying her. "Thanks," she added sourly.

He brewed a cup for each of them, took the seat across from her and pushed one of the mugs in her direction. "There's sugar. And creamer." Way back in ancient history, she liked both. He pushed the container of packets her way, too.

And then he just sat there, hardly knowing where to start. He drank the coffee he really didn't want as he watched her add a packet of sugar and creamer to her mug and take a cautious sip.

They shouldn't be here. Shouldn't be doing this.

And yet, if she got up and tried to leave right now, he would do whatever he had to do to convince her to stay.

Was he messed up over this woman or what?

Stupid question with an obvious answer.

Finally, she spoke. "Okay. I'm here. What did you want to say to me?"

Damned if he knew. "I just don't see why you're so mad at me. You said it's not about Myra."

"And it's not. It's just…it's everything, Derek. All these years and how much you hurt me and now it seems to me like you're just messing with me all over again."

Now, that was just wrong. "*I'm* messing with *you*?

What are you talking about? How am I messing with you?"

"One minute you act like we're completely over and done, the next you're bringing a picnic, showing me around here in the saddlery, kissing me. Twice."

He was in midsip when she mentioned those kisses, and the scornful way she spoke of them made him mad enough that he plunked his mug down hard. Hot liquid splashed on his hand. He swore under his breath as he whipped a paper towel from the roll in the center of the table and wiped up the spill. "Next you'll be claiming you didn't kiss me back."

She huffed out a furious breath. "That is completely and totally not in any way the point. Yes, I kissed you back. Yes, I loved that picnic and the tour you gave me here. I loved every minute I've spent with you this last week."

How did she do that? Drive him crazy one minute, and the next say something that had all his wounded fury draining right out of him. Carefully, he set the wadded ball of paper towel beside his mug. "You did?"

"Yes, I did. I even started thinking that maybe we could have a little something special together, that we could leave the past *in* the past and be together right now."

"Amy, I—"

She whipped up a hand. "Wait." And then she sat back in the chair and folded her arms hard across her middle. "Think back. What did you say when I suggested we see where this feeling between us might take us?" He would have answered. He even opened his mouth to do so, but she just rolled right on. "I'll tell you what you said. You said that I ought to think about it. You said that you would be thinking, too. Well, you know what? I don't believe you, Derek. I don't think you thought about it one bit since Tuesday night. Uh-uh. More likely you've spent all this time purposely *not* thinking about it, planning on going out this weekend and finding yourself some other girl, some *new* girl you don't have any baggage with."

"That's bull. I'm not looking for any new girl. And I did think about it—about you and me and seeing where it would take us. It's *all* I thought about." He lifted his left hand and wiggled the bandaged digits at her. "I practically cut all my fingers off thinking about it."

"Oh, please. As if you cut yourself because you were so wrapped up in pining for me."

"That is exactly what I did."

For a moment, her eyes softened and her mouth relaxed. But then she snapped right back to hissy-fit mode. "You just don't get it," she accused.

He threw up both hands. "And you're not listening to me."

She fumed at him, tapping her fingers on her crossed arms. "It took me forever to accept that you were never coming after me. Took me driving all the way back here from Boulder nine years ago, daring to hope that just maybe I might get a chance to talk to you. Took me stopping in at the Ace and chatting up the bartender, who told me all about what a player you were, how it was one girl after another with you. About the cute cowgirl you'd met there at the Ace the weekend before, how you danced every dance with her and left with her at closing time, how word in town was that you were off at the Missoula Stampede with her right that very moment."

He vaguely remembered the cowgirl in question, but a long-ago hookup wasn't what had him sitting up straight in his chair. "Wait. Are you serious? You came back?"

She scrunched her eyes tight and let out a moan. "Yeah. I came back and you were off with some other girl and I realized I needed to accept that you had moved on and to start finding a way to move on myself."

He pushed his chair back. "Amy…"

She glared at him as he stood. "What are we doing here? What is the point of this?"

Her words were not the least bit encouraging. But… she'd come back. She'd actually come back.

And he'd never even known.

"Amy…" He rounded the table. He just couldn't stop himself.

When he stood by her chair, she stared up at him defiantly. "Yeah, I came back. So what? I came back and you were with another girl."

"Amy, I didn't know. I never had a clue…"

"Don't do that, okay? Don't look at me like I'm so important to you. We both know that's just not true."

"But you are important. Always were, always will be."

She made a little scoffing sound. "Yeah, right."

He needed to prove it, needed her to know that he'd missed her, too. So, he went ahead and confessed, "I tried to find you, too. I went to Boulder, Amy. Like a lovesick fool, I went to CU looking for you."

Her eyes got wide and her pinched-up mouth went soft and full again. "You did?"

His chest felt constricted. His throat, too. "It was that first year after you left, in the early spring. I didn't know what the hell I was doing, how to go about getting in touch with you. I tried your old cell number. Some stranger answered, said it was his number now. I was afraid to ask the Armstrongs or someone who might know how to reach you. Afraid they wouldn't tell me. Afraid they'd tell *you* and you would refuse to see me. And there was zero access to social media around here at the time. I couldn't exactly look you up on Facebook."

She gazed at him across the table, her mouth softly parted, her eyes all dewy and so bright. "But you drove to Colorado anyway, to try and find me?"

"I did, yeah. I missed you so much. I couldn't stand it anymore. Drove all night and half the next day. It was snowing on and off, sometimes snowing hard, but I kept going. I had this idea that if you saw me, saw my face, knew how much I'd missed you, you'd maybe decide you couldn't live without me, either."

"But you never showed up."

"Yeah, I did. I mean, I made it to Boulder, anyway, to the main CU campus. I parked and went in to the administration building."

"And?"

"They wouldn't tell me squat. Turned out they have rules about that," he laughed, but it was a dry sound with very little humor in it. "I could've been a stalker or something. Hell, after driving fifteen hours in near-blizzard conditions, I probably *looked* like a stalker."

"Derek." Her eyes gleamed, wet now with unshed tears. "I'm so sorry. I didn't know."

He laughed again, humorless as the time before. "Pretty hard for you to know when I didn't tell a soul."

"What did you do then?"

"I went back to my truck and considered pulling out all the stops, paying a visit to your parents' house."

"You had my parents' address?"

He shrugged. "They were easy. I found a phone book. They were listed. But school was in session and I was reasonably sure you wouldn't be at your folks' house. That meant I'd be dealing with your mom and dad. They'd never been my biggest fans, your dad especially, though he was polite enough that last day."

"At the motel in Kalispell, you mean?"

He debated just going ahead and telling her the whole truth about that day. But what good would that do anyone, really? "Yeah. At the motel."

She pushed back her chair and stood. "You're such a bad liar."

He put up both hands and backed up a step. "I'm not—"

"Don't say it. I didn't believe you the first time, so there's no point in lying to me again." She shook her head. "I always wondered how my dad knew to follow us from the Armstrong house. I asked him about it more than once. He always just said he'd tried dropping by the Armstrongs' and he saw us drive away."

"It's ancient history, Amy."

She wouldn't leave it alone. "He got to you, didn't he? He went to find you at the Circle D and then he followed you to the Armstrongs' house and when you picked me up, he trailed both of us to Kalispell."

Derek couldn't believe he'd put himself in the position of defending Jack Wainwright. But at this point, she wouldn't believe him anyway if he insisted on keeping the truth from her. They were clearing the air, after all. Letting all their sad little secrets out of the closets.

"All right. Yeah. Your dad showed up at the ranch. He was worried sick about you. And I have to say, even though I didn't like him any more than he liked me, I knew he loved you and wanted the best for you. He was also no fool. He didn't threaten me or talk down to me. He took hat in hand, said he knew I loved you, said that you had a bright future in front of you and why would a man who loved you want to steal that future out from under you? He said he just wanted me to think about letting you go."

"Oh, Derek," she cried. "Why didn't you just tell me that you'd talked to him?"

"I thought about it, about us, about what your dad had said. I thought about it all the way from the Armstrong house to our dingy little honeymoon suite at that crappy motel. And the more I thought it over, the more certain I was that if I told you your dad had come looking for me, you'd just get mad at him. You'd dig in your heels and not admit that he was right."

She pressed her lips together. "I'm mad at him right now. He went behind my back and he never came clean to me about what he did."

"Amy, it's really old news."

"Still…"

"It's old news and he did it because he loved you."

"Yeah, well. Next time I see him, I'll tell him I know the truth now and I don't appreciate the way he lied to me."

"That's your call."

"Oh, yes, it is—and we're not finished talking about

the day you drove to Colorado to try to l find me at CU. Did you go see my parents that day?" Her eyes got stormy. "Because if you did, they never said a word to me about that, either."

"Settle down."

"Then answer the question, please." Her voice was clipped, tight.

"No, I didn't go to see your parents. I chickened out and just went home."

"Oh," she said, her outrage fading. "I see."

"And what did *you* do, after that bartender told you I was off in Missoula with some other girl?"

She scanned his face as though memorizing it. "Same as you. I chickened out and went home."

For a few seconds that seemed to last forever and a day, they just stood there, mere inches between them, gazes locked, neither even breathing.

And then he reached out.

And she stepped forward.

His arms went around her. She rested her head against his shoulder. He gathered her closer. Never would he get enough of the perfect feel of her in his arms.

When she finally looked up, she went on tiptoe and brushed a quick kiss on his chin. "Aren't we a pair?"

They laughed together. And he agreed, "Yeah. A matched set, no doubt about it."

"You really cut your hand thinking about me?"

"I did."

"Let me see." When he held up his injured fingers, she took them and kissed the bandaged spots. "Be more careful," she chided.

"Great advice." Though now that he was here, alone with her, the last thing he wanted was to be careful.

"Derek, I…" Those big hazel eyes searched his face.

"Yeah?"

"I still want to be with you. I want to spend every minute I can with you until the wedding. I don't know what will happen, really. Maybe you and I aren't meant for forever. But you told me to think about it and I have. And the answer's still the same. I want to be with you, to get to know you, to know the man you are now."

He wanted that, too—to know the Amy she was now—so damn much.

Yeah, she scared the hell out of him. She could hurt him so deep if he let her get too close. She'd probably break his heart all over again.

Too bad it was too late to walk away untouched. Somehow, she'd gone and worked her way back under his skin—or maybe she'd never left.

He wanted her so bad it hurt.

"It's only two weeks and a day till the wedding now," she said. "I would like to spend a lot of that time with you. I would like us to commit to being exclusive till the wedding."

She would like that? He would *love* it. "Exclusive, huh?"

"That's right. Yes or no? Can you give up the other women at least for the next fifteen days?"

"Amy, let me clear this up for you once and for all. There *are* no other women. Yes, I've been one of those guys who never sticks around for breakfast the morning after, but not in the past few years. I haven't been with anyone in a little over eight months and that was an actual relationship. Her name is Angela Bishop. She owns a diner in Kalispell." He added, with more sarcasm than was probably called for, "We went on dates and everything."

She scrunched up her eyebrows at him, an expression he recognized as concern for him. "What happened?"

"With Angela? Not enough. I mean, she liked me and I liked her and we had a good time together, but at a certain point we both realized it wasn't going anywhere. We broke up. End of story. So, would you please stop assuming I'm spending all my free time chasing women?"

She gave a slow, solemn nod. "Will do. I promise. And I'm sorry to have, um, made assumptions about you."

"You're forgiven. Now, about the next two weeks…"

She drew her shoulders back. "I would like to be with you."

"Got that."

"And to keep what we have just between the two of us. Because nobody else has to know."

Did that bother him? Not really. Rust Creek Falls was a very small town. People looked out for each other, but they also got way too interested in each others' activities. He could do without them all talking about him and Amy.

She went on, "It's partly to keep everyone out of our business. I mean, it's only two weeks and who knows what will happen? And until *we* know where we're going together, there's no reason to share what we have with the rest of the world. Also, I think it's important to keep the focus on Eva and Luke, where it belongs right now. We'll say we're just friends…" Her cheeks were pink and her eyes so wide and hopeful. "I mean, for the next two weeks, we could make time for each other and not date other people. And I'm hoping there could be, um, benefits if it works out that way. That's all I'm really asking. Would that work for you?"

He hid a grin. "I think I could manage it."

A little snort of laughter escaped her. "Stop joking. This is serious."

He put on his most somber expression. "Just friends, then. Friends who spend a lot of time together and don't go out with other people. Friends with possible secret benefits?"

"Well, yeah. I mean, you think?" She folded her upper lip between her teeth and nibbled on it. The sight was equal parts innocent and sexy. He wanted to grab her and kiss her, unwrap her like the best gift ever, get going on those benefits, secret or otherwise…

But he knew her, even with all the empty years away from her. She wasn't ready yet. And if it happened for them again—*when* it happened—he wanted it to be right.

"Is that too crazy?" Her voice was barely a whisper. "Am I totally on the wrong track here? Would you agree to something like that?" She stared up at him, anxious and adorable. "Derek, you have to tell me what you think."

"I do, huh?"

"Derek!" She whipped up a hand and batted his shoulder.

He caught her fingers before she could pull them away. "Hold on a minute."

"What are you doing?"

"I'll show you. But first, I think you should come closer."

Just like a woman, she hung back. "But I—"

"Closer." He laid her hand, palm flat, on his shoulder. "Don't move that hand." For that, he got an eye roll, but her palm stayed where he'd put it. It felt good there. It felt right. He almost let himself imagine a lifetime's worth of her soft hands touching him. But he didn't, not quite. No reason to get too carried away here. "Now, give me the other one."

"But, Derek, what do you—"

"Come on. Humor me." She offered her hand cautiously. He took it, opened her fingers and rested it on his other shoulder. "There."

She looked deliciously doubtful. "Now what?"

He clasped her waist. "It feels good." His voice came out gruff though he hadn't really meant it to. "It feels good to have your hands on me. To touch you. Nothing ever felt as good as touching you, Amy."

"Derek," she whispered, and somehow managed to put a thousand tender meanings into just saying his name.

"Amy." He swooped down and claimed himself a quick, sweet kiss, after which he announced, "I want to be with you, too. Exclusive secret friends, just the way you described it. With benefits—maybe. When the time is right."

She wrinkled her beautiful nose at him. "You're not just messing with me? You really mean it? You won't change your mind and stay away from me for days on end?"

He should have sense enough to let that stand. But

he'd never had much sense around her. "It was only two days—okay, three if you count today."

She tipped her head to the side and slanted him a narrow-eyed look. "You *were* staying away, though, weren't you?"

"I was thinking it over, as we agreed."

She blew out a hard breath. "I can see this is an argument you're never going to let me win."

"You're right. I'm not. I'm also not messing with you. I meant what I said. I've thought it through and, if you agree, I won't be keeping my distance anymore. I want to be with you, too. For the next two weeks, you and me."

"And if either of us is too busy or whatever and we can't be together, we'll keep in communication?" Her eyes were almost golden right then. Golden and shining.

"Yeah," he said. "We'll be together, be honest with each other, see where it takes us."

"Starting right this minute." She slid those soft hands up around his neck. Her cool fingers stroked the short hair at his nape. "Kiss me again."

He couldn't comply fast enough. Her lips were so soft and sweet. And her body fit against him as if she was born to be his. She opened for him eagerly and he tasted her more deeply, savoring the warmth and wet beyond her parted lips.

And that time, when he lifted his head, she asked, "Are you still in the bunkhouse at the Circle D?"

He touched her hair, so silky and warm. For the next two weeks, he would touch her a lot. Touch her everywhere, he hoped—eventually. When the time was right. "I built my own place a few years back. My brothers and cousins pitched in to help me, along with some friends who work in construction. It's not a big place, not fancy, but it's mine, you know?"

"I would love to see it."

"Now?"

"Yes." Her smile took his breath away. "I'll text Eva to let her know that I'll be out late. And then I'll follow you home."

Chapter Six

Once they turned off the highway onto Circle D land, Derek led the way in his pickup along the winding dirt ranch road past the main house, the barn and the bunkhouse.

Amy followed him, bumping along, trying her best to avoid the ruts. They skirted a pretty, rolling meadow. The house stood on the far side of the meadow, with a big cottonwood in the front yard. Sided in natural wood, it had a long front porch and three gabled windows breaking up the roofline.

Derek circled the cottonwood and parked facing back toward the highway. She followed him around the tree and pulled to a stop behind him. It was about eight by then, still light out. But the sun had gone behind the mountains and the pale moon rode high in the blue expanse of the Montana sky, the orange fingers of sunset beginning to color the wisps of clouds above the crests of the distant peaks.

An almost-white Labrador retriever came down the front steps, tail wagging. Derek, already out of his pickup, stopped to greet the dog, who gazed at him adoringly as he scratched the ruff at the animal's neck.

Amy got out and shut her door. "I didn't know you had a dog."

"I don't. Meet Buster. He belongs to Willa and Collin, but every once in a while, he takes off down the mountain and comes here or goes to the Christensen place."

The Christensens were Willa's family. Actually, Willa and Collin were kind of an unexpected match: Willa the good-girl kindergarten teacher and Collin Traub, who never met a rule he wouldn't break. "I was surprised when Eva told me that Willa and Collin got married."

"So were a lot of people. They got together during the big flood." The flood had swept through Rust Creek Falls and the surrounding valley. Half the town had to be rebuilt afterward. "And now Collin and Willa have a son named Robbie and a dog who likes to wander." He grinned down at Buster.

"He's a beautiful dog." Buster seemed to preen at her praise. He sat back on his haunches and stared up at her expectantly. She knelt to pet him.

"Watch out. He'll drool all over your dress."

"I don't mind." She scratched his head and let him swipe his big tongue across her cheek. "Why don't you have a dog of your own? Seems only right, now that you have your own place."

His gaze scanned her face, a look both slow and

appreciative. "I'm at the saddlery half the time now. Wouldn't be fair to keep a dog cooped up there." He held down his hand to her. She took it, loving the warm, intimate feel of his fingers closing around hers. "Let me show you the house."

Buster trailing along in their wake, Derek led her up the steps. At the door, he ushered her in first. The dog slipped around them both and headed off down the hallway that opened up to what looked like a great room at the far end.

They stood in the small foyer area for a moment. She admired the handsome oak staircase accented with iron balusters and asked, "How many bedrooms are up there?"

"None right now. It's an unfinished attic. I figure I can fix it up, divide it into bedrooms, even put in another bath if I ever need more living space."

If he ever needs more space...

Her mind went where it probably shouldn't—to the idea of Derek, married. Maybe with children.

Uh-uh. She blinked the thought away. It was too dangerous on too many levels.

"This way," he said.

He ushered her into the dining room, to the left of the entry and through there to the kitchen, breakfast nook, great room and two bedrooms. The furniture was basic, in a mishmash of styles.

"It's really nice," she said, "comfortable and inviting." There was even a big-screen TV above the natural stone fireplace.

He reached out and slid a hand under her hair, curving his strong, work-roughened fingers around the nape of her neck and pulling her in close to him. His lips brushed her cheek and his breath was warm in her ear. "You smell like heaven. Always did." An arrow of pure happiness darted straight through her heart at his whispered words. They shared a long, sweet kiss and then he lifted his head and captured her gaze. "Are you hungry?"

"A little."

At their feet, Buster whined and wagged his tail.

She leaned her head on Derek's shoulder. "I think you'd better feed Buster first."

He pressed his lips into her hair. It was an absolutely lovely moment and she let herself revel in it.

Too soon, he released her to fill one bowl with water and another with kibble. "Yeah," he replied to the question she hadn't even asked. "Buster stops by a lot and so I keep food on hand for him." He set the full bowls down and Buster went right to work gobbling his dinner. "I'd better let Collin know that his dog stopped by for dinner." Derek took out his phone and sent his friend a text.

When he stuck the phone back in his pocket, she said, "I want to help with the food."

"Works for me."

He made pasta with marinara sauce and Italian sausage. She tossed a quick salad with the lettuce and vegetables he had in the fridge, set the table and grated the parmesan.

Her phone buzzed with a text as they sat down to eat. She would have ignored it, but he said, "It could be important."

So, she checked. "It's Eva. She says we should have fun."

"Let me guess. There's a winky emoji followed by about ten hearts."

"I'm beginning to think you know her as well as I do."

He laughed. "Tell her I said hi."

As she typed a quick response, another text came in. She sent her reply to Eva and brought up the new message.

L.A. Noire. Tonight. Your house? I've got a nice Pinot Gris with your name on it.

She tapped out a quick reply. Sorry. Out of town for a few weeks.

Damn, woman. I was really in the mood to take you down.

Right. Like that's ever gonna happen.

Ping me.

Will do. Later.

She hit Send and glanced up to find Derek watching her. "A friend in Boulder. We play video games sometimes. He didn't know I was out of town."

Those green eyes were cool suddenly. "This friend got a name?"

"Jonas Baldwin." She picked up her fork again. "I met him in graduate school. We've stayed friends in a casual way." Derek just went on looking at her, his mouth a flat line. She thought of Myra, back at the Ace, and of how much she'd needed his reassurance that he had nothing going on with Myra. "Honestly, Derek. Jonas and I are in no way, shape or form, a thing and we never have been. We double-dated once—he took the girl he was dating at the time and I went with a friend of his. I see him maybe five or six times a year. He'll call and if I'm not doing anything, we get together, him and me and my Xbox One."

Derek just went on looking at her for several extremely uncomfortable seconds. Annoyance sizzled through her that he didn't believe her when she was telling the truth. He had no reason not to take her word for it—not to mention, he had zero right to be jealous. They'd only been exclusive for about two hours.

But then he asked, "Who wins?" and his mouth curved into that panty-melting grin.

Her heart lifted. "Are you kidding? I wipe the floor with him every time."

He tipped his beer at her. "Now, that's what I wanted to hear." The doorbell chimed. "That'll be Collin looking for Buster." He got up and pushed his chair in. "Be right back. Come on, Buster." The dog followed him down the central hall.

Amy let them go—and then felt uncomfortable. As though she was hiding there in the kitchen. From Collin Traub, of all people. Back in high school, Derek was every girl's handsome heartthrob. Collin was the dangerous one, the forbidden fantasy, with his jet-black hair and dark, knowing eyes. Just as many girls dreamed of him as wanted Derek.

Not Amy. It had always been Derek for her.

And right now, what mattered was that she knew him, knew Collin, and even if she and Derek were keeping this thing just between them, the least she could do was show her face at the door and say hi to an old schoolmate.

She slid her napkin next to her half-finished plate, pushed back her chair and followed the sound of men's voices to the front door.

Collin, just outside the door with his dog waiting patiently at his feet, caught sight of her first. "Amy Wainwright." He gave Derek a strange, narrow-eyed look, then aimed his killer smile at her. "How you been?"

"Hi, Collin. I'm doing well, thanks."

As she stepped up beside him, Derek shot her a questioning frown, which she'd kind of expected after she'd made such a big deal back at the saddlery about the two of them keeping their relationship on the down low.

Amy shook Collin's hand. "Good to see you."

"Must be your Audi, then," he said, shooting another significant glance at Derek.

Derek grunted. "Why are we standing here at the door? Come on in. I've got a longneck with your name on it."

"Better not. I have to get back." But Collin stayed where he was and his gaze shifted her way again, his dark eyes watchful. "It's been a long time."

"Yeah." She rushed into the usual chitchat, the stuff you say to people you never knew all that well and haven't seen in more than a decade. "So, you and Willa Christensen, huh?"

"That's right."

"I always liked Willa—and I know this is long overdue, but congratulations, Collin."

"Thanks." Collin's guarded expression relaxed a

little. "She really is the best thing that ever happened to me."

"And I understand you have a little boy—oh, and you're the mayor now, too?"

He smirked. "Never saw that coming, I'll bet."

"True." After all, Collin had been the classic high school bad boy. He partied hard, broke a lot of hearts, drove too fast and got in trouble with the sheriff more than once. "You never seemed like someone who would get into politics."

Collin laughed at that. "Talk about an understatement. Most of my life, not only would I never have considered running for public office, I never would have believed that anyone would vote for me."

"So, what changed?"

"I married Willa," he said with pride. "I had ideas for what I thought needed fixing around here and my wife decided I should step right up and make it happen."

"You're happy," Amy said softly, glad for him. "It's good to see how well things worked out for you."

"Can't complain."

Derek started to say something, but Collin went on before he got a word out. "What took you so long to come back to town?" He was looking faintly disapproving again.

"Long story," she said, and left it at that.

Collin's dark eyes seemed to look right through her. "I think I heard someone say you're here for the wedding?"

"I am." She rushed on. "It's been so good to see Eva, to get a chance to reconnect with old friends. Delphine and Calla and their families will be here next Friday. I can't wait to see them."

"And after the wedding, then what?" Collin didn't sound hostile, exactly. Just skeptical—and wary, too.

Derek muttered, "Come on, man."

Collin locked eyes with him and said almost gently, "It's a reasonable thing to ask."

Amy answered Collin's question, more or less. "I live in Boulder."

"So, a month in Montana *reconnecting* with old friends. Then back to real life." It was the truth, even if Collin Traub made it sound like something downright shady.

Before she could reply, Derek muttered, "Enough." He and Collin shared a look that seemed to speak volumes—about what, exactly, Amy couldn't be sure.

Collin took a step back. "You're right. I should get moving. See you Monday. Amy, you take care now."

"Thanks. You, too." She gave him a big smile. Because she really had nothing against Collin. No need to make an issue of his weirdly disapproving attitude.

Collin went down the steps, Buster at his heels, headed for the crew cab parked beside her SUV.

Derek shut the door.

She faced him. "Let me guess. Collin remembers that we used to be together in high school."

"Yeah." Derek headed to the kitchen. She fell in step behind him.

They took their seats at the table. He sipped his beer and she debated trying to go on as if the conversation with Collin hadn't happened.

He made the decision for her. "Go ahead. Ask me."

She took a fortifying sip of ice water and set the glass down with care. "How much does Collin know about you and me?"

He drank again. "That you were my girl and it ended when you moved away."

"That's all? He seemed a little too suspicious of me, like I did something bad to you."

"Maybe you're imagining things."

"Am I?"

He stared at her across the table for a few seconds that seemed to go on forever. And then he admitted, "The night I heard that you and your family had left for Colorado, I went out drinking."

"With Collin?"

"At some point, I met up with him. By then, I was really blasted. We ended up at this bonfire with a bunch of kids from Kalispell. I might've said a few stupid things to him and he might've gotten the idea that you ripped out my heart and chopped it into tiny pieces."

She had a strong urge to defend herself, to argue that he wasn't the only one who'd ended up with a ripped-out heart. But they'd been there, said all that—twice, as a matter of fact. No reason to hash it out all over again.

Instead, she asked, "So then, that night you got so drunk, you told him we'd been married?"

"No. I don't think so."

"You don't *know*?"

"Didn't I just say I got really drunk?" He glared at her. "In case you haven't heard, drunk people some-times say and do things they later can't remember."

Did she blame him for being annoyed with this con-versation? Not really. He had to be sick of rehashing the past. She certainly was. But she did want to under-stand Collin's attitude at the door. "So, you *might* have told him we were married, but you doubt it."

"That's right. I can't be absolutely sure of what I

said or didn't say. But if I'd slipped up and mentioned that we'd run off and gotten married, I'm thinking he'd have brought it up to me by now."

She poked at a slice of sausage with her fork. "He seems like he's a really good friend to you. A true friend, you know?"

"Look." His voice was hard. "Just tell me. Are you pissed off that I might have told Collin you married me once?"

"No. If you did tell him, I understand why."

"You sure?"

"Positive. I mean, it was a bad time. You probably needed to talk to someone and Collin's your friend." She thought of Eva. Of Delphine and Calla. They were her true friends, yet she'd never told them the truth about the past. Guilt jabbed at her, that she'd kept the secret for so long, that she would probably go right on keeping it. "At the door just now, Collin asked about my car. What was he getting at?"

"Before you decided to come say hi to him, he asked if I had company. I said, just a friend. Wasn't that what I was supposed to say?"

"I'm not criticizing you, Derek. I'm only trying to understand why he seemed suspicious of me—and protective of you."

"Yeah, well, you could have avoided all that by staying in here until I got rid of him."

She swallowed. Hard. He had a good point and she needed to explain herself. "It seemed tacky somehow, you know? To hide in the kitchen while you sent away someone we both went to school with."

"Amy, it's what you asked for. To be 'secretly, exclusively together.' Am I right?" And then he added, under his breath, "Whatever the hell all that even means."

She set down her fork with care. "You're upset with me."

"Yeah. You've got me all turned around here. You say we're keeping what we're doing a secret. Then you come strolling down the hall to greet Collin at the door after I've tried to cover for your being here. I don't know what you want."

"I guess I didn't think it through, when I proposed how we would be together. I just meant we wouldn't explain ourselves, okay?"

His strong jaw was set. "Uh-uh. Still don't get it."

"Well, I mean when we're together, we're together and people are going to see that. I don't want us to lie."

"Yeah, you do. You want us to lie and say we're just friends when we're more than friends and we always will be, whether we move on to benefits or not."

We always will be.

Her heart pounded harder and her skin felt too tight. He was right, and she knew it. And it made her ridiculously glad—that after more than a decade apart, she was still important to him.

She tried again to explain herself. "I only meant that we could just skip the PDAs and the declarations of our relationship, or whatever. We can just tell everyone we're friends and leave it at that. I didn't mean we would hide or pretend I'm not at your house when I am."

He pushed his plate away. "Okay. No PDAs and we tell everyone we're friends. And when your car's parked outside my house all night, we just say you stayed over and let them think whatever they want to think."

"Yes. That's it. Exactly."

"So, there is no secret, really. There are just zero explanations."

"Yeah. Is that wrong somehow, Derek?"

"We might as well get real about this. If we're not keeping our getting together a secret, they're going to talk anyway. In case you didn't notice, it's Rust Creek Falls."

"I'm just saying that this is none of their business. *We're* none of their business. It's just between us and they can talk all they want, but we'll just ignore them." He didn't reply so she pressed him. "I'll ask again, do you think that not explaining ourselves to other people is wrong?"

"No, I don't think it's wrong. And I do want to be with you, however we can make that work." He stared across the table in her general direction, but he wasn't really meeting her eyes.

"Well, okay, then." She waited for him to look directly at her so that she could try a coaxing smile.

But he only lowered his gaze and turned his empty beer bottle in a slow circle, staring at it as though deep in thought. "You realize I said '*When* your car's parked outside my house all night' and you didn't argue with me. You didn't remind me that at this point, the two of us making love is still more of an *if* than a *when*." He looked up at last. His eyes said it all. He wasn't mad.

And he wanted her to stay.

After the uncomfortable moments with Collin at the door and the difficult discussion over dinner, Derek was a little afraid that Amy might decide it was time for her go.

She didn't act like she wanted to go, but he couldn't

be sure. Maybe he was reading her all wrong and any minute now she would start edging toward the door.

As she helped him clear the table and load the dishwasher, he considered the various ways to get her to stay.

He knew one surefire method: offer to play video games. She'd always loved them and apparently, she still played them with some dude named Jonas in Boulder.

Yeah, she'd probably mop the floor with him. She used to beat him every time no matter what they played. *Zelda, Call of Duty, Super Mario Kart*, you name it.

But that was then. Maybe that Jonas guy just wasn't all that good a player. Maybe Amy had lost her touch playing with guys who didn't challenge her—not that he, Derek, was all that much of a challenge to her.

Still, he would like a rematch after all these years, a chance to beat her for once.

He shut the dishwasher door and started it up.

"Well," she said, looking gorgeous and nervous and not sure what would happen next. "I guess maybe I'd better be—"

"Grand Theft Auto V?" he asked.

Worked like a charm. Her grin was slow and full of evil. "It's your funeral."

They went into the great room, kicked off their boots and played.

Just like old times, she whipped his butt.

And then whipped it again.

After two hours of ending up riddled with bullets, buried in a pile of rubble game after game, he dropped his controller onto the coffee table and put up both hands. "I surrender. You win."

She cupped a hand to her ear. "What did you say?"

"You heard me."

"Yeah, but I want you to say it again."

"Amy, you win."

"Yeah!" She dropped her controller next to his, let out a squeal of triumph and did a double fist pump.

"Why don't you go ahead and tell me how you really feel?"

She squealed again and stomped her stocking feet on the floor. "Who's the man?"

"You're the man."

"Say it again! Say it again!" She bounced up and down on the couch, hair flying, eyes squinty, pumping both fists for all she was worth, her red skirt rising temptingly high on her smooth thighs.

Cutest thing he'd ever seen. Strangest girl he'd ever known.

He could not resist her. And why even try? They were together, right? In a nondeclared, open-ended, nobody's-business sort of way. For the next two weeks, at least.

Suddenly, it seemed like a bad idea to waste a single second of the time he might have with her. To hell with waiting. If she was willing, there would be benefits tonight.

He caught her fist in mid-pump. She let out a yelp followed by a goofy giggle as he dragged her close, cupped the back of her head and claimed that delicious mouth of hers.

Another sound escaped her then, breathless and wanting, as she pulled her hand free of his grip and wrapped it around his neck. Her hair was everywhere, glorious and wild around her flushed face, which he cradled between his two palms so he could kiss her some more.

Long, wet kisses. Short, hard kisses. Kisses light as a fleeting touch turning to kisses so deep he drowned in them.

How had he lived all these thirteen endless years without the taste of her mouth, the feel of her silky hair sifting through his fingers, the touch of her velvety skin beneath his hands?

He guided her down on the couch cushions, kissing her, touching her, smoothing her hair only to spear his fingers in it and mess it up all over again.

She gazed up at him, her eyes full of something he'd never thought he'd see in them again. "Oh, Derek," she whispered, as though his name said it all.

His pulse thudded in his ears and his blood seemed to burn in his veins. "Amy, I…"

"Tell me," she commanded.

"I need to touch you. All of you."

"Yes," she said, so eager. So sure. "Yes. Touch me. All of me. Please."

He wasted no time giving them both what they wanted. Slipping the skinny straps of her little red dress down over her shoulders, he eased the cups of her bra out of his way and buried his face between her soft breasts. She moaned and held him closer.

He needed so much.

All of her.

Naked.

In his hungry arms.

He lifted his head and looked at her, with her dress pulled down, her bra half off, her eyes dazed and dreamy. Her cheeks were a gorgeous shade of pink, her hair in a tangled halo across the nubby cushions of the old couch.

It was the finest sight he'd ever seen.

Something shifted within him. Something opened up wide.

One way or another, they were making it work this time. One way or another they were taking this hesitant, friends-with-benefits second chance all the way to forever.

He didn't know how exactly. Not yet.

But they were older now, and wiser, weren't they? All grown-up and ready to make the big choices and take the important chances, at last.

This time, somehow, they would get it right.

Chapter Seven

She pressed a hand to the side of his face and let out a soft little sigh. "Look at us. Is this really happening?"

"You'd better believe it."

She laughed, a giddy, happy sound. "I'm glad. I'm really glad."

He shifted on top of her. "I'm crushing you, aren't I?"

"Derek, I'm fine."

"This couch is too damn small. We're not kids anymore, making love in my pickup out under a tree in the middle of a pasture somewhere."

"Oh, I remember. I used to get bruises from bumping the steering wheel."

"Not anymore. I need to take you to bed, turn on all the lights, look at every inch of you and kiss you all over."

"Yeah." She tugged on his ear and grinned a goofy,

blissed-out little grin. "You should do that, all of it. You should do that right now."

He slid off the cushions and bent to gather her up. She raised her arms and wrapped them around his neck. He lifted her high. Kicking a random boot out of his way, he made for the central hall and the shorter hall off it that led to the bedrooms.

His door was wide open. He carried her through and set her down on the rug by the bed. Giggling a little, she readjusted her bra to cover those fine breasts, but left the front of her dress around her waist.

"Stay right there," he commanded. And he left her long enough to get everything right. He shut the curtains and turned on the lights—the standing lamp in the corner, the one on the dresser and the two on the nightstands. He grabbed a few condoms from the nearest nightstand drawer and set them by the clock. Last of all, he turned the covers back to reveal the white sheets.

"I like your house so much," she said. "And this is nice." Her gaze roamed the room, taking it all in. "That's beautiful." She pointed at the tooled leather headboard. "Did you do that yourself?"

"Yeah." He straightened from smoothing the sheet and turned to her. Taking her shoulders, he brought her to face him.

She gazed up at him with shining eyes. "Derek."

"What?"

"Nothing. Just Derek. I always liked saying your name. I still do. The combination of sounds is very satisfying. *D-air-ek*." She chuckled, a soft little whisper of sound. "You think I'm strange. You always did."

"You are one of a kind. Special."

Her bare shoulder lifted in a half shrug. "I'm just

plain strange. But thank you for giving it a more positive spin."

He dropped a kiss on that pretty shoulder. "Okay. You're strange—in a special, one-of-a-kind way."

"Derek?"

"Yeah?"

"Kiss my other shoulder."

"Happy to." He pressed his lips to the firm, silky curve, sticking out his tongue and licking the spot for good measure. She gasped just a little. He drank in that sound. "Now." He ran his palm down her arm, caught her fingers and kissed the tips of them. "Take off all your clothes."

"Hmm." She scrunched up her face and pretended to think it over. "I think you should take off my clothes for me."

"And I think that is an excellent idea."

She gazed up at him trustingly as he undid her red belt and tossed it on the bedside chair. Her dress and bra quickly followed.

Now she had only the pair of red socks she'd worn under her boots and little red panties trimmed in pink lace.

"Perfect," he whispered, and bent his head to press his lips to the gorgeous, sweet-smelling curve where her neck met her shoulder. She tasted so good. He couldn't get enough, so he bit her.

"Ouch!" She laughed and slapped at his shoulder. He hauled her against him—and bit her again. "That is going to leave a mark," she complained.

"Tell them we're just friends and it's none of their business."

"You're just asking for it, mister—and why is your

shirt still on? That's just not right." She started in on the buttons, her fingers deft and quick. In no time, she was pushing it off his shoulders. He tossed it toward the pile of clothing on the chair as she tugged at the T-shirt he wore underneath.

"Got it." He reached back over his shoulders and pulled it up and off.

"Oh, I do like where this is going," she said with her angel's smile, so completely at ease in her own mostly-naked skin. She'd always been like that with him, even their very first time. Eager and glowing. Adorably awkward. Open. Free. Not what he'd expected of Jack Wainwright's straight-A student, virgin daughter.

She spread her hands on his belly and slowly glided them upward. "I do believe this is an eight-pack you've got going on here."

"Hard work and clean living will do that to a man." Would he ever get enough of the feel of her touch?

Not a chance.

Those caressing hands glided up and over his shoulders. They met at his nape and kept going, her fingers sliding into his hair, massaging his scalp.

He had a feeling of stark unreality. That this was too perfect a moment to be true. "Am I dreaming?"

"If you are," she said low and achingly sweet, "so am I. We're dreaming this together and all I want is for us never to wake up."

He clasped her bare waist. "You're real."

"Oh, yes." She let her head drop back and closed her eyes. The feathery ends of her hair brushed his hands.

He slid his palms up over the cage of her ribs, bringing them around between them to cup both breasts, one in either hand. They were plump and so pretty, a little fuller than he remembered. She still had that tiny, heart-shaped mole over her left nipple.

No way he could resist bending to kiss that.

And then, well, he just went on kissing her, pressing his lips to the slope of her breast and then the beautiful swell on the underside. She let out a sweet, pleasured cry and pulled him closer, guiding him to where she wanted him.

His mouth closed on her tight nipple as her head fell back. She gave a low moan when he drew on her, using his teeth, circling with his tongue.

"Yes. Oh, please," she whispered as he moved to the other breast.

He still wore his jeans and his erection pressed almost painfully against his zipper, pulling even tighter as he went to his knees. Slowly, taking his time about it, he sank toward the rug, kissing his way between the delicate swells of her rib cage, down the velvety flesh of her belly. He paused to dip his tongue in her navel, bringing a sweet gasp from her.

Her lower belly was silky-smooth, with just that little bit of tempting roundness he remembered so well. He kissed the spot, his mind wandering briefly to the tiny, unformed baby that might have been sleeping there, once, long ago.

But that was the past.

Foolish to dwell on it.

Better to give himself up to right now, to the wonderful, womanly feel of her against his mouth, under his hands.

He scraped his teeth along her hip bones, and then,

bringing low moans from her, he took her panties in either hand and eased them down.

"Derek, oh, yes. That!" she cried, as he pressed his lips to the neatly trimmed strip of dark hair that led to the female heart of her. And then she sighed, "Oh, exactly *that*..."

And she didn't stop there. She added more tender, hungry encouragements as her fingers tunneled through his hair. She watched as he played her, as he drank in her sweetness, worked her with his tongue, using his fingers, too, both to stroke her and to hold her in place for his eager kiss.

When she broke wide open, he just went on kissing her, riding it out with her. He loved the sounds she made, the frantic, harsh rhythm of each ragged breath, the way her fingers dug into his scalp, yanking him closer as she pressed her core tighter to his never-ending kiss.

"Derek," she whispered. "Oh, Derek..." And she framed his face in her shaking hands and urged him to look up at her. For one glorious moment, he took in the sight of her, eyes dazed and shining, mouth softly parted, her hair on her shoulders, a few long curls veiling her pretty breasts.

"You are so beautiful, Amy."

With a yearning little cry, she urged him up.

He swept to his feet and she went on tiptoe to kiss him, laughing a little when she stumbled on her panties. They were tangled around one of her ankles. He dropped to the rug again, lifted her foot and removed both her sock and the twisted-up bit of satin and lace. She braced a hand on his shoulder as he slipped off her other sock.

Then she pulled him up again and got after the task of unhooking his belt and unzipping his jeans.

"Lie down." Hands spread on his chest, she pressed gently but insistently, until he let himself fall back across the mattress. It took her only a moment to pull off his jeans and get rid of his socks.

"Come here." He caught her hand and pulled her down next to him.

She landed at his side with a happy sigh, tucking her head into the crook of his shoulder, nuzzling his throat as her naughty hand strayed downward. When she touched him, he almost unraveled right there, with her hand barely brushing him. Even with his boxer briefs in the way, her touch thrilled and burned.

"Such a long time," she said softly, trailing her fingers back up his body to cradle his cheek.

"It's felt like forever," he agreed. He'd been so lonely without her, so empty inside. Should he admit that?

No.

A man had to have a little pride, after all.

"Forget everything," she whispered, her warm breath in his ear, the brush of her plump lower lip against his earlobe. "Let the world disappear. We'll stay here in bed and we'll never leave."

"I wish." But he couldn't quite make that promise. "Life...interrupts."

"Shh." She caught his earlobe between her teeth and gave it a tug. "For now, for tonight, pretend that it's possible. You and me, together in this comfy bed for all eternity."

As a fantasy, it rang all his bells. "Yes, Miss Wainwright."

She guided him to face her with the gentle pressure

of her palm against his cheek. "That's more like it." Their lips met, proving all over again that there was nothing in the wide world as good as her kiss.

He tasted her deeply, letting himself believe that he would never have to let her go, that the promise he'd made to himself—the two of them, working it out, getting it right this time—was bound to come true.

And when she took her lips from his to move down his body, he tried to hold her there, face-to-face with him, tried to kiss her some more. But she had other plans.

They were excellent plans, really. She got rid of his boxer briefs and took him in her hand.

And in her mouth.

It was so good. Too good.

He looked down his body at her head bobbing up and down on him, her hair caressing his belly, spilling like silk over his thighs. Bliss.

And if he didn't put a stop to this soon, he would lose it. He didn't want that. Not for their first time in all these years and years. For their first time, he needed to be joined with her, needed to feel her go over the edge again before his finish claimed him.

She made a sharp sound of disapproval as he took her under the arms and pulled her back up so they were face-to-face. Eyes low and lazy, mouth in a pout, she demanded, "What? I was busy."

"Too busy."

A slow grin tipped the corners of her red, swollen lips as she reached down and wrapped her hand around him all over again.

"Be good," he commanded.

She gave a snorty little laugh. "Oh, I am. You know I am. I am very, very, very good."

He felt for a condom, found it and reached down to capture that naughty hand of hers. "Here." He pressed the condom into her palm and folded her fingers over it.

"Well, all right, then." She brushed a kiss to his jaw. "Since you put it that way…" She got rid of the pouch and rolled the condom down over him, careful not to pinch or poke it, smoothing it nice and tight at the base.

Once that was accomplished, she met his eyes. "I've got an IUD," she said solemnly. "Double protection. We should be safe."

Safe.

Not really.

True, with a condom *and* an IUD, they had just about zero possibility of making a baby.

But there were so many other ways this was not safe—not safe at all. She'd cut his heart to pieces once. And this, now?

Talk about playing with fire.

So what? Some second chances a man just couldn't pass up. No matter how it all shook out in the end, he was in this with her now. All the way.

He had one arm around her and he used it to pull her closer, bringing his mouth a breath's distance from hers. "I'm just glad. You can't know how glad I am to be here with you like this."

She whispered his name again and then they were kissing, a deep and never-ending kiss. He rolled her under him and eased his thigh between her legs. She opened for him eagerly, lifting her body toward him as he sank into her.

Bracing on his hands, he lifted away enough to gaze down at her. She moaned in protest at the broken kiss. "Come back here."

In response, he pressed in deeper, but he didn't give her the kiss she demanded. He remained braced above her. "Amy."

She knew what he wanted. She opened her eyes.

"Real," he said on a harsh breath, staring down into her heavy-lidded eyes. Her pupils had blown wide with pleasure. They looked as dark as the middle of the night. Dark and deep and shining, promising all the things he'd stopped daring to dream of.

He wanted it all with her, wanted so much to believe that they could make it work together, at last.

But whatever happened in the end, right now, she was with him, her body soft and welcoming beneath him.

"Real," she agreed, surging against him.

The rest was a tangle of limbs and breath and seeking hands. He didn't know the things he said. She answered him in kind, pleading words, tender, too—and sometimes words of hot demand. They didn't really matter, the meaning in the words, the wildly whispered promises.

Only *she* mattered, her softness and her urgent sighs, her skin to his skin, her body holding him, owning him, taking him deep. Her scent like honey and citrus and roses and musk.

He held out against his climax, somehow, waiting for her, moving in her slowly, until she caught her ride to the finish, rocking faster when she needed a swifter, harder rhythm.

When she cried out, he stilled in her, pressing deep as her body pulsed so perfectly around him. Braced up on his hands again, he looked down at her. He watched her slow glide from the crest to afterglow.

Only then did he move again, propelling her into another rise.

That time, he went with her, to the top of the world and over. They rose together.

And together, they fell.

"I should go," she whispered.

He settled the covers more snugly around her. "It's two in the morning. Give it up. Spend the night."

"But Eva will—"

"Don't you even start worrying about Eva." He brushed the hair back from her forehead and dropped a kiss there. "She knows where you are and she's happy that you're here."

"Hmm," she said, which told him exactly nothing.

"Hmm, what?" He kissed her temple. She had so many good places for him to put his mouth.

She snuggled in closer. "Hmm, I think you might be right."

"You *know* I'm right." He kissed the side of her nose. "Now, go to sleep."

She yawned. "Do you provide breakfast?"

"Why? You hungry now?"

"No. I just wondered. I mean, you said it yourself. You used to be a guy who didn't stick around for breakfast."

"Used to be. Which means those days are over. Plus, if I don't stick around for breakfast, where would I go? This is my house."

She laughed. "Now you're confusing me."

"Let me make it crystal clear." He pressed his lips to hers. "Stay."

* * *

In the morning, Amy woke to the inviting smells of fresh coffee and frying bacon. The clock on the nightstand said it was a little after seven.

She shoved back the covers and pulled on her panties. Too bad her red dress, tossed in a wad across the bedside chair, was nothing but a bunch of wrinkles.

In the bathroom, she used the toilet and rinsed last night's mascara from under her eyes. There was toothpaste in the drawer by the sink. She used her finger as a toothbrush.

On the hook behind the door, she found a dark blue robe. It smelled like Derek's piney aftershave and was about three sizes too big.

Still. It was better than her wrinkled dress.

Derek, shirtless and barefoot in jeans that rode low on his narrow hips, was stirring scrambled eggs at the stove when she entered the kitchen from the central hallway. She had a few seconds to admire the gorgeous, hard curve of his shoulder and the sculpted muscles of his chest and belly before he glanced over and saw her.

His leaf-green gaze ran over her, stirring up sparks, hot little flares of sensation, reminders of all they'd done the night before. "You found my robe. It looks good on you."

She flapped the ends of the too-big arms at him. "Perfect fit." She shook her head. "Maybe I should have thought this through more carefully, though. I've got nothing but last night's rumpled red dress to wear back to Sunshine Farm. Talk about your classic walk of shame."

He turned off the fire under the eggs. "We'll figure something out." And then he was coming for her, his bare feet silent on the wide planks of the kitchen floor. He caught one of the sleeves she'd flapped at him and pulled her close. "Let's try this again. Say 'Good morning.'"

"Good morning." She gazed up at him, her heart aching in the best kind of way. To be here in his house, on a sunny Saturday morning, bacon and eggs and coffee waiting, his big hand brushing slow and lazy up and down her arm, thrilling her even through the thick terry cloth of his robe, his eyes for her alone. It was her own most impossible fantasy come true.

"Say, 'I had an amazing time last night, Derek. I can't wait to do it again.'"

"Yeah," she answered, thinking of his kisses, of how right it felt to be with him again, at last, in the most intimate way. "That's true. I can't wait."

He clasped the arm that he'd been stroking and pulled her in closer. His lips covered hers in a slow, perfect kiss. When he lifted his head, he turned for the stove again.

She stared after him, bemused. *Happy*, she thought. *Right in this moment, I'm as happy as I've ever been.*

"You hungry?" He picked up the pan full of eggs.

"Very." She glanced toward the breakfast nook. He'd already set the table.

"Pour yourself some coffee and let's eat."

Her phone, left on the central island the night before, rang as she was loading the dishwasher. Derek set down the plate of leftover bacon and got it for her.

It was still bleating out a ringtone when he handed it over. She looked at the display. "It's my mom." Stepping to the end of the counter, she put the phone back down and returned to her task. Derek hadn't moved. She probably should say something. "She'll leave a message."

"You don't want to talk to her." It wasn't a question. His gaze was locked on her face, reading her much too easily, the way he always had.

She opened the dishwasher, stuck in a plate and straightened. "All these years and they never told me that my dad went after you to convince you to call it off with me. I don't want to talk to either of them now. Not till I'm ready to brace them with the fact that I do not appreciate them keeping the truth from me— and don't even try to tell me that she might not know. Maybe she doesn't know. That's not the point. If I talk to her, I'm bringing it up and I'm not ready to get into it with either of them yet." As she grabbed the other plate, her phone buzzed from the end of the counter. She had a voice mail.

Derek stepped up close, gently took the plate from her and set it back in the sink. "Think about it. It wasn't a bad thing he did. He loved you and he wanted to make sure you had the best kind of start in life."

"He should have told me what he did—if not that very day, then later. He's had *years* to cop to it. And he's never said a word." She turned and picked up the plate again.

That time, he didn't stop her.

When they finished cleaning up the kitchen, he led her to the bedroom, where he found a Zac Brown Band T-shirt and an old pair of jeans for her. "The shirt's too big and you'll need to roll up the jeans," he warned as he handed them over.

"They'll be great, thanks."

He bent enough to brush a kiss across her lips. "I've got to meet up with Eli and a couple of my cousins in an hour. We need to move some cattle and burn out a ditch or two."

"Darn. I was kind of picturing us spending the whole day without a stitch on."

He rubbed the back of his neck, his expression rueful, the beautiful muscles of his arm flexing so temptingly as he moved. "Sometimes there's no upside to ranch life."

She went on tiptoe and kissed him again. "Tonight, then?"

He hooked his arm around her waist and brought her up hard and close. "Yes." The kiss he gave her then curled her toes and practically set her hair on fire. When he finally let her go, he asked, "How are we doing on the party supplies?"

"We've got everything we need, so at least the shopping part's done. But we still have signs to make and decorations and such to pull together before the big push next Saturday. We're talking several hours of crafting."

"Crafting." He faked a scared expression, all wide eyes and hanging mouth. "Now, there's a word to strike terror in the hearts of men everywhere."

"If you're not going to help me, I'll have to get Eva to pitch in."

It took him a moment to realize she meant that as a threat. "Wait. I get it. She's the bride and having the bride pitch in on the bachelor party would be wrong. Am I right?"

She reached up and patted his warm, beard-scruffy cheek. "Give that man a gold star. So I was thinking that a couple of hours an evening should do it."

He had that look men get when women sign them up for things they're just going to have to endure. "How many evenings?"

"Well, how about we start with tonight and see how it goes? I would bring the stuff we need and we can put it together here, if that works for you."

"Two hours of crafting? Here? Tonight?"

"I'll bring takeout," she coaxed.

He guided a swatch of her hair behind her ear and then skated the back of his finger down the bridge of her nose. "I've got some steaks. We're good for tonight."

"Steaks would be excellent."

He took her hand, pressed a key into her palm and folded her fingers over it. "Now you can come on in whether I'm here or not."

Was a key too much, too soon? "I don't know if I feel comfortable taking—"

He stopped her with a finger to her lips. "Between the saddlery and the ranch, I've always got something going on. If you get here before me one of these nights, I don't want you having to wait on the porch."

It was thoughtful of him, really. And to keep arguing would just be making a big deal of it. "Okay. Um, thanks, then. What time works for you tonight?"

"That's the thing. I could be back here at two or three—or it could be later."

"Six?" she suggested.

"That'll work for sure. And after the steaks and the crafting, you'll stay over?"

She kissed him again. "I thought you'd never ask."

Eva was lying in wait for her at Sunshine Farm. "Nice T-shirt. I never made you for a Zac Brown fan."

"I love the Zac Brown Band. 'Chicken Fried' is my favorite song—and aren't you supposed to be at Daisy's?" Eva worked at Daisy's Donuts, sometimes serving customers, but mostly producing an endless array of totally amazing baked goods.

"I've been cutting back my hours lately, what with the wedding and everything. Today, I'm off." She grabbed Amy's arm. "Come in the kitchen. We need to talk."

Amy tried to hang back. "I need to put my wrinkled dress away. And a shower would be so nice."

But Eva just took the red dress from her, plunked it on the entry table and kept on pulling her toward the other room. "This won't take long." About two seconds later, Eva had her sitting at the table with a full mug of coffee. "Jumbo caramel-banana-nut muffin?" She set a plateful of them on the table.

The nutty, caramel-banana scent was amazing. Amy took one. Who could resist? "Oh, Eva." She moaned in pleasure at the first bite. "They're still warm."

"Enjoy." Eva gave her a dessert plate and a fork, pulled out the chair beside her and plunked down into it. "And tell me *everything.*"

Amy sipped coffee and gobbled her muffin and explained the basics. "Derek and I are going to be spending some time together, that's all. Just for while I'm here. I mean, we have the party to plan and—"

Eva let out a musical trill of laughter. "Oh. Right. You spent all last night together working on the bachelor party. You must be exhausted."

Amy groaned. "Fine. We've kind of...reconnected."

Eva tipped her head to the side with a puzzled frown. "Reconnected. That sounds a little clinical, don't you think?"

"You don't like *reconnected*?"

"No, I do not."

"Well, all right, then. What should I call it?"

"Oh, let's see. How about *fated forever lovers re-united at last*?"

"Eva Rose, you are a hopeless romantic."

"And proud of it, too. Tell me more about this 're-connecting' you've been doing."

"Well, I mean, we're going to see where it takes us. Because we still get along."

Eva scrunched up her nose as though something smelled bad. "You 'get along'?"

"Yes, we do." Amy sipped her coffee and ate more of the delicious muffin.

"Ugh." Eva threw up both hands and plopped them back into her lap with a loud slapping sound. "That's it? That's all you're going to tell me?"

"Eva, I love you. But this is private, you know?"

"Private is fine," argued Eva. "I won't tell a soul. Come on. Please. You have to give me *something*. I'm your friend forever and I'm dying to know what's going on."

Amy relented—marginally, anyway. She did trust Eva and she hated disappointing her. "Well, I'm going back to his place for dinner tonight."

Eva's frown vanished. "Okay, I love the sound of that."

"We'll spend a couple of hours putting props and decorations together for the party. We'll be doing that pretty much every night this week—at least, until we finish the job."

"And of course, you'll be staying over at Derek's place afterward. I mean, it's just a bad idea for you to drive all the way back here when you're all worn out from making party decorations."

Amy blotted up delicious muffin crumbs with her fork and ate them. "Yes. That's right. I'll be staying over at his place. At least for tonight."

Eva put her hand on Amy's arm and gave it a squeeze. "I'm so grateful the two of you are working so hard on the party. It's going to be such fun, I just know it." She giggled.

Amy couldn't help it. She giggled right along with her. "I do, um, like him, Eva. I still do like him a lot."

"He's a good man," said Eva.

"He is, yes."

"I'm so glad you're giving it another chance with him."

Amy drew back a little. Eva would keep her confidence, absolutely. But still, she'd made such a big deal with Derek about keeping things just between the two of them. "Friends, Eva. Derek and I are friends."

"Of course, you are," agreed Eva. "And friends have sleepovers, now don't they? I'm seeing a lot of sleepovers at Derek's in your future and I am very, very happy about that."

Chapter Eight

Derek was waiting on his front porch when Amy arrived that evening.

He ran down the steps and pulled open her door. "I thought you'd never get here." His hair was still damp from a shower, his cheeks freshly shaven. He was and always had been the best-looking guy she'd ever known.

She reminded him, "We said six. I'm right on time."

He didn't argue, just grabbed her hand and pulled her out from behind the wheel. Right there by the car, he wrapped his arms around her and kissed her until her head spun, after which he bent to slide one arm under her legs and scoop her up against his chest.

She let out a laughing cry. "Derek!"

"Let's go inside."

Still laughing, she hooked one arm around his neck and pointed through the back window of her Audi.

"I've got my overnight case and all the party stuff we need to bring in."

"Later for that." And he kissed her again—kissed her and went on kissing her as he carried her up the steps and into the house. He kicked the door shut with his boot and took her straight to his bedroom, where they remained for the next two hours.

At a little after eight, they put their clothes back on and went out to unload the car. They brought everything in and then got dinner ready.

It was after nine when they finally started working on the signs for the casino and the scavenger hunt. When those were done, they wrapped party-favor prizes. Midnight had come and gone by the time they carted their finished work into Derek's spare room, where it would remain until the day of the party.

"Tomorrow, we'll figure out all the questions for The Nearly Newlywed Game," she said as they left the room. "We need twenty for Eva about Luke and twenty for him about her." He pulled the door shut behind them and took her hand. "They need to be funny questions, kind of hard, but not *too* hard…" He wrapped their joined hands behind his back, which brought her right up tight against him, and gave new meaning to the word *hard*. All the breath left her body and a thousand fluttery creatures took flight in her belly.

"No more party talk tonight," he growled as he nuzzled her ear.

"Poor baby." She went on tiptoe to feather a line of kisses down the side of his throat. "You must be exhausted."

"Yeah. We should go to bed."

She had zero objections to that suggestion. He kept

a firm grip on her hand as he turned for the open door
to the master suite.

Once inside, he started peeling off her clothes.

"You know, Derek. Suddenly, you don't seem the
least bit tired."

And then he kissed her and she forgot everything
but the glory of his touch.

Sunday morning after breakfast, they came up with
The Nearly Newlywed Game questions for Eva and
Luke.

As they made sandwiches for lunch, Amy got a text
from Eva. "She wants us to come to dinner at the farm
tonight. Six o'clock."

"I'm in."

Amy texted back that they would be there and returned to slicing tomatoes for turkey-on-rye.

But Derek took the knife from her and turned her to
face him. "I want every minute I can have with you."

She wasn't sure what he was getting at. "Didn't we
already agree to that?"

"We did, but tonight when it's time to come home
and whoever else Eva invited notices you're going with
me, don't chicken out on me and suddenly decide you
might as well just stay at Luke and Eva's. I want you
with me."

Her heart kind of melted. "No, I won't back out.
When it's time to go, I'll follow you home."

He brushed his warm lips against hers. "That's what
I needed to hear."

The evening was a lot of fun. It was just the four of
them and Bailey, who was thoroughly charming when

he chose to be. They had Eva's amazing roast chicken with herbed potatoes and a chocolate trifle for dessert.

Eva and Luke were so cute, exchanging random quick kisses, holding hands every chance they got, sitting extra close to each other on the couch, two people truly together and deeply in love.

Watching them, Amy felt just a little bit wistful. To be in love like that, to be half of a private world inhabited by two—she and Derek had been like that once. No other guy had ever made her feel the way he had, that she was the only one he'd ever wanted, the only one for him.

Which was why she needed to be careful with him, not let herself get too carried away. Now and then, she would catch herself about to reach out and touch him, wanting to lean close and whisper something tender in his ear.

But she didn't. Throughout the evening, she and Derek kept to their agreement. They played it friends-only, with zero PDAs.

Amy had brought the two lists of Nearly Newly-wed Game questions. She gave one to Luke and one to Eva. "We'll need these back tomorrow, if possible, so we can get going on making a proper display for this game. There will be two sets of boards, one set without the answers, so everyone can read your questions and guess the answers, then another set to put out when we announce the winners. Those will have your answers on them. I'm putting you two on the honor system," she warned. "I want your word you won't share your questions with each other or cheat on the answers."

"Don't be scared, you two," Derek advised with a

grin. "It's just that Amy takes her party planning seriously."

As if there was anything wrong with that. "Yes, I do," she said, "and I'm proud of it, too."

Eva put up a hand like a witness swearing an oath. "I do solemnly promise to answer all my questions myself and not to help Luke with his no matter how hard he begs me."

"Excellent." Amy turned her gaze on Eva's fiancé. "Luke?"

He put up *both* hands. "Okay, okay. I promise, too."

Bailey grumbled, "I gotta say it. Amy, when it comes to this party, you're definitely scaring *me*."

She pinned Luke's brother with a severe frown. "Don't you start in, Bailey Stockton. Party planning is a tough job and you are one of the groomsmen, which means you really ought to be helping Derek and me pull this thing together."

Bailey, who'd taken the leftover seat at one end of the sofa, bent at the waist and thunked his head against the coffee table. "Anything but that."

Everybody laughed as Eva got up to get the coffeepot in case anyone wanted one more cup.

When it was time to go, Amy slipped away to run up to her room and grab a change of clothes for tomorrow. She and Derek thanked Eva for the great meal and headed for the door.

"Good night, Luke," Amy said. "Bailey…" She turned to give Bailey a smile.

He glanced from her to Derek and back again. He didn't say anything, but he didn't have to. The speculative look on his face said it all.

Which was fine.

To be expected.

People were going to notice that they were together. And they'd agreed on how to deal with that: no PDAs and continued denial till after the wedding.

And then?

She'd been thinking about that. A lot. And she really did hope that after the wedding they could talk honestly about the future, about ways that maybe they might really try again.

But as for now, Amy did love a good plan and so far, this one seemed to be working just great.

She was having the time of her life with her secret ex-husband and every hour that passed had her feeling more certain that this time, they would get it right.

It was going so well.

What could possibly go wrong?

Monday morning, Derek woke next to Amy.

He rolled over and gathered her close, spoon fashion. "Derek…" He could hear her sleepy smile in her voice. She snuggled right in with a happy little sigh and drifted back to sleep.

In a few minutes, he had to get up. It was his turn to open at the saddlery and he needed to be there by eight.

But a few minutes went by and a few more after that, and he lay there in bed with Amy in his arms, her hair a shining, red-brown tangle across the white pillow, her breathing shallow and slow.

What was it about her? He couldn't really put his finger on it. She was bossy, strong-minded and really smart. Maybe too smart for a small-town cowboy like him. She made him laugh. She made him think—about what he wanted and how to get it.

She made everything better, somehow.

No other girl had ever compared.

He was beginning to face the truth that if he didn't have Amy, well, he probably wouldn't have anyone. Not in the way that really mattered, the forever way, the way Collin had Willa, the way Luke had Eva.

All these years, he'd been telling himself he was slowly getting over her, that at some point, it would happen. He'd look in the bathroom mirror one morning and see a man who didn't love Amy Wainwright anymore.

But now, here she was, back in town. And miracle of miracles, back in his bed.

And all he could think about was how he was going to keep her here, his own bossy little angel, sleeping beside him for the rest of their lives.

Collin's crew cab was already parked in front of the saddlery when Derek got there at 8:10.

"You're early," Derek said when he found his partner sitting at the table in the break room, a full mug of coffee in front of him.

Collin pointed at the chair across from him. "I was hoping we might have a chance to talk before the kid comes in."

Derek brewed himself a cup, though he'd already had two back at the house. He was stalling, putting off the inevitable just a little bit longer.

But it only took so long to brew a pod of coffee. He set the mug on the table and dropped into the chair. "Okay. Got a problem with my work or something?"

Collin barked out a dry laugh. "You wish." He aimed a brooding look at his full cup, but didn't pick it up. "So. Amy Wainwright?"

"Saying her name with a question mark after it doesn't count as an actual question, Collin."

"She's a nice girl. I always liked her. I got nothing against her."

"Yeah? So, then what's this about?"

Collin tipped his head thoughtfully—and then went on as though Derek hadn't spoken. "Her father was kind of a douche nozzle, though. Snotty rich guy. Had to get back to the land, or some such, but always kept himself above the rest of us."

"Jack Wainwright wasn't so bad."

Collin scoffed, "Really? You're going to defend him?"

Derek rubbed the bridge of his nose between his thumb and forefinger. "Whatever it is you're trying to say here, you need to just come out with it."

Collin did sip his coffee then. "We never talked about that night of the bonfire, the night you got wasted and told me all your secrets." Collin stared across the table at him, dark gaze unwavering. "Don't worry. I never said a word to anyone about any of it and I damn well never will."

Derek's gut kind of felt like a big boot had kicked it. "I always wondered how much I told you."

"You said that you and Amy thought she was pregnant and so you'd gotten married, but then it turned out she wasn't pregnant. You said that the original plan was for Amy to go off to college and since there was no baby after all, it was back to the plan. She was moving to Colorado to go to school and you expected you'd be getting divorce papers in the mail. You said that you loved her and you always would, but you hated her, too, for walking out on you."

Derek swore. "I had no right to say that she walked out on me. I told her to go."

"But you didn't think she'd really leave you, did you? You thought she'd fight to keep your marriage together."

"I'll say it again. I told her to go."

"You were wrecked over her. That girl ruined you. I didn't understand then, how deep she'd cut you. But now I have Willa. If Willa ever did something like that to me, I don't rightly know if I would ever recover." Collin fell silent. He stared into the middle distance.

Derek almost dared to hope his friend had said all he meant to say.

No such luck.

"Guys like you and me, we go from girl to girl. And people judge us. They think we haven't got deep feelings. But could be it's the opposite. Maybe our feelings run too damn deep and if we ever give in and give a woman everything, and she turns around and leaves us..." Collin let that thought finish itself. He asked, "You sure you want to go tempting fate all over again?" Derek just looked at him. Collin didn't need an answer anyway. He already understood. "I know. I do. She's the one for you and at this point, while it's good between you, before it gets down to where the rubber hits the road, you can't walk away. But you need to remember how good you are at leaving. You need to remind yourself what a natural talent you have for letting go. It's what you know how to do. Don't let your bad habits rule you. Don't fold before the game's even over. Step up and just say it. This time, when you're ready to run, tell the woman straight out that you love her and you want her to stay."

* * *

After Derek left for the saddlery that morning, Amy went back to Sunshine Farm. She had work to catch up on and spent most of the day at her computer.

When she went downstairs to make a sandwich at noon, Eva joined her in the kitchen.

"Here are both your questionnaires." Eva handed them over. "They're all filled out and ready to go— and don't give me that look. Luke gave me his to give to you, but I have not even glanced at it."

"Good." Amy took them.

Eva let out a wry little laugh. "Bailey may have had a point last night. The good Lord have mercy on anyone who messes with your plans."

"Nothing wrong with careful planning. Just watch. This party is going to be amazing."

"I know it will be—and I keep forgetting to tell you that Friday night, after you left the Ace, Viv asked me if you needed help with anything."

"Not a thing. We're so on it. And I have kept in touch with her. Just this morning, I texted her a suggested playlist for the band." In her back pocket, Amy's phone rang. It was the ringtone she'd assigned to her dad and she ignored it, letting it ring until it stopped. She answered Eva's questioning glance with, "It's my dad. I'll call him back later. Right now, I need lunch."

"How about a roast chicken sandwich with mayo, walnuts and cranberry sauce?"

"I thought you'd never ask."

That evening after a beautiful hour in bed together, Derek said that he and Collin had talked. "Turns out, I did tell him pretty much everything that night I got so drunk." He put a finger under her chin and tipped her face up so she was looking at him. "I'm sorry I broke my promise not to tell anyone."

She lifted up higher—enough to press a reassuring kiss on those fine lips of his. "Well, when I left, I kind of gave up my right to ask for your silence. You were on your own and I'm really not upset that you told him. I think it was good that you had someone to talk to. And Collin clearly knows how to keep a confidence. I mean, *you* didn't even know he knew."

He chuckled, a rueful sound. "True."

"Did he…warn you off me?" Should she even ask him that? Probably not. But she really wanted to know.

Derek's silence lasted just a moment too long. "He was just being a friend, you know? Showing his support."

She got the message. Derek had said all he wanted to say. Pushing him to reveal more wouldn't be right. She left it at that, tucking her head in under his chin as he pulled the covers up closer around them.

Amy spent that night and the next and the next after that at Derek's.

Their nobody's-business, one-day-at-a-time relationship was working out so well. She spent four or five hours a day at Sunshine Farm, being with Eva and keeping on top of her work with Hurdly and Main.

In the early evening, she would meet Derek at his house. They would have dinner and put in some work on the party, after which they would watch a movie or play video games—sometimes not finishing either and having glorious sex instead. Eventually, they would go to bed, where yet more gloriousness ensued.

Every moment with him was better than the moment before and she never wanted it to end.

Which they would have to talk about.

Eventually.

But at this point, they were living firmly in the now and she wouldn't have it any other way.

Wednesday night, they finished the party prep. There was literally nothing more to do until setup on Saturday.

Thursday, they met at his place at two in the afternoon. They tacked up a couple of horses and rode out across Circle D land to a private spot on Rust Creek, a bend in the stream where the water ran slow and deep.

They hobbled the horses. And in the shade of a river birch, they spread a blanket and stripped down to their birthday suits. The water was cold and they laughed and splashed each other, chasing each other back and forth across the slow-moving stream. He dunked her twice and she managed to shove him under once, just to prove that she could.

They ended up on the blanket, making love in the dappled shade of the tree. Afterward, they put their clothes back on and lay side by side, holding hands, staring up through the wind-ruffled cottonwood leaves at the wide blue sky.

She had so much to tell him, all the secrets of her heart, the longing in her soul. She needed him to know how much she had missed him all the years they'd been apart, needed to confess that she couldn't help dreaming of a possible future with him.

Too bad she had no idea how to even start saying all that she yearned to say.

She rolled her head toward him. He was already

watching her. She drank in the sight of him, his square, beard-scruffy jaw, his eyes, green as shamrocks right now, the perfect, sexy dent in the center of his chin. "I never want to leave you. I want to stay here forever, Derek, just you and me."

He gave her that smile, the one that made her heart stop and her belly hollow out. "Right here under this tree?"

Should she go for it, go all the way right here and now? Was it too early?

How did people do this? Start over. Really begin. She hardly knew how. She'd done it so badly the last time. She hadn't been brave enough.

Hadn't been true enough.

And now she had another chance—or at least, she hoped that was what this might be. She didn't want to blow it. She didn't want to push too fast.

Or miss the moment when it was finally upon her.

Would she mess it up this time, too, and lose him all over again?

Her heart knocked against her rib cage and her pulse raced.

He used the hand that wasn't holding hers, reaching across his broad chest to brush a slow, wonderfully rough finger along the line of her jaw. "You all right?"

Not yet! screeched a terrified voice in her head. *Don't say anything yet! Get a grip. It's way too soon. You'll ruin everything.*

"Yeah." Her heart rate slowed and she dared to breathe again as she chose the easy way out. "I was thinking we could make a little shelter here, a hut of sticks and pine branches."

He lifted their joined hands and pressed his lips to

her knuckles, one by one. Gladness filled her so full, she felt she might burst apart. She said, "It could get mighty cold when winter comes."

"Well then, we'd have to get under the blanket and hold each other really tight." To demonstrate, he rolled toward her, reaching for her, gathering her close, sheltering her in the strength of his arms.

I love you, Derek. I always have. You are the only man for me. It sounded so good inside her head. So good and so true.

And she *would* say it. Just not now, not so soon.

Later. When the time was right.

Friday, Eva's sisters were due to arrive: Delphine, her husband, Harrison, and their three boys from Billings; and Calla, her husband, Patrick, and their two kids from Thunder Canyon.

Amy planned to spend the day at the Armstrong house in town. It would be so good, to get some quality time not only with Delphine and Calla and their families, but also with Marion and Ray Armstrong, who'd been like a second mother and father to her while she was growing up.

She saw Derek off at his house early that morning when he went out to cut alfalfa with Eli and his cousins, and she promised to meet him back there after the big family dinner at Ray and Marion's.

"It might be late," she warned him. "Delphine and Calla and I have a lot of catching up to do."

"I don't care if it's the middle of the night when they finally let you out of there. We agreed every night for as long as you're here, remember?"

Had they agreed on that? She wasn't really sure.

But whether they had or they hadn't, she wanted every night she could get with him. "Well, all right then. I'll be here. Leave the porch light on."

He kissed her, a long, deep one. And then she stood in the yard, waving and grinning like a lovestruck fool as he started up his truck and headed off down the dirt ranch road toward the main house and the barn.

Eva was already at the two-story Armstrong family home in town when Amy arrived at nine. Delphine and Calla and their families had set out long before dawn. Of the two older sisters, Delphine got there first at a little after eleven. Calla and her crew arrived just before noon.

They all shared lunch out in the backyard. It was just like old times, except with even more of them, now that Calla's and Delphine's husbands and active youngsters had been added to the mix. Amy could almost grow wistful with her friends' children all around. At ten years old, Calla's daughter, Fiona, was becoming such a young lady. And Delphine's oldest, Tommy, was already nine. Amy marveled at how fast they were all growing up.

And she couldn't help feeling a little bit sad. If she and Derek had stayed together, they would have recently celebrated thirteen years of marriage. Their might-have-been baby would be twelve now, the oldest of the children in the Armstrong backyard.

Luke showed up at a little after five. He came in the door and Eva ran to greet him. Amy felt a sharp, painful tug on her heartstrings that Derek couldn't somehow be there, too. Eva and her sisters had all found love. Amy was the only single adult in the bunch today.

They all looked so happy, with their lives, their loves, their families.

What would they say if they knew she'd been married before any of them?

Married and divorced before she was even nineteen.

Nobody was going to congratulate her for that.

As they gathered around the big dining room table to sit down for dinner, there was a knock at the door.

Luke said, "That's Derek. I'll get it."

Amy's heart leapt—and she didn't miss the sly grin that Eva tried to hide.

Yep. No doubt about it. Her lifelong BFF was matchmaking like crazy.

And at this point, all Amy felt about that was love and gratitude.

When he returned to the room, Luke said, "You all remember Derek, my best man."

Derek's hair was still damp from his shower and he looked so hot and handsome in a green-and-black plaid snap-front shirt and dress jeans.

Delphine and Calla both jumped up to give him a quick hug of greeting. Introductions were made to the husbands and kids—reintroductions really. Derek, it turned out, had met both Delphine's and Calla's husbands over the years and more than one of the kids.

"Have a seat, everyone," said Marion.

Eva piped up with, "Derek, there's a free chair next to Amy."

Derek came right over, pulled out Amy's chair for her and then sat down beside her. She leaned toward the man who owned her nights—at least until the wedding—and greeted him teasingly, "Derek. So nice to see you again."

"Yeah." His gaze held hers and a delicious little

shiver skittered down her spine and tickled the backs of her knees. "We need to get together more often."

She didn't look away. "I think that can be arranged. How come you didn't tell me you were coming for dinner?"

"Because I didn't know I was coming until Luke called this afternoon and invited me."

Amy slid another glance at Eva, who was still watching them, still trying to hide her self-satisfied grin. "Did you have to skip Friday happy hour at the Ace?" Amy teased the man beside her.

"To tell you the truth, I wasn't planning on dropping by there anyway. Hanging out at the local bar kind of loses its appeal when you have someone special right there at home." His gaze held hers and sheer joy shimmered through her.

Marion beamed down the length of the table at Ray. "Honey, please say the blessing. Everyone, join hands."

Amy offered one hand to Harrison. Derek took the other, his grip warm and firm. Ray said grace, amens echoed around the table and then everyone was talking at once, passing overflowing bowls and piled-high serving platters, dishing up the food.

Derek's hand brushed Amy's again, this time where it rested in her lap. She sent him a soft smile, turned her palm up and linked her fingers with his. Just long enough to share their own private moment with no one the wiser.

He had to pull away to serve himself a giant spoonful from the heaping bowl of mashed potatoes, but the warmth of his touch still lingered, soothing the old hurt for all the time they might have had together if things could have been different somehow.

* * *

Amy and Derek left the Armstrong house at half past eight. She followed him back to the Circle D.

They were barely in the door before he tossed his hat on the small entry table and grabbed her close.

His kiss…

Nothing compared to it.

She melted against him, her heart full of longing, her whole body burning, sparks of awareness popping and flashing all through her, her belly hollowing out, every inch of her skin on fire for him.

And then her phone rang.

She tried to ignore it, but Derek took her by the shoulders and pulled his thrilling, hot mouth from hers.

"Come back here." She slid her fingers up into his hair and fisted them, surging up to claim those lips again.

But he just held on to her arms and stared in her eyes as the ringtone finally went silent. "That was your dad, am I right?"

She yanked the phone from the back pocket of her favorite jeans and dropped it on the narrow table next to Derek's discarded hat. "My dad can wait. I'll call him later." The voice-mail alert chimed and she pretended not to hear it. "Now…" She slid her hands up over the crisp fabric of his shirt, enjoying the muscled strength in the hard flesh beneath. "Where were we?"

He just continued to stare down at her. "You ever call your mom back?"

Talk about a mood-killer. "I don't want to get into this." She dropped her hands and turned away.

But she didn't get far because he pulled her back.

"You need to at least let them know that you're fine and you'll be in touch when you're ready."

"I don't need to do any such thing." She yanked free of his hold. "I'm thirty-one years old. It's up to me when and how I reach out to my parents." She turned on her heel and headed toward the great room.

"Thirty-one, huh?" He spoke to her retreating back. "Well, you're acting like a spoiled brat."

She whirled on him. "I don't want to talk to them right now."

He put up both hands. "Then don't talk to them. But let them know you're safe and well."

"Why are you worried about them? They've never been anything but mean to you."

He was trying not to grin. She could see the slight quiver at the corner of that sexy mouth of his. "They weren't *that* mean."

She let out a little growl of frustration. "I'm so mad at my dad for never telling me that he went after you that day, that he got you alone and worked on you. If he'd just stayed out of it—"

"What?" He raked his hands back through his beautiful, messy hair. "I mean, think about it. Yeah, he made it clear what he wanted and how he knew that what he wanted was right. But *we* made the decision, the two of us, you and me. You wanted to go—and I told you to go."

"But he didn't tell me what he did. For thirteen years, he didn't tell me. And he knew I was coming to town for the wedding, knew that I would be here for a whole month and that I would more than likely run into you. And *still* he didn't tell me what I had a right to know. That's what I'm so angry about."

Derek picked up the phone and held it out to her. "A text. One sentence. 'I'm fine. Don't worry. I'll call you when I'm ready to talk.'"

"Actually..." she said, wrinkling her nose at him, "that's *three* sentences."

"Oh, come on, Amy. Can't you do that much for the poor guy who thinks the sun rises and sets on his little girl, and who's probably worried sick that you're dead in a ditch somewhere? Can't you just put his mind at ease?"

She wrapped her arms around her middle and fumed at him for a good fifteen seconds, feeling brattier and more mean-spirited as each second ticked by.

"Please," he said so very gently, melting her heart to a puddle of goo.

"Oh, all right." She marched back to him, grabbed the phone from his hand and typed out the exact three sentences he had suggested. "There." She held up the phone so he could read it for himself. "Satisfied?"

"Send it."

She hit the icon, closed the window and set the phone back down by his hat. "Now, I want you to make mad, passionate love to me, please. Do not make me hang around to see what he sends back."

"Deal." He took her hand, lifted it to his mouth and pressed his lips to the back of it. "God. You are so beautiful. All evening, at the Armstrongs', I kept thinking how I'm the guy who gets to bring you home."

Her pulse fluttered madly and her tummy got those butterflies—but she sulked anyway, as a matter of principle. "Flatter me all you want, but you kind of ruined the hot, sexy mood. You know that, right? You're going to have to make a serious effort to seduce me now, so stop fooling around and get to work."

He guided their joined hands around behind his back, pulling her up nice and close. He felt so warm and big and solid. And he smelled of leather and soap and that outdoorsy aftershave he favored. They had tonight and then one more week of nights. This impossible, wonderful time they'd agreed to be together was racing by much too fast.

"Just give me a chance," he teased.

"A chance for what?"

"To kiss it and make it all better." His rough, husky tone sent tendrils of heat curling down her spine.

She went on tiptoe, caught his earlobe between her teeth and gave it a tug, loving the low, needful sound he made in response. "Okay, you're forgiven. And yes, please, I would love it if you would kiss it and make it all better."

Her phone lit up, wrecking her mood all over again.

She glared up at him. "Don't ask me to check that."

"I wouldn't dare." He dropped a quick kiss on the end of her nose.

She unlaced their fingers and stepped back from him. Muttering a few choice words, she took the phone and brought up the text from her dad.

All right, then. Thanks for letting us know you're okay. Your mother and I send love.

She flashed the phone at Derek. "Happy now?" He just looked at her, all manly and tender, everything she'd ever wanted and lost somehow during the turbulent summer of her eighteenth year. "Grrr," she said, trying to drum up the outrage that kept draining away because he was so thoughtful and wonderful and good. "Ugh." And then she turned the phone back around and punched out, Love you, too, reading the words aloud in a singsong as she typed them. "And..." She hit the little envelope icon. "Sent and done." And then she grabbed his hand and pulled him down the central hall, detouring to the right when she reached the open doorway that led to his bedroom.

Feeling like the luckiest man alive, Derek smoothed Amy's hair back and pressed a kiss to the flawless skin of her forehead. "You realize we have to be up by five at the latest." It was after midnight. They'd used two condoms and were discussing the wisdom of using a third. "We need to get some sleep."

"Yeah, I know." Her sigh was resigned. "Tomorrow's going to be a very busy day."

They still had to load his pickup and her Audi with the party stuff stored in his spare room. Bailey would bring everything that was still in the barn at Sunshine Farm. Everyone in the wedding party was on board to help— except the bride and the groom, who would have pitched in gladly if Amy would only allow that. Several other friends and family members had volunteered, as well.

They would all converge on Maverick Manor at 6:00 a.m. sharp. With everybody pitching in, Amy predicted they would have the setup complete by early afternoon.

She snuggled in closer to him, all gorgeous curves and velvet skin. He could hardly believe his good fortune, to have thirteen years' worth of dreams come true right here in his bed—for the next seven days, anyway.

Her breath brushed his neck and then her soft lips, too. She made a throaty, sexy little sound and traced his collarbone with a soft, lazy finger. "You feel so good. I love just touching you. Always. And forever. And even longer than that…"

Then stay with me. Never leave.

God. He wanted to say it.

But they'd only been together for a week. He needed to wait—at least until after the wedding. Then, one way or another, before she left for Boulder, he would ask her to consider a future for the two of them, ask her if maybe she might be willing to stay.

"Sleep." He settled her in closer and nuzzled her hair. It was everywhere, a net of silk, trailing over his shoulder, pooling against his bare chest, catching in his beard scruff that came in too fast no matter how often he shaved.

I love you…

For a moment, he was certain he'd said it aloud and he didn't know whether to be glad that the words were out of his mouth after more than a decade of not being able to say them—or terrified that she might not take him seriously.

That could happen. He had to be ready for it. She could so easily say something gentle and regretful, about how they couldn't go there. How this was just a fling for as long as she was in town, how they both needed to accept this beautiful time together for what it was and not ruin a good thing.

Glad or terrified…

He didn't know which to be.

And he needed to stop obsessing about it. He wasn't going to say a thing about love and the future to her, anyway.

Not for another week yet, at least.

Chapter Nine

"This party is perfect," Viv Shuster announced.

Amy beamed with pride. Things were going so well.

It was ten o'clock on Saturday night and the Jack and Jill bachelor party was in full swing. The guests, who added up to just about every adult in town and a lot of friends and family from other parts of the state and beyond, filled the public rooms of the gorgeous log cabin resort.

The last time Amy checked, every table in the casino room had been full. And in the giant, high-ceilinged lobby, the band played an upbeat Brad Paisley song and a lot of people were dancing, most of them wearing the straw cowboy hats offered at the door, hats decorated with a band of hearts and *Eva & Luke* written in glitter on a bigger heart where the crown met the brim. The Nearly Newlywed Game was a hit. Everyone seemed to be stepping up to bet on Luke and Eva's answers, dropping a buck in a giant pickle jar for each entry. The winner would go home with the pickle jar of dollar bills and a really nice bottle of champagne.

"To you and Derek, Amy." Viv raised her champagne flute high. "Just a completely amazing job."

"Thank you." Amy tapped her flute to Viv's. "I mean, you're the expert, so a high five from you is especially appreciated." And then she gave credit where it was due. "We had a lot of help. And the worksheets and suggestions you gave us definitely got us off to a great start."

Derek, every cowgirl's dream in dress jeans, fancy boots and a snow-white shirt, appeared out of the crowd and grabbed her hand. "Dance with me."

With a quick wave to Viv, she followed where he led her, to the windows that looked out on the Manor grounds. The wide square of open space there had been designated as the dance floor for the night.

They two-stepped and they line danced and during the slow ones, they held each other close. Amy could dance with him all night long.

But when the second slow song ended, she pulled away regretfully. "We should check on the games and make the rounds of the casino room."

"I'll take the casino," he said, and kissed her. Yes, it was breaking their no PDAs rule. So what? She kissed him back and didn't give a damn who saw. It was a bachelor party, after all, and the whole point was to break a few rules.

He headed for the casino and she wandered the other rooms, checking that the champagne station still had plenty of bubbly and the water table remained well stocked. She straightened the display at The Nearly Newlywed Game table.

And she entered the bar area just in time to see Brenna O'Reilly Dalton jump up onto her husband, Travis's, back. With a loud, "Wahoo!" Brenna wrapped her arms and legs around him. Amy laughed at the sight as Brenna tossed the bartender her phone so he could snap a picture of Travis running in a circle giving his wife a piggyback ride. It was one of the challenges in the Jack and Jill Scavenger Hunt. When the bartender returned her phone, Brenna passed it to Travis, who caught the shot as she kissed the bartender's cheek—another scavenger hunt challenge met.

Amy applauded, along with everyone nearby. Travis and Brenna were not only perfect together, they were both enthusiastic competitors. No wonder they'd stolen viewers' hearts on *The Great Roundup* reality TV show last year.

There was a tap on her shoulder. "Amy."

She turned to the bride-to-be, who looked absolutely gorgeous in a bright pink halter dress. "Eva! Love that dress. Having a good time?"

"Best. Time. Ever. And I have someone I've been wanting you to meet." Eva slipped her arm around the shoulders of a pretty dark-haired woman in a floral print maternity dress. "This is Mikayla Brown. She just arrived from Wyoming today and she'll be living with us at the farm for as long as we can convince her to stay."

Mikayla smiled, but her big, dark eyes remained watchful and serious. "Hi." She added kind of wearily, "Great party."

Eva's smooth brow crinkled. "Maybe I shouldn't have pushed you to come. Is it too much for you?"

"Of course not." Mikayla patted Eva's hand where it rested on her shoulder. "I feel fine and it's nice to get out and mix it up a little."

Dana Stockton, who'd arrived from Oregon two days ago, waved from down at the end of the bar where she sat with Bailey. "Eva! We need you!"

"Coming!" Eva turned to Mikayla. "That's Dana, Luke's youngest sister. I'll introduce you."

Mikayla put up a hand. "I'll meet her later. Go ahead and see what's up. I'm fine, really."

"You sure?"

"Positive."

Amy said, "Stick with me, Mikayla, I'll introduce you around—not that I know everyone, but I'm working on it."

"Terrific." Mikayla made shooing motions at Eva. "Go."

Eva took off to find out what Dana wanted and Amy offered, "Let's get you something cold to drink."

They each got a ginger ale and then wandered the party together. Amy kept an eye on the various events and refreshment tables, and made sure Mikayla met plenty of the locals, including Derek's brothers, Eli and Jonah. Eli introduced them to a bunch of Dalton cousins. Zach, Garrett, Shawn, Booker and Cole Dalton, Viv's fiancé, were the sons of Derek's uncle Phil. They all had thick dark hair and killer blue eyes.

Amy kidded, "You guys have my head spinning. There's a Dalton everywhere I turn."

Booker said, "And there are more on the way. Our Uncle Neal Dalton is moving to town along with his boys Morgan, Holt and Boone." He leaned close to Amy and stage-whispered, "Take my word on this, Amy. You gotta watch your back around Uncle Neal's boys."

"Come on, Booker," said Eli, frowning. "They're not *that* bad."

Booker scoffed. "They're bad enough," he muttered. "But you're right. I should shut up and go find another beer."

Amy took Mikayla's arm. "Let's see how it's going in the casino."

The casino room, done up like a saloon in an old Western movie, was wall-to-wall with guests shooting craps, playing poker and rummy, baccarat and black-jack.

Derek had gotten stuck filling in as croupier at the roulette table. He called out "Place your bets!" and then spun the wheel, which Amy had picked up for practi-cally nothing on eBay. After he paid the winners, he glanced over and gave Amy a wink, causing her pulse to speed up and her heart to do the happy dance. All the Dalton boys were handsome, but Derek really was the best-looking of all of them. Everyone said so, and everyone was right.

"Let me guess," said Mikayla. "That's your guy."

"Oh, yes, he is." And then she remembered the agreement they'd made. "Correction." She couldn't help giggling. "We're just friends."

"Oh, yeah. And if you think I believe that, I've got a uranium mine I can sell you." The golden light from the wagon wheel chandelier overhead put tired shad-ows under Mikayla's big dark eyes.

Amy took her arm. "Come on. Let's go someplace more comfortable where we can sit down for a while."

They went outside and found an unoccupied bench waiting for them under the star-filled Montana sky.

Mikayla set her empty glass on the ground beside her and sat back with a little sigh. "It's nice out here."

"Yeah. Just right." The evening was warm, with a hint of a breeze. "So, you're from Wyoming, Eva said?"

"Cheyenne, specifically." Mikayla stared off down the twisting path that led deeper into the resort grounds. "Luke and my cousin Brent are longtime friends. Before Luke came back here to Montana, he and Brent both had jobs on the same big spread not far from Cheyenne. As for me, the past few years, I've been working at a day care. My job ended several weeks ago and I...needed a change of scenery, I guess you could say. Brent called Luke. Luke said I should come stay at Sunshine Farm. So here I am, with the room next to yours, according to Eva. Till the baby's born, anyway. Maybe longer. I really can't say."

"Knowing Eva and Luke, they'll be glad to have you for as long as you want to stay. They're the best."

"Yes, they are." Mikayla folded her hands on the mound of her belly.

For a few minutes, they were quiet together, a companionable sort of silence. Amy could hear the sounds of the party from back inside the Manor, the band playing a ballad, people laughing and chatting.

Then Mikayla said softly, "You might have guessed that I'm on my own with this." Her dark head was tipped down and she stroked her stomach as though soothing the little one within. "The father...well, I kind of made a bad choice with him. Long story short, he cheated. I wanted more than a guy who couldn't even be true to me. I wanted love. *Real* love. The kind that curls your toes and fills your heart and lasts till the day after the end of forever."

Amy thought of Derek, of their not-quite-baby, of how much he'd wanted to marry her, of the love and hope in his beautiful green eyes when he'd dropped to his knees and begged her to be his wife. Even though it all spiraled into heartbreak later, she'd been so lucky with him—*was* so lucky with him.

Whatever happened between them now, she would always know that Derek Dalton, the first love she'd never really gotten over, was a hero in the truest sense of the word.

She said, "Good riddance on the cheater."

"Thank you," Mikayla replied dryly. "I couldn't agree more."

"And you won't be on your own for long, believe me. Everybody will tell you that Rust Creek Falls is the place to come if you're looking for the love of your life."

Mikayla let out a husky laugh. "Well, I *was* looking and it didn't go well. Now it's me and my baby and you know what? That's just fine with me."

Amy glanced toward the Manor. As though her yearning heart had conjured him, Derek emerged. Every molecule in her body lit up at the sight of him. She waved. He saw her and came toward them.

Mikayla said, "Here comes that 'friend' of yours. Go on, now. Dance and have fun."

Amy held out her hand. "Come with us."

But Mikayla shook her head. "Uh-uh. Go. Dance. And have a glass of bubbly for me."

Amy did dance. And not only with Derek. She danced with Bella's multimillionaire husband, Hudson

Jones, and his equally rich brothers: Walker—who was married to Derek's cousin, Lindsay—and Gideon and Jensen who were visiting from out of town. She danced with the Strickland boys, L.J., Trey, Benjamin and Billy, who lived in Thunder Canyon. She also danced with their brother Drew Strickland, an obstetrician. Rumor had it that Drew might soon be moving to Rust Creek Falls.

She even danced with Collin Traub as his wife, Willa, danced with Derek. Collin was friendly and kind. He said what a great job she and Derek had done on the party and not so much as a word about what he knew of the past.

Much later, after two in the morning when the party was slowly winding down, when her poor feet were aching from hours of dancing, Amy took off her high-heeled sandals and ran barefoot with Derek along the twisting paths on the Maverick Manor grounds.

"Wait," he said, his boots going still. "Listen."

She paused in midstep—and she heard it, too. Slow and sweet in the distance, back in the Manor, the band was playing, "Hey, Pretty Girl."

Derek reeled her in and pulled her close. "I believe this dance is mine."

She gazed up into his eyes. They gleamed in the darkness, endlessly deep. "Yes, this dance is yours, Derek. All yours."

And he whirled her around under the moon in a pool of starlight. It was pure magic. Her tired feet had never felt so light, as though she was floating right off the ground.

At four thirty in the morning, when the last guest finally left the party, Amy changed into the jeans, T-shirt and trusty high-tops she'd brought along to wear for the cleanup.

She and Derek and Luke's brothers stayed on to help the staff break everything down. Nate Crawford and his partners in the resort would be keeping all the props and decorations. Amy and Derek were happy to give the Manor every last poster, banner and baggie of wedding ring confetti. They had no use for any of it and the Manor had been beyond generous, letting them use the venue for nearly nothing. The owners planned to host a lot of parties in the future. Decorations and party props and a ready-to-assemble saloon-themed casino would be bound to come in handy.

As the sun peeked over the crests of the mountains and lit up the morning sky, she followed Derek back to the Circle D. All night, she'd been looking forward to getting him alone. Every dance they'd shared had reminded her of how precious this time was—*their* time, together again at last. She couldn't wait to unzip his jeans, pull off his fancy boots and unbutton that snowy white shirt.

When they finally got to his place, it was eight in the morning. They'd both been awake since 5:00 a.m. the day before. She turned off the engine of her Audi and then just sat there in the driver's seat, staring blankly out the windshield.

The sun was fully above the mountains now, the sky so clear and pure and blue. About fifty yards away, a couple of horses had ambled up to the fence that ran along the dirt road leading off toward the main house. They shook their manes, snorting and whinnying and then wheeled and took off back the way they had come.

Such a beautiful place.—Rust Creek Falls, the mountains all around, the wide, rolling valley. She'd stayed away much too long. Being back felt so good. It felt like coming home.

She heard the pickup door open and close and then boots crunching gravel.

Derek leaned in her open window. "You're dead on your feet."

A laugh bubbled up and she corrected him, "I'm dead on my butt is what I am."

He pulled open her door. "Come here, pretty girl."

She fell sideways out the door, still laughing. He caught her—and suddenly, her throat was tight, her vision blurred with tears. She wrapped her arms around his neck as he scooped her high against his chest. "Oh, Derek. We killed it, didn't we? It was a great party."

"The best ever," he answered solemnly. She tipped her head back enough to see his eyes under the brim of his hat. His brow furrowed. "You're crying. What'd I do?"

She snuggled her head under his chin, her hair catching on his beard scruff the way it always did. "This is happy crying," she explained, causing him to mutter something about women and all the ways a man could never understand them. She pressed her hand against his shirt, right over his heart. "Honestly, I am happy. So very happy—and I waited all night to get this shirt off you."

His lips touched her hair. "Let's go inside and you can get busy on that."

She reached out and pushed her door shut. He turned for the steps leading up to the porch.

Inside, he carried her straight to the bedroom.

When he set her down, she fell back across the bed,

arms outstretched. "Gonna close my eyes, just for a minute…"

"Yeah." She heard the warm humor in his voice as he untied her shoes. "You do that, Miss Wainwright."

"I believe I will, thank you very much." She let her heavy eyelids drift shut and thought about all the naughty things she would do to him. Sexy things. Delicious things.

It was going to be so much fun…

When she woke, she was alone in the bed wearing only her lacy panties and bra from the night before. The nightstand clock said 4:00 p.m.

"Derek?"

No answer. And the house felt strangely silent.

She saw the note sticking out from under the clock.

Gone to round up some stray cattle. My mom called. She says we're going to dinner at main house. Just casual. Be back for you by six at the latest.

Back when she and Derek were high school sweethearts, Amy had been to more than one Sunday dinner at Charles and Rita Dalton's house. She remembered the rambling, two-story ranch house. In those days, Sunday dinners were crowded, every chair taken.

But all of Derek's brothers and sisters were married now and none of them had come to Sunday dinner this particular evening. It was just Derek, Amy, Rita and Charles.

Derek's parents seemed happy to see her. They asked about her life in Boulder and her work for Hurdly and Main. Charles seemed pretty interested in how she tracked financial fraudsters on the internet. Rita listened politely, but her eyes got that glassy look, the one most people ended up wearing when she tried to explain about stopping data breaches and the lengths some tech-savvy crooks would go to steal what didn't belong to them.

Rita plied her with roast beef, broccoli and cheesy potatoes and asked, "Have you been to the saddlery?"

"Yes. Derek gave me a tour."

"Isn't he talented?"

"Mom," Derek groaned. "Don't."

Rita gave him her sweetest smile. "Well, I'm your mother. I'm allowed to be impressed with you."

"His work is beautiful," Amy said, and meant it.

"He's an artist," Rita declared with pride. "He gets commissions, did you know that? From people in Europe, from all over the world. And they pay a *lot*."

"Mom." Derek pinned his mother with a flinty stare. "Stop. I gave Amy a tour of the shop and I told her all about it."

Charles chuckled and Rita ate a bite of tender beef.

"So, Amy," Rita said when she'd finished chewing and swallowing. "It's wonderful to have you back in town, to hear that you've been spending time with Derek again. I always thought that the two of you—"

"Mom," Derek said for the third time, the single syllable freighted with warning.

Rita widened her eyes, all innocence. "What I meant to say was, I hope we're going to be seeing a lot of you."

"Well, I'll be here until the wedding, that's for sure."

"And after that?"

Amy couldn't stop her glance from sliding to Derek.

For a moment, their gazes locked. She dared to think he wanted her to stay, that when they finally really talked about it after the wedding, they would be discussing how to blend their two lives into one. "I...ahem. I guess you never know what will happen, do you?"

Rita arched an eyebrow. "You're a cagey one, Amy Wainwright."

"Leave her alone, Mom," Derek said.

Rita sighed. "It's a thankless job, being a mother. Your children grow up and they won't tell you anything."

Charles reached over and put his hand on his wife's. "Be patient, my love."

Rita leaned his way and kissed him. "All right, then." She smoothed her napkin on her lap and picked up her fork again. "Don't mind me, Amy. I'm just glad to have you here again at last."

The next week just plain didn't have enough hours in it. It felt like a whirlwind, with the wedding coming up and all the Armstrongs in town.

Monday, Eva and her bridesmaids drove into Kalispell for their final fittings. It was Amy, Eva, Delphine and Calla, plus Luke's sisters, Bella and Dana, and his sisters-in-law, Fallon and Annie. They took over the wedding boutique and shared champagne and snacks as they tried on their dresses for the big day.

They snapped selfies like mad. The full-length gowns were gorgeous, each one in a different color and style. They'd all brought the cowboy boots they would be wearing on the big day. At first, Eva had wanted them in dressy nude pumps, but the boots were a better choice for a barn wedding, especially with the ceremony itself being held outside on uneven scrub grass.

When Eva tried on her dress, all the happy laughter and chatter stopped. She emerged from the dressing room and everybody sighed. Her sleeveless gown had a fitted bodice and a full skirt of ruffled tulle, and it was perfect with her teal-blue, white-tooled cowboy boots.

"You are a vision," Calla said reverently at last. They all burst into enthusiastic applause and more than a few tears.

The next day, Amy went with Eva to check in with Viv. The lists of things still to do before the wedding went on and on.

"Don't forget to break in those pretty cowboy boots," Viv advised. "Get plenty of sleep. Practice your vows out loud. Keep on top of your email just in case someone has something important they have to tell you about their part in the wedding. Pack your honeymoon bags well ahead and check them the next day to make sure you haven't forgotten anything. Confirm that Derek has his toast prepared, and your dad. As for the cake—"

Eva cut her off. "I have the cake completely under control."

"I just worry it's too much for you. You're the *bride*."

Eva stood taller. "Yes, I am. The bride who happens to be a baker by profession. I've always dreamed of baking my own wedding cake and that is exactly what I'm doing."

Viv had the good sense not to argue the point further. She turned to Amy. "How about your toast?"

"I'm on it," Amy promised, her fingers crossed behind her back.

That night, she and Derek worked together on the toasts. She helped him write his and he gave her a few great pointers on hers. And then they went to bed and stayed awake too late, making love, whispering together, laughing a lot. At one in the morning, they got up and raided the freezer. They ate cappuccino-chunky-chocolate ice cream straight from the carton and then went back to bed and made love again.

Suddenly, it was Wednesday.

Before accompanying Eva to a final check-in with the caterer, Amy had a long Skype meeting with her supervisor and his boss at Hurdly and Main. It took some convincing, but they finally agreed that it didn't matter whether she worked from her home in Boulder or in Montana. They said they would want her at the Boulder office for a few days a month, minimum, and to remain available several times a year to give expert testimony when certain cases she'd developed ended up in court.

She signed off the Skype call knowing she could make her job work long-distance and she couldn't wait to get with Derek and talk it over.

But then she started thinking how that would be jumping the gun a little. After the wedding, that was the time to discuss whatever might happen next. They would talk then about their desires and intentions for the future. That would be the time to tell him she could telecommute, the time to prove how much she wanted to be with him by showing him how she was prepared to make that happen.

Thursday, during the two hours she spent at Sunshine Farm supposedly working, she picked up her phone out of the blue and called her father.

"Jelly Bean, I'm so happy to hear your voice."

Jelly Bean. The silly nickname made her tear up a little. She could hear his love for her in the way he said it and right now, she didn't want to feel his love. She wanted to yell at him for the things he'd done thirteen years ago—the things he'd done and never copped to. "Hey, Dad."

"Still in Rust Creek Falls?"

"That's right."

"Having a good time?"

She had no idea where to even start with him. So, she came right out with it. "Dad, I'm in love with Derek Dalton and I always have been and I'm going to give it my whole heart this time around. I'm not positive how it will work out yet, but my plan is to move back here and make a life with him." *That is, if he wants a life with me.*

The silence was deafening. "I see," Jack Wainwright said at last. "What about your job?"

"I've handled that. I work mostly from home anyway. It's not going to be a big deal. And Dad, I'm telling you this because I want you to know how I feel and how I hope things will work out. Don't you dare approach Derek behind my back."

For a long count of five, her father said nothing. Then, at last, he answered quietly, "I won't."

"Promise?"

"I do." There was another endless silence, after which he shocked the hell out of her by saying, "Your mother and I had a feeling this might happen, that with a month back in Montana, you and Derek would…reconnect. I expected this. And I'm glad. Your mother will be, too."

A silly sputtering sound escaped her. She stammered, "Wh-what did you just say?"

"I said I'm glad and I meant it. I know you really loved that boy."

"*Love*, Dad. Present tense."

"All right. *Love* him, then. I know you love him and over the years, I've regretted my role in tearing you two apart. I've realized we could have found a better way, a way for you to get the education you deserved and still be with the boy you love."

Tears clogged her throat and burned her eyes—and that made her furious. "I've talked to Derek about that summer. He finally admitted that you came to find him at the Circle D, that you begged him to let me go."

Her dad said simply, "That's true."

"Why didn't you even have the integrity to tell me what you did?"

"It's hard to explain…"

"Try me," she insisted through clenched teeth.

"Well, at first, I thought the main thing was to get you away from him and Rust Creek Falls, to get you back to focusing on your education, on your new life in Boulder. But then, over time, I felt guilty. I knew that at the very least, you did have a right to know that I had convinced your boyfriend—"

"Husband, Dad. Derek was my husband." *And the father of the child I never had.* She considered just saying it, confessing that last sad little truth right out loud.

But her dad didn't need to know, not really. And bringing up the baby now would only confuse the issue at hand.

"Yes," said her dad. "Derek was your husband. I know. And I promise you, Amy, at the time I thought I was doing the right thing for you."

"Well, it *wasn't* right."

"I see that now. But it seemed right at the time. And later, over time, I saw the sadness in you. I saw that what you felt for Derek really did run deep. And somehow, I just never could find the words to tell you what I'd done. Then every year I didn't tell you, it only got harder to decide how to come out with it, how to admit to you that I'd convinced Derek that if he really loved you, the only choice was to let you go."

If he really loved me... All her anger just leached away. She felt only sadness, for what was lost, what might have been. "So. I guess he really did love me, huh?"

"Yes, sweetheart. I believe he really did—and still does, from what you're telling me now."

Oh, she did hope so.

"Maybe in time you'll come to forgive me," her father said.

Of course, she would forgive him. But some stubborn part of her refused to make it too easy for him. "I'm not happy with you about this."

"I understand."

"But, Dad, I do love you. Mom, too."

"And we love you. So much. We just want you to be happy, that's all. Please tell Derek I look forward to seeing him again, to having a chance to apologize in person for the wrong I did him thirteen years ago."

"I'll tell him."

They said goodbye, after which she sat staring

blankly at her computer monitor, longing to tell Derek everything her dad had just said.

And she *would* tell him, once the wedding was over and it was finally time to talk about the rest of their lives.

Chapter Ten

Friday afternoon, the wedding party gathered and did the walk-through outside under the clear, sunny sky, in front of the big, wide-open doors of the yellow barn. That evening, Bella and Hudson hosted the rehearsal dinner at their house.

Amy and Derek didn't get back to his place until after midnight. They were so close now to the end of their friends-with-secret-benefits agreement. After tomorrow, it would happen at last. They would talk about the future, decide what came next for them.

If anything, she thought and shivered a little. But that was just fatalism rearing its ugly head.

She wasn't going to be negative. Uh-uh. Because she definitely believed they did have a future, she and Derek. She wanted it so much. And she was almost positive that he wanted it, too.

She longed to get going on it, get her dreams for the future out in the open. But really, the best thing at this point, she decided, was to stick with the plan, to get through the wedding tomorrow, to enjoy the party afterward.

And then, over breakfast Sunday morning, she would do it. She would tell him that she loved him, that she'd realized now she'd never stopped. She would say she wanted another chance with him. She wanted to stay here in Rust Creek Falls with him and get busy on the rest of their lives.

"You're really quiet," he said, holding her close after they'd climbed into bed.

She wavered. Why not just tell him everything right now?

But in the end, she chickened out. "I keep going over my toast in my head. I hope I get it right."

"It's a great little speech," he soothed, stroking her hair.

"Little is right. Because short is always best." *And I love you and I want it to work out for us this time. At last. Oh, Derek. I want that so bad...*

"It's gonna be fine," he promised, catching a random curl and wrapping it around his finger.

She lifted her chin and captured his gaze. "You sure?"

"No doubt." His eyes were bottle-green in the light of the bedside lamp, and beneath the covers, she felt him stirring, growing hard against her bare hip. He said her name, "Amy," like a promise. Or a plea. His wonderful mouth dipped down and claimed hers.

She kissed him back with all the love and yearning in her heart.

It was going to work out this time.

It *had* to work out.

There was no other possibility but happiness for them now. After all these long years apart, they deserved to share a future together. And Sunday morning, over coffee and pancakes, they would start planning the rest of their lives.

At three o'clock the next afternoon, beneath the blue Montana sky, the groomsmen and the groom took their places at the makeshift altar in front of the yellow barn. The six-piece band launched into the traditional wedding march and the bridesmaids, in a rainbow of bright dresses, took their walk down the aisle. They carried bouquets of sunflowers and lavender phlox. As the maid of honor, Amy came last.

When she took her place with the other bridesmaids, three cherubs appeared—Jamie Stockton's two-and-a-half-year-old triplets, Jared, Henry and Kate. Kate came first in a ruffled blush-pink dress, tiny cowboy boots on her feet. She scattered petals as she went. Jared and Henry, the ring bearers, were right behind her, perfect little cowboys in jeans, boots, blue shirts, tan vests and hats to match. The three made it almost to the bridal party assembled at the end of the aisle.

But a few feet from their destination, something caught Henry's eye. "Horsie!" he cried, veering off at the end of the white carpet and racing toward a gray gelding standing at the pasture fence twenty yards away. A murmur of laughter rose from the guest.

Fallon, the triplets' stepmother, moved fast. She caught little Henry before he made good his escape. Jamie corralled Jared, just in case he got ideas from his brother. Kate never wavered. She took her place with the rest of the wedding party, head high, her angelic face composed.

Then the music changed, and a lone guitarist played Pachelbel's *Canon in D*. More than one pair of eyes brimmed with tears as Eva, a vision in white except for the teal-blue toes of her cowboy boots peeking out beneath her skirt, her bright hair covered in a filmy veil, emerged from the bride's tent set up a few yards from the foot of the white carpet. She carried sunflowers, purple phlox, white roses and yellow snapdragons.

Not far from the tent, Ray Armstrong waited. He offered Eva his arm and whispered something to her. She murmured a reply. Even through her veil, her pretty face seemed to glow.

Ray walked his youngest daughter down the aisle, stepping aside at last to leave her facing her groom. A sigh went up from the rows of white chairs as Luke turned back her veil.

Their eyes only for each other, they said their vows and exchanged their rings. Then, as Luke kissed his bride, Amy's gaze strayed to Derek. He was already watching her. They shared a secret smile.

Tomorrow. The word echoed in her head.

Tomorrow would be their day, hers and Derek's. She couldn't wait to tell him everything, to open her heart to him, to claim again what they'd lost all those years ago.

For the wedding dinner and reception, Viv Shuster had worked a miracle in the old barn, with twinkle lights and long plank tables. She'd hung gorgeous old crystal chandeliers from the overhead beams and created a bower effect with yards of filmy white fabric draped from the rafters. There were flowers in mason jars everywhere.

It really was perfect, Amy thought. Eva had never looked so radiant, so gloriously happy.

As for Derek, he was sweet and attentive. But as the afternoon became early evening, he seemed to grow distracted—distant, even. As though something was preying on his mind.

Derek couldn't quite put his finger on what was bugging him. A lot of things, really. Amy had been too quiet the last couple of days. He wasn't sure what was going on with her, but it kind of made him nervous.

He had hopes, he really did, for a future with her. And he'd made a secret trip to Kalispell two days before because this time, he intended to offer something a whole lot better than an imitation diamond when he made his big move. But maybe he'd jumped the gun.

Maybe she was only thinking that it was almost time for her to go.

Or maybe it was this perfect country wedding messing with his head. It was like a dream, with Luke and Eva so happy, their whole lives ahead of them and nothing standing in their way. And it reminded him too painfully of how different his own wedding day had been, of him and Amy at the courthouse with strangers for witnesses, of the forty-dollar wedding ring and the tired-looking bunch of daisies she'd clutched in her hand as they vowed to love and care for each other as long as they both should live.

This wedding brought all the old hurts to fresh life again, reminding him how much he'd loved her and how wrong it all went, how little he'd had to offer her then.

His plan was to speak of the future with her tomorrow, to tell her he still loved her and always would. How was that going to go? He couldn't be sure what she'd say when he asked her to be his again in front of the world—forever this time, no matter what.

He tried to take heart from the tender looks she gave him, but playing the "just friends" game was really getting to him. He hated it now. He wanted to shout to the world that she was his. That they were together.

At dinner, it was open seating for everyone but the bride and groom, who sat at a smaller table up on a dais. Derek and Amy sat together. He rested his arm across the back of her chair and she didn't remind him that he was pushing the boundaries of their friends-only act.

Instead, she leaned close to him and whispered how handsome he looked in his jeans and dress boots, his blue shirt and tan vest. She even straightened his white rose boutonniere, the way a woman does for her special guy.

He was feeling pretty good about everything, gaining confidence about how it would go between them tomorrow when he asked her for forever.

But then Brandi Foster, who lived in Kalispell but sometimes spent her Friday nights at the Ace, pulled out a chair across the table from them. "Derek! How have you been?" She raised her mason jar of wedding punch. "Been a while, huh?"

Yes, it had. About five years, if he wasn't mistaken. They'd hooked up at the Ace one Friday or Saturday night back when he was spending too much time meeting women in bars. She'd given him her number before he left her place. He'd never gotten around to calling her back.

"Hi, Brandi," he said, going through the motions, being polite. "I'm doing well. How 'bout you?"

"Can't complain." She kind of scowled as she said it. Her gaze shifted to Amy. "If it isn't the maid of honor. I'm Brandi." She offered her hand across the table.

Amy took it and gave it a quick shake.

Brandi had a million questions for Amy. Did she live in town? Oh, well, then, if she didn't, where *did* she live and when was she going back? How did she know Eva? And no kidding, she went to high school in Rust Creek Falls and graduated the same year as Derek? "So, you were schoolmates, you two."

"Yes, we were." Amy leaned a little closer to him and sent him a fond smile. The warmth in those golden-green eyes eased the knot of tension gathering in the center of his chest. Amy didn't seem all that bothered to be fielding endless questions from a woman she didn't know.

But then Brandi snickered and drank more punch. The tension in Derek's chest fisted tight again. Brandi seemed a little buzzed. He wondered if eccentric old Homer Gilmore, famous for spiking the punch at weddings with his dangerously powerful moonshine, might be up to his old tricks again. Brandi craned across the table and stage-whispered to Amy, "Well, if you went to school with Derek, I guess I don't have to warn you about him."

Amy only shrugged. "Of course not. I'm sure I know him a lot better than you do."

Brandi tossed her blond head. "Oh, you think so, huh?"

"I *know* so."

Brandi grabbed her empty mason jar and swept to her feet. "Just don't expect a phone call afterward, if you know what I'm saying. I need more punch." She turned and flounced away without giving Amy a chance to say anything more.

Amy sent him a sideways look. "I get the impression that Brandi is not very happy with you."

Feeling like a first-class jerk, he eased his arm off the back of her chair. "Yeah. Well, she's right. I never did call her."

"How long ago was this?"

"Five years or so."

She leaned in and nudged his shoulder with hers. "Come on. Don't beat yourself up. It was a long time ago and everybody just needs to move on."

God, she was amazing, the way she took the awkward, ugly encounter in stride. He dipped his head to hers and whispered, "Thanks."

She caught his hand under the table. "Hey. It's okay." She wove their fingers together, her eyes steady on his, letting him know that Brandi hadn't bothered her in the least.

It helped, her kind words, her soft hand in his. But not enough, really.

Brandi was living proof of what a dog he'd once been and that made him feel…less. Cheap. Like he wasn't quite good enough, somehow.

He really needed to buck up. Take Amy's advice and shake it the hell off.

Dinner was served. And then it was time for the toasts. Derek thought his went over well enough.

Amy's was so sweet and funny. She had great stories about Eva as a little girl who followed Calla, Delphine and

Amy around the Armstrong backyard, asking a thousand questions: *How do you know when you're in love? Does a girl need a good job before she gets married? I know you're all bigger than me and teenagers and everything— but still, can we please play My Little Pony and can I be Princess Twilight Sparkle?*

After the toasts and dinner, there was dancing at one end of the barn. People lingered at the tables or wandered around outside, where the white folding chairs and rows of hay bales provided plenty of seating. The sun sank below the mountains and the outside party lights came on, endless strings of them, looped between the exterior walls of the barn and the nearby trees.

Derek and Amy stayed together. They danced and they visited with friends and family. He was having a great time and had almost forgotten the depressing encounter with Brandi.

But then, after dark, as they sat together on a hay bale under the loops of lights, a guy he didn't know wandered over.

"Hey. You're Amy, right?" He offered his hand to her and they shook. "And…?" He turned to Derek.

Derek stood. "Derek Dalton."

The guy shook his hand, too. But his attention remained on Amy. "I'm Joe Armstrong, Eva's cousin. Uncle Ray's my dad's brother."

Amy got up, too. "Marion has talked about you."

Joe grinned. "All good stuff, right?"

"Absolutely. She said you live in Denver."

Joe was a good-looking guy if you liked the executive type. He wore a pricey suit and tie—and cowboy boots. It was a barn wedding, after all. A guy never knew what he might step in. "I'm an attorney," he said, "with Bartles, Downey and Smart. Ray said you live in Boulder."

"For the past several years, yes."

"We should get together." Joe whipped out a phone bigger than Amy's. "Give me your number or an email." Derek wanted to punch the fool. "Or wait. Are you on LinkedIn?"

Amy started to say something. But before she got an actual word out, Derek took a step forward. "Back off." The warning was out before he let himself think twice about how rude he sounded or what Joe-freaking-Armstrong might think.

Joe almost dropped his enormous phone. "Hey. Whoa, there." He actually put up both hands like Derek had a gun on him. "No offense, man. Seriously."

Derek knew himself to be a jealous fool. He stuck his hands in his pockets to keep them from grabbing good old Joe by the throat. "Sorry. That was out of line."

"Derek?" Amy sounded worried.

Joe muttered something in a neutral tone.

But Derek didn't hear it. He needed a serious time-out—like go sit in a corner with his face to the wall. Spinning on his heel, he walked away.

"Derek!" She was coming after him.

He felt like crap and just wanted to go. But no way could he leave her like that, calling his name, trying to catch up with him. He stopped and waited under the night-shadowed branches of a hackberry tree.

She ducked in there beneath the leaves with him. "Derek? Are you okay?"

He had so much to say to her and no idea where to start.

Not that this was the time or the place for it.

The least he could do was apologize. "I…look, I really am sorry. I'm an ass and I don't know what the hell's the matter with me."

Cautiously, moving with slow care, like someone soothing a spooked horse, she brushed her palm along his arm. Her touch soothed him. He got a hint of her perfume and relaxed a little more.

When he didn't pull away, she stepped in close. "We, um, have a lot to talk about. Maybe we should—"

"Not now." He just wasn't ready. And what if she said no? Through the darkness her eyes gleamed so bright. "I'm sorry, I really am. I don't know what I was thinking to jump on that guy like that."

Her pretty white teeth flashed with her smile. "Well, Ray's nephew seems a little pushy. But I think he's harmless, really."

"I got jealous." There. He'd admitted it, even though it made him look like even more of an ass.

"Don't be. I've got no interest in getting anything going with Ray's nephew. You're the only one I'm looking at."

"Even when I act like an idiot?"

"You're not an idiot. No way." Her gaze didn't waver. "You're the best man I know."

"Well, I *am* the best man," he teased lamely and tugged on a loose curl of her pinned-up hair. "You're kind. A good woman."

"It's only the truth." She caught his fingers, brought them to her lips and pressed a kiss into his palm.

He could have stayed there under that tree with her

forever, just looking into her big eyes, feeling her velvety cheek against his hand. But the evening wasn't over yet. "We should go back. They haven't even cut the cake."

"You sure you're okay?"

He traced the curve of her ear, ran the back of his finger down the side of her throat—and for no logical reason, out of nowhere, the hard things Collin had said that morning at the saddlery filled his mind.

Guys like you and me, we go from girl to girl. And people judge us. They think we haven't got deep feelings. But could be it's the opposite. Maybe our feelings run too damn deep...

You were wrecked over her. That girl ruined you. I didn't understand then, how deep she'd cut you...

Back in the barn, the band was playing "Lost in This Moment," that Big & Rich song about getting married. Would he ever get there again with the only woman for him?

Yesterday, he'd believed he would. But somehow, tonight, with Luke and Eva's happiness reminding him of how it all went wrong before, with tomorrow coming on too fast, he just didn't know anymore.

"Derek?" There was worry in her eyes again.

"I'm good," he lied. "Never better."

They went back to the party. They danced some more. They hung out with Derek's brothers and sisters and their wives and husbands.

Eva and Luke eventually got down to cutting the gorgeous cake that Eva had insisted on baking herself. It was enormous, that cake, a tower of white frosting and twining frosting flowers, with a cowgirl bride and her cowboy groom perched on top. Inside, the cake it-self was yellow swirled with bright ribbons of rasp-berry filling.

Amy and Derek sat inside at one of the tables to shovel it in.

Bailey strolled up with a giant slice of his own. He took the place across from Amy. "You two." He smirked at them. "Worst kept secret in Rust Creek Falls." He pointed with his fork at Amy, then at Derek. "I can't believe it's really happened. I never thought it would. But it looks to me like Derek Dalton has fi-nally met his match."

Derek slid a glance at Amy. She was grinning. He looked back at Bailey and played his part, deadpan. "No idea what you're talkin' about, man."

"Oh, give me a break." Bailey stuck a big bite of cake in his mouth, chewed it and swallowed before continuing, "You two are together and you're fooling nobody."

Amy laughed. "Are you kidding?" And then, cool as the middle of a long winter's night, she said, "No, we are not together, no way."

The hair on the back of Derek's neck stood up. *She's dumping you tomorrow, fool*, said a flat voice inside his head. *She's just playing her part, playing the friend game.*

What was he, blind? It was all right there in front of him and he needed to open his damn eyes and look at the truth: *her laugh, that cold way she'd said that we aren't together...*

Derek knew then with absolute certainty that he'd read this situation all wrong, that he'd been thinking forever but she wasn't thinking about anything but right now and she never had been.

She'd been honest with him from the first. *Friends with secret benefits.* That was what they were.

It was *all* that they were.

And what about Joe Armstrong? The more he thought about the way she'd acted when Ray's nephew put the move on her, the more he thought that just maybe she was kind of interested in that guy.

Yeah, she'd run after him when he took off like some little boy with a big crush who couldn't handle his own damn feelings. But that was because she had a kind heart. In a situation like that, she would have run to offer comfort to anyone.

Bottom line: she was just waiting for the damn wedding to be over so she could get back to Boulder and her real life.

What did he have to offer a girl like her? A little house on the family ranch, an ordinary life in the small town she'd left behind years ago.

Past and present were all mixed up together, suddenly. He'd had this dream of a certain girl and now was the part where the dream turned to a nightmare. It had hurt so bad to lose her last time.

And now it was about to happen all over again.

The evening wore on, the party lights twinkling, the band playing one corny love song after another, everyone laughing and chattering, just happy to be there as Eva and Luke claimed a lifetime together.

"You're quiet," she said, same as he'd said last night. They were dancing to Jason Aldean's "Staring at the Sun" and he wished from the bottom of his soul that the damn band could play something that wasn't about loving a woman forever.

He didn't answer her, just pulled her closer and leaned his cheek against her soft, sweet-smelling hair and wished that the end wasn't coming on so damn fast.

"Derek, I have so much I want to—"

"Shh," he whispered. He kissed the tender indentation just below her temple and pulled her closer still. "Just dance with me. Just dance…"

She made the sweetest, softest little sound and rested her head on his shoulder. They danced on.

At midnight, Eva climbed up to the hayloft to throw her bouquet. All the single women—and more than a few girls nowhere near old enough to get married—gathered beneath the hayloft doors, each one eager to make the catch.

Derek stood with the men, watching the age-old ritual, listening to Bailey grouse about ridiculous traditions.

"Wait!" Amy called from the middle of the tight knot of women.

Above, Eva laughed. "What now?"

"Where's Mikayla? I don't see Mikayla!"

Eva held her bouquet high. "Go get her, Amy. I'll wait. She's not missing this chance."

Amy wriggled free of the jostling crowd of eager females. "Mikayla!" she hollered.

The very pregnant little brunette stepped reluctantly forward. "This is just silly."

But Amy only grabbed her hand and dragged her into the middle of the crowd of women and girls. "Ready!" she shouted to Eva when she had Mikayla where she wanted her.

Derek looked up to the loft and saw Eva turn around as though to throw the flowers blind. But at the last second, she whirled front again and threw them straight for Amy's outstretched hands.

With a whoop of triumph, Amy seemed to catch them—but then everyone was laughing and shouting. The knot of women loosened and he saw it.

There was Mikayla in the center of the circle with the flowers clutched tightly in her hands.

Yeah, okay, Derek knew it was only an old superstition. No woman really got married next just because she ended up with the flowers that had been the bride's.

But still, women fought to make that catch. Amy hadn't. Instead, she'd made sure that Mikayla got lucky.

Because Amy had no intention of getting married to anyone anytime soon.

A half an hour later, Eva and Luke drove away from the barn in a horse-drawn cart covered in flowers. Viv Shuster had passed out bubble wands and plastic jars of soap and water, along with paper cones of dried lavender for everyone to blow and throw as the bride and groom rode away.

They weren't really going anywhere. The flower-covered cart only disappeared around the far side of the farmhouse. Eva and Luke would spend their wedding night in their own bed and leave for their honeymoon on Monday.

The party continued. There was more dancing and horsing around. Derek kept up his front pretty well, he thought. He and Amy hung out and joined in the fun.

Around two, as things were kind of winding down,

Amy leaned in close. "Let me grab a few things from the house and I'll follow you to the ranch."

One more night.

He really wanted that.

But if he got it, he just knew he'd make a damn fool of himself in the morning. When she told him she was leaving, he would beg her to stay. Bad enough she was going. No reason to embarrass himself when she left.

"Listen," he said.

She gazed up at him through those innocent eyes. "Yeah?"

"Not here."

"Um. Okay…"

He grabbed her hand and started walking away from the party, out of the glow of the strings of lights, out of sight of the remaining guests.

"Derek?" She sounded confused, like she didn't have any idea what the hell was going on. He just pulled her farther on, back to the hackberry tree and the deep shadows provided by its leafy branches.

Once they were sheltered from any prying eyes, he let go of her hand and stepped away.

"Derek, what is going on?"

He rubbed the back of his neck which was suddenly stiff and aching. "Look. We don't need to drag this out, do we?"

Her face was only a shadow, but her big eyes got bigger. "I don't understand what you're—"

"What I mean is, I had a great time these last couple of weeks with you. The best time. You're beautiful and sexy and just about perfect and it's meant a lot to me, that we could spend this time together, kind of put the past behind us. I think we've done that. I really do. I also think it's better if we just call this over now."

"Over?" Those eyes shone so bright. "But I thought we were together. I thought we might—"

"Uh-uh." He couldn't stand to hear her say those things. He couldn't let himself *believe* those things, couldn't get his hopes up that if he let her keep talking, she might tell him what he longed to hear. That wasn't going to happen. He wasn't that kind of guy. "No. You have a life. I have a life. It's not going to work and it's better if we just face that now."

"Derek, please…" She reached for him.

"Don't." Hands up, he backed off another step. "I don't want to hear it, okay? I don't need to hear it. I just need to get going."

"But I thought that we understood each other. I thought we wanted the same things. I want to *be* with you." She reached for him again. "I want to—"

"Knock it off." He pushed her hand away. "I mean it. I don't know what you're talking about. I just want to wish you well and say goodbye."

Her face changed. Even in the darkness he could see it. Her eyes gleamed with tears, but they were furious tears. "Derek Dalton, this is such crap. You've been freaking out all night and you really need to stop that. You're acting like a coward. I don't believe you're doing this. I don't believe you actually think you're going to—"

"Enough." He cut her off again. "I can't take this anymore. I'm leaving now and that's how I want it, that's who I am."

"But we—"

"Goodbye, Amy. Have a great life."

And he turned and started walking fast, out from under the branches of the tree, straight for his pickup parked along the winding dirt driveway on the far side of the house.

Did she follow? He had no idea. Because he never once looked back.

Chapter Eleven

Amy stood alone in the dark under the spreading branches of the big, old tree and felt her heart breaking all over again.

How could this be happening? It was just like thirteen years ago.

She considered going after him, begging him to reconsider.

But he didn't want her following him. He'd made that more than clear.

He didn't want her, period.

She'd been living in a fool's dream. He didn't feel the way that she did. It had all just been a fling to him.

The man had crushed her heart to bits all over again.

What to do now?

No way could she return to the remains of the party.

Her arms wrapped around herself, shoulders

hunched, eyes squinted hard to keep from letting the tears fall, she ducked out from under the tree and made for the house.

She got all the way across the dark yard, up the steps and inside without meeting a single soul. The house was quiet. She dropped to the straight chair in the foyer to tug off her boots. Then, on stocking feet, she ran up the stairs to her room and quietly shut the door. Leaning back against it, she let go of the boots.

They thudded to the floor. The sound of them dropping finished her somehow. She broke.

Her knees buckled. She slid down the door, buried her head in her hands and let the tears fall.

How long did she crouch there, knees drawn up under her chin, crying like a silly twit for a guy who didn't want her?

Way too long.

Finally, on shaky legs, she pushed herself upright again. She should wash her face, brush her teeth.

But she had no energy for any of that. Instead, she peeled off her maid-of-honor dress and fell across the bed in her lacy underwear.

She tried to sleep. Maybe she did sleep a little, dropping off exhausted. But then she jolted awake to remember that it had all gone bad and she could only stare at the far wall through another bout of sheer misery. She couldn't wait for daylight when she could pack up her stuff, throw it all in her Audi and get out of town.

At the crack of dawn, she snuck down the hall for a quick shower and to finally brush her teeth. Back in her room again, she packed like a madwoman, only pausing to wipe away the damn tears that wouldn't stop falling.

In fifteen minutes flat, she was ready to go. Her crammed-full suitcases waited against the wall. Her computer equipment was unplugged, unhooked and disassembled, stacked beside her bags. As she glared at it all and tried to decide what to haul downstairs first, someone tapped on the door.

"Amy?" Mikayla. "Eva's got breakfast ready downstairs."

Amy stood frozen. If she opened the damn door, Mikayla would see it all—her red, runny nose and bloodshot eyes, the stupid tears that kept spilling over and dribbling down her blotchy face.

Mikayla rapped on the door again. "Amy, are you in there?"

"I'm here," she gave out reluctantly. Her voice sounded like a couple of pieces of coarse sandpaper rubbing together.

"Amy, what's going on?" The real concern in Mikayla's tone had the tear factory going great guns all over again. "Why didn't you go to Derek's for the night?"

She yanked the door wide. "Don't mention that name." She glowered at the woman she'd begun to think of as a friend.

Mikayla's pretty face scrunched up with sympathy and concern. "Aw, honey. What's happened?" She held out her arms.

That did it. Amy threw herself against Mikayla's big belly and sobbed out brokenly, "Derek ended it. I thought we were together. But, he called it off with me. I left some of my stuff at his house and I still have his key and I don't even have the energy to go over there, get my things and throw the key in his face. Everything is… I don't know how to even tell you. It's awful. Terrible. So much worse than bad…"

"Oh, sweetie. Oh, hon…" Mikayla stroked her back, ran her hands down Amy's arms. "Whatever it is, you'll work it out. It'll be okay."

"No, it won't. It never will. He hurt me so bad. He did it again, because, you know, I guess once just wasn't enough."

Mikayla took her by the shoulders and guided her backwards to the bed. "Sit down." Amy obeyed. Grabbing the box of tissues on the nightstand, Mikayla took Amy's hand. She plunked the tissues in it. "Blow your nose and stay right there. I mean it. Do. Not. Move."

"Fine," she replied—except it came out "Fide" because she really did need the tissues.

Mikayla took off through the door. Amy heard her footsteps going down the stairs.

Two minutes later, Mikayla was back, this time with Eva. They hovered in the doorway.

"Amy, what's happened?" Eva cried, which only caused Amy to burst into tears all over again.

The two women flew to her side. They sat on the bed, Eva on her right and Mikayla on her left, and wrapped their arms around her while she cried some more.

At least that storm of weeping didn't last long. "I think I'm pretty close to cried out," she confessed after blowing her nose for about the hundredth time.

"Talk," ordered Eva. "Tell us everything so we can help."

Amy looked from one dear, concerned face to the other. All these years and years she'd told no one what had happened the summer she was eighteen.

And look how well that had gone.

Not well at all.

So, she blew her nose one more time and she did what Eva demanded. She talked.

She told them everything, about the past, the baby that maybe wasn't, about the wedding at the courthouse, about how true Derek had been to her, right there for her when she needed him most, about the cheap motel and the trucks going by on the highway. About how it all ended, about how she came back nine years ago to talk to him and he came to CU to find her, but neither of them knew the other had tried to reach out.

About how it all started up again when she came back for the wedding, about how she'd really believed they would make it this time. How she'd made arrangements with her boss so she could live right here in Rust Creek Falls, how she'd braced her father and he'd ended up admitting that he believed Derek really did love her, that her dad had wished her happiness with the man she'd never stopped loving.

And then how, last night, Derek had broken her heart all over again.

"He doesn't want me. He doesn't love me. He told me he had a great time the last couple of weeks. He said to have a nice life and he left me under that big tree between the house and the barn." Amy gave one last sniffle and wiped her nose.

Eva asked gently, "Is that it? Is that all?"

"Isn't that enough?" Amy cried.

And Mikayla said, "Well, there's just one little problem…"

Amy slid her a suspicious glance. "What?" she grumbled.

Mikayla wrapped an arm around her. "Well, honey. The problem is that you've got it all wrong."

Amy sputtered in outrage, but before she could argue, Eva backed Mikayla. "She's right, Amy. Derek loves you."

"No, he—"

"Yes." Eva sat tall and spoke firmly. "His love is written all over his face every time he looks at you."

Mikayla took Amy's hand and put it on the round crest of her own belly where her unborn baby slept. "A man who stands by you, who makes you know that you're wanted when things get rough… A man like that is worth fighting for. And he did stand by you, way back when. He was there when you needed him the most. Try looking at it from his point of view, why don't you? Your father finally told you what really happened. Derek stepped aside so that you could have the education you'd worked so hard for."

Amy gulped and nodded. "I know. I realize now that he did what he did then for me and that I was too hurt and confused to see it at the time."

"Kind of like now?" Eva suggested gently.

"No!" Amy argued. "It's not like now—okay, yeah. I'm hurt and confused now, but I *told* him I don't want to go. I told him I want to stay, to be with him."

"That's lame," Mikayla said.

"Lame!" Amy practically shouted.

Mikayla didn't even flinch. "Yeah, lame. If you want to make it work this time, I think you're going to have to say right out loud that you love him and that you're ready now to stand by him like he once stood by you. You have to be strong and you have to be clear. You have to know in your heart that what you had with him—what you *could* have again if you don't give up now—is what matters most. Love. That's what you had and that's what you still have. Just don't quit on love. Because a guy who steps up, that's a guy worth fighting for."

Eva asked, "Last night, did you tell him in so many words that you love him? Did you say that you want to stay here in town, that you've talked to your boss and you can work right here and still keep your job?"

"I never got a chance. He didn't let me."

"Make the chance," Mikayla and Eva insisted in unison.

"But what if he just says no to me again?"

"Then you'll know for sure," replied Mikayla.

Deep down, Amy did understand what her friends were trying to tell her, but the brokenhearted, scared little girl inside her just had to ask, "I'll know what for sure?"

"That you gave him your all. You gave your love every possible chance. If you go all the way and he still turns you down, at least you'll always know that this time you did everything you could to make it work."

Eva's hand, light as a breath, stroked Amy's hair. "We know you're scared. You wouldn't be human if you weren't. It's okay to be scared. What's not okay is to give up without first giving love everything you've got."

"I just…what if I'm only asking for more heartache?"

Mikayla snort-laughed. "Have you seen yourself? You're about at max heartache now. Giving your all is only going to make you stronger."

Was it? Really?

Amy had serious doubts on that score.

And yet, she knew the truth when she heard it. Her

friends were right. She hadn't gone all the way last night, hadn't really put her heart right out there. She'd failed to declare her love out loud.

She needed to do that, once and for all.

If she didn't, she would never know if, just maybe, they could have made it work.

"Okay," she said to no one in particular as she jumped to her feet.

The two women on the bed stared up at her. "Okay, what?" demanded Mikayla.

"Okay, I'm going for it."

"Yes!" Eva shoved both fists high in the air as Mikayla muttered, "Finally."

Amy strode to the foot of the bed. From there, she paced back and forth. "Chances are he's at the ranch. But no matter where he is, he'll have to go home eventually. When he gets there, I'll be waiting for him and I'll pull out all the stops this time to get through to him."

Eva got up and came to her. With a cry, Amy grabbed for her friend. And then Mikayla was there, too. The three of them held each other good and tight.

"All right then," Amy said at last as the other two stepped back. She smoothed her hair and straightened her shirt. "I know I look like I cried all night."

"You look beautiful," said Eva.

"Not true. But I'll take it. Wish me luck."

"We wish you love," said Mikayla. "Because that's what matters most."

They walked her downstairs. She hugged them once more at the door and went out alone—and got only as far as the top step that led down to the yard and her dusty Audi waiting in the morning sun.

She stopped when she heard a truck approaching. The sun was wicked bright, so she brought her hand up to shade her poor, tired eyes.

And she saw Derek's red pickup barreling along the driveway, coming right for her, kicking up a big plume of dust in its wake.

She stood there with her mouth hanging open as he skidded to a stop at the base of the steps. He flung his door wide and jumped out.

"Amy," he said, his mouth grim and his jaw set. He strode up the stairs to her.

Oh, had any man ever looked so handsome, in good jeans and dress boots, a tan plaid shirt and a fine, gray hat?

"Amy." He swept off his hat, tossed it over his shoulder and dropped to his knees. "Amy, I love you."

Was he really here, kneeling before her? "Derek?" she asked, her voice barely a whisper, half-fearing she might be hallucinating from exhaustion and a long night's worth of brokenhearted misery and crying jags.

He put a hand to his heart. "Amy, I was a pure coward yesterday and I didn't sleep a wink all night. I've just been afraid, that's all. Afraid that I was living in a fool's dream, afraid that if I asked you to stay or offered to come live in Boulder with you, all I'd get was a flat no. I was so sure I was only going to end up losing you all over again. So, I went and beat you to the losing part. I said goodbye before you could. I told you it was over.

"Because I'm an idiot who tried to escape getting his heart broken by walking away first. An idiot who spent the rest of last night realizing that all I'd accomplished was the breaking of my own damn heart. So yeah. I'm an idiot, but I'm *your* idiot, Amy. If only you'll have me."

Her throat was clutching, more tears rising—but this time in the good way. This time with joy. "Yes! Yes, I will have you and love you and be yours. It's all I ever wanted, Derek Dalton. I love you, too. And I want to move here, to Rust Creek Falls, where I've always dreamed I might someday make a home again. I want to move here and be with you—which reminds me, I failed to mention that I've got that all arranged. I talked to my bosses and they agreed I can make the move to Rust Creek Falls and still keep my job. And I talked to my dad and he admitted what he did, how he begged you to let me go that summer we got married, how he convinced you that my being with you would hold me back. He also said he'd had a feeling we would get back together and he was glad for us.

"Derek, I should have told you last night. I should have stood up and fought to make you see that I really do love you and want to be with you, only you. And I was coming to see you, just now, when you drove up, coming to tell you I want to move into your house on the Circle D with you. I want to love you and take care of you and have you take care of me and I want to do that for the rest of our lives."

He gazed up at her, his gorgeous, messy hair flopping over his forehead, pure love in those incomparable green eyes of his. How could she not have seen it before? How could she not have known that he was hers if only she would reach out and claim him? "Wait!" he said with teasing urgency.

"What?" she asked, alarmed.

"Amy Wainwright, did you just tell me yes?"

"Derek, *yes*." A goofy trill of laughter escaped her. "Yes, I said yes." He pulled something from his pocket, something that shone so bright. She gasped. "Derek, is that…"

"Amy." He reached out. "Will you give me your hand?"

"Yes." She giggled again. "Somehow, I can't stop saying yes." He slipped the ring on her finger. It was perfect, with a large central diamond in a halo of smaller stones. "Oh, Derek. It's just beautiful."

He looked so earnest, staring up at her. "If you'd rather make the choice yourself—"

"No way. It's mine and I'm keeping it. I love it." She wrapped her other hand around it and brought both hands against her heart just as he swept upward to his full height. She swayed toward him.

"Amy. My love." He gathered her close as she lifted her face to him. "I have a powerful feeling we're going to make it this time."

"Oh, Derek. Yes. Yes, we will make it. You and me and the rest of our lives. A home on the Circle D with you, and children, I hope. That's what I want, Derek. That's what we will have."

He bent close and his lips touched hers. She surged onto her toes then, sliding her hands up over his broad shoulders to clasp them around his neck.

The kiss was long and slow and deep, sealing their promise, each to the other.

When she dropped back to her heels again and opened her eyes, he said, "I gave up on us twice, Amy—thirteen years ago and then last night. I'm done giving up. This time, it's forever. I will never walk away again."

She stroked the hair at his temple, traced the shape

of his ear. "Good. Because I'm sticking with you now, no matter what. You are mine, Derek Dalton, and I am never letting you go."

"That reminds me..." He reached in his breast pocket a second time, bringing out a thin gold chain with another ring at the end of it, a ring with a gold-tone band and a square-cut imitation diamond.

She let out a cry. "Oh, Derek. You kept it. You kept my ring for all these years." She waved her hand in front of her face. "Now, just look at me, crying all over again."

"Turn around," he instructed. Dashing away the pesky tears, she turned and lifted her hair off her neck so he could hook the clasp. "There," he said. His warm lips brushed her nape.

She curled her fingers protectively over the old ring with her left hand, cherishing the feel of it, as her new ring glittered in the morning light. "So it was never lost, after all." She turned to him again. "Thank you."

He tipped up her chin and kissed her—first, her tear-wet cheeks and then her lips, a chaste kiss, infinitely sweet. As he lifted his head, she heard a sound from the house.

"Don't look now," she warned, "but I think we have an audience."

The door was open just a crack. A grinning Eva pulled it wide. Behind her stood Luke, Mikayla and Bailey, too.

"About time," muttered Luke.

"Congratulations," said Eva. "Love wins out. It always does."

Mikayla started clapping, causing the other three to follow suit.

Derek laughed, put his arm around Amy's shoulders

and pulled her close to his side. "She said yes," he announced proudly. "She's going to marry me—again."

"I'm so glad," Mikayla said.

"Again?" Bailey grumbled. "I'll bet *that's* a good story. And didn't I tell you last night that you guys were fooling no one with your friends-only act?"

"Come on inside, you two." Luke swept out a hand toward the house. "Eva's got breakfast on."

"French toast stuffed with cream cheese and blackberry jam," Eva tempted them. "With whipped cream on top and your choice of syrup—oh, and hickory smoked bacon, because what's a decadent after-wedding breakfast without a little bacon?"

"You're on," said Derek. "But give us a minute, okay? We'll be right in."

When Eva shut the door, Derek tugged Amy close again for another lovely, lengthy kiss. "Does it get any better than this?" he asked at last.

She beamed up at him. "I don't see how it can, but I know that it will. Because we're together now, for real. And I do honestly believe in us now. I know in my deepest heart that at last we are strong together, you and me, Derek. And I also know that through the years, we will only get stronger."

He bent close and whispered, "I love you, Amy Wainwright, and that means forever. From this day forward, nothing and no one can tear us apart."

A few minutes later, they went inside together, into Eva's warm, busy kitchen, hand in hand.

Mikayla asked to see the ring and Amy proudly held out her hand.

Eva left the stove to have a look. "Just beautiful," she said.

"Gorgeous," Mikayla agreed.

Luke got up to clap Derek on the back. "Way to go, man."

Then Eva waved a pot holder. "Sit down, you two. Your breakfast is ready."

Derek pulled out Amy's chair for her, stealing a quick kiss as she took her seat. He sat beside her.

"Two more damn love birds," Bailey complained. "Everyone in this town's gone love-crazy, and that's a plain fact."

"It's Rust Creek Falls," said Eva, as if that explained everything.

Mikayla laughed. "Watch out, Bailey. You'll be next."

Scowling, he muttered, "Never again."

Amy brushed Derek's arm under the table. He turned his hand over and she twined her fingers with his.

It was a moment she would treasure forever: a bright, summer morning at Sunshine Farm with good friends around her, the love of her life right here beside her, her hand in his. This was true happiness.

After too many long, lonely years away, Amy Wainwright had come home at last.

* * * * *

COMING SOON!

We really hope you enjoyed reading this book. If you're looking for more romance, be sure to head to the shops when new books are available on

Thursday
26th July

To see which titles are coming soon, please visit
millsandboon.co.uk